FORSAKEN THRONES

THE FORSAKEN KINGDOM SERIES
BOOK 1

L. L. STILES

*To all who like to escape from our world
by getting lost in another.*

TRIGGER/CONTENT WARNING

Graphic violence, Death, Mature Content, Mature
Language, Death of a Parent, Misogyny.

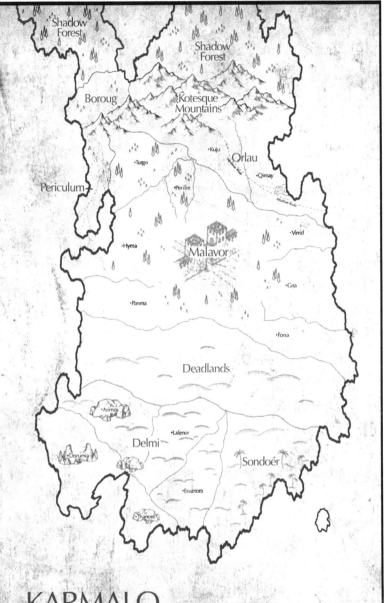

KARMALO

A swift kick to the chest had Ellie Batair falling to the ground. Her pride, and the thin veil that held back her anger, fell with her. Gasping for air, she quickly rolled to the right, dodging a stomp that would have left her shoulder aching for days.

In a smooth motion, she gracefully lifted herself, dirt and hay from the barn floor now covering her. Sweat rolled down her back as she dodged another blow from her older sister.

Cammie's manic smile sent a chill up Ellie's spine. Her sister's golden-blonde hair had been tied up before the start of their sparring, but large strands had escaped and were now stuck flat to her sweaty face. Cammie's wild green eyes stared at Ellie as she contemplated her next move.

"You know you can't dodge me forever, sis," Cammie taunted, her arms stretched out as if welcoming an attack.

Cammie was the tallest and strongest of the three Batair sisters, but what Ellie lacked in strength, she made up for in speed. Her sister often had trouble tracking her movements, and years of practice made her evasions and strikes nearly unpredictable.

Ellie sucked in a breath, pushing back at her growing anger. "If you're getting tired, Cam, just say the words and we'll stop."

Her sister howled then lunged forward, fists at the ready. Ellie dodged the first punch that flew towards her face, but in doing so failed to track the trajectory of the second fist that landed swiftly into her left side.

She stumbled back, holding in the gasp of pain. The delight in her sister's eyes caused Ellie's own to blur with rage.

Anger.

It was a constant battle. Controlling it had only gotten more difficult with age, and her eldest sister thrived on that anger, pushed at it any chance that she could, but Ellie never let it take over.

Cammie's arrogant attitude from the lucky blow she'd landed left her careless and unaware of her wide, welcoming stance. Ellie sent a vicious smile towards Cam before swiftly sliding underneath her legs. Seeing an opportunity, Ellie grabbed an old rake that leaned against the barn's only window. She stomped off the metal head, leaving four feet of wooden hilt swinging in her hands.

"Woah! No weapons!" Cammie's protests were nearly drowned out by the rage ringing in Ellie's ears.

Breathe. Breathe. Breathe. She blinked away the blur in her eyes and shook her head to clear it. With a steady breath, she replied to Cammie's plea, "What is Grandpa's number one rule and first lesson?"

"Never fight fair, just win." Cammie rolled her eyes but knew she couldn't argue against the advantage that Ellie now held. Using items and their surroundings to their benefit was just one of her grandpa's many, many lessons.

She swung the makeshift staff towards Cammie's face, who blocked it with her forearms. Ellie smiled, knowing the hit would definitely leave some bruising. Cammie pushed it off, and Ellie immediately swung towards her legs. Cammie tried to jump but wasn't fast enough. Ellie made contact with her ankles, leading her sister to fall hard on her side. She went in for one more blow.

"HEY!" Their grandpa's voice boomed through the small wood structure. Ellie stopped the splintered hilt just inches above Cammie's panicked face.

"Ellie, did you break a perfectly good rake? Just to have an upper hand?" His voice was reprimanding, but Ellie could see a glimmer of pride hiding behind his angry facade.

Since the age of five, their grandpa had been training the three girls in a variety of physical combat—along with an assortment of lessons. Lessons on war strategy, on observation, on poisons and their many effects, and lessons on alliances and inevitable betrayals. Years of schooling and training led to three fierce, beautiful weapons.

"Was it a *perfectly* good rake, Grandpa? It was rusted, and the hilt snapped off like a twig. Admittedly, though, this rake was the only thing that kept me from saying those two horrible words." Ellie turned to her sister, who still lay flat on the dirt ground. "Actually, Cammie, I think I need to hear those words from you. I clearly would have won if Grandpa hadn't so rudely interrupted us." She swung the hilt to point at the slender, yet muscular old man, hoping she didn't misread the glimmer of pride in his eyes.

"Fine." Cammie sat up and dusted the dirt from her

arms. *"You win."* Her annoyed growl was music to Ellie's ears. "Whatever. I'm bathing first."

"Bathing may need to wait. It seems you both have forgotten what day it is."

"We didn't forget, Grandpa. We just chose to ignore it as long as possible." Ellie's gut twisted at the thought of the coming event. This annual occurrence never got easier for anyone.

It was three days after Summer Solstice, which meant it was Designation Day.

2

It had been nearly a century since the Queen of Sondoér arrived on Karmalo soil. Where she came from, no one knew. Nearly two decades ago, she decided Sondoér wasn't enough, and she began the first battle in her bid for more land. Southern Karmalo had all been claimed, but her forces still fought for those further north. To ensure the queen never ran out of capable men for her endless conquest, she decreed an annual Designation Day for all who lived under her reign.

Designation Day had been the same year after year for as long as Ellie could remember. One man between the ages of fifteen and fifty from every family in Southern Karmalo must enlist and undergo multiple brutal trials to find out his strength, and therefore his placement among the Queen's forces. The first took place on the day of designation. However, this year was different.

On the night of Perilin's Summer Solstice celebration, the town's arbitrator, Captain Cormel, announced a new decree from the Queen.

"My dear children of Perilin,

Though our efforts have been grand, and thus far rewarding, we have yet to convince our northern brothers and sisters to lay down their arms and join us in peace. Fear not, my children, for we will continue to bring more northern territories to our side. We will not give up the fight for peace, despite the fact that they continue to murder more and more of our people in a senseless war that could so easily conclude with their surrender.

To replace the lives taken from us, I decree that no longer should just one male from each family be given the privilege of joining our cause, but either one female or male, in the required age restriction, may volunteer his or her services for your queen. I understand the hardship this may present, but I assure each and every one of you that the joys of winning this war will far outweigh the sacrifices made from this decree.

Forever,

Your Eternal Queen"

Perilin was known for being a peaceful territory. The people of Ellie's small town were excellent farmers, and their surplus of crops and willingness to provide was the only reason the self-proclaimed Eternal Queen had yet to fully restrict their town. Former designates, now turned loyal arbitrators to the Queen, occupied most of Southern Karmalo. While most villages had a handful, or even dozens of the Queen's men stationed among the citizens, there was only ever one arbitrator placed in Perilin.

But the night Captain Cormel read the Queen's newest decree, the once peaceful people of Perilin had rioted. Extra forces were brought in, a curfew was set, and word spread that the rioters were punished.

"You've yet to tell us who will be enlisting, Grandpa." Cammie's words felt like a physical punch to Ellie's gut. At fifteen, eighteen, and nineteen, all three Batair sisters were of age, and all three would sacrifice themselves for each other.

"The answer to that currently lies in your room." Their grandpa hung his head, unable to meet any of their gazes. "Go. We need to leave in a few hours, and your sister is still nowhere to be found."

A small voice spoke from right above Ellie. "I'm up here, Grandpa."

Maisie swung down from the barn rafters, landing between her elder sisters on all fours like a cat. Standing, she tucked deep auburn ringlets behind her ears. She was the only one of the three to get the most beautiful dark-red hair. Ellie's ice-blonde locks were a stark contrast to the warmth of her younger sister's.

"Geez, Mai, how long have you been up there?" Cammie inspected Maisie, trying to decipher exactly how she and Ellie had failed to notice the silent sister. Maisie simply shrugged in reply. She had always been a child of little words. A constant observer, she spoke only when she wanted to.

And when she spoke, Ellie made a point to listen.

"Alright, all three of you, go. Grams will want you fed before we leave."

The sisters slowly made their way down a worn dirt path towards their home. Each one dragged their feet, not wanting to face the decision that waited for them in their shared bedroom.

It wasn't enlisting or fighting in the war that scared each of them. It was being separated.

"So—" Cammie broke the silence. "—I don't know about

you two, but I sure as hell am not entering that house covered in hay and dirt. Grams will have a heart attack." Cammie stepped off the path into the field of wildflowers that surrounded their farm.

"Grams will have a heart attack if we don't leave on time." Ellie knew the direction Cammie was trailing towards, and admittedly was tempted to follow her. "We can't risk being late, Cam, nor can we wander off into the woods so close to the designation time. There are too many arbitrators around for that."

"Come on, El, this could be our last time seeing Henry together."

Maisie tentatively smiled. "It would be nice to say goodbye to the big guy."

Damn. It was two against one. Ellie knew there was no point in trying to argue with both sisters. "Fine, but we're just going long enough to rinse off in the stream and say our goodbyes."

A gleam Ellie knew all too well twinkled in Cammie's eyes. "Race you."

The three sisters were speeding through the wildflower-covered fields well before Cammie finished speaking.

3
_____

It wasn't long before they reached the fence surrounding the farm. They had sped through the pastures, startling horses and cows, and easily weaved through the beautiful pecan orchard that they had played many strategy-enhancing games in, like capture the chicken.

Each sister had a chicken, and whoever captured all the chickens first, won. Ellie used to be the most proficient in the game, but more recently Maisie and her stealth skills had dominated the contest.

Ellie, the fastest of the sisters, hopped over the fence without breaking speed. Her sisters were only a breath behind her. She hit the forest only a few steps from the fence. The trees were thick and grew close together, leaving little room for mistake, but Ellie had run this path a hundred times. She dodged clusters of leaves, hopped over roots, and swung off sturdy branches. In no time, she was splashing through knee-deep water and standing on a moss-covered boulder that the sisters' younger selves named Henry.

"And once again, I won." Ellie beamed down at her

sisters, who were panting and splashing their hot faces with water.

"I have longer legs, yet you still beat me. I don't understand it." Cammie drank handfuls from the brook.

"You have more muscle. It weighs you down," Maisie said matter-of-factly.

"And what's your excuse, little sis?"

Maisie shrugged. "I didn't want to deal with your anger today. I thought it best to just let you win."

Cammie doubled over in laughter. A spark of that anger Maisie referred to clawed its way up Ellie's spine. She jumped into the water, splashing both sisters in the face. "Is that your excuse for the dozen other times I've beat you here, little sis?" Maisie smirked but didn't reply.

They each washed off, Cammie and Ellie taking extra time to pull hay out of their pale hair, then climbed up Henry and settled into the soft moss. It grew in an odd way, leaving what looked like eyes and a smile on the side of the enormous rock. It was why they were so determined to name it. It was so long ago, Ellie couldn't remember why they had chosen Henry.

Maisie laid her head in Ellie's lap, letting her separate Mai's wet coils. Cammie sat close, leaning into her right side. "When we get back, I'm telling Grandpa that I'm the one enlisting." Maisie stiffened at Cammie's words.

Ellie rolled her eyes. They had had this argument what felt like a hundred times now. It always led to the same conclusion. "Cam—"

"No, Ellie. I can't let either one of you go. As the oldest sister, it's my job to protect you. If either of you left...if you... if you died in the war—died for *her*." Cammie choked out the final word. "I could never recover from that failure."

Ellie's chest tightened at her sister's words. She kept her

voice calm despite the thundering of her heart. "I have a feeling each of our fighting starts today. No matter who stays or goes. If any of these new arbitrators stay here, it's only going to get worse. Especially once fathers and husbands see their daughters and wives leave on that dirt path towards Malavor. This is what Grandpa trained us for."

"*You will one day put an end to this war.*'" Maisie quietly added the statement their grandpa had said many times throughout their lives. He had said it any time they felt their lessons were too hard or their training too painful.

Ellie could feel Cammie thinking of a solid argument against the reality she had laid out for her. Eventually Cam sighed, lying back on the boulder's surface.

As the silence stretched on, Ellie picked up a white pebble and rolled it in her callused fingers. They needed to head back soon, but Ellie wasn't ready to be the voice of reason quite yet. A strange breeze whispered in her ears, harmonizing with the brook that flowed before her. She became entranced by the movement of the rushing water. It flowed effortlessly over and around rocks. She moved her dexterous fingers around a pebble as if they were the flowing water. She could feel the stream's strength and adaptability. Feel its power as it continuously coursed over both small and large stones.

She was so entranced, she barely noticed the snapping of twigs and crushing of leaves under large feet. Cammie and Maisie shot up on either side of her, pulling her completely back to reality. She stood, taking in her surroundings.

"Do you think it's an arbitrator?" Maisie whispered, her face cold and focused.

More rustling came from directly across the brook. "Whoever it is, they're coming from the direction of the farm. We should run." Ellie began bouncing on the balls of her feet.

"Why would we run when we could kick their ass?" Cammie wasn't wrong, but fighting an arbitrator would only lead to more problems.

"Would you three calm down!" The familiar voice sent a wave of warm comfort over Ellie. Her sisters also visibly relaxed when the handsome familiar face and gentle smile appeared through the thick forest.

4

"Nate!" Ellie jumped down and threw herself at her best friend. He wrapped his arms around her waist and easily lifted her from the ground. "I thought I taught you better. I should not have been able to hear you approach so easily."

Nate let go of her and laughed. "I may not be extremely smart, El, but I'm smart enough to know not to sneak up on the three of you."

"Wise indeed." Cammie swung her fist at Nate's shoulder, and he caught it only to take a knee to the gut. He grunted, but Cammie must have held back, as he was laughing only a few seconds later.

Ellie's grandpa had instructed the sisters not to share their training with anyone, but Nate's family, like her own, were refugees to this town. And after witnessing years of bullying towards Nate, because of his more northeastern appearance, Ellie decided an exception had to be made. For years, on every third night of the week, she had secretly been training Nate.

"What are you doing here?" Ellie pushed back the dark hair that had fallen in Nate's umber eyes.

His smile faltered only slightly. "My dad had some things he needed dropped off to your grandpa. I figured since I am to join one of you in enlisting, I might as well deliver the goods and accompany whoever it is to The Ring."

Ellie dropped her gaze from Nate. Her chest tightened, and she swallowed down the knot forming in her throat.

A few months ago, Nate's family received a letter informing them that his older brother Wesley had died in battle. The rule was that only one man in each household had to serve in the Queen's Army at a time, but once their "service" ended, another must sign up on the next Designation Day. Mr. Gadeu, Nate's father, was ineligible to join due to an old injury, so at eighteen years old, it was now Nate's turn. Ellie wasn't sure what was worse: possibly going with Nate and being separated from her two sisters, or staying and losing both a sister and her best friend.

Maisie placed a gentle hand on Ellie's shoulder, and her sorrow eased. "How did you know we were here?"

"Oh, that's easy. I dropped the bag of things on your front porch and heard your grams in the kitchen yelling obscenities to your grandpa about the three of you disappearing again."

Shit.

"I couldn't find you near the barn, so I figured you'd be here saying your goodbyes to Henry."

"We need to go. Now." Ellie grabbed Nate's wrist and ran after Cammie and Maisie, who had taken off the moment Nate mentioned Grams's yelling.

"Wait." Nate pulled her to a stop. "I need to talk to you, El."

Ellie's heart sank. They had promised not to say goodbye, but she knew Nate would break that promise. "Can we walk and talk? If I'm to go with you today, I'd rather not leave with Grams angry at me." That was true, but Ellie also needed an excuse to not look at Nate while he said what he needed to say.

"I just—I wanted to give you something." Nate ignored her request and pulled out a black silk pouch. "It's tradition in our family, and culture, to give a gift to the most important person in our lives before leaving for war. We give it so we know someone will always remember us, even if we don't return. It's a way for us to be at peace with our journey ahead."

Ellie sucked in a breath. She avoided Nate's gaze to hide the tears building behind her eyes. "I cannot accept whatever this is, Nate. I may be joining you in this war." Her voice caught several times as she spoke.

Nate poured the contents of the silk pouch into his hand, a long silver necklace with a blue pendant hanging at the end. Not just a blue pendant. A small teardrop-shaped glass pendant filled with the bluest liquid Ellie had ever seen. A sudden breeze blew the pendant towards her, as if urging her to reach out and take it. She clenched her hands into fists, fighting the odd desire.

"This necklace was given to my grandmother by her brother before he left for war. I asked my parents, and they agreed to let me give it to you. It's filled with the water of my country's healing rivers, so I've been told." The necklace continued to sway temptingly towards her over and over again. "I know you may enlist with me today, but I still want you to have it. It's to be given to the most important person in my life who's not going off to war, and after the events on the night of Summer Solstice, that's just not possible. The people in this town have joined the war, whether they realize it or not. Please, El, take it."

Ellie looked at the swaying glass pendant in front of her. She reached for it faster than intended and placed the long chain over her head. The silver was cold against her skin, but the liquid inside the glass was like ice. It felt oddly comforting to her.

She tucked the chain and pendant under her cotton tunic, keenly aware of Nate's lingering gaze to where the pendant now lay.

"Thank you."

He looked up, his olive cheeks becoming a rosy red. He cleared his throat. "We should hurry back."

They caught up to Cammie and Maisie, who had stopped to wait for them, as the two sisters admitted that they didn't want to take the brunt of Grams's wrath without her.

Not to Ellie's surprise, Mr. and Mrs. Gadeu, Nate's parents, sat on the steps of the house's decrepit front porch. Nate and his family were a constant on their farm. Mr. Gadeu supplied any leatherwork her grandfather might need, and Mrs. Gadeu enjoyed cooking and gossiping with Grams.

"We felt it was best to wait out here until things calmed down a bit." Mrs. Gadeu winked just as the sound of something shattering echoed out the kitchen window.

The sisters ran inside to find a very disgruntled Grams sweeping up the remains of a plate. She shot her gaze up to the three of them, and Ellie felt like she shrunk three sizes. Grams's eyes were red and puffy, but the rest of her features were set in a hard mask of anger.

"Where have you girls been! I thought the worst had happened and one of those despicable arbitrators found you! I've been a nervous wreck!" Sure enough, Grams was shaking, the most likely cause of the shattered plate. Her usually tight bun was also loose, and wisps of gray hair fell in her face. "Oh, I should have known!" She pointed down to their sodden, muddied boots. "If you three didn't have to hurry and get dressed, I'd make you clean up my now muddy floors!" Grams stood up, waving her broom at them. "Go! To your room!"

The sisters ran to the hallway but stopped before their closed door. Once they opened it, none of their lives would be the same. Maisie grabbed Ellie's hand, and a lot of her trepidation disappeared. She pushed open the door and walked in first.

The small bedroom was simple, cozy, and smelled of the lavender that grew just outside their open window. Across from the window stood a large oak dresser, a small glass perfume bottle, and a white vase filled with wildflowers sat on top. Nothing looked out of place until she noticed the pile of things laid out on top of the middle of the three beds that lined the far wall.

Her bed.

The reality of Ellie's situation didn't pierce as harshly as she thought it would. Deep down, she knew this would be her grandfather's choice, and she would gladly accept it to protect her sisters. Though, she couldn't help the fear and rage that coiled up her spine. She would endure several brutal trials, be separated from her family, and be forced to fight for a queen she hated.

"No." Cammie's denial was a demand. "I will not—"

"Though you are an excellent fighter, Cammie, your sister has excelled in more than just combat." Their grandpa spoke from the opening of their doorway. "She is a strong strategist, a natural leader, and charismatic enough to gain many allies within the Queen's forces."

"No. No! Despite the anger she fights against, Ellie is too kind. She trusts too easily. It will be her downfall!"

Ellie couldn't help but be hurt by Cammie's words, though they weren't the first time she had heard them from the sister who built up walls upon walls around her heart.

"She can control her anger as she has always done. She will be brutal when she needs to be, as I have taught each of you but your sister's kindness will be her strength, not her weakness, Cammie. I will not discuss this any further; my decision has been made." Before turning to leave, their grandpa instructed Ellie to grab Nate and meet him in his study once she was dressed.

Cammie reached out and placed a palm on each side of Ellie's face. "Please, Ellie. Tell him he's wrong. Tell him you won't go."

Ellie could see the tears her older sister fought to hold back. She wanted to do what Cammie asked, but she knew she couldn't. "I'm sorry, Cammie, but he's right. I need to be the one to go."

At her words, Cammie's pain turned into a mask of anger. She ripped her hands away as if Ellie's skin physically burned her. "Fine. Give up your life for a queen we all hate." Cammie turned and left, slamming the door closed behind her.

"She didn't mean that." Maisie's whisper sounded far away. Ellie found her younger sister sitting on her bed, her shoulders hunched and her features flat and distant. Maisie often detached whenever emotions ran high around her.

Ellie sighed, making her way over to wrap Maisie in her

arms. "I know." Her words still hurt though. "Cammie has every right to be upset, as do you, Mai."

Maisie stiffened in Ellie's hold, but she didn't drop the mask of indifference. "I will miss you." Ellie's words caught in her throat. Maisie didn't reply, and that hurt more than Cammie's cruel words.

"It seems Grandpa and Mr. Gadeu have been hard at work these last couple days." Maisie waved a hand behind her to the pile of things on Ellie's bed.

Designates were allowed to bring anything they could carry during the long journey to Malavor. An empty pack hung from her footboard. She would fill it with basic necessities, an extra change of clothes, and what seemed to be a handful of new weapons. Ellie's eyes lit up at the sight of twelve silver blades tucked safely in a new leather knife holder.

Throwing daggers. Her weapon of choice.

Two vambraces with single dagger sheaths on each sat beside the holder, and a garter featuring double dagger sheaths sat to the left of the vambraces. It was all made from the finest leather in the southern continent, soft to the touch yet incredibly durable. Definitely the work of Mr. Gadeu.

On the surface of her pillow sat a new pair of leather pants, a loose long-sleeve cotton blouse, and new black boots.

Ellie quickly changed into the fine gifts, pulling on the tight leather pants and buckling the double-sheathed garter around her waist and right thigh. Over the new light-blue cotton blouse, she placed the two vambraces and filled each empty sheath with a dagger. She rolled up the leather dagger holder and placed it in her pack. After sliding on the new boots, she walked over to their standing mirror. She brushed through her wavy blonde hair and braided the front of it back, leaving the bottom half down.

Once fully finished, the woman in the reflection before her was both stunning and terrifying.

"Are you going to war or to assassinate the Eternal Queen yourself?" A teasing smile graced Maisie's lips, though it didn't reach her navy-blue eyes.

"It's a bit much for the first trial, isn't it?"

Ellie pulled at her blouse, wishing the neckline was cut just a little higher. It barely hid the pendant that now lay cushioned between her breasts. In addition, the tight leather pants left little to the imagination, as each curve, dimple, and muscle were on display.

"At least lose the vambraces," Maisie suggested. She fingered the sleeve of Ellie's new blouse and studied the quality of the leather placed all over her body. "You look good, El. You're just missing one thing." Maisie walked over to their shared dresser and pulled the beautiful glass bottle of perfume down. It was a gift from Grams to all three of them at the last Winter Solstice.

The perfume smelled of citrus blossoms, parchment, and warm tobacco. There was something comforting and familiar about the aroma, but none of them could pin down what it was.

"Despite rinsing in the brook, you still smell horrible." Maisie sprayed the perfume onto Ellie's neck and wrists. Ellie closed her eyes, letting the smell fill her senses.

A faded scene of a man reading by an open window flashed through Ellie's head. He gazed across the room at something on the floor, and a clear, stunning smile flashed across his blurred

*face. Silent laughter shook his body. He stood, showing his great
height.*

*Then a blinding blue light behind her eyelids blurred the
vision away.*

Ellie rubbed her eyes, clearing the fog from her head. She
couldn't stop the dread that seeped through her bones.
Maisie stared up at her, her face once again free from any
emotion.

"You saw him again?" she asked, still staring blankly. It
would be concerning if it wasn't something she did so often.
"The same vision?"

"Yes," Ellie replied simply.

"It's happening more often. The vision. Do you think it
means something?"

"No. I'm sure it's nothing." Ellie shrugged her shoulders,
willing herself to believe her own words.

The gift of sight was rare, especially among humans. But
Ellie only ever had this one recurring vision, a vision she felt
was from the past, so she didn't feel the recent "blessing," as
Maisie had once called it, was of enough concern to tell her
grandparents. If she did hold power, no matter how slight,
Ellie knew it meant trouble. There was a reason all who
held magic had disappeared. They were not welcomed
under the Queen's reign.

Maisie looked at her, clearly contemplating before
taking a deep breath. Her face relaxed. "You should hurry.
Grandpa is waiting for you."

Ellie leaned towards her younger sister and gently kissed
the top of her auburn head. "I love you," she whispered and
left her childhood room without looking back.

Ellie wasn't surprised to find Nate sitting next to his father on the worn-out brown couch. The hideous thing sagged at the back and off-white stuffing popped out of the left arm rest. Nate sat cross-legged on the middle cushion, knowing it was the most comfortable of the three.

Her best friend was close to an exact copy of the man beside him, both adorned with black wavy hair, currently stuck flat to their sweaty tan-olive brows. Nate's slightly longer hair curled around his ears and sat gently at the base of his neck. Both men shared broad faces, square jaws, a flat, bridged, round nose, and upturned brown eyes. Nate, once a tall, lanky child, had filled out, as he now made his well-built father look small by comparison.

He was definitely handsome, and no small number of the girls in town had taken notice. Anytime the two of them were in town together, he never seemed to acknowledge the innocent flirting from the market saleswomen or the distant giggling from younger, less-brave admirers. In truth, he might have just chosen to ignore it, given a relationship seemed futile in their current environment.

Nate looked up at her, and to her surprise, he seemed shocked to see her standing armed and dressed for enlistment. "I selfishly hoped I wouldn't have to part from you but still wished that you wouldn't be the one to go with me."

Mr. Gadeu stood, pulling a long leather sheath from the floor. "Here. You will need this as well. The weapon it is meant for is in the study with your grandfather."

She took the extraordinary sheath. The edges were excellently woven, and a long-stemmed rose was branded into the front. She ran gentle fingers along the detailed pedals.

"The rose," Mr. Gadeu began. "A complicated flower. Its beauty and scent are beyond comparison, and often it's a symbol of love and hope. One wrong touch, though, and you will be in a great amount of pain. It is one of the few species of flowers that knows how to not only protect itself, but others."

Not fully understanding Mr. Gadeu's words, Ellie shifted uncomfortably under the scrutinizing gaze of the elder man. "The seedmen of my home would often plant stems of a rose bush among young plants as a way of protecting them as they grew. But, if not carefully watched and removed at the proper time, the bush would over grow and choke out the plants. Without the beauty of the rose blossoms, the stems can become chaotic and unbalanced. Their blind desire to fight takes over, leading to death and destruction."

Mr. Gadeu placed a gentle hand on Ellie's cheek. "There is more to war than just brutality. It can bring out the best and worst in a person. Show their darkest desires and the depth of their true selves. Just remember my sweet girl, you have more beauty and light than darkness. Don't let this war change that."

Tears pricked at the back of Ellie's eyes. She felt the weight of Mr. Gadeu's words settle on her shoulders. She could be a vicious fighter, and she knew how easy it would be to fall into her anger. She could easily become a monster and wondered if she would.

Pushing down those thoughts, she quickly swung the sheath around her back. She fastened the straps that ran diagonally and horizontally across her chest. Once on, she stretched, turned, and bent. It was perfect. It moved and stretched where it needed to and stayed secured where it was supposed to.

"It's perfect. Thank you, Mr. Gadeu. For everything."

He bowed his head to leave but caught the gleam of silver around her neck. "May I?" he asked with his hand held just inches from her chest.

She pulled the pendant from underneath the shirt and harness and placed it in his hand.

"My mother claimed this necklace held immense power. That the liquid inside had the ability to heal all ailments." He stared at the blue liquid, tracing his fingers over the cold glass. "For years I searched for someone that knew more about it. I found an elderly gentleman, from your home of Malavor, who claimed it was filled with the liquid of the Heuleun River. Do you know the tale of the Heuleun River?"

Ellie shook her head in reply.

"Hmm. Perhaps we'll see each other again someday and I'll tell you the story." He released the pendant, and its cold touch sent shivers along her chest.

"It suits you." He again smiled softly. "I have no doubt you will have better luck discovering its powers."

With that, Mr. Gadeu bowed his head and left Nate and

Ellie alone in the sitting room. Nate stood from the couch, his gaze running up every inch of her again. This time, she didn't miss the heat that ran across his cheeks. Her stomach flipped. "We shouldn't keep my grandpa waiting."

A knowing smile crossed his lips. "Lead the way."

Ellie could smell burning tobacco before she even opened the study door. Passing over the threshold, the smell was so overpowering, it threatened to cloud the rest of her senses. In the center of the room sat an ornate wooden desk that their grandpa had built himself. The far wall behind the desk was lined with hundreds of books, most acquired in Perilin, though a select few were brought from their long-abandoned home. A home she was too young to remember.

Ellie spent many nights sneaking into this small study. She read every book her grandfather owned on the many magical beings of Karmalo: races that still lived and roamed the lands, and those that hadn't been seen or heard from in almost two decades. A few, like the Nokken, hadn't been seen in centuries. Their way of life had been...strange.

Grandpa sat in his large leather chair behind his desk, letting out large puffs of smoke from his ivory pipe and reading from a piece of parchment. More parchment was scattered across the top of his desk. Ellie glanced at one rolled up and crested with a blue eagle holding a dagger in its talons. Encircling the eagle was a halo of olive branches. It felt familiar, but she didn't know why. Above the mess of parchments were two brilliant gleaming swords.

Closest to her was the smaller of the two weapons. The blue-silver double-edged blade was no longer than sixty centimeters. The silver hilt was wrapped in fresh leather and featured the head of a doe at the end. The larger sword was also freshly wrapped, but it's blade and hilt were black as onyx and featured the head of a stag. Ellie ran a tentative finger over the silky blue metal in front of her. Before she could do the same to the onyx blade, her grandpa placed his parchment down, emptied his pipe, and stood.

"The blades before you were supposed to be gifts from me to your parents, Ellie." She sucked in a shallow breath. Ellie's grandparents never spoke of her parents. Losing their daughter, her mother, was a pain they wished to never remember. She couldn't help the quickening of her pulse. "I had commissioned them just weeks before the attack that took their lives. It seems a waste to let them rust here on this farm." With a soft smile and a shaky hand, her grandpa passed Ellie the doe-handled sword. "The blade on this sword is made from blue steel. It's incredibly durable and quite beautiful."

She waved the sword around. Its weight was perfectly balanced, and the iridescent metal gleamed in the soft morning light that poured through the small study window. For the first time in her life, she felt a strange connection to the mother she couldn't remember. To the woman she never had the chance to know.

"The blade on this sword," he continued as he lifted what would have been her father's blade. "Is made from elysium. The toughest metal found in these lands." He stared for a long time at the stag on the hilt. With tears in his eyes, he offered it to Nate. "The deer was your father's family sigil, Ellie. The doe and stag represent gentleness, mindfulness, and protection. I give these to you both, knowing you will each watch over one another with those qualities in mind."

Nate held the elegant sword in his hands. "I cannot accept this. Nor am I worthy to carry a sword from—"

Grandpa silenced him with a wave. "You are more than worthy to carry this sword, Nathaniel Gadeu. And my grand-daughter's training has made you more than capable of wielding such a weapon." He smiled and winked at their shocked faces. "I trained you in everything you know, and you thought I wouldn't notice you two sneaking around the farm every few nights to beat each other up. Ha!"

Ellie laughed and lunged for her grandfather. Even with no weapon, he easily disarmed her, moving too swiftly for any normal seventy-year-old.

Clang. Ellie's new sword fell to the ground. She swung her arms around his neck, taking in one last embrace.

"Thank you, Grandpa." They released each other, and she picked up her fallen sword and slid it into the sheath hung from her back.

"Your Grams and I had hoped we could protect you from this war for a little bit longer, but alas, we cannot. There are events and trials that you are about to experience that the years of training I've given you could never prepare you for." He paused, packing his pipe with more tobacco.

He slumped back down into his leather chair. His face was worn, and dark circles and deep lines surrounded his eyes. He held his pipe in his left hand and drummed the fingers of his right on the desk. After a deep breath, he continued, "Ellie, I need you to go and find out anything and everything you can while training in Malavor. There will be designates there who come from places completely loyal to the Eternal Queen, eager to do more to serve her, and there will be others like us, waiting and hoping for a way to fight against her rule. Win over what arbitrators you can. Make allies. Find out any information that could be crucial to ending this war, and her reign. And lastly—" His eyes lined with silver, and his hands began to shake. He set his pipe down and stood from his leather chair.

"You will be in Malavor, Ellie. What was once our home."

Yes, they were refugees from the once-great kingdom, but neither Ellie nor her sisters remembered a thing about it. She knew it was once a kingdom of peace for all races of Karmalo, but that was a very long time ago. "Ellie, learn what you can about what it was, what it could be again, and decide what role you want to play in this war."

His voice broke as tears spilled down his face. She had never seen her grandpa show such sorrow. It shocked her in a way that had her own emotional barriers crumbling to dust. He slowly walked around his desk, slumped and broken. Placing both hands on her shoulders, he looked into Ellie's misted eyes. Pulling her into an embrace, he whispered, "You are my granddaughter, and I am so proud of you no matter what happens. I love you, my sweet Ellie."

She sucked in a breath at his words. Unable to hold it in any longer, she sobbed into his shoulder. Her chest tightened, her head throbbed, and she willed herself not to shake from the fear and anger threatening to consume her.

Everything was about to change. Everything.

He released her, his normal stone mask set back in place. "Go. I need to have a quick word with Nate."

She wiped her face and gave a reassuring smile to Nate. She didn't know what her grandfather needed to say to her best friend, but she couldn't focus on anything but the instructions her grandpa just gave her. She needed to get out of the tobacco-filled room so she could think more clearly.

Once out in the hallway, Ellie took a cleansing breath,

but it didn't clear away the knot in her throat or the stream of tears running down her face.

"So you will be the one to go?" Ellie jumped at her grams's question. She stood at the end of the hall, a teacup wrapped in her small wrinkled hands. Ellie wasn't surprised that Grams was not involved with her grandpa's decision. Ellie simply nodded, her tears beginning to flow harder.

"I-I don't understand what Grandpa is asking of me. If I do all that he has instructed, what then? Running or outright opposition will lead to my—to all of our deaths!"

"Fight." Grams reached out to grab her hand. The warmth of her grasp seeped into her bones. "Fight, my girl. Fight as we will fight. Do not worry about your decisions affecting us. We can take care of ourselves." She lowered her voice to a whisper. "You are Ellienia Batair, you are a warrior, and you *will* fight."

Ellie loosened a breath at the sound of her full name. Her vision blurred at the edges and Grams's words echoed in the back of her mind.

A young Ellie squealed and giggled as Cammie ran after her with a makeshift stick-sword. Her own makeshift sword swung aimlessly behind her. They played in front of their house, running and jabbing at each other and laughing with every clash of their pretend weapons.

Their grandfather walked out of the house, his face nearly as grim as the man who walked behind him. Ellie stopped abruptly at the sight of the man. Cammie slammed into her, causing both girls to fall into the soft grass.

He ran up to them, dusting off grass and dirt and lifting them back to their feet with ease.

"Are you leaving?" Ellie's small voice trembled. She'd known this man. Was fond of him.

"Yes, little warriors." His eyes were swollen from tears, his voice rough and raw, as if he had been screaming. Dark soot and ash covered the hand that picked grass from her blonde hair.

She swung her tiny arms around the man's neck. Cammie did the same, and from nowhere, a toddling Maisie followed suit. They held the man as the vision blurred and a blinding blue light burned her vision.

Ellie's vision cleared. A wide-eyed Grams stood staring at her. "No, it's too soon..."

Ellie's blood heated with terror. Not from the vision, it seemed both lovely and sad, but from what it would mean, that she may have just experienced another vision, one completely new and different from the one she had been having for the past few months.

She shook her head, pushing away the fear and ignoring what she might be.

Nate stepped out from the door behind her. Grams shook her head. "Come, my dears. It's time to go."

6

I n the center of town, Ellie and Nate walked next to each other in complete silence. Nate had emerged from her grandpa's study with a stone mask replacing his usual expressive face. That mask remained, and Ellie didn't dare ask what her grandfather had said to him.

They ignored the many eyes that trailed them through town. They knew that compared to the rest of today's recruits, they would look overly prepared. Unfortunately, Perilin did not have a blacksmith, and Mr. Gadeu's work was worth more than a few coins.

Ellie clenched her fists at the sight of windows boarded up and arbitrators lining the dirt streets. Perilin was once beautiful, filled with lively people and lush gardens. In just three days, it had turned into a town she no longer recognized. Many of the beautiful gardens were trampled, and every gaze she met was filled with deeper anger and sorrow than any Designation Day before.

A few feet ahead, hushed cries and angered whispers surrounded a tall, thick poll. "We should go around," Nate urged.

Ellie ignored his suggestion, needing to know what had the usually kind citizens so distraught. She easily pushed her way through the crowd, and what she saw nearly had her emptying the contents of her stomach.

Hung from the pole by bound hands was a limp, lifeless body. The person was barely recognizable. Intense bruising covered a pale face, parts of their body looked as if birds and beasts had fed on their flesh throughout the night, and strange black marks spiderwebbed across their bare chest. What gave the person's identity away, and had Ellie holding in a shaky breath, were the intricate silver braids cascading from the top of the man's head.

Mr. Remal. A kind father and husband who once saved a young Ellie and her sisters from a perverted Mr. Pevingsonton. He had followed them on their path home from the town's market, and through panicked breaths, Maisie led the sisters past the Remals' home. They were always outside working on their garden or fences. Mrs. Remal had taken them inside while Mr. Remal gave Mr. Pevingsonton a nice black eye. The next day, Mr. Pevingsonton was nowhere to be seen, and the rumors around town were that Mr. Remal and a few other men had driven the depraved man from town.

"What happened?" Ellie could hardly talk through the knot in her throat.

"Mr. Remal has been unable to enlist due to his heart problems." Though treated by the local healer, Mr. Remal had a weak heart and struggled with tremors and fainting spells. As a result, he was ineligible to join the Queen's Army. "Unfortunately, with the new decree, that meant Mrs. Remal would have to enlist." Nate grabbed Ellie's hand and squeezed. "He was among the townsfolk that fought on the night of Summer Solstice."

And his heart couldn't handle the punishment the arbitrators dealt out to those who rioted. A tear escaped Ellie's eye as she thought the words Nate left unsaid.

"I've heard some of the men talk about a new weapon the arbitrators carry." Nate pointed to the strange black wound on Mr. Remal's chest. "I think that's what caused the mark."

"Were there others hit with the weapon?"

Nate nodded. "I'm not sure if their wounds were fatal or not."

A cold shock of fury ran up Ellie's spine. She clenched her fists at the thought of many more citizens of Perilin ending up like Mr. Remal. "What's going to happen to Mrs. Remal and her daughter?"

"She is now a sole caretaker, making her ineligible to join."

"That is until her daughter turns fifteen." Ellie's words came out like a growl.

"Come on." Nate pulled on her hand.

They walked quickly to the east gate of The Ring. It was once used for the town's center for entertainment. Artists, instrumentalists, and storytellers would come from all over to perform in the small arena. After years of designations, however, it no longer felt like a place where one could find joy in the entertainment, no matter who was at the center.

A dirt path led the way to the grassy ring, and stone arches covered in dark-green vines marked the entrances: one on the west where sullen families entered to watch the first trial, and one on the east where designates waited to sign their lives away. Both entrances were currently manned by an arbitrator adorned in a red-velvet uniform.

Nate and Ellie stepped into line; many others filed in behind them. She felt their stares before she heard the first vile voice. Most of those in Perilin were kind, but there were always a few Ellie and her sisters knew to stay away from.

"You sure you can handle all them pretty blades, missy?"

An angry heat rushed to Ellie's face. She ignored the man's hollering but didn't miss the snickering that came from both ends of the line. She looked over to see Nate's fist tighten around the pommel of his sword.

"Hey, you! Why don't you tell your girlfriend to hand her weapons to a man who'll know how to actually wield 'em!" Another man joined in on the heckling. She heard his heavy footsteps head towards her. She began to slide one of the small daggers from her holster, but Nate grabbed her wrist. "Don't."

"Fine, but if he gets any closer, I'm knocking him to the ground." She clenched her jaw, grinding her teeth through each steadying breath. Seeing Mr. Remal, beaten and brutally strung up for all to see, had snapped something in Ellie. The weapon her grandpa had created was itching to be released.

"I wouldn't come any closer, sir," Nate warned. "We wouldn't want to cause a commotion on the first day of the trials, would we?"

The man laughed and kept walking. "The weapons are a bit much for you, darlin', but I will say, them leather trousers are real nice to look at."

Nate's knuckles went white as he grasped the hilt of his onyx sword.

"Now?" she asked, near deaf by the sound of her thundering heart. Nate simply nodded, his own muscles seeming ready to snap.

Ellie let her body settle into a calm rage, ready and waiting for the man to step closer. Four more steps, three more, two...She turned, swinging her right leg around, making contact with the back of the man's knees. She pushed him down, simultaneously sliding one of the daggers free from its holster on her thigh. Moving her leg out of the way, Ellie followed the man to the ground with the blade grazing his neck.

They landed with her knee digging into his groin and her dagger drawing just a drop of his blood. Silence struck the entire line of people.

"You look at my ass one more time and I'll pop your eyes out and feed them to the birds. Understand?"

"Y-yes," he squeaked.

"Good." She stood, giving a nasty snarl down the line of terrified faces.

She ignored the man's struggle to get up and took her place next to Nate. "How was that?" He smirked, allowing clear amusement to break his stone facade.

"Fun," she mused, her heart still pounding and her anger only slightly assuaged. "Though I feel like the bird thing was a bit much."

Nate huffed. "Yeah, I think just a bit."

After what seemed like an eternity, they were next to sign their names on the long scroll of parchment that was nailed to the left of the east stone entrance. Captain Cormel observed as each person wrote their full name. Signing with anything but your full given name was forbidden. There was power in a name, and the Queen understood the power of signing it away.

"Ellie Batair. Nathaniel Gadeu." Captain Cormel nodded in greeting, handing Nate a freshly-inked quill.

Nate stepped up to the parchment and began carefully writing his name. Cormel walked a few steps closer to Ellie. His tan skin and dark hair were stark against the arbitrator's bright-red-velvet uniform. Jade-green eyes looked at her with intense thought and consideration. Ellie couldn't deny that the captain was handsome. He was broad shouldered and towered over most of the men and women in Perilin. Ellie once admired him, as he had never demanded respect but still earned it from the small town. However, any regard that Ellie once held for the striking officer disappeared the moment she saw Mr. Remal's lifeless body.

He leaned towards Ellie and, with a soft, lowered tone, said, "I am sorry you have to leave your family—your sisters."

His words were like lead to her ears. She stiffened, holding back the urge to send a fist towards the man's handsome face. "Are you also sorry for the murder of Mr. Remal?" Her voice was stern and not hushed, and she let her own crystal eyes glare into his like daggers. Cormel took a step back, jaw clenched and gaze averted.

"I did not participate in the punishment of Mr. Remal."

"You outrank every man here, and yet you didn't stop it. And what of the others with him? I have yet to see any of their faces today. Did you stand aside in their murders as well?" Nate was back at her side, a look of concern breaking through the cool indifference that blanketed his features.

"Mr. Remal stood against a direct order from the Eternal Queen. He and the ones who foolishly fought with him, unfortunately, had to be punished. As for their absences, they were not killed but asked to stay home and not attend the events today."

"I'm sure their injuries would keep them from attending even if they wanted to." She yanked the quill from Nate and wrote down the name Captain Cormel and everyone else in the town knew. *Ellie Batair.*

She shoved the quill back in Cormel's hand, nearly spilling the ink bottle he held in the other. Standing tall, she viciously whispered into the captain's ear. "You knew of his condition. You knew what those new weapons would do to him. You knew he would not be able to fight back or properly defend himself. You allowed his broken body to be displayed, mutilated, and openly mocked by your men. Your actions, or lack thereof, helped murder a husband, a father, and a good man. I hope you are able to live with that for the rest of your miserable life."

She stepped back and glared at the hard mask Cormel now wore. Any expressions of guilt or sincerity were long gone. "As for your regrets towards my leaving, I can assure you that my sisters and I will meet again...as will you and I, *captain*."

She walked off, her threat lingering in the air. Her rage coiled and twisted in her chest, begging her to act. She needed to feel the pain of each arbitrator that dared to lay a hand on the people of Perilin. The pendant hanging between her breasts seemed to burn with similar desire. Her grandfather may have chosen her to join this army for her ability to easily make allies, but she was capable and more than willing to destroy her enemies.

7

Entering The Ring, it was hard to miss the large new addition to the center. In place of the small wooden box that once held tellers of tales and musicians was a large wooden stage. Ellie and Nate sat on a wood plank that was dug into the side of the steep grassy hill. The hill created a natural U-shape opposite of the stone wall that connected the east and west entrances. The entire east side was blocked off for designates, while the west was open for families and friends to watch as their loved ones joined a war for a queen they all despised.

Once they got settled in their spots, Nate leaned over to her. With his face nearly touching the side of hers, he delicately brushed her hair behind her ear. Onlookers would have mistaken it as simple flirting.

"Though I fully support you putting the captain in his place, I thought you were supposed to win over your superiors," he said quietly, his lips lightly brushing against her cheek. Her heart quickened. Nate was her friend, and they never once crossed that line beyond more than that, but Ellie couldn't deny how good it felt for him to be this close.

"I intend to win over our superiors once *in* Malavor. Captain Cormel will not be joining us. I also know he won't share my outburst with his men. The only harm that'll come from our little conversation will be towards the captain and the captain alone. Now, if you don't give me some space, I'm going to send my elbow through your stomach." She sweetly smiled at him with a piercing gaze. He scoffed softly but didn't move, as if reading the lie hidden in her voice.

"How else am I supposed to secretly talk to you when we're surrounded by people? Affection makes people uncomfortable, and therefore not listen."

His warm breath against her cheek sent her stomach fluttering. Ignoring it, she sternly replied, "It also makes us look weak and could put potential targets on both of our backs. It's dangerous to even allude to the arbitrators that we're friends. It only gives them a way to hold something and someone against us."

Nate sat back. A flash of hurt showed across his face before he returned to his emotionless demeanor. "So your grandpa was right," was his only quiet and short reply.

Before she could react to his statement, a short, round arbitrator struck his sword hilt against the wood stage. The sound was louder and more effective than yesterday's wooden box. The crowd settled. She scanned the western side, looking for her family, but there were too many people, too many worried faces.

"Good afternoon, Perilin!" A tall, well-built arbitrator began to speak from the round one's right side. His crimson jacket was missing and his sleeves were rolled up, exposing his tan, muscular arms.

He wasn't the only one missing the arbitrator's signature jacket. Three other men, including the round one, all wore their simple white linen shirts rolled up to their elbows.

"We have decided to do things a bit differently this year," the tall man said with a rough voice and a cruel smile. "Agility will still be your first test. However, quickly jumping over rocks, avoiding swinging flour sacks, and crawling through some mud isn't a great way to test agility for war. On the battlefield, you will have to move quickly enough to avoid a swinging sword, a flying arrow, or even a simple fist from your enemy. So this year, your agility test will be dodging us." He held his hands outright as some of the arbitrators whooped in excitement.

The man waited until the sickening cheers of his fellow men died down to continue. "You will come up to this stage four at a time, and each of you will stand across from one of us." He gestured to himself and the three jacketless arbitrators. "You will try your best to dodge the blows we send your way. After three hits, you're out. You will find that we are a lot less predictable than the normal obstacle course. This will truly test your agility."

Two of the arbitrators walked down from the stage and began picking designates to be tested. The first four included the man Ellie had encountered in line, two other men, and a young girl around her age. Ellie recognized the girl as one she often saw giggling in the market whenever Nate walked by. The girl's dark-ash hair had been tied in a bun, revealing a round, freckled face. She wore canvas shoes, twill pants, and a light cotton shirt, none of which were suited for the long journey ahead.

The girl faced the small arbitrator. He swung for her nose, and she quickly stepped back to dodge it. He swung again, and though she dodged underneath the fist, she wasn't prepared for the knee that swooped up into her chin. Hit one. She fell to the ground, cupping her face in her hands. Ellie's muscles stiffened. She clenched her fists at her sides, resisting the urge to rush on stage and brutally beat each arbitrator that supported this vile trial.

"This is cruel and just an excuse to hit us," Nate said through bared teeth.

The girl stood again, mouth and chin bleeding. Tears fell from the corners of her eyes as she readied for another attack. There was a fierce determination in her gaze, one that Ellie understood and admired. Though without proper training, will alone would not help the young woman.

"What's our strategy for this, El?" Nate asked, not looking away from the continuing trial.

"My grandpa once said it's best to let our enemies underestimate us. If we're underestimated, we won't be seen as much of a threat." Therefore, having the element of surprise for when they do show their true strength. She hated this particular lesson. She hated being underestimated. As a petite, wide-eyed young woman, that was already one thing men often did to her.

The girl took another blow to the stomach. Hit two.

"So, we dodge a few then let them take us out?"

"Maybe. Maybe not. I assume we'll be traveling with most of these men all the way to Malavor. It may be beneficial to win some of them over now rather than later. There's a total of ten arbitrators on the stage right now. Look at the three standing with Captain Cormel."

Hit three.

The young girl now lay unconscious on the wood stage. Cormel seemed to look anywhere but at the brutality that was occuring in front of him. None of the three men standing with the captain looked amused. The older, red-bearded one even looked disgusted and uncomfortable as he shifted in his spot.

"They just look bored. And like one of them has to relieve himself," Nate commented.

"Exactly—well, not the relief part—they're unamused. They clearly want to be entertained, so that's exactly what we're going to do." She smiled at Nate.

"Sounds like this might actually be some fun." The smile he sent back caused her stomach to twist again.

She quickly looked away. "I'd be willing to bet this new 'agility test' wasn't agreed on by all of the arbitrators. I personally don't want to ally or win over any arbitrator that sides with this kind of trial."

The three remaining designates got their three hits soon after the girl. One of them was forced to carry her limp body off the stage.

Captain Cormel and one of his bored, yet very attractive, comrades picked four more designates.

This process went on for some time. Not many people lasted long against the well-trained officers. A few older gentlemen, and even one girl with insane speed, lasted an impressive amount of time. After about eight rounds, Captain Cormel walked towards Ellie and Nate.

He simply pointed at them then gestured to the stage. The plump, short arbitrator leered and licked his lips as he pointed his stubby fingers at Ellie.

"I want that one." His smile showed crooked yellow teeth. Sweat and grease dripped from his dark brow, and his smell...It took everything in her not to gag. "You sure are dressed like you're ready for a fight." He ran his eyes down her entire body, stopping a little too long at her chest.

"I assume the use of my weapons is forbidden? The rules were a little vague," Ellie replied coolly.

"Seeing as how I have none, it would only be fair to refrain," the short man quipped back. "I wouldn't be opposed to some love taps, though, if you can land 'em." His wink was grotesque, but she didn't let her disgust show.

Ellie noted that, while his sword and whip were indeed missing from his belt, a peculiar buzzing black box still remained. Apparently, it didn't count as a weapon, so she simply smiled and replied, "Good."

They squared up, arms at the ready.

Nate stood against the tall, well-built arbitrator. He wasn't the worst-looking man with his tan skin, dark eyes, and square jaw. Upon closer inspection, however, Ellie could see he had a raised scar that ran from his left cheek to the middle of his neck. Another flat, discolored scar ran down his right forearm, and a small chunk of his right ear seemed to be missing.

Ellie was so focused on analyzing the man, she almost got hit by the small one's right hook. She swiftly dodged back just in time.

He came in for another. Avoiding his blows was step one. She easily evaded every hit that came her way, ducking, bending, rolling, and playfully spinning. It was a dance that she was clearly leading.

From the corner of her eye, Ellie could tell she had grabbed the attention of the onlooking arbitrators. They were mesmerized by the scene in front of them, so was the crowd as they began to cheer for every dodge Nate and her made.

The two other designates that were pulled on stage with them became distracted, and each received what remained of their three strikes. Their arbitrators now stood back watching as Nate and Ellie evaded each oncoming strike effortlessly.

Step two, taunt.

"Still waiting on those hits, sir...What was your name?"

The robust man gnashed his crooked teeth in anger. He came in for another sloppy hit. He was getting tired.

She twirled out of his way. "Not going to tell me, eh? That's fine. I'll just call you...the small one...or round one? No, I'll stick with the small one." She sent a sweet smile his way.

She heard a tiny huff from one of the men in Captain Cormel's direction. She looked their way and winked with a flirtatious smile. They each smirked and smiled back, clearly entertained. She found herself distracted by the soft, devilish smirk of one of the arbitrators. A truly handsome man with long golden-brown locks.

The husky arbitrator's voice snapped her back to focus. "You will call me Officer Schmilt or risk punishment." He struggled to not sound out of breath.

"My apologies, officer, but you seem tired. Would you like to take a break?"

"AGH!" He lunged, clearly planning a full-on tackle.

She sidestepped at the last moment, clipping his ankle and sending him face-first towards the wood ground.

At the same time, she glanced to see Nate take a hard hit to the gut. His arbitrator was clearly more skilled than the brute she faced.

Before Nate could recover, the arbitrator landed another hit to his face and ribs. Three strikes. He swayed but stayed standing. He took his place off stage with the other two defeated designates. It was impressive Nate had lasted this long.

"Bitch!" Schmilt picked himself up and wiped his now bleeding nose.

"Will this only end when *you* have landed three hits? Or could I end this now and distribute those three 'love taps' you seem to be waiting for? Again, the rules of this were a bit unclear."

His red-stained nostrils flared. "You continue to disrespect me and I'll make sure your body hangs in the middle of town alongside that worthless sack of a man."

He struck a chord; her face heated and hands shook as her anger rose.

Ellie knew she was playing with fire. If she let her rage take over, the small brute before her would be lying unconscious. Regardless of how vague she claimed the rules were, that could only lead to serious retribution.

Schmilt smiled at the clear agitation on her face. He attacked again, his right fist aimed for her face, while the other headed towards her gut.

Instead of avoiding the hits, she blocked each one with her forearms then quickly, and effectively, swung her knee into his groin. He fell to the ground like a sack of flour. The crowd roared their approval, while the three other whiteshirt arbitrators grabbed for their buzzing boxes. With a simple flick of their wrists, the box extended to a long metal rod with bright blue and white sparks blinking at the end.

Captain Cormel stepped in, hands raised towards the three arbitrators ready to attack. "She is right!" he yelled. His voice was commanding and stern. "The rules to this trial were unclear and seemed to be made with the underestimation of the designates."

He turned directly towards the tall, scarred arbitrator. "Officer Ballock, since you are the headmaster of this trial, shall you clarify some things?"

Officer Ballock nodded with a sneer, clearly displeased with the captain. He stepped towards the still whimpering Schmilt and dragged him off to the side.

"You will face me now," he said to Ellie with a poisonous

grin. "You may evade only. No blocking and no return blows. This is a test for agility, not a spar or combat test. Got it?"

"Got it." She returned the same poisonous grin, but before she knew it, Ballock's right leg was swinging towards her. She barely moved in time before it slammed back to the ground. Without missing a beat, he came at her with fists and elbows flying left, right, up, down.

All her years of training screamed to block, to hit, but she continued to duck, dodge, roll and spin, narrowly avoiding every potentially painful blow. Ballock was faster, larger, and stronger. His long reach made each evasion more difficult and exhausting.

He swung upwards towards her chest. She spun left only to be met by a kick landing in the exact spot the fist had originally aimed for. She flew back, landing just barely away from the edge of the stage. The air escaped her lungs, and her vision blurred.

She knew he'd try for the second and possible third blows while she was still down. She heard his heavy, quick pace head straight for where she lay. She rolled, barely avoiding a stomp that would have landed directly on her face.

New plan. She quickly jumped back up on her feet. Her lungs still burned, but her vision began to clear again. *Allow two more hits that won't kill or seriously injure me.*

Ballock came at her again. His speed had not wavered in the slightest.

"You seem to be less talkative with me, sweetheart. Am I proving to be too much for you?" He spoke smoothly between punches and kicks.

Yes, Ballock definitely had more training. Lethal training. He did have a pattern, though. One she was starting to become familiar with.

"I assume those scars are from the one who trained you. Was it a fellow arbitrator?" She jumped and rolled, avoiding another deadly hit. "Or was it a family member?"

He slightly clenched his jaw but let little other emotion show.

"I'm leaning towards family. Mom? Maybe a brother? Or was it dear old Daddy?"

Pain and anger quickly flashed across his face. *There it is.*

He came for her with rage-filled eyes. His anger made him sloppy but less predictable, and hopefully less lethal.

She saw an elbow head her way and allowed it to land against her cheek. She did her best to move with the hit, to avoid serious injury, but the man was incredibly strong.

The final hit came faster than Ellie expected. Ballock brought his foot up into her gut, thrusting her off her feet, towards his fellow arbitrators, and into the wood deck. It splintered and cracked below her, as did her head.

She tried to stand but only sat up as far as her arms could push her. Her head throbbed and the world around her spun.

Captain Cormel's voice boomed from behind her. "NO!" he yelled as intense, hot pain suddenly coursed through Ellie's body.

She tried to move, breathe, or just scream, but all she could do was feel pain.

"ELLIE!" She locked in on Cammie's distressed face among the crowd before being taken by complete darkness.

8

The smell of herbs and bark filled her dizzy head. The feeling of canvas pressed against her skin. Both the smell and touch were familiar.

She was on a cot in the healer's home.

Her face throbbed, her chest burned, but nothing hurt more than the fire she felt from the center of her back. She didn't dare move or breathe too deeply.

Hushed whispers came from her right.

"You saw how she fought, captain," one man voiced.

"And the fact that her two other sisters most likely have the same training...It's incredible. You had no clue she could fight like that?" Another deeper voice spoke. It sounded slightly amused.

"No, and I understand your concern, Ames, but her training makes her even more valuable. It's best if you two and Officer Shea earn her loyalty quickly. And make sure the other arbitrators stay clear of her. Do you understand? I've already sent word to the generals, reporting the actions of Officer Schmilt." Captain Cormel's voice was strong. Assertive. Not at all like how he spoke with the folks in town. The voices continued to speak, but darkness took over.

Pain shot through her spine as she again came to.

"She should not travel in this condition." Agilta, the town healer, spoke firmly. "Her external and internal wounds were only worsened by that horrid weapon you carry. I cannot and will not release her. It goes against every oath I've given as a healer."

"If you give us detailed and proper instructions, we can assure she will be well taken care of." The deep-voiced officer spoke in a calm tone, trying to ease the tension that swirled in the room.

"Ha! I did trust you! I even helped some of you! Despite once being free citizens of these lands, you arbitrators are all the same. You come to this town, killing and injuring more than half of its people! I've treated more patients today than I have all year! Now you expect me to hand over to you a young lady that was nearly killed just hours ago?"

"Ma'am, I—"

"No! Get out! Get OUT!" The last word echoed in Ellie's throbbing head. She groaned as she tried to lift herself from the hard cot.

"Oh, dear...No, no darling. Please, you must lie down and rest." Agilta shoved a foul-tasting liquid into her mouth. Seconds later, she welcomed the dark once more.

Ellie came in and out of consciousness for what she had to assume was days. There were moments where water and other liquids were being shoved down her throat. Moments where she could feel the sun beating down on her and could hear the crunching of rocks and dirt beneath wood wheels. A moment where she could smell the dews of the night and feel the warmth of a larger body sleeping next to her.

All of these moments were short, and as hard as she

tried to fight it, the darkness would take her. Over and over again. Until she finally awoke to the touch of a hand rubbing something cool and soothing onto her back.

Her head no longer throbbed, but her face felt stiff and bruised. The salve now being placed on her back took the edge off the intense stinging.

In circular motions, a strong, gentle hand melted away the pain.

"Mmm." She couldn't control the relief that escaped her throat.

"Hey. You finally coming to?" Nate's voice sounded strange, gravelly, and strained.

"Mmm," was her only reply. He removed his hand from her back. She grumbled in protest. "How long?"

Talking took more effort than she thought it would. Her tongue was dry, and her throat felt like sandpaper.

"Three days," he replied.

Three Days! She had been out for *three* days. "What happened? I need every detail." She pushed herself up to sit. Every muscle screamed and ached in protest. Her arms shook under her own weight. Three days of unmoving recovery inside the back of a large wood wagon had taken its toll.

A flat mat and blankets lay underneath her, and she was surrounded by packs of supplies and some weapons, including her own. Light was beginning to fade, bugs began to chirp, and a light breeze blew on the back of her neck, all indications of evening.

She took her first look at Nate.

These three days must have been hell because that was what he looked like. His eyes were sunken in, hair disheveled, and dust and dirt covered him from head to toe.

"You need to eat first. I will inform Officer Shea that

you're awake and see if there is any food left from supper." Nate walked off, his steps unsteady and weaker than usual. As if...As if he'd been the only one pulling her and this wagon for the past three days.

She looked for straps and reins that may be used to attach the wagon to a horse, but there were none. The handles to the wagon were wrapped in leather, and that leather had two large, familiar handprints worn into it.

Scattered around the dirt path, far from the wagon, were the rest of Perilin's designates. Some sat, still picking at their supper, while others found a patch of dirt to sleep for the night. They all looked the same as Nate: tired, disheveled, and dirty.

A young girl with beautiful brown skin and dark coiled hair locked eyes with Ellie. She jumped to her feet, despite the exhaustion that showed on her petite face, and ran Ellie's way. She was the girl with the speed. The one who had lasted a surprising amount of time against her arbitrator.

"Hi!" She smiled, her lip and cheek still a bit swollen and bruised from one of the arbitrator's hits. Her kind, hazel eyes examined Ellie's body as if to make sure she truly was alive.

"I'm Kiarhem. I just wanted to say, you are AMAZING! I have so many questions! But I don't want to get in trouble with the arbitrators. I just wanted to introduce myself. Hopefully we can talk more and you could maybe teach me a few things."

There was a slight inflection in the way the young girl spoke. Ellie couldn't quite focus on it through the speed that also apparently applied to how Kiarhem talked.

"Get in trouble?" Ellie looked at her, confused and a little overwhelmed.

Kiarhem was bouncing on the balls of her feet, seemingly unable to control her nervous energy. Ellie had never seen her anywhere before, which for a small town like Perilin, was nearly impossible.

"We're not supposed to come near you." Her bouncing stopped as she looked around for arbitrators. "Only a few arbitrators and your handsome friend are allowed to be near you and this wagon."

"Why?"

"We don't know." Kiarhem shrugged her shoulders. "I think they're afraid of you."

Ellie looked around and noticed there were many eyes watching her. Some whispered to each other, while others met her gaze with a tired, yet revering expression.

"We admire you, though. All of Perilin does." Kiarhem turned and ran back to her spot among a few other women and young men.

Moments later, Nate returned with a plate of food in hand and an arbitrator on his heels. The redheaded arbitrator wore his full uniform despite the summer heat. His bearded face was aged and wrinkled, and a gentle smile grew as he came closer.

"Hello, Miss Batair." He grabbed her hand gently and cupped it between his. She tried not to cringe at the touch or the quiet humming that came from the black box on his right hip. "I am Officer Shea, and I would formally like to apologize for the actions of Officer Schmilt. Now tell me, how are you feeling?"

Actions of Officer Schmilt? She still didn't know what happened to her. The last thing she remembered was pain. Utterly indescribable pain.

Ellie had questions upon questions, but Officer Shea's kindness and overall presence caught her off guard. His downturned, teal eyes sat closely to his crooked nose. Ellie could tell that nose had been broken and reset one too many times. His fiery beard was trimmed and well-groomed, but the hair still covered most of his thin lips.

"Uh, I'm fine. Just stiff."

"May I examine you? I'm no healer, but I've been in enough battles to know when something's healing and when it's not." His teal eyes were locked onto hers as he patiently awaited her answer. His voice was oddly comforting, and Ellie thought there was some familiarity to it. Like she had once heard it a lifetime ago.

She simply nodded in reply, too deep in her confusion and thoughts to form a verbal response.

Nate stood nearby, monitoring every move Shea made. He first examined the bruising on her face, then her ribs, gut, and finally back. He touched the center of her spine, and she nearly blacked back out from the pain.

It shot through her entire body, burning and stinging like a million fire ants had made their home in the cracks between her bones. She fell towards the mat, screaming in agony.

"I'm sorry! Oh, my. I'm so sorry." Shea backed away with arms raised.

Nate dropped the plate of food and rushed to her side. He held Ellie's head as tears fell from the corners of her eyes.

"Why would you touch it!?" Nate yelled.

"I apologize, but I needed to see how far she had recovered. The fact that she is still conscious means the spot is in fact healing."

"Or you've just agitated it and made it worse!" Nate shook with rage.

"What spot!" Ellie cried. "Please, what happened to me?" Her broken sobs were less from the pain and more from the unknown. Her training had made her quite adaptable to pain, but this agony—this pure suffering—was like nothing she had ever experienced before.

"I-I assumed you had told her." Shea's eyes glazed over with sadness, and he looked down at the food that lay in the dirt. "I will fetch you more food."

Nate pulled out a silver jar from her pack and scooped a small amount of thick salve onto his hand. "Turn onto your side. This will help." She did as he asked. He began to gently rub the tonic in circular motions along her lower back and up until he reached the center. It immediately soothed the burning pain once more.

"How are you able to touch my back without it hurting?" She couldn't help it as her body relaxed into his caress.

"Agilta. It's one of her concoctions. Thankfully, it seems to work."

She took deep breaths, releasing the lasting ache as she exhaled. "Nate. Please, what happened?"

He pulled his hand away and let it fall to his lap. "Schmilt. He used his flare baton on you."

"Flare baton?"

"It's what they call those new weapons. The ones with the blue and white sparks at the end. When you went to get up after Ballock knocked you down the final time, Schmilt stabbed you in the back with the baton. He was whimpering on the ground for most of your fight with Ballock, so no one noticed when he got up and pulled out the weapon. Captain Cormel tackled Schmilt to the ground, and he's been in shackles since."

"Why was I affected so badly? There were others in town hit with these same weapons the day before, and Cormel said they were fine."

"No." Nate helped her sit up but refused to meet her eyes. "They were not fine. They all died, El."

Her heart sank at his words. "What? H-how would you know that? Cor-Cormel said they were fine." The wood wagon beneath her seat suddenly felt unsteady. The world seemed to spin as she thought of the dozens of men and women of Perilin that no longer walked this land.

"The captain was unaware of their statuses when we were at the trial. It wasn't until he took you to Agilta that he was told about their deaths."

"And how did you find out?"

"Agilta refused to release you. She was willing to give her life to keep you there. The arbitrators wanted us to start traveling almost immediately after the trial ended, but they wouldn't leave without you. After only a couple hours of Agilta tending to you, Cormel came and got me. We assured her that I would be your sole caretaker. That only Shea and I would be allowed near you until you awoke. She eventually agreed and walked me through everything that had happened to the others, and everything you would need to have a fighting chance at recovery."

"Wha-what happened to the others, Nate?" She recalled each face that could have stood against the arbitrators that day. Perilin was small enough that she knew most by name. It was almost too hard to believe they no longer lived and breathed.

Nate's jaw tightened and throat bobbed. "They each were hit with the weapons in different areas, but the spots where they were hit were all marked the same: a black cluster of lightning that grew and grew each hour. Agilta said they were unconscious until the last moment when the mark would reach their hearts. They would wake up silently screaming in pain and agony until it killed them. She found that this tonic was the only thing that slowed down the spread of the mark, but she couldn't figure out how to stop it completely."

Nate grabbed her hand. It was rough and blistered from the past few days of pulling the wagon. "Your mark, El. It's only inches from your heart, but it hasn't grown. It's slowly getting smaller. Agilta monitored you for hours, and she could not tell me why it has affected you differently or why you're still here." Nate's eyes lined with silver. His head drooped, and his breathing became uneven. "I thought...I thought I lost you, El. For days now, I expected you to wake up screaming and that would be the end. I would've had to do all of this without you."

Ellie's chest and throat tightened. Seeing Nate so tormented was worse than any pain she could ever feel.

She placed his arm around her neck and wrapped her own arms around his torso. "I'm sorry you have had to deal with this alone. I promise, I'm here now and I'm not going anywhere." He squeezed ever so slightly, aware that any more would put her in a great deal of pain. She could feel his shoulders relax and his breathing ease. "And thank you. I'm sure pulling me in this thing hasn't been easy."

"That would be putting it lightly." His words were a guilt-filled poison. He saw the hurt and squeezed her once more. "It's fine. I just wish I could take small rests throughout the day. No one is allowed to stop. We walk from first light to early evening. Except for the first day. We left as soon as Agilta released you and walked through half the night."

That was odd. Designates usually left the morning after the first trial, giving them much-needed rest before the long journey. They weren't allowed to see their families once enlisted, so designates were forced to camp out in The Ring.

Of course, Ellie and Nate had planned on breaking that rule when it was just him enlisting. The plan they had spent weeks making became useless when the decree was read and she knew her grandpa would be sending her to join Nate on this risky journey.

Ellie didn't question the unusual departure. "What happens if you stop?"

"Ballock." Nate's shoulders tensed. "The first full day of travel, an older man fell from the heat and exhaustion. When two other men tried to help him up, Ballock stabbed the man who fell, leaving him to bleed to death, and flogged the other two for stopping to help. Shea claims if Cormel were here, his actions would have him shackled next to Schmilt. But they're all ranked equally here, which allows Ballock to do what he wants with no repercussions."

Her gut burned with deep hatred towards the cruel arbitrator. "Has he killed any others?"

"No. Just whipped a few that he felt weren't walking fast enough. Honestly, with the order to keep away from you, I probably could have rested for a few seconds here and there. It just didn't seem fair if I did."

Ellie nodded in agreement. "You should get some rest. I'll eat once Officer Shea has returned and then rest as well."

A warmth entered his eyes as he lifted a hand to tuck a tangled piece of hair behind her ear. "You have no idea how happy I am that you're okay."

Nate's words should have unwound the knot forming in Ellie's gut, but instead, it tightened. An unexplainable uncertainty gnawed at her. Was she really alright? If so, why? She was struck by a weapon that should have killed her. With the amount of pain the wound still inflicted on her, she wondered if it still could. Officer Shea seemed to think she was healing, but he was an arbitrator. One she didn't know if she could trust yet. He had touched the wound, willingly agitating it. If the mark was poked at enough, would it start to grow? Would it eventually take her like it did the others?

Nate lay down, unaware of her turmoil, and was sound asleep within minutes.

Shea returned with a plate of stale bread, some kind of meat, and a few berries. Ellie took it tentatively. He examined her face again, making sure there were no signs of infection. With the man's face close to hers, she searched it more thoroughly for a crack in the kind exterior he wore. But she couldn't find one, and the more she looked, the more familiar the man seemed.

"It's good to see him rest peacefully. He has hardly slept in days." He eyed her closely to make sure she choked down the old food. Ellie wanted to believe this man was genuinely kind but was hesitant to trust any arbitrator.

"Did you help kill the men and women in my town?" Ellie abruptly asked, unable to hold in her question. She needed to know if she could trust *this* arbitrator, and she couldn't ignore her gut screaming at her to do just that.

His eyes filled instantly with sorrow. "We were not aware of what these weapons would do. We're not even sure how they work. Fortunately, no. I do not hold that burden in my hands."

"Why would you use a weapon that you know nothing about?"

"Because our queen and her generals told us to."

"That's foolish."

"No. That is service." He glared down at her, though his

teal eyes still glittered with a hint of kindness. "It would be wise of you to think more before you speak. Calling any of the other arbitrators here a fool would have resulted in more pain for you."

"My apologies, sir." Ellie knew he was right.

Shea sighed, hanging his arms by his side. "I too used to have your fire, many years ago, on my Designation Day."

"It's hard to see arbitrators as once-fellow designates. I forget you all were once taken from your homes too."

"It is easy to forget when brutes like Schmilt and Ballock exist. Cruel and obsessed with power."

"I've heard that most arbitrators are like them."

"Mm. Yes, most are. The cruel and hate-filled designees are the ones the generals choose for duties like town watch or designate collecting. However, every now and then, they mess up and enlist a good egg for those positions." He smiled, deepening the wrinkles around his eye.

The generals came with the Queen from wherever she came from. They were present for the next trials and chose where each designate was placed among the Queen's Army. They also chose when and if you were ever promoted.

"So, what were you? Before all of this, Officer Shea?" She waved a hand around at the designates.

His teal eyes softened. "Before joining the war, I was a husband, and..." He looked away, clenching his jaw. Ellie heard the hurt that filled his voice. She didn't need him to finish speaking to know he was going to say he was a father. *Was.*

She then remembered what she had overheard in Agilta's hut. She recalled the words of Captain Cormel.

Earn her loyalty.

Officer Shea was doing a good job at following orders at this moment, and she wondered who Ames and the other deeper-voiced arbitrator were. Why did they want her loyalty? And would they return that loyalty to her?

"You should rest. I shall check on you in the morning." He grabbed the now empty plate from her hands and turned to leave, but Ellie stopped him with a gentle hand to his wrist. He looked down at the hand that held him, a distant memory seeming to flash across his face.

"You said I was healing. Do you truly believe that?"

Shea met her gaze. She was shocked by the tenderness that blanketed his features. "Like I said, there is not much we know about these weapons or the wounds they inflict. But yes, I truly believe you are healing, Ellie. It would take a force much stronger than the power in these weapons to end a Batair."

Officer Shea turned and walked away, not giving her a chance to see the truth of his statement written on his features. But it was there, in his voice and the way he spoke. There was respect, pride, and undeniable sincerity.

Ellie lay down next to Nate, scooting close for his warmth.

Shea was right. Other than the generals, every officer in the Queen's Army was once a designee, so why had this gone on for so long? The arbitrators, captains, and designates outnumbered the generals a hundred to one. Everyone knew the Eternal Queen held immense power, but there were rumors her generals did as well.

Many more questions ran through her head, calculating, theorizing, and speculating, when sleep took hold.

Ellie stood watching a beautiful dark-haired woman. She held a small infant in her arms and lifted the storage compartment of a carriage. *Two small children climbed in. The woman placed the baby atop them.*

"Make sure she stays quiet, my girls. They mustn't hear you." Before closing the compartment, she placed blankets and a few other items in to further conceal the girls. The woman ran to sit next to a tall man with silver hair.

Ellie's grandpa.

The woman to his left, though much younger, was her Grams. "Go."

They took off on a dirt path. Smoke and fire raged all around them. Beautiful homes were burning to nothing but rubble. Invisible screams from women and children rang through Ellie's ears.

The carriage began to disappear into the distance as smoke filled and burned her lungs. She ran after it, wanting to see more, know more. She ran but did not move forward. The air around her filled with the thick black smoke. She couldn't breathe. She couldn't see. She was suffocating.

A sudden blue light flashed, and from it a voice cried out.

"Find me!"

9

Ellie shot up.

Her body screamed in pain at the sudden movement. It took a moment to get her bearings. The intense sun had already passed the center of the sky, making it late afternoon. On both sides, dense forest and old dilapidated burnt homes passed her by. The same homes she just saw burning in her dream.

"Why didn't you wake me? Where are we?" she called up to a sweaty Nate.

"You needed your sleep," he said through ragged breaths. "And we're in Malavor, just an hour or so away from the training center."

Shit.

Ellie swiftly strapped on her gear and pack. Thankfully, her back harness hit just above the mark on her spine. After a deep breath, she readied herself to jump out of the moving wagon. She couldn't arrive at the training camp looking weak and already injured.

*Alright. One. Two...*She jumped on three.

Normally, it would have been an easy graceful leap to the ground. Unfortunately, her injuries and days of lying on her ass led to her crumbling towards the dirt. Her legs instantly gave out beneath her. She reached her arm out to catch her fall, but it, too, failed. She instinctively rolled onto her shoulder, the silver hilt of her sword clanging against the rocky dirt.

"WHAT THE HELL!" Nate yelled, slowing his pace.

She pushed through the stiffness in her joints and the agonizing pain of her injuries, both on her back and now on the hands and knees that failed to break her fall. Through gritted teeth, she crawled alongside the wagon, attempting to grab onto the side every few steps.

Nate stopped. "Get back in. *Now!*"

His face was red from more than just the heat. With the wagon stopped, she grabbed the side's edge and pulled herself up.

"I'm fine. Keep going before we get in trouble."

His clenched jaw was Nate's only protest as he began walking again. She leaned into the wood with her arms hanging inside the wagon, putting nearly all her weight on it.

Every step was excruciating. Her legs shook, her chest burned, and her back screamed in protest. An arbitrator on horseback rode up seconds later.

"Is everything alright here?" His familiar deep voice sent shivers over every inch of her skin. It was the same deep voice she had heard in Agilta's place. Light-gray eyes stared down at her, almost hidden beneath the shadow of his shoulder-length golden-brown hair. This was the same handsome arbitrator whose smirk had nearly distracted her during the first trial. The same mischievous smile currently looked at her.

"We're fine, *sir*," Nate snapped back without even a glance at the breathtaking broad man.

A low, feral growl vibrated out from the man. Eyes like daggers stared at the back of Nate's head. The sound ended as quickly as it started. Ellie blinked and the officer's gaze was once again on her, his coquettish smile not matching the remaining fire in his eyes. This man was undeniably dangerous. And despite the warning bells ringing in Ellie's head, she couldn't help but be intrigued by him.

In a swift movement, the arbitrator dismounted from his horse. He left the reins lying loosely against his horse's neck. With a click of the tongue, the silky brown mare followed close behind him.

"May I?" He held an outstretched hand towards her. He did not wear the velvet arbitrator coat over his white tunic. A few buttons were left undone, showing a sliver of bronze muscle. More surprising than the relaxed way he wore his uniform was the absence of a black buzzing box.

He noticed her gaze on his empty hip. "I have no need for that weapon, at least not right now." She looked at him, needing more reasoning for the missing weapon. He continued, "The flare batons are meant to quickly deal with traitors or deserters, not to be used on women who bruise a small man's ego."

He moved closer, that wicked smile growing more gentle with each step. Ellie thought through the advantages and disadvantages of taking the man's arm. Having an arbitrators' help showed her weakened state. She knew this man was one of the arbitrators that Captain Cormel spoke with. This officer wanted her loyalty and only offered his hand now as a way to gain it, but she could hear Nate's labored breath. Her added weight and the unbalanced position it took on the wagon was making things harder for him. A questionable part of her tugged at her gut, pulling her towards taking the man's outstretched hand. The pendant pressed against her chest reacting to that pull; it grew colder, causing her skin to prickle.

Ellie nodded, taking the man's hand. "Just avoid touching my back, please."

She pushed up against the wood beneath her. The instant his strong arm looped underneath her's, a strange breeze caressed her ears. It carried with it the crisp scent of autumn and the whisper of leaves and branches rustling in the wind. The sound called to her very soul. It was comforting, yet freeing. Like it could sing her to sleep or encourage her to fly. But when she looked around, there were no trees that swayed, and the stale summer air was utterly still. She shook her head, ignoring the odd sensation.

At first, they walked arm in arm in silence. She focused on her steps, as if learning to walk all over again. After a while, her steps became stronger and the pain in her back lessened. She was able to put less weight on the man next to her. He silently looked onward as his mare still followed close by.

"I've never seen a horse follow its owner like that. It must have taken a lot of work and training to trust her off reins in such a way."

"Animals are always trustworthy. We are the ones that must earn their keeping. Tabat follows because she trusts me, not the other way around." His voice was like silk, wrapping her in the warmest of blankets. His deep, soothing tone kept her distracted from the aching in her back. An aching that he seemed to notice.

"I am sorry for the events that took place at your first trial." He looked at her with true regret in his eyes, as if he himself struck her with the flare baton. He shifted his gaze away for a moment then half smiled. "However, I would be lying if I said I didn't enjoy seeing Schmilt taken out by a lethal and absolutely stunning woman."

She whipped her head to meet the arbitrator's gaze. Her face flushed with heat at the devilish grin he gave her. She suddenly became very aware of the strong hand she held. Of the muscles beneath her arm.

"Whoever trained you did an excellent job," he added. Amusement danced in his gray eyes at her visibly heated face.

Arrogant ass, she thought, angry at the effect this stranger had on her. Ellie removed more of her weight from his hold, no longer wanting to be so close to a man who so easily got under her skin.

She contemplated her next words. She needed to win over as many arbitrators as she could. That was one of the only clear actions her grandfather asked of her. She needed their loyalty, just as much as this officer needed hers, for reasons she couldn't even begin to speculate or understand.

"My grandpa."

"Sorry?"

"My grandpa. He's the one who trained me and my sisters." The officer was already somehow aware of her sisters' training, as he was the one to mention it to Cormel. "He trained us knowing one day we would have to fight in this war."

He stared fervently at her still red and bruised face. After some time, he replied, "I am sorry for that as well. Though it is quite an attractive quality when a woman can fight and take care of herself."

"I'm sure you are quite used to a woman having to take *care* of things herself." She slammed her mouth shut. His teasing smile and rain of compliments begged for the snide remark, but he was an arbitrator that she should only speak to with respect.

The officer's eyes widened at her insinuation. Not in shock, but delight. The slight pull at the corner of his mouth revealed the laugh he held in. He lowered his voice, drawing nearer to her ear. "I assure you, Miss Batair, *that* is one thing I know exactly how to take care of."

Her heart seemed to beat out of her chest. He straightened back up, his eyes not leaving hers. Her gut twisted with a bit of terror and slight intrigue. Ellie had verbally sparred with many men, but this one was the most beautiful man she had ever met. Each corner of his full lips remained pulled up as she unashamedly studied every inch of him.

Ellie slowly brought her gaze forward, ignoring the officer's delighted smile. Nate glared back at them, his entire body tense and rigid as he pulled the heavy wagon behind him. She ignored both men, bringing her focus to the charred homes and destroyed lives that surrounded her. "The Queen's men did all this?" Ellie barely even whispered her question.

"Yes," the arbitrator answered to her surprise. "Many years ago. The destruction on the outskirts of Malavor has been untouched as the generals focused mostly on building the training camp in and around the old castle."

The single dirt path they walked started to branch out in multiple different directions, all leading down paths with more destroyed homes and buildings. All except one lonely path to her right.

It was overgrown with grass and weeds, but it was unmistakably still a path. A path that led to a house still standing in the far distance. A strange urge to walk towards the house pulled at her skin. The pendant hanging from her neck grew colder in answer to the strange call.

"Ah. I wouldn't even think about going that way."

"Why?" Ellie snapped her attention back to the officer. He looked at her with a playful smile. His arrogance was grating on what little restraint she had on the anger growing in her gut.

"If the stories are true, it's best to stay clear of that house. Let's just leave it at that."

She looked up at him with wide, questioning eyes that begged to be told more. Question without questioning. Another one of her grandfather's lessons.

Find out information without it seeming like you're in search of that information.

The young officer lightly laughed at the curious expression she wore. "Well, we know that the people that once resided here in Malavor were of many different races, but most residents were indeed Fae."

"Really?" She knew this already, knew of the Fae and of their incredible strength and power, but she wanted him to keep talking. She wanted to see how much he knew, and how much he was willing to share.

The people of Fae descent were said to have all but disappeared years ago. Some people even claimed they were all killed when the Eternal Queen took over Malavor. The thought of a race holding such power was truly intriguing, but information on them was limited. Since their disappearance, not many people still talked of the Fae, and her grandfather's study had little to no books about them.

"Yes. The King and Queens of Malavor were in fact very formidable Fae." He looked down at her, his gray eyes lingering on hers for a moment. "The last person who lived there was said to be an extremely powerful Fae. With their dying breath, they placed a curse around the house, so that anyone who goes near it becomes, well...They become so distraught that they kill themselves."

Ellie's chest tightened, and she was unable to hide her wide, horrified eyes. "That's awful."

"The Eternal Queen sent multiple groups of men to the house. They all ended up killing themselves. At one point, the Queen herself went to the house. She didn't get close enough to be affected by its magic. She just tried to get close enough to break the curse, but as we all know, only the blood of the one that cast the curse can break it."

She, in fact, did not know that and was truly surprised he did.

"The Queen came to Malavor? I've never heard of her leaving her throne in Sondoér."

"She was here for the entire attack on Malavor. I doubt it would have happened without her presence."

"How do you know so much about this?" Truly. The man holding her upright knew more about the attack on Malavor than anyone she had ever come in contact with.

"We all have our hobbies," he said with a wink that sent her empty stomach flipping. "The city seems to hold on to its history despite the many years the Eternal Queen has spent trying to erase it."

His gray eyes looked into hers once more. For a moment, she didn't feel the aches and pains that ran through her body. She only felt fierce strength and something...different from those gray eyes. "You may find many places in Malavor where magic still runs free."

"Officer Reuel!" an arbitrator called in the distance, breaking their gaze.

"It seems I'm being summoned. Your steps appear to be stronger," he said, looking down at her dust-covered pants.

"Will you be alright with the wagon as your support, Miss Batair?"

"It's Ellie," she blurted, shocked by her own extension of familiarity. His jaw clenched slightly, as if the sound of her name pained him. The line of tightness in his face disappeared as quickly as it had appeared, replaced only by his pompous smile.

"Yes, I think I can manage." He guided her to the wood side. "Thank you, Officer Reuel. For your support and overall company. It was unexpectedly nice," she said with a flirtatious smile.

If this officer wanted to play games, she would gladly engage. With one hand on the wagon, she untangled her other from his. Slowly, she took a moment to pass every line, scar, and callus. It was his turn to become the slightest shade of red. Her own devilish smile widened at what she had done to him.

Before she could pull her hand completely away, he grabbed it back. Ever so gently, he brought her hand to his lips. Releasing it, he smiled broadly. "I hope to have more conversations with you, Ellie."

He walked off with his mare following close behind.

She watched him saunter away, annoyed that he had the last word, until the wagon ran over a rock that shook the wood beneath her. She leaned into the side, barely keeping herself upright.

"Sorry." Nate grimaced back.

She scooted forward to the front of the wagon. Her added weight to the lifted front didn't seem to bother Nate.

"These arbitrators aren't what I thought they would be. You've been around them longer. What is your opinion?"

Nate filled his lungs. "Shea is decent. Reuel..." He

grimaced at the name. "I'm not sure about. But Ames...I'd like to stay as far away from him as possible."

"Why? Which one is Ames?" She stiffly looked around the group.

"You won't find him. He likes to stay...*hidden*." Ellie furrowed her brows but didn't ask more about the officer in question. "The other officers, though less aggressive, are still just as cruel and hostile as Ballock." Nate's breath was deeply labored. His arms shook and sweat dripped from every inch of his body.

She lifted herself from the wagon. Her back throbbed, but her legs held true. Each step became easier as the muscle memory returned. She walked up next to Nate, placing a hand over his.

"I can try to help you pull—"

"No. I'm all right." But he wasn't. She knew he wasn't. No body, even one as young and fit as Nate's, should endure the labor his had in the last few days.

"I'm sure we're almost there. You'll be done with this wagon soon."

They were closer than she realized as a tall stone wall peeked above the trees and worn-down buildings.

10

People in front of them began to slow down. The path up ahead was met with multiple other paths that were filing in hundreds of people, with designates from other places all over Karmalo. Some groups traveled fully on horseback, while others traveled in large wooden carriages. Very few traveled on foot like their group. They squeezed themselves within the crowd.

"Hey! You!" a voice yelled from their right. A lean arbitrator atop a horse pointed down in Nate's direction. "Bring that wagon over here!" Nate didn't hesitate.

He placed the wagon next to a large canvas tent. After a nod from the arbitrator, he returned to beside Ellie. His arms hung stiff as he opened and closed his fists, stretching his tired fingers.

"I hope I never have to touch another wagon again." He now rested a hand on the black stag hilt that swung from his hip. The two of them and their weapons no longer stood out among the new individuals that surrounded them. Many other designates wore similar garb and carried well-made and hand-crafted weapons.

Every few moments, the crowd would inch closer to the large stone wall. For ages they stood in line, squished and surrounded by people, all of whom could use a wash. As they got closer, Ellie scanned her new surroundings.

Dozens of large canvas tents lined the exterior wall. Atop of the wall were multiple arbitrators who stood guard, keeping an eye on every new designate below. The sun was on its descent as they finally reached the massive entrance built into the stone wall.

Multiple small wood tables were blocking the entrance. At each table sat a beautiful woman, some young, some old. Designees stood across from each woman. After some time, a lady would nod and wave them past to the area beyond the wall.

"I thought this was the first year women were forced to sign up," Ellie whispered to Nate. A large man to her left stood so close that his sweat was now dripping onto her shoulder. He heard her comment and replied.

"They're not women. They're witches."

"Witches haven't been seen since the Eternal Queen's first attack on Karmalo soil." Nate looked in the man's direction.

"Most covens dispersed and hid all throughout Karmalo, keeping their powers hidden from the Queen. All except one." The man nodded towards the women. "This coven freely joined the Queen's cause."

"Why?" Ellie asked, trying not to cringe at the growing moisture on her shoulder.

"I heard it was because they're not as strong as their sister clans. They were tired of being overlooked and gladly jumped at the opportunity to be used. This is all talk from the healers in my town. I don't know where they got their information, so it could be all hogwash."

Ellie doubted that. Healers were not ones to spread misinformation.

Three arbitrators stood at the front of the line. When a place was freed up across from a witch, they called the next designate to move forward. After a few minutes, it was Nate and Ellie's turn.

She was called forward first and pointed to an elderly witch seated in the center of the line of tables. The witch's hair was white, her face was covered in small lines and deep wrinkles, and her dark-purple eyes were lined with charcoal.

She did not speak as Ellie slowly approached her small wood table. Scrutinizing eyes studied up and down her face and toned body. The witch furrowed her brows, pursed her lips, and looked into Ellie's crystal eyes with clear concern written all over her features.

After ages of her staring, she signaled to a witch standing hidden among the shadows of the entrance. Another young witch emerged from a different shadow, cutting off the first.

"I can take over from here, Mother Ubel." The elder witch looked at her skeptically, but the young one just stared blankly back at her. After a moment, Ubel stood, whispering something into the young witch's ear.

She turned to give one more questioning look before heading to the shadows, where Ellie was sure many more witches waited and watched.

"Sorry about that. Mother Ubel has never trusted a pretty face." The young witch smiled, showing overly-white teeth between deep-red lips. She, too, wore charcoal around her emerald-green eyes, which popped against her unbound raven-black hair.

She pulled a small glass vial from a drawer below the wood table. "Here. You have to drink this," she said, handing Ellie the vial filled with a thick brown liquid. "It unfortunately tastes worse than it looks."

"What is it?" Ellie asked, swirling the goo inside. All witches were known to be exceptional potion and tonic makers. At one time, they were the teachers to the healers of this world, traveling from town to town, sharing their gifts and knowledge. But the witches were one of the handful of races who were prone to have stronger forms of magic. From the research Ellie had done in her grandpa's study, witches were one of only two races who studied and used the origin tongue. The language of the gods. They used it to guide their magic, forming it to their will.

"I am not at liberty to say, but I assure you, every new designate has to drink it." That wasn't as comforting as Ellie was sure the witch thought it was.

Sure enough, designates to her left and right were drinking from small brown-filled vials. She took a deep breath, pinching her nose as she lifted the vile to her lips.

It didn't help. The brown sludge tasted of bile and rotten eggs with a hint of...*Vanilla?* she thought, forcing herself to swallow.

Instantly, she felt off. Her heart raced, palms clammed, and every hair on her body stood on edge.

"Good. Let's begin. What is your name?"

"Elll—"

Oh, gods. What did she give me?

Every ounce of her being wanted to scream her full given birth name. She clenched her fists and breathed deeply.

"Ellie Batair."

The witch looked at her skeptically, with a hint of

delight. "And where were you born, Ellie?" she continued. A smile now formed at the corner of her mouth.

"P-Perilin."

"Will you be a threat to our queen?"

"N-no" Every answer, every lie was agony. The witch leaned further onto the wood table between her. With a poisonous smile, she asked one final question.

"What blood runs through your veins?"

"What?" Ellie's hands were beginning to tremble.

"What are you? What blood runs through your veins?"

"Human." Ellie's body relaxed as the truth left her lips. It was such a relief, she almost missed the look of slight shock from the young witch. The witch sat back, a wicked smile now plastered onto her pale face.

"Interesting," she said, looking Ellie over.

"What?"

"Nothing. The tonic should wear off in a few, so you're free to go." She waved her hand behind her.

Nate stood just beyond the wall of witches in a crowded courtyard. Ellie rushed to his side, ready to discuss the events that just occurred.

"Oh! Wait!" the young witch yelled behind her. "I forgot to give you your mark!" She signaled to the shadows, where another witch appeared to take her place. She glided gracefully towards where Ellie now stood. Her black-velvet cloak billowed behind her, displaying tight leather trousers and an extremely revealing red corset blouse.

"Mark?" Ellie questioned.

"All designates are given a number. I apologize; this may hurt a little."

"A little?" Nate scoffed as he rubbed the palm of his hand. She looked at him with a scrutinizing glare then turned her gaze to Ellie, then at him, then once again to Ellie.

"Let me see." she finally said to Nate. He held his left palm up to her. Now carved and scarred just underneath his thumb was the number twenty-four. It was small but perfectly raised and clear to see.

"The number tells the arbitrators what group you are in. You will eat, sleep, and train with this group." She gestured towards Ellie. Ellie laid the back of her left hand into the palm of the witch's. "Would you like to be placed in the same group?"

"Would it get you in trouble?" Ellie asked.

"No. I'll just give someone else the number I would have given you. Decide quickly though." She looked around as if to check for any watching eyes.

"Do it."

The young witch smiled her wicked smile. Holding up her index finger, she placed her long, black, rough nail to Ellie's palm. With a whisper of unrecognizable words from her lips, tiny golden embers flared within the nail as little puffs of smoke rose from it.

Ellie grimaced, trying not to give any indication of the searing pain coming from her hand. The coal-like nail carved the numbers into her palm, cauterizing the wound before any amount of blood could escape. After a short minute, she was done.

"There." She released her hand. "Now you owe me."

"Owe you? For giving us the same group number?"

"Witches never give out favors for free, darling, no matter how big or small the favor may be. But we all three know how important it is for the two of you to stay together. Don't worry though, I won't ask you to kill anyone for me... well, maybe."

"And if I refuse to return the favor?" Ellie asked, her anger starting to grow.

"Mmm. A witch's curse is a nasty little thing. I, personally, wouldn't risk it." She smiled her evil smile then glided off, back into the shadows of the entrance walls.

Nate examined his newly-engraved palm. It still stung, but so did the many blisters caused by the wagon.

"I don't know if I should hate or admire her." El scoffed. "What now?" She turned to him. Her crystal eyes were clearer than they had been just yesterday.

Thank the gods.

"After being marked, the witch told me to find my tent. I assume it will have our number posted nearby for indication. Let's move farther into the courtyard to see if we can get some bearings of this place."

They headed for the center. Hundreds of people walked among the massive castle square, so massive the castle itself was yet to be in view. Closer in, they found an arbitrator yelling out directions to the chaotic crowd.

"NUMBERS ONE THROUGH FIFTY ARE SOUTH BEYOND THE CASTLE GARDENS! FIFTY-ONE THROUGH ONE-HUNDRED LOWER WEST CORNER OF THE GROUNDS! ONE-HUNDRED-ONE THROUGH ONE-FIFTY YOU'RE IN THE LOWER EAST CORNER..."

His yelling continued as they headed in the southern direction.

Beyond the crowds, the walls of the Malavor castle appeared. Though it looked slightly neglected, the castle was still beautiful. Green vines covered the red stone that made up the front building, while the rest of the castle was built with glistening gray and white stones. A different animal made of gold sat atop each peaked tower. Each window was filled with cerulean blue glass and lined with the same gold as the animals. The castle was so large, it was hard to see every intricate detail.

They walked along the west edge of the castle, staying in what light the evening sun provided. More vines climbed the walls of the impressive building. Their right was lined with the same large canvas tents as the ones out front. Arbitrators stood at the entrance to each tent as designates shuffled in and out. Each tent had a large black number painted on the side. They turned a corner and found themselves surrounded by well-kept gardens. They were filled with herbs, odd flowers, and frightening weeds. This was not a garden for royals, but one for witches. They made their way through the maze of plants, finally a good distance from any intruding ear.

"It's beautiful," Nate said, admiring the backside of the castle. An enormous concrete terrace protruded below a wall of blue and gold windows. "These grounds and this building are so beyond massive, I don't understand how the Eternal Queen took it so easily."

"The King and Queens of Malavor were powerful, and Officer Reuel said they were 'formidable Fae.' Yet the Eternal Queen still defeated them."

Officer Reuel. His name on El's tongue was like a dagger to the gut. He was an arrogant albeit charming man, who had been looking at El like some kind of prize since her first trial. She had impressed him, and even when she lay unconscious, he would look into the wagon with a sense of claiming then up at Nate with a feral grin that promised death to him if El did not make a full recovery. As if it were Nate's fault she lay half dead, and not one of his fellow arbitrator's.

"King and queens? There was more than one?" Nate asked, ignoring his need to grimace at the thought of the arbitrator.

"Malavor was always ruled by three. No more, no less. The first three children to be born among the three rulers would be next in line. I don't know how the last rulers were related to one another, but I know they weren't all siblings. I think one was a cousin."

"Confusing. And why three? Did they each have separate royal duties?"

"I don't know. That is all my knowledge on the subject. I only know what I do from the bits and pieces I've gathered from those in Perilin willing to discuss their past rulers."

"It's odd your grandparents never taught you more about Malavor. My parents never stop talking about our home in Orlau." Or how they regretted fleeing when they did. Being a northern country, Orlau was taken much later than Malavor and its territories. However, Nate's parents had heard of Perilin and its peaceful transition to the Eternal Queen's reign. Nate's father had seen enough war and felt fleeing to Perilin before the queen's forces reached Orlau was the safest and wisest decision. It had kept them out of direct conflict for many years, but at the cost of leaving their extended family, friends, and way of life behind.

El interrupted his thoughts. "What did your witch ask you after you drank the brown tonic? And how did you feel?" She grabbed at Nate's arm as a sudden ache seemed to shoot through her back. He didn't hesitate to put that arm underneath her shoulder. His eyes filled with guilt for not offering the help sooner. "I'm fine," she assured, leaning into his hold. "Answer the question."

"I felt relaxed. Like she could have asked me anything and I'd easily let it slip. Thankfully, she only asked my name, age, and what town I traveled from. To be honest, she looked bored, tired, and not at all like she wanted to be there. Why? How did it make you feel?"

"Not relaxed, that's for sure. My heart is still racing from it."

"And her questions?"

"She asked where I was born and if I'd be a threat to the Eternal Queen."

Nate's eyes widened. "What did you answer?"

"I answered Perilin and no."

"But how? That was clearly some sort of truth tonic."

"I don't know, but it wasn't easy. Every lie felt like my bones were melting. She asked one more question. *'What blood runs through my veins?'* When I answered 'human,' the pain stopped."

"Do you think she knows you were lying?"

"I think she suspects it, but no, I don't think she knows for sure."

El also mentioned to Nate the peculiar Mother Ubel and her request for a younger witch. The overall interaction had El's face scrunched in deep thought and frustration.

They walked slowly through the gardens. Nate took a moment to enjoy how close El was as she leaned deeper into his hold. Despite the green and yellow bruising that covered her face, she was still incredibly beautiful. She didn't seem to notice his extended gaze as she admired the thousands of different plant species around them. El had once shared with Nate that knowledge of plants and their uses was part of her early lessons as a young girl. Her grandfather had especially focused on the ones used to poison and kill.

"The cowards kill," El said, as if hearing where Nate's mind had wondered. "If Cam were here, she would be listing off the name of every single plant." Ellie softly smiled at the thought of her older sister.

"Some of them are quite beautiful," Nate said, admiring the pedals of a rose.

"Mmm. The beautiful ones are usually the most dangerous." She winked at Nate, sending an ache of longing through him. He sucked in a breath, shaking off the feeling. She removed herself from his hold, and the absence of her touch pulled at a dull gnawing in his chest.

"Like this one." El walked towards a familiar flower, one that Nate had seen grow wildly around her farm in Perilin. "A perfect white pedal, bright yellow center, and an extremely unique-shaped leaf." She violently snapped the stem of one of the delicate flowers. Thick red sap sprayed at the breaking point. "It's called a bloodroot, for obvious reasons."

Red liquid dripped from the stem, staining the rocky dirt beneath. "The sap from this flower is anything but beautiful. A small amount into a person would cause immediate vomiting, extreme temperatures, and permanent loss of site. Large amounts would end in a painfully long death."

"Geez, El! Are all the plants here that dangerous?" Nate stepped back farther from the deathly liquid.

"No. Most look like plants used for healing and medicinal purposes. Though, I would suggest only drinking water and mead while here and smelling it beforehand. If it smells sweeter than normal, it's best to stay clear of it."

"Great," Nate sneered. They continued their walk, quickening their pace some as the daylight was quickly ending.

The garden's end was marked with a line of tall green hedges that were split, opening a path every few meters. Beyond those was the line of white canvas tents with numbers one through fifty painted on their left side. Just like the other tents, an arbitrator stood at the entrance, checking the hands of each designate.

Standing at the entrance of tent twenty-four was Officer Reuel.

"Fantastic," Nate grumbled.

Ellie could see the anger in Nate's eyes at the sight of the young, handsome officer. She ignored it as she prepared herself to play in the arbitrator's flirtatious games.

"You *both* got group twenty-four?" A wicked smile graced the officer's full lips. "Am I to assume this was coincidental? Or did it involve a raven-haired green-eyed young witch?"

"How—" Ellie's mouth hung gaping in confusion.

"Layla is extremely gifted. I would say the most gifted witch here. She has a way of making her presence known when she feels it is needed. Let me guess, you now owe her?"

"Yes, or risk a witch's curse."

The officer's deep laugh shook the air between them. When he finished, a playful gleam remained in his gaze. "More than half the arbitrators here 'owe' Layla. Including myself. She has yet to call on a return favor from any of us. Trust me. She's harmless."

Trust me. A simple phrase, easily said but hard to do. Ellie also wouldn't call Layla "harmless," but if the witch was willing to give favors behind the generals' backs, she was a possible ally.

"So, are you here to just check our numbers, or is there more?"

"I am your assigned arbitrator. I will eat, sleep, and train with you for the entirety of your stay here, as well as keep you in line if need be."

"Yes, *sir*." Reuel's eyes widened in delight at the coquettish way she spoke. Ellie hid her own surprise at how alluring she had sounded.

"Careful, Miss Batair, or I might think you're happy to be *under* my command."

The way he said "under" made Ellie's stomach flip. "I'd rather be under you than anyone else."

A bit of pink appeared on the officer's cheeks, "And why is that?"

"Officer Shea reminded me that you were all once designates like us, and not all of you are as cruel as Ballock or Schmilt."

"What makes you think I am not as cruel or even worse than those officers?" An arrogant, playful brow rose at Reuel's question.

"My grams once told me you could tell a lot from a man by the way he treats his horse, or any animal for that matter. Despite your arrogant appearance, you are kind and gentle to Tabat." Reuel's sultry smile softened to something more appreciative. "I also refuse to believe someone as handsome as you could be so cruel."

The laugh that Reuel voiced was soft, and any trace of arrogance or flirtation had disappeared for only a moment. "Thank you, Ellie."

The appreciation was genuine, as if she had just

reminded him that he wasn't just an arbitrator, but a decent man.

Nate released an annoyed sigh. "Should we assume your presence is also coincidental? Or did you somehow weasel your way to our tent specifically?" Nate's question sent a cold wave of shock through Ellie's spine, causing her injury to ache and burn. She shot him a warning glance.

Not only could Officer Reuel strike Nate for the clear disrespect, but Ellie needed to win over the arbitrator's trust to gain information. She needed to know what he knew of the generals and Eternal Queen. She needed to know why Cormel ordered him, Shea, and Ames to earn her loyalty.

The feral rage in Reuel's eyes told Ellie that Nate was ruining her chance at earning any of that information. Reuel gripped the crow head of his sword, his knuckles turning stark white against the gold pommel.

"Not that I need to explain anything to you." Reuel ran a murderous gaze up and down Nate's stiff body. Ellie began to wonder if she had been wrong in her earlier observation of the arbitrator. Maybe he could be just as cruel as Schmilt and Ballock. "The horse stables are just beyond those trees to your left. I convinced one of the more lenient generals to place me somewhere in the southern groups so I could stay close to Tabat. It is, however, a nice twist of fate to be placed specifically at *your* tent."

The smile Reuel gave was a promise to make Nate's time in Malavor a living hell. To Ellie's surprise, Nate didn't balk at the look. He only held his shoulders back farther and met Reuel's gaze with a glare filled with a hateful promise of his own.

Before Nate could open his mouth in retort, Officer Reuel turned his attention solely towards Ellie. The brutal look on his features softened and returned to his playful gleam.

"How are you feeling, Ellie?"

She could see Nate tense at the clear disregard.

"I'm surprisingly well." *Lie.* Her legs begged to rest, and her entire back burned. She couldn't allow anyone to see her struggling, though. Ellie spoke again before Nate said something else stupid. "Is there anything we should know before entering the tent, sir?"

"Wash up, get settled, and get to know your tent mates. We'll head to dinner in the Great Hall in an hour."

"Thank you, Officer Reuel." Ellie showed her freshly-engraved palm to him, then pushed Nate towards the front flaps of their tent. He entered, but Ellie was stopped by a strong hand wrapping gently around her wrist.

"Ellie." Reuel's voice was soft, but when she turned to face him, that hard line in his jaw had returned. Ellie was almost certain it was pain that caused it. "You can call me Auden, just not in front of the generals, officers, or other designates."

She softly smiled, which seemed to deepen the clench in his jaw.

"Thank you, Auden."

12

Two rows of six mats lay lining the sides of the large canvas tent. Only seven were currently claimed. Six were men, including Nate who strategically picked a mat near the rear exit flaps. The seventh designate was none other than Kiarhem, the mysterious girl with quick feet. She jumped from her mat, hair bouncing as she did.

"Hi!" Her voice amongst the silent tent made the men jump. All eyes were now on Ellie.

Brows raised as a few eyes trailed every inch of her body. One middle-aged man let out a low disgusting whistle. Her heart raced, stomach dropped, and the hairs on the back of her neck stood. Men looked at her and her sisters in this way for most of their lives. It was something a woman would never get used to.

Nate watched from his mat, knowing Ellie could handle herself, but was available if need be.

"Wow. Where are you from? And are all the women there just as beautiful?" a young man said. His sneer sent bile into her throat, but the look in his eyes seemed less lethal than those of the man who whistled at her.

She was in no mood to deal with any of the men who looked at her, but she knew ignoring them wouldn't help. She walked up to the brown-haired, green-eyed, dimple-cheeked man, allowing the anger that always lingered inside to boil up some as she did.

Eyes glared and lips curled. With one simple, quick motion, she sent her palm straight up into his large nose. She kept the force minimal, so as not to cause serious injury, but that did not stop the blood that now gushed from his face. She began to walk away before he could even comprehend what happened.

"What the hell! You little bit—" Before he could finish, she turned, releasing a dagger into the air. The blade grazed his cheek and landed perfectly into the wood beam behind him. His eyes widened, and he let out a high-pitched squeal as his hands covered both his nose and bleeding cheek.

"What is going—" Auden entered the tent, assessing the situation before finishing his reprimand. "Carry on."

He walked back out as quickly as he entered.

"If you speak to me that way again, I'll make sure that dagger lands between those green eyes. Understand?" She stared at his now regretful face. He simply nodded his head in agreement.

"Good. Now hand me my dagger."

He quickly pulled her knife free of the wood and handed it to her. She glared around at the other men, who quickly returned to their business. All except one elderly gentleman. Eyes filled with kindness, he softly smiled and nodded his head in approval of her actions. She returned the nod then headed to the empty mat next to Nate, dropping her pack onto it and removing a few weapons from her sore body.

"I'm sorry." A quiet voice came from behind her. Ellie turned to see sad hazel eyes staring up at her. "I didn't mean to bring so much attention to you."

Ellie smiled, sitting down on her mat. Gods, it felt good to sit again.

"It's fine." She began stretching, bending and moving her body as best as she could. She turned in a way that had her back burning again. She quickly straightened, holding back a groan.

Ellie studied the young girl standing in front of her. She couldn't be older than twelve, but that would be against designate rules. "Kiarhem, if you don't mind me asking, how old are you?"

"I'm sixteen. Though—" She looked at Nate, unsure if she should speak freely.

"Nate is my most trusted friend and ally. Anything you choose to say to me will be shared with him. If you are not comfortable with that, I understand."

She looked between the two of them then sighed. "I know I look much younger, but my people age differently than yours."

Ellie looked closer at her features. High cheekbones lay just below her almond eyes, eyes that seem to glow in the dull tent lighting. Her thick, curly hair mostly covered her ears, except for the left ear slightly sticking out, revealing a thin point.

Ellie grabbed her wrist, pulling her in close.

"You're an elf, aren't you?" she whispered. Kiarhem nodded with a slight smile.

Ellie had read of elves and their colonies south of Malavor. "And you're not from Perilin, are you?"

"It's complicated," she whispered back. "I'm originally from an elf colony south of here. I could tell you more, but not here." She looked around at the men that surrounded them. Ellie nodded, releasing Kiarhem's arm and leaning back.

"We desperately need a wash. Could you show us where?" Ellie pulled out a fresh change of clothes, a small cloth, and some oils and soaps from her pack. She followed Kiarhem out the back canvas flaps. Nate soon followed after.

Behind the tent was a tall single rusted standpipe that arched over a few large stones placed strategically for standing on. A tiny mirror hooked to the tent, and a bucket for relieving oneself sat just a few meters away.

Ellie didn't expect much, but she definitely expected more than this. She looked at the other tents around them, noticing the same setup as theirs. "Did you wash and change in the open like this?"

Kiarhem shook her head then pointed to a group of very large trees behind them.

"I washed myself fully clothed. It wasn't ideal. Then I changed behind those trees. There's drying lines placed between each tent." She pointed at her clothes that now hung on a line that ran from one of our tent beams to our neighboring tent's beam.

Ellie needed a decent wash, and she wasn't going to settle for anything less.

"Nate, could you go grab one of the blankets from the tent?" He nodded then returned within seconds. "Would you two mind holding up the blanket to conceal me?"

They both agreed and took separate corners of the blanket. It wasn't perfect, but if anyone walked by, they would have to try hard to see anything good. She laid her clean clothes and cloth on the ground far enough away to ensure they stayed dry then slowly undressed herself, being careful to avoid her more bruised and injured areas. Once wearing nothing but the blue pendant around her neck, she looked at herself in the small round mirror. Some of her hair stuck out along the crown of braids, and she was covered in dust and dirt. As for her injuries, her face had mostly healed, with just slight yellow bruising left around the eye and cheek.

Her chest was fully mended, but her back...Her back was worse than she could ever expect. Blotchy blue and purple bruising covered every inch of it. In the center was a black, burn-like wound that branched out like lightning bolts in every direction. She couldn't hold the shock in and began to weep.

"How big is it, El? From one bolt at the top to a bolt at the bottom?" Nate's voice was concerned but steady. He looked up at the darkening sky, not daring to look at her exposed body.

"Uh–um..." Her voice shook through a ragged breath. "T–two, maybe three inches."

"Good."

"Good? H–how big was it before?"

"Double to triple that." He looked over his shoulder, scanning for onlookers.

"May I see?" Kiarhem asked, her curiosity getting the better of her.

"Yes," Ellie answered, fully aware of her exposure.

A line of colorful words left Kiarhem's mouth. "How are you even standing right now?"

"We don't know," Nate answered for Ellie. "We should hurry. It's getting dark, and we'll be leaving for supper soon."

Ellie let down her hair, combing through it with aching fingers. She then grabbed the lever next to the pipe and began to pump. She allowed the cool water to hit every inch of her.

Grabbing her oils and soaps, she dispersed them among her hair and injured body. After a good long rinse, she washed her dirt-covered clothes. Once clean and dressed again, Nate and Kiarhem dropped the blanket. She swung her dripping clothes over the line and took Nate's place.

They tried their best to conceal him, but he was quite a bit taller than the two young women.

"So what colony in the south are you from?" Ellie whispered to Kiarhem.

"I come from the Dorumia colony in Delmi."

"And how did you end up in Perilin?"

Kiarhem bit her inner lip, shifting her weight as she surveyed for listeners. "My colony is home to elves and many refugees. Most are powerful Fae from here in Malavor."

Her words sent a wave of shock through Ellie's body.

"The Fae. They're alive?" Ellie questioned in disbelief.

"Yes. They've been hiding and living in one of our more expansive areas. Only the Fae truly know where and how to find it. They continue to stay there, hoping the Eternal Queen never finds out about their whereabouts. They've succeeded this long because of Delmi's special alliance with the Queen."

"What alliance?"

"Back when the Queen first arrived on these lands, she met with our colony leaders. She was aware of how powerful our armies could be if all pulled together as one. The details of how are clouded, but she won over three of the five colony leaders. They pledged to provide their armies to her whenever needed, and in return, she promised all of Delmi would be free of her generals and exempt from any war decrees. That was until three years ago when she found out the two colonies that didn't pledge to her had sent their armies north. The following year, she sent decrees that all of Delmi would have its first Designation Day, and all families from every colony would have to attend." A dark shadow crossed Kiarhem's eyes.

"My brother was forced to join that year. We were sent a letter a few months ago that he had died dishonorably for not following orders."

"I'm sorry," Ellie said, truly meaning it. Kiarhem nodded her head in reply then continued.

"After we got the letter about my brother, we were called on by a seer. By one of the last remaining Fae seers."

"Seer?" Ellie's stomach dipped, and she tried not to shift at the word.

"I was told that seeing powers among Fae, though still more common than a human seer, are extremely rare. He says he's one of only two left."

"And what did he call on you for?"

"He had a vision about me." She took a deep, cleansing breath. "He saw me joining the war as a designate. My parents, at first, didn't believe him. Women were not forced to join the war, but he projected the vision into their minds. My parents panicked. They had just lost their son, and now they were being told they were to lose their daughter as well. Their only thought was to run north." Kiarhem's voice became shaky. She struggled to control her breathing.

"In a town west of Perilin, my parents were attacked. A few arbitrators heckled them for money, saying their taxes were due. When my parents refused and tried to explain that we were just visitors, the arbitrators began to beat them. They fought back, and during the exchange, my father screamed for me to run and to keep running. I did. I ran until I reached Perilin, just days before designation.

I slept behind houses and ate from their gardens until Agilta found me. She took me in and listened to this same story. She advised me about seers, saying it was best not to try and avoid my destiny, so I joined. And now I'm here, holding up a blanket to conceal what I am sure is to be an incredibly hot body." She smiled, a joke to make light of the story she just told. Though, the shadow in her eyes remained.

Nate coughed, tugging the blanket from their hands, revealing his shirtless self.

Ellie's stomach jumped into her throat as her face flushed with heat. She quickly looked away, unsure if it was alright for her to admire her friend's very attractive build. He hung his wet clothes on the wire then turned to Kiarhem.

"Does this mean there will be more elves coming here?" Ellie asked, keeping her gaze on Kiarhem and away from Nate's glistening torso.

"Yes. Only a dozen or so though. Elves are hard to kill." Kiarhem beamed.

From what Ellie had read of elves, they were incredibly fast and excellent warriors. Unfortunately, Kiarhem's colony would have deemed her too young to train.

"Most of the elves that joined the Queen's Army a few years ago are still alive and fighting."

"The ones that are coming, are they from colonies loyal to the Eternal Queen?" Nate brushed back his dark waves from his face. Gods, he was distracting.

"Some." Kiarhem's face turned somber. "My people are hurting. After the alliance was broken, there have been rumors of war in my lands. A war the Queen would no doubt use to tear my people further apart from one another."

"I'm sorry." Nate placed a strong hand on Kiarhem's shoulder. "Kai, you are welcome to stay near us. We'll protect you, if you do the same for us."

She nodded with relief on her face.

He then turned and headed for the tent.

Ellie splashed her face with a little more cool water then picked up her oils that still lay on the ground.

"You two are just friends?" Kiarhem asked, staring at Ellie's still-flushed face.

"We've known each other since we were small children. I trust him with every ounce of my life. So, no we're not 'just' friends. I guess it's—"

"Complicated?"

"Yeah. Complicated to say the least."

13

They made their way to the Great Hall in one single line. Two more designates arrived at the tent while they were bathing. More would come in the following days, but their group was mostly full, with only one mat remaining empty.

The benefit to being in groups one through fifty was the short walk to the castle's Great Hall. They made their way through the gardens, up the back stairs, onto the large concrete terrace, and through a massive cerulean glass door. It led directly into the Great Hall, where smells of spiced meat and warm bread wafted in the air.

The hall was lit with warm candlelight and lined with intricate mahogany tables. Auden led the group to a table where food and drink was brought directly to them by very young witchlings.

"Witches serving us our food. That seems safe," Nate whispered into Ellie's left ear.

Auden warned that they only had twenty minutes to eat before they were to leave and allow the next groups to enter.

There was not enough space for all groups to eat at once, so they rotated.

Ellie shoveled every morsel of food in her mouth. It was surprisingly delicious. The meat was tender, the bread still warm, and even the greens were bearable. She finished before most. The others at her table clearly never had to eat quickly and fight for second helpings against siblings.

She sat patiently, taking in the beauty of the Great Hall. The back wall where they entered was top to bottom cerulean blue glass with gold trimming. The three other walls were the same white and gray glistening stone from the outside, but every few feet were large wood beams that connected to beautiful wooden arches above them. The beams were carved with the most intricate depictions.

"They're stories," Auden whispered to her right. "The carvings on the beams, and even on these tables, are all stories from the Fae's past. Most are stories of great battles; some are of great love." He looked at her with intense passion in his eyes. Not for her, but for the history in the room.

She ran her fingers along the wood before her. A doe was running away from a sun that was setting between two connected mountain peaks and towards a raging fire.

Ellie's vision blurred as her focus changed to something else.

The Great Hall, empty of tables but filled with terrified screaming people. Large brutes in complete black rammed their swords into innocent men, women, and children. Ellie tried to scream, tried to warn people of oncoming attacks, but her voice was silent. She tried to physically stop one of the attackers, but he walked right through her as if she were mist in the wind. She ran through the people, trying to find a way out, only to find herself at the foot of three thrones. She looked up to see three faceless crowned heads sitting lifeless and unmoving.

The blank middle face glowed a bright blinding blue.

"Ellie. Ellie!" Nate shook her shoulders. Her face was wet, her heart pounded, and her breath was short and quick. Ellie still stared at the carving before her, now displaying a few drops of her tears.

"Are you ok? What's wrong?" Nate's voice was quiet but filled with panic.

"I-I 'm fine." She ran a trembling hand down her face. Kiarhem sat across from her, face rigid. Ellie ignored the confused stares of others at the table, while Auden looked at her with focused eyes. He stared as if something in his head just clicked. His thoughts were quickly interrupted by the man that walked in from the east entrance of the room.

"Schmilt. What the hell is he doing here?" Nate growled.

"I don't know, but I'll ask around." Auden left the table, making friendly rounds to the other arbitrators, their voices a faraway echo in her head.

Ellie thought of the vision that just passed through her, her second different vision in one day. What she told herself was just a dream both the day of her designation and early that morning, she now positively knew was something so much more.

"Nate, I need to tell you something," she whispered through a ragged breath. His rust-lined brown eyes looked straight into hers.

The sudden appearance of Officer Schmilt had no effect on Ellie, as her head and body was still reeling from the current experience. Her chest ached as she failed at controlling her breath. She felt as if an invisible force were pushing her deeper and deeper into the chair beneath her, trapping her against the hard wood. He reached under the table to squeeze one of her shaking hands.

"Breathe with me, El." His voice was calm. They breathed in then out slowly. In and then out. Over and over again. "You're safe, El. I will always ensure you are safe."

"I don't know what's happening to me, Nate."

"Just breathe. We can talk about it later." She stared into his eyes, breathing in and out. His wavy black hair fell into his face. She pushed it back, running her fingers slowly through the strands. She was aware that it gestured towards affection. Affection that she reprimanded Nate for just days ago.

So many things had changed since that day. The man beside her had kept her alive for days. The arbitrators and generals were already well aware of what happened, and who took care of her through it all. Any target she was trying to avoid was now plastered onto their foreheads.

"Nate. What did you mean on Designation Day when you said, 'Your grandpa was right?' What did the two of you talk about that morning in his study?" Ellie moved the hand that was being squeezed by him and slowly laced her fingers between each one of his. Though his breathing stayed steady, his body tensed.

"Your grandpa, he...uh...he—"

"Alright." Auden sat back down beside her, interrupting Nate. "It seems Schmilt pleaded his case in front of the generals, and most deemed his actions forgivable but not fully without punishment."

"What does that mean?" Nate did not watch his tone with their group arbitrator. Ellie wondered if he even realized how disrespectful he sounded.

"It *means*—" Auden's growl towards Nate had Ellie's heart thundering again. "He'll most likely have a few more chore duties and a few less training privileges for the next couple weeks, but that's it. There were some other things said at the hearing, but overall, Schmilt is a punishment-free man." He looked at Ellie's flat, expressionless face. Schmilt getting a pass for almost killing her was not in the least bit surprising. They were among the Queen's Army after all. "He's been warned to stay away from you until the trials. Though, I think he would do so even without the warning." Auden smirked before giving a five-minute warning to the rest of the table.

In a straight line once again, they walked towards their tent. The three brought up the rear so Nate could slowly and strategically fall just far enough behind from listening ears.

"What's going on, El. If you're not ready to talk about it. We can wait," Nate said, still looking ahead.

"I'm fine. The fresh air helps." She took a deep cleansing breath then told them of her visions: the same recurring one she's had for the last year, the one she had the morning of Designation Day, and the two she had that day.

"You're a seer?" Kiarhem asked. A hint of fear lined her voice.

"Maybe. I only see visions of the past, and I'm pretty sure only Fae seers have the power to look into the future."

"Today's visions were both triggered by being in the same place as where the vision occurred, correct?" Nate asked.

"Yes. The one from this morning occurred on the same dirt road that I woke up on, and the one tonight occurred in the Great Hall." The vision she had on Designation Day occurred near her home, close to where she stood. The only vision that was not triggered by her location seemed to be the one that had been on replay the last few months.

"Why are they happening though? And what about the whole 'find me' thing. What do you think that's all about?" Kiarhem pointed out.

"I don't know. The only thing I do know is it will most likely happen again. What did I look like when I was having the vision tonight?"

"Your body went to stone. Your face went blank, emotionless, yet your eyes began to weep. It looked as if you were trapped inside your own body, unable to move or talk."

"It was terrifying," Kiarhem added.

"Good. You'll know when it's happening then."

"And what do we do the next time one occurs?" Nate asked.

"I guess just try to snap me out of it like you did tonight." They agreed then picked up their paces to close the growing gap in the group line.

Ellie lay on her mat, staring up at the canvas ceiling. Light snores came from one of the men at the other end. Her body begged for rest, but her mind refused.

Kiarhem had moved from her previously picked mat to the one to Ellie's right. The small elf slept peacefully, her face seeming even younger in the dull moonlight that leaked through the cracks of the tent.

Ellie turned to face a still-lucid Nate. "Can't sleep either?" she whispered.

"No."

Ellie stared at Nate, memorizing every curve and line of his strong jaw, every dip and curl of his wavy hair. "I need to apologize."

"For what?"

"I was wrong. Affection. Our friendship is not a weakness. It will be the strength that gets us through this whole ordeal."

"What changed your mind? Was it all the flirting with Officer Reuel, or something else?" His tone was not playful. This subject had clearly been bothering him for a while.

"I don't know if Auden is a decent person worthy of friendship, or even a possible ally yet, but your attitude towards him could ruin any chances we have to build trust and find out needed information. Yes, I flirted with him, and I will continue to do so if it gets us closer to where we need to be."

Nate stayed silent, his body tense and rigid. "*Auden?*" he finally ground out.

"Yes. Auden. That's his name. What is your deal with him?"

"I don't like the way he looks at you, but you're right. I'm sorry." His tone did not match the final words he spoke as he turned over. They lay there in silence for a moment.

She wasn't sure what possessed her, but she sucked in a breath and said, "I can flirt with you too, if that'll help you feel better. After seeing you shirtless, it definitely wouldn't be hard." She held in a nervous laugh at the bold statement.

"Your face was so red, I thought your head would explode." He smiled broadly, clearly proud of the effect he had on her. She reached over to punch his arm, but he caught it and pulled both her and her mat towards him. Back on his side, they now lay only inches from one another.

Her heart raced as he softly brushed his fingers through her hair.

"When you were out, those three days on the road, despite being told to stay away, *Auden* checked on you... often. Shea would remind him of his orders to stay away, but without Captain Cormel there to enforce the order, there was no stopping him." Nate continued to run his hand through her hair. "He would check on you every evening before dinner. He'd ask questions about your mark, your breathing, your heart rate, and the entire time, he would look at you like, like, I don't know. I just didn't like it."

The back of Nate's fingers slowly traveled from her hair to her cheek, down to the chain around her neck.

"He was concerned." Ellie's words were barely heard over her pounding heart.

"Yes. He hardly knows you, and he was *deeply* concerned." Nate picked up the chain around her neck, pulling out the cold pendant from beneath her shirt and placing it in the palm of his hand. "You want to know what your grandpa said to me?"

Ellie furrowed her brows at the sudden change in conversation. "Yes."

"He said I couldn't allow my feelings towards you to get in the way of your mission. That this journey and your discoveries were far too important. Any realization or declarations of love would have to wait."

He set the pendant down. The weight of it crashed onto her mat.

Love. The tightness in her chest returned.

"Nate, I—"

"He was right, El." He turned onto his back once more. She was caught off guard by the slight sting of rejection.

"Getting out of this army and this camp alive has to be the only thing on our minds. We have to focus."

Her anger rose at his words. Her hands shook from the rage she pushed deeper down.

Focus. Fight. Survive. Everything she's been taught and forced to do her entire life.

14

"E verybody up!" Auden shouted.

Ellie shot up, instantly regretting her sudden movement as pain roared down her back.

"Let's go! Your second trial doesn't start for a week, but your training starts now!" With the tip of his boot, he tapped the feet of a few men who were slow to wake. "You will be in a line and out of this tent in five minutes!"

He made his way to her already-dressed, weapon-adorned self.

"Ellie, come with me." His face was unreadable. She looked at Nate for a second, and the worry in his eyes matched her own.

Auden and Ellie made their way towards the front of the tent and out into the cool morning air. It was still mostly dark as the sun barely peeked above the far horizon. It was so early, the birds had yet to begin their morning songs. Standing just outside the garden hedges was another arbitrator. The distance across the grassy knoll towards the garden was wide, so Ellie couldn't place the scarlet-clad figure.

"What's going on?" she asked in a calm, relaxed tone. She was anything but.

"General Dolion has requested your presence. Shea will escort you. That is all I know." The playful gleam that was in Auden's eyes just yesterday was now replaced by poorly-disguised fear. It was all the information she needed about Dolion.

She was being called on by a general not even a full day after arriving. Despite the slight intrigue in meeting one of the Queen's generals after never seeing one before, Ellie was quite terrified. She needed to distract herself from the panic growing in her gut, and Auden's unusual silence mixed with the quiet morning air only made her fear grow.

She walked closer to the handsome officer, matching her steps to his. "You know, Nate was right to question your presence as our group arbitrator. It does seem a bit too...*coincidental*."

Ellie ran a long side-eye over the officer, hoping he would take the bait. At first, she thought he would remain silent and brooding. She kept her brows raised, and a cool, coy smile remained fixated on him.

After a moment, the left corner of Auden's mouth rose. Amused mischief danced in his gray eyes. "I did not lie when I said I convinced a more lenient general to place me closer to Tabat. I got my orders to be stationed in the southern groups weeks ago during the preparation for the trials. However, I may owe more than just one favor to Layla and her witch sisters."

Ellie couldn't hide the shock on her face. She was only placing innocent blame on him to create distracting banter. She hadn't considered he actually did "weasel" his way into being their group arbitrator. Into being *her* arbitrator. "How? And why?"

He shrugged. "I can't give away all my secrets, Ellie. You may start to lose interest in me."

"How very pompous to assume I was ever interested in you, Auden."

His laugh was low, forcefully quiet, in the early morning stillness. Ellie had indeed forgotten all about her panic, but it was now replaced by frustrated confusion. They walked closer towards where Shea stood still and strong, like a true soldier.

"I would never assume anything when it comes to you, Ellie. I learned that after seeing your abilities in the first trial."

"It's a shame you were not the one I faced during the trial. I would have enjoyed embarrassing you."

"We would have all enjoyed seeing that." Ellie would have bumped right into Officer Shea if Auden hadn't pulled her to a stop. She looked up to her left to see specks of white glistening throughout dark-red hair. The wrinkles on Shea's forehead deepened as he raised his brows in amusement. Shea was definitely the oldest of all the officers here. Ellie had thought most men his age either died in battle or were promoted to a higher standing. "Unfortunately, I've yet to see anyone knock the arrogance from Officer Reuel."

"I'll gladly take that as a challenge." Ellie's focus was solely on Auden. His playful smile wavered a bit. That flicker of tense pain ran across his jaw, and a bit of fear slowly forced its way through his features once again.

"Thank you, Officer Reuel. I've got her from here."

Auden gave her one last worried glance then headed back to the tent.

"Good morning, Miss Batair. This way." Shea held out his hand, directing to the gardens.

"Am I free to ask you questions, sir?" Ellie asked in the silent, empty gardens.

"Of course. Though I may not be free to answer them in full."

She nodded her head in understanding. "I understand I am to meet with General Dolion. Where exactly will I be meeting him?"

"In his tent beyond the stone wall."

"His tent? Do the generals not reside in the castle?"

"No. Most of the castle is abandoned, except for a few areas that the witches occupy."

"What does the general want with me?"

"I do not know." His words were calm, but his eyes gave way to fear for just a moment.

They walked in silence for some time. His pace was steady but not quick. Ellie had the feeling that he was taking his time leading her there. They passed the lower west group. Their tent flaps were open, revealing their emptiness. They, too, would begin training today, and it would continue every day until all the designates arrived. Then the trials would begin.

"How long has it been since you joined this army, sir?" Shea was far from elderly, but the wrinkles around his eyes and brow were deep and true.

"Hmm. It has been some time since I thought about that." He contemplated his answer. "I think this will be my thirteenth year."

Thirteen. The designation decree had been around for thirteen years.

"You've been here since the beginning. How are you still alive? And why are you still just an officer? Captain Cormel is much younger but ranked higher than you." Shea let out a soft laugh at her spew of words.

"*Much* younger, eh?" His smile was sweet. Contagious. She couldn't help but smile too. "To be honest, I don't know how I'm still living. I've fought in more battles than all the men here, including the generals. I guess I'm just lucky...or unlucky. It depends on how you look at it. As for my ranking, I've been offered promotions a few times, but each time I request to stay an officer."

"Why?"

"Officers never have the...*privilege* of meeting the Eternal Queen."

"Smart." She was impressed. Shea was a true survivor. "Does that mean Captain Cormel has met the Queen?"

"No. This is only his first year as a captain. It's really more of a probationary period. Once he proves worthy as a captain, she will call on him."

"Mmm. She is wise to only meet with ones who have proven their loyalty."

"Wise? No. Only good leaders are wise. She is smart. Strategic. Paranoid. A leader who keeps her people at arm's length. That is not the sign of a wise leader, but a cruel one." Shea grimaced as if in pain. He reached up to rub a spot behind his left shoulder.

Ellie was both shocked and confused by his outright disdain for the queen he claimed to serve. For the queen he killed and fought for. If he truly believed the Eternal Queen to be cruel, then he might indeed be a loyal ally.

"Where are you originally from?" Her question brought a soft smile to his face.

"Perilin."

Perilin! Hundreds of questions ran through her mind. If Shea was from Perilin, he would have lived under the original rulers of Malavor. They would have been his king and queens.

If asked, would he find her questions to be that of an innocently curious young woman, or something more? She decided to take the risk.

"Do you remember the King and Queens who used to rule over Malavor and its surrounding territories?"

"Yes." His eyes filled with sadness.

"Could you tell me about them?"

"If you ask the right questions, maybe." He rubbed his shoulder more. Ellie ran through the list of questions in her head, deciding which to ask first.

"The Eternal Queen's men had been on this land for months, fighting and taking power in the southern countries. Why didn't the rulers of Malavor call upon their armies to help fight against her initial rampage?"

"Honestly, I do not know. No one seems to. I know their advisors demanded they join before her armies reached these borders, but they didn't listen."

"If the King and Queens were such powerful Fae, how did the Eternal Queen and her men take Malavor so easily?"

"Again, I do not know. Knowledge of that day is limited. None close to the royal court survived, leaving most of what happened a mystery."

"How were the King and Queens related? And what were their powers?"

"Mmm. If I remember correctly, there were three queens who ruled before the King and two Queens. All three were sisters. The eldest sister bore the first Queen. Queen Odina. Only a year later, she also bore the King. King Vedmar. The second sister, though she tried dearly, was never able to bear a child. However, just after the King was born, the youngest sister had the final heir to the throne. The second Queen. Queen Akéra. Queen Odina had the power of air. She was incredibly skilled with the bow and would use her powers to assure she hit her mark every time. Queen Akéra had earth powers like her mother before her. Some claimed she actually moved mountains. Last, King Vedmar had the power of water."

"Water?"

"Yes. Not many had the privilege to view the King's power. Those who did said it was truly something to behold."

They passed the center of the castle courtyard. She only had time for a few more questions. She had to choose wisely.

"Were there more?"

"More?" Shea stitched his brows together.

"Did the three sister Queens have any other children after the three heirs?"

"Oh, yes. King Vedmar and Queen Odina had a younger sister, and Queen Akéra, their cousin, had two other siblings as well."

"Were they all killed during the attack?"

"Yes." His eyes looked at Ellie, anticipating another question. She felt she had enough information about the royal family, at least for the time being.

"The house on the outskirts of town, the one with the curse, do you know much about it? About the Fae that lived there?" This question did come from pure curiosity. She couldn't ignore how she felt called to go there. She didn't know why, but she needed to know more about it.

"No. There are theories, of course, but I know nothing for sure. I would advise to stay away from it though. Fae curses are far worse than any of the curses these surrounding witches could cast on you."

They walked through the enormous stone archway, leaving the castle grounds behind them. Witches sat at their tables and hid among the shadows, all waiting for the next group of designates to arrive.

Turning from the entrance, they walked among a grassy path. The large canvas tents to their right sat stark against the dark-stone wall. They walked almost to the end of the line, where twenty to thirty arbitrators stood guard, one at each tent. They passed three guarded tents before stopping in front of the fourth.

"Please inform General Dolion that Ellie Batair is here as he requested."

15

The arbitrator disappeared through the tent's flaps. A few seconds later, he returned, holding the flaps open for them to enter.

The inside of the tent was much more pleasant than the tent she slept in. Covering most of the ground was an ornate red and gold rug. Similar depictions to the ones found in the Great Hall were stitched along the border. In the back right corner stood a large bed atop a dark-wood, four-poster frame. On it hung multiple holsters filled with an amassment of weapons. In the center of the room sat a matching wood desk. These were all pieces stolen from the castle walls.

Despite the homely look of the tent, the air around her felt wrong. Dangerous. She dragged her gaze from the desk to the beast that sat behind it. Her breaths became heavy and labored. The sounds around her became muffled and hollow. Shea's own breathing sounded far, far away. A dark beard covered most of the male's scarred face. His black, soulless eyes bored into her. Ellie's skin crawled and stomach sank at the sight of both the man and the raven-haired witch who leaned on the front of his desk. Layla.

She forced herself to take steady breaths to control the race of her beating heart. Had Layla reported her lies to the general? Is that why she was here?

"Ellie Batair. What a pleasure to finally meet the beauty that I've heard so much about." His words were laced within a poisonous tone. Ice filled her veins. "Please remove all weapons. You will not need them here." He forcefully waved a hand.

She fearfully obeyed, handing each weapon carefully to Shea.

"It seems you are quite a mystery girl. Reports from all over our territories claim the power of our new weapon. Anyone touched by the baton dies a true traitor's death. Yet you stand before me. Quite odd." General Dolion stood from behind his desk, revealing the true mass of the man.

Peeking out of his black, flowing cloak and rolled-up sleeves were large tan arms covered in dark-black hair. Greasy black locks hung just below his shoulders, and from his long muscular waist hung a flare baton, ready for use.

"Turn around and remove your shirt." His soulless eyes gleamed with evil intent. She hesitated only for a moment before doing as he commanded. All that was left on her exposed upper half was a thin cotton undergarment. Shea respectfully looked away.

She focused on her breathing, willing her body not to move, not to show any sign of fright. A light gasp came from Layla's direction.

"Interesting." Dolion walked closer, his steps heavy against the ground. Despite her best efforts Ellie's hands began to shake.

"It's horrendous," Layla whispered.

"It's beautiful," Dolion said in a cruel tone. "Tell me. What did it feel like when you were struck?" He bent down, so close his breath warmed her skin. She controlled every urge that begged her to run.

"I just felt pain, sir. Intense, hot pain. I was unable to move, speak, or cry out. Then darkness took over." Ellie forced her words to be clear.

She would not let the cruel man see her fear.

"Wonderful." He placed a large, overly warm hand on her lower back. She tensed. A cold dread washed over her.

It took everything in her not to turn and strike the large man. He slowly trailed his rough fingertips up her spine. Her breath quickened.

"What happens if I—"

Pain. Burning, stinging pain took over her body. She fell to the ground. His hand followed, and he pressed his fingers deeper into the mark. A piercing scream left her lips. She wanted to beg, plead for him to stop, but she could not form the words.

"Sir!" Shea stepped forward. Dolion removed his hand from her back and swung it across Shea's face.

Ellie lay on the ground sobbing, trembling, and wishing for darkness to take her. For anything to stop the agony that continued to rage through her body. She reached for her chest, grabbing onto the liquid-filled glass pendant. She forced herself to focus on the freezing cold and not the excruciating pain.

"Interrupt me again and I'll test the accuracy of my flare baton on you, Officer Shea."

"Yes, sir." Shea took one step back.

"Layla." Dolion knelt next to Ellie's broken body. "You were the witch to question Ellie, am I correct?"

"Yes, sir. I was." Layla's voice was clear and steady.

"What were your questions?" She relayed both her questions and Ellie's answers to the general. "Were her answers honest?"

Silence filled the room. All Ellie could hear was her shallow cries and the thunder of her beating heart. Finally, Layla answered.

"The tonic we provide would make anything but the truth impossible, sir."

"Unless she herself were magic. Am I correct?"

"Yes, but I assure you, general. She is human. If there was any lie laced within that answer, I would have felt it." Ellie could feel Layla's eyes attached to her mutilated back.

"Is it true? Are you merely a human, Ellie? Are you just simply lucky to be alive?" Dolion taunted.

"No," Ellie answered through ragged breath. Shea dared a glance down at her. His confusion only showed for a moment.

"No?" Dolion drawled.

"I'm not lucky. My town's healer. Sh–she helped mend me."

"A healer?" Dolion flashed a glare at Shea. "I was not told there was a healer involved."

Shit. Her stomach sank. Shea and the others left Agilta out of their report, and Ellie just exposed them for it.

"It seems I do not have the full story. Interesting." Ellie continued to feel his grotesque stare on her back. "Layla, help Miss Batair back to her group. For now, Ellie, you will remain a mystery, but I will be keeping an eye on you. Shea, stay. We must go over your report once more."

Layla removed Ellie's body from the rug. Her back screamed and twanged in pain. Layla helped place the shirt back over Ellie's head and assisted in delicately looping her arms in the sleeves. Officer Shea handed over her weapons, which she took with shaking hands. She looked at him with regretful, terrified eyes. He returned the look with unshakable confidence, as if to say it would be alright.

Layla dragged her out of the tent, as the legs beneath her were weak and shaky. Once out of Dolion's reach, they stopped to readjust. Layla looped her arm underneath hers, and Ellie focused every ounce of strength she had towards her legs.

If anything happened to Shea, she would now be to blame.

No.

The only blame fell on these disgusting, cruel generals. She had no doubt they were all just as bad, if not worse than Dolion. The fear that had taken over her body now turned to rage. She knew once she uncovered all there was to discover in Malavor, she would gladly end Dolion's life, and anyone who stood in her way.

"W-we need to go back to my tent. There's a tonic in Nate's pack that will stop the pain." She dug her fingers into Layla's arm.

She nodded her understanding and began the long walk. Every step was the hardest of Ellie's life, but she refused to put too much weight on Layla. Refused to let onlookers see anything more than just two friends taking a stroll. She would not look weak. She could not look weak. She focused only on her rage, letting the pain in her spine be an afterthought.

Arbitrators and designates were all around the castle courtyard. One group learned defense tactics, one worked on strength building, while another ran up and down the front steps of the castle. An arbitrator with chestnut hair pulled his whip on a young girl who could do no more push-ups. Ellie looked away, adding his face to the list of men she would kill before leaving this place.

They walked as quickly as her legs would allow. Layla silently supported her weight. They made their way through the courtyard, along the side of the castle, past the lower west group of tents, and through the gardens. The lengthy walk was tortuous. Finally, they passed through the flaps of tent twenty-four, and Ellie collapsed to the ground.

"Which pack?" Layla's tone was flat, revealing little of what she was thinking.

Ellie pointed to the back corner at the brown pack sitting on Nate's mat.

"It's the silver jar." Ellie lay on the tent floor, refusing to move. Layla carefully pulled out the jar.

Ellie pulled her shirt up, allowing Layla's cold hands to rub a large amount of thick salve onto her. The pain instantly began to melt away.

"Thank you." Her shoulder relaxed in relief.

"For the tonic, or for lying for you?" Layla removed her hand from her back. Ellie sat up, looking into her deep-emerald eyes.

"I didn't—"

"Stop. We both know your answers were shit. If you truly are human like you believe you are, how were you able to control yourself through the tonic? Who are you?"

Ellie remained silent. Unable to decide whether to trust the witch or not.

"Ellie, if I wanted to turn you over to the generals as a traitor, I would have already done so. I lied for you. I protected you. I will continue to do so, but in exchange I need you to tell me who you really are."

"I don't know."

"Who are y—"

"I DON'T KNOW!" Irate tears dropped from Ellie's crystal eyes. She no longer trembled from pain, but from the continuous rage and confused frustration. Layla looked at her in shock. Ellie released a long exhale, calming herself down, forcing herself to keep her anger at bay.

"I don't know why the flare baton mark hasn't killed me yet, I don't know why I'm still alive, and I don't know why your stupid truth tonic didn't work on me...I swear." She made herself stand and held a helping hand out to Layla. She took it after some time of consideration.

"Then tell me what you do know."

16

The two young women slowly walked through the witches' gardens. Bees and butterflies fluttered all around, and the early morning sun shone brightly down upon them.

A shadow of pain still ached in Ellie's mid back, but it was bearable once again.

"I trust that you have not told anyone else of my lies?" Ellie asked quietly.

"No. No one that would harm you knows. However, Mother Ubel felt something from you. She could not say what, but when asked what I felt, I told her nothing."

"Why? Why would you help me?" Ellie looked at the young rave- haired witch. Layla's hands grazed a flower of a rose bush. She gently picked a petal from its bud.

"Is it true? What they say about your first trial? You easily took down Schmilt and held up well against Ballock?" Ellie nodded, choosing not to point out that she could have taken Ballock down as well if she were allowed to strike back.

Layla looked at her as if she were a puzzle. A puzzle she

desperately needed to solve. "Do you know of the witches' history, Ellie? Of our origin Mothers?"

Ellie's grandfather had only a few books on the witches, and none contained much information about their history. They focused on their magic. The books were interesting, but not nearly as enjoyable as the writings about the Nokken or the elves. She didn't want to mention any of that to Layla. Instead, she said, "I don't even know of my own history. It's best to assume I know nothing of yours."

Layla smiled at the clear snarkiness. "We witches believe we are direct daughters of the goddess of life and magic. The Mother. At the beginning of time, she first created healthy, enriched soil. From that, she grew every variety of plant and herb. Plants that could be used for good. Plants that could heal and produce life." Layla rubbed the velvet rose petal between her fingers.

"Our histories claim that the god of death grew jealous of her garden. Jealous that he could not produce something so beautiful. So to spite her, he poisoned the soil of her most favored and beautiful flowers. Their roots soaked in his poison, flourished from it, and though they remained beautiful, the flowers only produced tonics of pain and death.

"Unaware of his treachery, the goddess formed the five origin Mothers from her garden: Mother Érra, Mother Hekat, Mother Jayr, Mother Galé, and Mother Zye. Mother Érra was blessed to be born from the goddess's most healing and life-giving plants. She gave birth to a strong and kind coven: the Érra coven. Mother Hekat, Jayr, and Galé were born from mainly good herbs and flowers, but a few petals from the cursed flowers were mixed among them. To this day, their covens are strong and powerful but struggle with the evil inside them.

"Lastly, Mother Zye was formed. The goddess took her

time creating her, raising her from her favorite, most beautiful flowers. The same flowers that were full of the god's poison. When the goddess finished, she instantly saw the evil she created. She saw the darkness in Mother Zye's soul. She tried to remove her evil, tried to form her over again, but she could not undo her creation. The goddess's power formed with the god's and was impossible to destroy. Instead, the goddess stripped Mother Zye of her powers, cursing her to live as a black sheep among her sisters. Over the decades, a few Zye witches have earned the goddess's favor, and she blessed them with some of the magic she originally took away."

"So your coven, it's the Zye coven?" Ellie asked.

"Yes." She placed the rose petal upon her lips, whispered something onto it, then put it in her mouth, fully consuming it before she continued her story.

"Unfortunately, the elder Mothers of my coven no longer feel they should earn the favor of the goddess, but the favor of the god of death. Our father. They tire of being the lesser coven and feel our alliance with the Eternal Queen and her reign of death will bring favor upon us."

"And do you agree?" Ellie asked as they reached the back stairs of the castle. They slowly climbed each step.

"No. I grew up here, in these castle walls. At first, our coven thrived. Many Mothers were blessed with daughters to carry on the magical line, but that blessing soon faded. Each year, as I watched thousands of innocent men be dragged off to war, I also watched witch after witch give birth to still children. The older generation of my coven believes the work we are doing for the Queen is honorable. They believe it to be the only path towards restoring our powers to their fullest. I believe it to be our ultimate end."

"Are you the only witch here who feels this way?"

"No. There are a few others like me. Others who also wish to find a way out of these castle walls." She looked at Ellie with hope in her eyes. "Ellie, I believe you to be our way out."

Layla stared at her, a vulnerable expression blanketing her pale face. Ellie contemplated the witch's alliance. Her words and desire for something better felt honest and true. The benefits to trusting the young witch before her far outweighed the possible drawbacks.

"I do not feel I can share everything with you, but here is what I can." She told her of her training, that she was a refugee from Malavor, and what her grandpa asked her to do while here.

Layla's eyes widened at the information she freely gave. When Ellie finished, Layla stood staring out from the concrete terrace over into the gardens. Her silky black hair flowed with the light, warm breeze.

"What will you do when you learn everything there is to learn here? Will you leave under the shadow of night? Try to escape this place unnoticed? If that is your plan, I assure you, it will not work. Even if you were to get past the witches that are placed all around the surrounding wall that currently traps us, they will go after you, they will catch you, and the generals will surely kill you."

Hurt shone from her eyes, eyes that longed to escape in the ways she just mentioned. Layla would know every inch of these grounds, every possible exit. If it were truly possible to leave and not be chased, she would have done it by now. Ellie grabbed the witch's hand.

"I plan to fight, Layla, and not alone. Will you help me?"

Layla gazed upon her face, emerald eyes staring down at her. Ellie could see her mind working, see it contemplating every action and the possible reactions. Layla grabbed her other hand and fully embraced both between her own. Lifting them to her mouth, she whispered upon them in a language Ellie was unfamiliar with: the origin tongue. The prayer was short and beautiful to hear. It flowed over her skin like the rays of an early-morning sun. She could feel each syllable, each harsh and soft sound in the depths of her bones. It was a comfort like nothing Ellie had ever felt before.

Still holding hands, she looked sternly into Ellie's eyes. "Yes. I will help you, Ellie, but I must warn you. I sense great power within you. Power like none I've ever felt before. You are not simply human, my friend, but someone—*something*—more. When you discover it, discover who you are, you may not like it."

Layla's words were like stones placed upon her chest. She could crumble from the weight now placed on her.

Powers. Ellie already knew she was a seer, but did Layla sense something more?

She forced herself to release a cleansing breath.

"I will be ready for whatever is revealed to me. I have no choice but to accept it." Her words gave relief to the unknowns. She could not control what would happen from here, but she could control how she reacted to it.

"Well then, if you are going to gather an army to fight against the Queen, you're going to have to look like a woman worth fighting for."

Layla looked Ellie up and down. She had quickly thrown on leather pants and a cotton shirt after Auden's early wake-up call this morning. She hadn't had time to comb through her hair, so she was sure it looked a mess.

"What does how I look have anything to do with this? And I didn't say anything about an army, Layla."

"Well, you will at least need more than just a few infatuated men, a young elf, and some witches as allies. A few more infatuated men will do." She winked at Ellie's red, flustered face.

"How—Nate is just a—and Officer Shea and Auden aren't...You know what? Never mind." Ellie rolled her eyes at the uncomfortable subject. Layla softly laughed before getting to work. She tucked in Ellie's loose cotton shirt, pulling and tugging it until it lay exactly how she wanted it to.

"There is not much I do not know, Ellie. I have small eyes and ears everywhere." Ellie looked around at the nearby shadows cast by the large castle walls. "Do not worry. It is just you and me right now. I can sense when another is present."

"Can other witches do that? Sense when they're not alone?"

"No. Just me." She continued to fiddle with the shirt by rolling up the sleeves and pulling on the collar. "They're all excellent allies, especially Officer Reuel, or Auden, as you so comfortably call him." She raised a mocking brow. The smile on her lips was anything but sweet.

"He has his own *powerful* secrets, but I have no doubt we can trust him. Anyhow, do you think the Eternal Queen merely built her army from just fear and strength? No. She started with a few men who followed her for her intense, powerful beauty." Layla pulled something thin and black from her back pocket. "You need to start presenting yourself like a worthy leader. One with power, strength, and fierce beauty."

She brought the black stick close to Ellie's eyes. She tried to back away, but Layla held the back of Ellie's head with her free hand. "What are you doing? What is that?"

"Stop moving. It's just charcoal. I'm going to put a very thin stroke along the water line."

"It will just end up running down my face as I sweat in this heat!" She pushed Layla's hand away, but the witch brought it back with true determination.

"We witches can create a tonic that heals any ailment, yet you do not think I can create a stick of charcoal that will last through your nasty sweat?"

Ellie conceded her struggling "Fine. I still don't see why it's needed."

Layla then carefully ran the charcoal stick along her upper eyelids and softly along the outer corners of the lower lid.

"This is why." Layla pulled out a small circular mirror. Ellie was instantly drawn to her intense crystal-blue eyes. They looked fierce and unyielding.

"When you look powerful, you feel powerful." Layla handed her the charcoal stick. "This one is yours. I'll find some rouge for your lips and cheeks tomorrow." She looked Ellie up and down again before heading to the back of her head.

With gentle fingers, Layla brushed through her knotted hair. "We look to be about the same size. I will provide you with more appropriate blouses, some leather corsets, and a few extra pairs of leather pants like the ones you're wearing, but cleaner." Ellie used the small mirror to see Layla's nose scrunch in disgust as she gathered all of her hair up to braid. She was not subtle in her opinions.

"My clothes are just fine, Layla, and please don't pull it all up. I hate when my hair is pulled fully away from my face."

"They cannot see your beautiful face if you hide it! You have magnificent bone structure and need to show it off. Plus, this style will make you look older and more elegant." She yanked and pulled. After just a few minutes, she finished the hairdo by tying it up with a string that was wrapped around her wrist.

Two thick braids ran down the top sides of Ellie's head and back into a detailed bun. Layla pulled out small strands of hair to hang, framing Ellie's petite face. It was nothing like Grams or her sisters ever did, and she reluctantly didn't hate it.

Layla stepped back, admiring her work. "Now you're a woman I would follow to an early death." An accomplished smile stuck to her beautiful face. "Let's see what the men think." Her hand gestured to the large glass doors behind them.

"You missed the first bit of training this morning, so your group is most likely just sitting down to eat their first meal. If you get a reaction from both Nate *and* Officer Reuel, you have to wear whatever I provide. Deal?" Her smile was wicked, but one of a clear new friend.

"Deal." Ellie doubted either men would notice any difference at all, especially Nate, who never seemed to care what she wore or how she looked. Layla crossed in front and held the large glass door open.

"Shall we?" Her smile filled with pure joy and amusement. Ellie couldn't help but return the smile.

They entered the Great Hall to lines of men and some women just sitting down to eat. All of tent twenty-four sat at the same table as the night before. As they walked closer, a sudden wave of nerves hit Ellie's gut. She began to notice many eyes following where the two women walked. Ellie stood tall, trying to emanate the confidence of a leader. She could see Layla smirking from the corner of her eye.

They approached the table where Nate and Auden sat

next to each other, seemingly ignoring each other's existence. When Ellie and Layla were only a few steps from the table, they looked up and noticed her presence. As if on cue, they both shot up from their seats, eyes wide, nose flared, and jaws clenched. Oh, gods.

Layla could not control her amusement. Her cackle caught the attention of most everyone else in the Great Hall. Ellie shot her a blank glare that quieted her some, but Ellie's red burning face only brought Layla more joy.

"I hate you," Ellie whispered through a forced smile.

"No, you don't." Layla leaned in close to Ellie's ear. "Meet me outside your tent after everyone else is asleep. I think a trip to the castle library would be beneficial for you. I'll also have your new clothes in hand."

Layla's last words shook through her laughter. She sent one final wink to the two gawking men across the table before turning on her way.

17

Ellie couldn't get out of the Great Hall fast enough. Apparently, the only "training" she missed was a short run and horse stall duty.

For most of breakfast, Kiarhem rambled on about the horses, her favorite being a multicolored pinto horse. Nate and Auden took turns staring in Ellie's direction, and they weren't the only ones. Men and women from almost every table glanced her way throughout the entire meal. When it was finally time to leave, she quickly jumped to the front of the line. They headed to the front courtyard for weapons training.

Thank the gods.

Instead of his usual place in front, Auden walked side by side with her. "How was your meeting with General Dolion?" He kept his eyes forward, his expression flat.

"Painful." She bit her lip, trying to ignore the shadow of hurt that still lingered from the horrible man's touch. Auden's eyes glanced down at her before he quickly returned his gaze to the front. He did not voice his response, but the anger that radiated off of him was the only reply she needed. Auden cared if she was hurt. It wasn't a full admittance of his loyalty or allegiance to her, but it was enough to know he at least didn't want her to be in pain.

"I'm fine. Layla helped me back to the tent where she rubbed Agilta's tonic onto my back. I would be more worried about Officer Shea right now. I said something...I-I didn't know—"

Auden nodded ever so slightly. "I'll ask Ames to check on him later, but I wouldn't worry. Shea has a way of always turning up fine."

They made their way down the front castle steps and to the west side of the courtyard where lines of dull swords and daggers lay.

"If you don't have a sword, find one! I will be partnering you up for duels! We will be practicing disarming techniques only! If you try to harm your opponent in any way, I will have you on bucket cleaning duty for a week! Got it?"

"YES, SIR!"

Bucket cleaning duty, though vile and disgusting, was a gentle threat compared to the beatings she'd witnessed other arbitrators dole out when designees disobeyed. Auden partnered them up: Kiarhem with the elderly gentleman with kind eyes, Nate with a tall dark man, and her with the man she bruised and cut just a day earlier. Auden walked by with an amused glare.

"Be nice," he said with a wink that sent her eyes rolling and her gut twisting. "And good luck." He eyed the blue-and-black-eyed man. The man was not in the least bit amused. In fact, he looked downright terrified.

"Swords up! Let's first see what each of you can do! I'll instruct as I see fit for each person! Ready? Parry!"

The man in front of her hesitated. She took one step

forward, and he took two clumsy steps back. She relaxed her sword arm.

"I'm not going to hurt you. Cleaning out fecal matter for a week is literally the last thing I want. Come on." She held her blue-silver sword upright. He hesitated for one more moment, but when she advanced, he stood his ground.

She swung her sword at his, testing the strength and power of his block. It stood mostly without movement. Good, this wouldn't be a total bore. He swung back with decent strength. She blocked with ease. Back and forth they parried, gaining trust and her learning his weaknesses.

She decided to take it up a notch. She came in stronger and faster, swinging down at his head. He blocked and pushed back with focused eyes. She came in again and again. His feet fumbled to keep up with her speed, and as a result, his blocks became sloppy. After a few more hits, she easily knocked the sword from his hand.

Clang.

"Your blocks are good, but your footwork is terrible. If there's no strength at the foundation, there will be no strength at the top. Can I show you?"

He looked at her with a puzzling stare but slowly nodded his yes. She showed him what he was doing versus what he should do. Then shared some exercises her grandpa gave to help build strength, agility, and balance at the base.

"How do you know all this?" He looked at her with both respect and admiration, a far cry from how he had looked at her the day before.

"My grandpa started training me at just five years old." She examined his cut, dimpled cheek and bruised eyes. "Sorry about the...you know...face." She waved her finger, circling and pointing at the wounds she provided.

"Don't be. I deserved it. I was just trying to look 'manly'

in front of the others. Clearly, I was in the wrong. My name's Collern, by the way." He held out his hand in greeting.

"Ellie." She shook his soft, callus-free hand.

"Glad to see you two figured things out," Auden said, walking up the line towards them. "Alright! Let's mix it up!"

Ellie now faced the middle-aged brunet man who whistled at her yesterday. He snarled at her, which she took as a clear invitation to humiliate him. After just a few seconds, his sword lay at her feet. He picked it up to begin again, rage filling his eyes. Again, after a few more seconds, his sword was on the ground.

Auden gave him some pointers, but he did not hear them through his anger. He came at her with intense speed and rage. Instead of blocking his attack, she simply stepped aside. His forward momentum brought his blade crashing to the stone ground, shattering the dull weapon to pieces.

"FILTMON! THAT'S ENOUGH!" The entire line stopped to stare at the man. "Bucket duty and laps around the courtyard until we are finished with weapons training! Go! Now!" Filtmon didn't move. He glared at Auden with flared nostrils. Auden had already unbuckled the whip from his belt. "I will not ask again." Filtmon looked down at the weapon, and after a split second, he began his jog around the outer square.

It would have been invisible to most, but Ellie saw the slight exhale and relaxation of Auden's shoulders. He slowly placed his weapon back in its holder. "Let's mix it up again!" he yelled, partnering them up and filling in the gap Filtmon left.

Auden started with facing Nate. The arbitrator upheld his earlier promise and did not go easy on him. Auden disarmed Nate over and over again with surprising ease, seriously bruising his pride, but when Auden instructed him, Nate listened.

Ellie parried man after man, also leaving a line of slightly bruised egos. Most handled it well and took her critiques with appreciation. The elderly gentleman softly smiled during their entire encounter. Though gray with age, he held himself against her quite well, lasting longer than most everyone else.

Kiarhem used her speed against Ellie. Her foot work was phenomenal, but she lacked skill in her blocks and swings. After assessing her for some time, Ellie disarmed her with ease.

"Not bad." She smiled at the young elf. She lit up, her grin going from pointed ear to pointed ear. Next, she faced Nate.

Finally, a challenge.

He returned the amused grin plastered to her face. He lunged first. She blocked the attack to her head. Ignoring the growing ache in her back, she pushed him off with an immense amount of effort.

Nate's strength was her weakness, but her speed was his. They met their black and blue blades over and over again, spinning and turning with each strike—a beautiful dance that they had performed hundreds of times. Their battle led away from the group's line and closer to the center of the square.

She could feel the eyes of many onlookers. Nate's own heated gaze met hers, sending her gut into a frenzy. The sparing went for some time before she finally twisted her blade with Nate's, knocking it free from his hand. She playfully swung her sword, stopping inches from Nate's neck. He laughed, knocking her blue blade away with his hand.

Clapping erupted from designates and arbitrators alike.

She was unaware they had gathered the attention of everyone in the square. Her face flushed with heat. Nate held out his hands, presenting her to the entertained crowd. She playfully smiled and bowed before returning to their group's line. The crowd died down as arbitrators yelled and demanded their groups to get back to work.

"Next time stay within our group's area." Auden's gaze met Ellie's. The muscles in his jaw tightened again.

"Yes, sir," Ellie replied.

"Mmm. She can fight and obey. Interesting." A silky voice spoke from behind Ellie.

She turned to see a slightly-familiar, tall, slender officer. His thin lips pulled up at the corner as his sapphire eyes gleamed down at her with delight. He pushed his dark hair back from his face, revealing a thin jawline and angular brows. He was beautiful. Terrifying, but beautiful.

"Ellie, this is Officer Ames." Auden cooly gestured to the man. Ellie bowed her head slightly in greeting.

"It's nice to finally meet you, Officer Ames. I remember seeing you at my first trial, but I've only heard mention of you since." He smirked at her in a way that urged her to take three steps back, but she only shifted her weight.

"Ames has a way of only being seen when he wants to be," Auden explained.

"The generals must find that quite useful." Ellie's tone was polite, but Ames's continuous stare made her want to either run or shove a dagger in one of those piercing eyes.

"Quite. They have their witches to hide in the shadows here, while I use my gifts...*elsewhere*." The drawl on his last word sent a chill through her injured spine.

"Ellie and Shea had a meeting with General Dolion this morning. Shea may need to debrief with you later."

Ames finally removed his gaze from her to nod his

understanding to Auden. He then bowed his head towards her, revealing a final grotesque sneer before turning on his way.

"I understand now why you wanted to keep your distance from him," Ellie murmured to Nate, though it was loud enough for Auden to hear.

"Ames is harmless. A little odd and unpredictable, but still harmless," Auden assured them before turning back around to the rest of the group. Ellie hadn't even noticed their eyes watching the quick interaction.

"I apologize, Ellie, but our turn to duel will have to wait until next time." Auden looked at her, that devilish gleam shining in his eyes. "Alright, twenty-four! Let's head back to the tent! More designates will be arriving soon, and I'd rather not greet them smelling like sweat and horse shit!"

He was right. They did all smell like sweat and horse shit. She prayed they would not be on stall duty tomorrow.

18

She let most everyone else wash up before her, seeing as she didn't have to endure the early hours of shoveling hay and manure. Though, she would have rather suffered that over the torture placed on her by the hand of General Dolion.

Most of the men refused to don shirts after their wash, including Nate. He claimed it was because of the heat and to avoid sweat. Ellie knew it was because he enjoyed seeing how flustered it made her.

After washing up herself, leaving her hair untouched but reapplying the charcoal Layla gave her, she filled both Nate and Kiarhem in on her morning events.

No one seemed to pay them any attention in the back corner of the tent. Some men took afternoon naps; others played with a worn deck of cards while talking chummily as they ate the bread and cheese that was left mysteriously on their mats.

"So, Layla is our ally?" Kiarhem asked with giddy excitement.

"Yes. A strong one at that. She knows more about these

castle walls than most of the arbitrators here," Ellie answered. "She's taking me to the castle library after everyone else is asleep."

"You mean she's taking us. You're not going alone, El. You may trust her, but I'm going to need more proof on where her loyalties lie." Nate sat, polishing his sword.

"Fine. You can both come." She shoved a huge piece of bread in her mouth.

Auden opened the back flap, his dark-golden hair still dripping from his washing. His shirt adorned him. *Thank the gods.* But it hung loose with only a few bottom buttons looped, leaving the shirt open to his very broad, muscular chest. Ellie realized she was staring, mouth slightly gaping and full of bread. She quickly closed it.

"That is the most attractive man I've ever seen." Kiarhem giggled. "Too bad he's an arbitrator."

"This is only his second year," Nate voiced, a little on edge.

"How do you know that?" Ellie looked up from her mat to see Nate shrug.

"We mucked the same stall this morning, and I asked him how long he's been an arbitrator. I was making light conversation. I was trying to be...*nice.*"

Nate was trying to repair the bridge he had already stupidly burned.

"We still can't fully trust him. Not yet. There's so much we don't know about the generals and how they keep, or force, the officers' loyalty." Ellie lay down on her mat, stretching her tired, sore back.

"Just as we can't fully trust this witch," Nate added, rubbing a finger over his scarred palm. He was right, though Ellie's gut told her differently.

"She lied for me, Nate. She has wanted to get away from

these castle walls for far longer than us. I believe we can trust her."

Whooping and hollering came from the other end of the tent. She sat back up to view a few of the men slap Collern on the back.

"What are they playing?" she questioned. Both Nate and Kiarhem shrugged in reply. She stood up and walked over to the gathered group of men.

"Can I join you?" she asked, standing behind a smiling Collern. Both him and the kind-eyed, elderly gentleman next to him made room between them. She reached her hand out to the white-haired man. "I'm Ellie."

He shook it with delight. After letting go, he began to make motions and intricate symbols with his hands.

"He's saying his name is Belig." A dark-skin, black-haired man spoke. Belig nodded then continued to sign with his hands. "He says we're from Turgo and wants to know where you're from."

"I traveled here from Perilin. What's your name?" She turned to the man translating for his friend. His face was young but strong.

"I'm Doal. This is Keir and Myer. And you've met Collern."

"Keir, Collern, and I are from Hyma, a territory southwest of here," Myer interrupted with a gleaming smile. His fiery-orange hair was cut short and lay flat against his forehead. "Have you ever played three card tussle?" he asked, shuffling the card deck in his hand.

"No, I'm afraid I haven't."

"It's pretty easy. I'm sure you'll catch on," Keir, the tan, bright-eyed friend reassured. His curly ash hair was tied into a tight knot on the top of his head.

Myer began to distribute the deck among them. "So

Collern tells us your superior handling of a sword comes from the training of your grandfather. Did he teach you anything else?"

"Yes," she answered simply, giving the men a coy smile. They soaked it in.

"Did your dad have the same training? Did he fight for the Queen's Army?" Collern eagerly asked.

"No. Both of my parents were killed during one of the Queen's initial conquests. I'm the first of my family to be designated." She picked up the pile of cards that lay before her, stacking them in her hand facedown as the others did. Collern looked away, regretting his question.

"Both Keir and I lost our dads this past year. They died on the battlefield, which is why we're here now," Myer explained. Both men looked to be about her age.

"My older brother lost his life on a mission for the Queen," Collern added. "He enlisted at just fifteen years old. He lasted seven years. I doubt I will be able to do the same."

"I'm sorry for each of your losses." She reached and gently squeezed Collern's soft hand. Belig began to sign again to her right.

"We've all lost so many loved ones to this endless war," Doal translated. "The only one who should apologize is the Eternal Queen."

The kindness in the elder man's light-blue eyes faded. All five men flipped three cards from their hand onto the mat before them. She did the same. Myer had the highest number card and took the pile, adding it to his own hand.

"I don't mean this to sound disrespectful, but I thought the cutoff age for joining was fifty?" Belig laughed softly at her question. Doal did not.

"Belig turns fifty next month. All three of his sons before him joined and fell in this war. Other than his wife, he was the last one left in his family that could sign up on Designation Day." Doal's words were filled with pain. Her heart sank for the man who sat beside her.

"That's terrible," she whispered through water-filled eyes. The elder man patted her cheek with a rough hand. He removed it to sign once more.

"One day," Doal whispered, "her rule will end."

"And what about you, Doal? Why are you here?" Ellie asked.

"I am the oldest of five children. My father is still alive and serving somewhere in the Queen's Army, but I recently married. Legally, we are now a separate family from our parents, so I had to enlist. Knowing what I know now, I'd still marry her." Doal smirked to himself. He was older than the three from Hyma; Ellie guessed mid-thirties.

The rest of the game was played with lighthearted talk and wordful jabs at one another. Once the round was over, she stood from the group.

"Thank you for allowing me to join. I think I need to get a bit of rest before supper. Belig, if there is more free time this week, will you teach me some of your language?" His eyes lit up as he nodded his yes. She smiled at each of the men before turning away.

"You are welcome to grace us with your presence anytime, Ellie," Myer voiced behind her. She turned back and winked, causing his freckled face to blush.

She crawled onto her mat, smiling slightly from the interaction. Finding allies was proving to be easier than she initially thought it would. She relaxed and instantly fell into a deep rest. One her broken body desperately needed.

19

One more designate arrived in the tent, filling the last mat. To Nate's shock and displeasure, it was a chestnut-haired boy who looked much too young. Not younger than his new elf friend, but definitely young for a human. The boy's eyes were filled with a sadness that everyone living in Karmalo was all too familiar with: the gaze of loss and death. He ignored the rest of the tent, only eyeing El before secluding himself to his mat.

He stayed silent through dinner, ignoring El's new friends Myer and Keir, who seemed eager to pull the kid out of his shell. Nate wasn't sure what to think about how easily it seemed for El to win these men over. The way they all looked at her had his teeth grinding.

Worse was the way she looked at Officer Reuel as he translated a story carved into their dining table. It depicted a war that had happened centuries ago. A war that only ended once the three pillars of royalty were seated on their thrones. It was Malavor's origin story, one that led to the downfall of one king and the rise of three.

A soft smile remained plastered onto her face as she kept her eyes on the annoyingly handsome man. He mentioned the three Kings filling their armies with the most beautiful and fiercest of Fae women. "An army you would have easily fit in with, Ellie." Her cheeks reddened, and Nate had the sudden urge to ram his fists right into Reuel's perfectly-chiseled jaw.

After dinner, they waited silently on their mats. After a few hours, the sound of faint snoring and soft breaths filled the tent. Nate followed El and Kia out the back flaps. Staying in the shadows of the tent, they slowly made their way along the side. The sudden appearance of a dark form emerged from the shadows.

"Holy sh—" Ellie nearly jumped back into Nate.

"Shh!" Layla held a finger to her elated mouth. In her other hand was a large black sack. She smiled wickedly, handing the bag over to Ellie. She reached in and pulled out a lace brassiere that instantly had heat rush through Nate's body. *What the hell is that for?*

El shoved the garment back in the sack, giving Layla a flat glare. "That should provide more support and volume under the very...*tasteful* blouses that I provided for you," Layla whispered and grinned, her too-white teeth gleaming in the moonlight. El placed the sack next to the tent, leaving it to be retrieved when they returned. "Alright, let's go. I've never shadow cloaked so many bodies at once, so stay close."

After a strange murmur of words from Layla, a cold prickle ran up Nate's spine. Suddenly, the world was cast in an unfamiliar silver sheen. He looked at El and was shocked by the glow of her eyes. Gods, she was beyond beautiful even in the strange colorless world that Layla cast them in. She looked around, smiling, absolutely delighted at what

Layla had done. Kia released a quiet squeal of joy. "Witches are amazing."

Layla shrugged, but her face failed to hide the pride she clearly felt at Kia's statement. "No one will see us while we are cloaked. However, if another witch is also shadow cloaked nearby, she will be able to see us. Thankfully, I have the power to sense when one of my Mothers or sisters is near enough to view us."

They walked close to one another in silence, keeping to the edge of trees, hedges, and the castle walls where shadows were darker and deeper. The journey outside the castle was easy, but inside would be a different story. From outside the cerulean glass door, Nate could see candles burning brightly in the Great Hall at one of the tables near the kitchen as multiple witches sat enjoying a late meal. The rest of the room was cast in darkness, but they would not be able to enter through the large glass door without being noticed.

Layla led them further down the outside wall to the last cerulean window. Like all the other windows along the back entrance, it ran up the height of the wall and connected to the next window beside it.

"I'm going to be honest with you," Layla whispered. "I've only done this a few times, and it's never gone super well. The first time I attempted this spell, I might have cut off the tip of one of my sister's fingers."

"Might of? What exactly are you going to do?" Nate kept his voice low despite the urge to yell at the witch.

"You'll see." Layla turned to the window, placing both palms of her hands on it. She again whispered in the strange language Nate had never heard before, and after a moment, the glass began to ripple around her palms like rocks dropping into a lake. "Hurry, I'm not sure how long the spell will last." She stepped through the glass as if it were a curtain of silk.

Kia and El rushed after the witch. Nate took a second before doing the same. The glass formed around him like water, but it did not leave him feeling wet as any normal liquid would. He ran into the side of El, and it bumped him back into the window. However, it was no longer liquid, but solid once more. The window didn't return to the smooth clear glass it once was, though. It rippled and waved, leaving it starkly different from the rest of the windows.

"I'll have to fix that later. At least none of us were caught in the glass before it rehardened." Nate assumed that was how one of her fellow witchlings lost a finger.

They continued walking, staying against the wall and far away from the witches and their candlelight.

"Did you hear about the new designate? The young girl from Perilin?" an elder witch with gray hair said to a few others as she sat down with a plateful of sweet bread.

"That's what we're talking about. She made quite a commotion this afternoon during training," said another. Nate sucked in a breath. They were talking about El.

"I heard Ubel got a slight power reading from the young girl."

"Ha! Ubel wouldn't be able to feel power even if the old King and Queens of this court stood right in front of her! Either way, the girl's fighting skill alone shows a great threat to the generals. I doubt they let her get through the trials alive."

"Such a shame to let all that beauty go to waste. If I had that beauty at her age, I'd use it to be sitting on the throne our Eternal Queen now sits upon."

"Mmm. Another reason for the generals to end her. With the right amount of confidence and power, that girl could easily have thousands of men and women fighting for her." The four witches sitting at the far wood table nodded in agreement, and Nate's gut dipped at the thought of the generals targeting El.

They reached the large oak door at the end of the Great Hall. How they would open it without drawing attention to themselves was beyond Nate. Layla looked at El with a crafty gleam in her eye. She held up three fingers. Two fingers. One.

The oak door swung open. A young witch with strawberry-red hair swiftly passed them by, leaving the door wide open for them to pass through. Once through the door, they stood in a dark, empty hallway. The slight hue of silver moonlight cast through the windows to their right.

"Hannabella can't refuse the temptations of late-night sweet bread. She makes her way to the Great Hall every night around this time," Layla whispered. "Come on. We still have quite a way to go."

One after the other, they walked silently through the stone hallway. Layla warned that their bodies would reappear every time they stepped through an unavoidable gleam of moonlight. It didn't seem to matter, as the hallway stayed empty and quiet, until they came upon a door where sounds of lovely music and soft laughter radiated from behind it. A large beam of moonlight shone directly in front of them.

"One at a time," Layla quietly instructed. She silently ran across the light. Her body reappeared without the silver glow to it then disappeared once more into the shadows.

"Your turn," El whispered to Kia. Nate doubted the light could catch the elf. Sure enough, Kia was through the beam of light within one blink.

El prepared herself to run. She jumped forward when the doorknob inches from her arm began to turn. Nate grabbed her wrist, yanking it back and twisting her into his chest. He held one arm around her waist, the other hovered over his sword. Neither one dared to breathe as a large dark-haired man emerged from the warm, lit room.

"Thank you for your time and knowledge, Mother Ubel. I will relay your findings to the other generals."

This beast was a general? This was the first one Nate had seen, and he was undeniably terrifying. His presence sent a chill up Nate's spine. The air felt thick and strange.

El leaned further into Nate's hold. The sound of both their beating hearts was deafening.

"Of course. Goodnight, General Dolion." Mother Ubel closed the door to her chambers, leaving the general lit only by the light of the moon. Not just any general, but General Dolion. The same general that got off on torturing El earlier that day.

"Useless witch," he spat. He stormed down the hallway towards the Great Hall. Once his heavy footsteps echoed farther away, they both released a heavy exhale. Nate pulled El's waist closer, enjoying their proximity more than he should in the moment. To his surprise, she nuzzled deeper into his neck.

"I'm sorry," he whispered, knowing she was remembering her terror from the morning. He burrowed his face in her hair. She smelled of wildflowers and rain. It was intoxicating, and when she lifted her gaze to meet his, it took all his willpower not to brush his lips against hers.

"You first," he whispered, breaking the hold she had on him. He instantly regretted it.

She swiftly ran through the bright moonlight, and Nate followed seconds later.

20

The farther up they went, the more relaxed Ellie felt. They had no other close calls as they walked down hallways and up flights and flights of stone staircases. After a final flight of stairs that led to one short hallway, they reached another large oak door. An enormous intricate owl surrounded by a border of thorns and thistles was carved upon it.

"This was the King's personal library. It's the only royal room that wasn't destroyed and has stayed in pristine condition all these years," Layla whispered.

"Why was it spared?" Nate asked.

"King Vedmar was said to be one of the wisest and most knowledgeable men in history. There are stories, ideas, books, and scrolls all found here and nowhere else. Some say the Eternal Queen understood the value of this library, therefore chose to spare it. Others say there's a book hidden deep within the library—a book that she longs to find. One that would lead her to even more power."

"And what do you believe, Layla?" Ellie questioned.

"There is a witch by the name of Talmi. Mother Talmi

has been assigned to the library. She comes here during the day and leaves in the evening. No one knows what she does in there, only that she was given a task by the generals many years ago. A task she still performs to this day." She looked at the three of them. "I believe she looks for the book the Queen desires."

The hairs on Ellie's arms stood. If there was such a book and the Queen found it, all hope of defeating her would be lost.

"Well, are we going to go in or just stand here talking about it?" Kiarhem asked impatiently.

"Let's go." Ellie led the way through the large owl door.

At first glance, Ellie only saw darkness. Soft moonlight from a few windows and a small lantern hung on the wall to her left were their only light. The small lantern held a tiny flame atop clear liquid. Layla walked closer to it. With her lips near touching the flame, she whispered in the origin tongue.

In an instant, lanterns were lit in every direction, on every wall, and in every corner.

Now that the library was lit, they could behold the mass of the room. It was nearly the same size as the Great Hall, yet every inch of the twenty-or-so-foot wall was covered in books or scrolls. A large wooden table, identical to the ones they dined at, was placed in the center of the room. On either side of it were standing shelves that, again, were filled to the brim with books.

"Wow," Kiarhem exhaled.

"If this was his personal library, what was the main library like?" Nate jested.

Ellie walked towards the large wooden table, where scrolls and books lay open upon it. A quick glance told her there was nothing important in them, so she moved towards the south end of the room. Layla followed as Ellie ran her fingers against the spine of every book she passed.

"I saw you at dinner this evening, surrounded by what looked to be more enamored men," Layla purred from a few steps behind Ellie.

She shot her an annoyed glare. "I have to live with these men. I might as well befriend a few."

"I also saw you speak with Officer Creepy this afternoon."

Ellie softly laughed at the proper description of Officer Ames. "Are you following me, Layla?"

"Yes."

Ellie scoffed, "Auden seems to think Ames is harmless."

"I wouldn't call the general's assassin and whore harmless." Layla's tone became utterly serious. Ellie stopped walking to face the young witch. "Most of the generals prefer entertaining themselves with the witches, but some prefer the company of men."

Ellie cringed as she remembered the feeling of Dolion's hand on her bare skin. She couldn't imagine *entertaining* the general in the way Layla was referring to.

"The generals allow Ames a bit more freedom than most other officers. He's the only one to go on solo missions for them, and in turn, he provides a few with his company."

Bile burned in Ellie's throat. The thought of having one of those monsters near her like that was enough to bring up every bit of her dinner.

She shook the thought from her head, and both women continued walking.

At the end of the room, they found a corner where a small desk sat. Behind it was a narrow wall of small portraits. Dozens hung from ceiling to floor, just like the surrounding books. Ellie walked closer to them.

Each frame held a portrait of a young Fae. They all had long, angled ears, sharp bone structures, and immeasurable beauty.

"It's all of the past crowned royals." Layla spoke softly behind her.

"Do you know who they all are?" Ellie asked, reaching towards a picture of a young woman. Her blonde hair was cropped short, and she stared back at Ellie with glittering green eyes.

"I assume the bottom three would be the last King and Queens of Malavor."

"So this would be King Vedmar?" She pointed to an icy-blond bearded man who wore a silver jeweled crown atop his head. Most of his features were broad, yet his cheeks and nose were sharp and angled. His gaze held equal strength and gentleness.

"Yes. King Vedmar the Wise. The two women on either side of him would have been Queen Odina the Warrior and Queen Akéra the Just. I apologize, but I'm not sure which is which." Layla pointed to the two beautiful women. Their golden locks were pulled up like Ellie's currently was, but the braiding was different, less elegant, and more...Feral was the only way Ellie could explain it. It was the vicious beauty she strived for.

"They were beautiful," she whispered.

"Yes. They had phenomenal genetics." Layla waved her hand at the rest of the royal portraits.

Ellie turned to face the small desk behind her. She pulled out the wooden chair and sat. Running her fingers along the wood, she stopped at the drawer to her left. Upon opening it, she found another portrait, one with the faces of a Fae male and female. She focused on the female's face, on her curly auburn hair, and her intense green eyes.

Her vision began to blur.

"It doesn't have to happen this way, Vedmar! We can fight now and end this!" a woman yelled.

Ellie stood behind the desk once more. The silver-crowned King sat in his chair just inches from her. The auburn-haired Fae from the portrait in his desk stood across from him. Her face was worn, and her eyes were full of fear.

"Please, Vedmar. There has to be another way." Her eyes were lined with silver.

"There is no other way. I am sorry." His voice was soft. Tired. "This is the only way to ensure their safety and our entire country's return to peace." He pulled a thick book from his top drawer and placed it on the desk in front of him.

"You've been wrong before." The woman's voice shook.

"Yes, but I am not wrong now." He slid the large book closer to her. The binding was dark emerald green and engraved with gold accents. "You need to take this and hide it in a place she cannot find. A plan has been made by your guard. When the time comes, do everything that he has instructed."

"So that's it then. You will allow this foreign queen to come into our home. To tear apart our land, murder your people, your children, your sisters, your cousins, even you?"

"Yes. I have to. This queen, she is too powerful. They are the only ones who will have the abilities, the powers to stop her. To end her." Lines of tears ran down King Vedmar's face as the female Fae sobbed into her hands. She continued to sob as she grabbed the book that lay between them. The King placed a gentle hand on top of hers. "I am so sorry, my sweet Millie."

Their joined hands blurred and burned into a blinding bright-blue light.

.   .   .

"ELLIE!" Layla screamed in Ellie's face. She blinked, clearing the fog from her eyes, then shot up from the chair. "WHAT THE—"

"Where's Nate?" Ellie spoke calmly despite the over-whelm of questions that swarmed in her head.

Who was that female? Why did the King trust her with the book? The book. It had to be the one the Eternal Queen had been searching for all these years.

"Nah-uh. No. What the hell was that, Ellie?" Layla grabbed her wrist, forcing Ellie to look at her face.

"It was a vision. One of the past and the third one I've had since arriving in Malavor." Ignoring Layla's shocked face, Ellie pulled her arm free. Nate and Kiarhem rounded the corner straight towards them. Nate held a scroll rolled and crumpled in his clenched fist.

"What's going on? We heard Layla yelling," Nate said with slight panic to his tone.

"I didn't know what else to do! She just sat there like— like stone! Like someone had put a spell on her, trapping her in her own body!" Layla's breath was short and quick.

"Another vision." Kiarhem gasped quietly.

Ellie nodded softly in conformation. "It was clearer and filled with more information than the last two. It was of the King and this female Fae." She handed Nate the portrait, who held it low enough for Kiarhem to also see. She relayed the vision in exact detail, from the conversation to the description of the book.

"They knew the Queen was coming, and the royals allowed Malavor to be taken. Why didn't they at least warn their people? Give them more time to escape?" Nate questioned.

"They did," Kiarhem voiced. "The leader of my colony and the other leader not fully aligned with the Eternal

Queen received a letter from King Vedmar. He asked for their help in hiding the Fae. My colony leader agreed to allow the Malavor people to find refuge in Dorumia. Some of them started to arrive weeks before the attack. The King and Queens only allowed a few families at a time to leave. A mass exodus would have alarmed the Eternal Queen. Unfortunately, I think the attack still came sooner than the Malavor royals expected."

"How do you know all this?" Layla questioned.

"My aunt. She's uhh...Well, she's Dorumia's leader or chief, as we call her." Kiarhem shifted her weight uncomfortably. "It's why I'm one of the very few elves to even know the Fae reside somewhere in Dorumia. I've never seen the city they've built, or any of its people. Neither has my aunt. She felt it was safer if even she did not know where they chose to hide."

"So you're like...royalty? Should we bow, or?" Nate made a curtsy motion towards Kiarhem, who sent a swift elbow into his side. He softly laughed. "Alright, then what should we be focusing on, El? The book? The woman?"

"Both," she answered. "The two go hand in hand. We have to find the book before the Queen does, and to do that, we have to figure out who the female is."

"Were there any words on the binding of the book?" Nate asked.

"No. It had gold lines framing the front and horizontally placed on the spine, and..." She closed her eyes to focus. There was more. "A tree. There was an oak tree filled with and surrounded by animals. It was pressed into the leather front of the book."

"And you're sure this is the book the Eternal Queen has been looking for?" Layla asked. Shock still remained on her face.

"Yes. King Vedmar somehow knew the Eternal Queen would look for it and told the female to hide it."

"Is there anything more you can tell us about her?" Nate asked.

"Just what she looked like, and that the King called her, um...Millie."

"Mill—"

Their conversation was interrupted by the creek of the library door. Ellie's stomach sank as they all froze in panic.

"Hello! Who's in here!" an elder woman yelled into the lit library.

"*Hide!*" Layla hissed.

"Just shadow cloak us!" Ellie muttered through clenched teeth.

"I can't! My powers are too drained! Hurry! Go!" She waved them off as she made her way to the front of the library. Kiarhem and Ellie hid underneath the King's desk, while Nate stood concealed behind a shelf filled with books. He had stuffed both the scrolls he held and the small portrait into his pants pockets.

"Mother Talmi! Hi!" Layla yelled out to the librarian witch.

"Layla? What on earth are you doing here?" Talmi's tone was stern and angry.

"Well. I...er...I—"

"I asked her to come." The deep voice that echoed through the library walls had heat traveling through Ellie's body. She shifted under the desk, ignoring the sudden urge to run towards the owner of it.

"Officer Reuel. My gods. Hello." The elder witch's voice softened and flew up two octaves at the site of the handsome arbitrator.

"My apologies, Mother Talmi." Ellie could hear the

slight lift in Auden's tone. He spoke quietly, but there was no mistaking the flirtation behind his words. Ellie scrunched her nose and stuck out her tongue to Kiarhem in disgust. Kia covered her mouth, concealing her laugh.

"I know it is late, but I was having trouble sleeping. I saw Layla in the gardens and asked her to retrieve a book for me. Only, I believe I told her the wrong volume."

"Oh, no worries at all, officer. You know you are welcomed here whenever. It is late though, so I will leave you to find it. Please make sure all flames are extinguished when you leave."

"Of course, Mother Talmi. Thank you." Based on the sounds of Talmi's slight giggles, Ellie could only imagine the smile Auden shone her way, one Ellie found herself wishing she could see. The wood door creaked once more as it shut.

"All right, you three. Come out. *Now*." The demanding tone to Auden's voice was surprising but not unexpected. They were caught, and Ellie wondered what the arbitrator might do. Should she be afraid of his reprimand? Her gut told her no.

They did as he commanded. Once in view, Ellie saw the anger plastered on his face. Terrifying anger. She saw both Layla and Kia flinch at the rage-filled daggers that stared at them. But it wasn't fear that Ellie felt, it was—*intrigue.*

"Layla, go extinguish the lanterns." His demand was near guttural. His shirt was barely buttoned again, clearly thrown on in a hurry to follow them. Every hard, sculpted muscle beneath the shirt was tense and waiting. Ready to be released at a moment's notice. "We will not leave the way you came in, so stay close. I assume since you were all hiding, Layla's powers are now drained."

They each shamefully nodded.

"*Great.*" He snarled through clenched teeth. "Let's just

pray we don't get caught then, shall we." Layla returned quickly, and they all headed out the large wood door into the dark moonlit hallway.

They followed Auden in complete silence. After the first flight of stairs from the library, they turned east, opposite of the direction they came. He led them down another flight of stairs and another long hallway until they reached a small wooden door. Auden opened it and ducked in. It was a windowless winding staircase that led down farther than the eye could see.

"Watch your step," Auden whispered as Nate closed the door, leaving them in complete darkness.

She hated the pitch black and the feeling of the complete abandoned loneliness that came with the darkness. She quickly reached back to grab Nate. She accidentally ran the tips of her fingers along the ridges of his muscled torso. "Sorry," she whispered.

Nate snagged her hand. "Never apologize for touching me, El." His whisper was hot against her ear. She couldn't control the heat that jolted through her. A barely-audible growl sounded from ahead, and Ellie swore it had come from Auden.

She ran her free hand along the wall to her right. They slowly made their descent down the small spiraling staircase. A few minutes went by, and she became dizzy from the constant turning. She shook her head, trying to clear it from its daze. It was never-ending. No wonder Layla risked taking them the other way. She wondered if Layla even knew of this secret staircase before now.

"Almost there." Auden spoke, breaking the silence After a handful more turns, they finally gathered onto a small landing. A strange, comforting tingle ran up the center of Ellie's spine, caressing the mark on her back but not causing it to hurt. A soft glow leaked through a small wooden door in front of them. Auden shoved his shoulder against the door, opening it with force. Dust and debris from years of little use swirled in the air.

"What is this place?" Ellie stepped in after Auden. A nearly-empty stone room surrounded her. Discarded shields, intricate armor, weapons, and some jewelry brown and green from oxidation were scattered along edges of the walls. A small ball of yellow light floated in the far corner. Ellie sucked in a breath, realizing the light was a wisp. A ball of magic created by the Fae. Ellie had once read that Malavor was covered in the small globes of light. Her grams had even once reminisced about the beauty the small lights created through the streets of the city. She had said it was like walking through the stars.

Ellie hadn't seen any other wisps left in the castle; candles and lanterns took their place. Why had this small bit of Fae magic remained in a place taken over by witches? Walking closer to the orb, an odd sense of familiarity washed over her. The sound of a small breeze and rustling leaves caressed her ears.

"It looks to be one of the royal treasure rooms, but I've never been to this one." Layla crossed over to a pile of shields. She dug through them, pulling out necklaces, rings, and other bits of jewelry, then she carefully placed them in the pockets of her cloak.

A twist of anger pierced Ellie's gut. The witch was stealing from the Malavor kings and queens. She was taking what little remained of the Fae people. She was doing what all the other witches had already done to so many parts of this castle.

"*Stop.*" The growl in Ellie's demand was unrecognizable. Nate and Auden were instantly to her, positioning themselves on either side. The movement seemed practiced, like they'd done this a hundred times, yet they hadn't. Kiarhem stood frozen in the middle of the room, unable to decide what to do. "Those are not yours to take, *witch*."

Layla rose, one eyebrow pulled up as she smirked at the three lethal warriors that faced her. "Interesting." Her smile grew, ignoring the danger she was in. Layla's smile was kindling to the fire growing in Ellie's gut. She needed to push it down, needed to gain control over it before someone got hurt. The wisp in the corner grew brighter, as if feeding off her rage.

Layla waved a hand and rolled her eyes. "Calm down. I'm not stealing. I only wish to clean them and restore them to their original beauty. I'll bring them back when I'm done, or perhaps I'll return them to the royal they belong to."

Ellie took a deep breath, cooling down her anger. She didn't miss Layla's subtle glance at Auden. "It's late. We need to keep moving." Auden placed a strong hand on her lower back, guiding her towards the door at the other end of the room. A shiver of delight ran up her spine at the contact.

They exited the room only to enter into another pitch-black maze of hallways. The warm hand on Ellie's back never strayed, bringing a sense of comfort Ellie had only ever felt with Nate and her sisters.

Finally, streams of moonlight leaked through the cracks of the stone wall ahead of them. "Wait here," Auden said as he pushed the secret stone door open just enough for him to fit through. He came back a few moments later, waving them through. They emerged from the southeast walls of the castle. The gardens were just a few steps and around the corner.

"Layla, are your powers strong enough to get them from here to the tents?"

"Yes. I think so." Layla grabbed Kiarhem's hand, and Kia grabbed Ellie's. After a deep breath, Layla began their walk back to the tent. They, again, stayed in the shadows of the hedges of the garden and trees in the field that spanned between their tent and the garden. There were a few moon beams that they could not avoid. They could only hope and pray no one noticed them in those split seconds of reveal.

Back at the side of their tent, Layla released Kiarhem's hand and slumped her shoulders forward. She breathed deeply, clearly exhausted. Auden walked up moments later.

"Nate, Kiarhem, head inside," Auden commanded through a whisper. They didn't hesitate to follow his command. Kia grabbed the sack of clothes Ellie had left and headed through the back flaps. "Layla, do you sense any witches in the trees beyond us?"

Layla closed her eyes and reached her magic out beyond her. "No. They are all currently gathered at the back wall." Her voice was ragged and tired.

"Good. Come with me, Ellie." He walked off towards the trees. Layla looked at her, worry filling every inch of her beautiful face.

"It's fine. Go. Rest," Ellie whispered to her, though she was not convinced it was fine. Auden was holding in his anger, and she was about to be at the receiving end of its release.

She followed the tall, broad man. His golden-brown hair reflected the moon's rays as he faded into the trees. Her heart raced as she walked, unaware of where the man now waited. A few steps in from the tree line, he grabbed her wrist, twisting her to face his infuriated gray eyes.

"What the hell were you thinking!" He seethed through bared teeth. His jaw was so tight, Ellie didn't know if his usual pain caused him to clench or if the clenching caused the pain that seemed to radiate from every inch of his body.

"Do you know what could have happened if you had gotten caught? A girl with mysterious healing, immense training, now snooping around the castle? No. No. Not just around the castle. In the King's personal library! They would have killed you and your friends on the spot! Seriously, Ellie! What the hell?!"

Ellie ripped her wrist from his grasp, though she was sure Auden could have held on if he wanted. Ellie tried to stay levelheaded, pushing down the anger he was pulling out of her. The fact that he was yelling at her and not whipping her or taking her straight to the generals was a good sign. However, his gray eyes were filled with so much pain and fury, she was truly struggling to keep her own anger in check.

"I don't know what you want me to say. I'm sorry? No, because I'm not." A stubborn truthful reply. She kept her features flat and calm despite the anger she felt.

"Of course. Why would you be sorry for putting both your life and others in danger? Why did you even go to the library in the first place?"

She stayed silent, forcing herself to stare down the enraged man in front of her. Ellie wouldn't dare reveal it was Layla's idea.

Auden released a frustrated groan. "You truly know nothing, don't you?" he grumbled to himself. "That is the only reason for taking such a ridiculous risk." Rubbing his temples with one hand, he paced back and forth. When he removed the hand on his face, Ellie was a bit shocked to see the gentle concern that lined every inch of his features. "Ellie. More than a few of the generals view you as a threat.

They don't want someone in their army that they know they can't control."

Ellie knew this to be true. She had heard what the witches had to say in the Great Hall. She was aware that more than a few generals felt the same way. "And what do the other generals think? Am I a threat in their minds too?"

Auden stiffened. "They have not made a decision yet, which is why you still stand before me. They believe they can use you as a weapon for the Queen if you show enough fealty."

He rubbed a spot on his right shoulder, just as Shea had done earlier that day.

"I am begging you, Ellie. Please act with more caution. No more late-night strolls through the castle, no more displays of grandeur in the courtyard, no more drawing attention to yourself. Please. If there are answers you seek, I will help you discover them." The pleading in his voice was a true shock. His light-gray eyes glowed down on her.

"No," she breathed.

"No?" That pain-filled clench in his jaw returned. He took a few steps closer, causing Ellie to back up into a large tree. The smell of spice, crisp air, and dry leaves assaulted her nose. She closed her eyes, ignoring the broad chest that was inches from her heated face. Auden was truly intoxicating.

Breathlessly, she replied, "There is already a target on me. Hiding now will not change that. I need to continue to prove I can be the weapon the generals on my side think I can be. In the end, if they decide they want me dead, then they will try to kill me during the trials. Not before. And I cannot simply trust you to give me the answers I seek."

He sucked in a breath at the mention of her distrust. He shook his head. "You don't know that for certain, Ellie. Any one of the generals could see your skills during training, decide you're too much of a threat, and end you before the trials even begin."

"They *will* do it during the trials in front of everyone to show their strength against anyone who may try to go against them. Well, if they want to try, let them."

She held her hands open, no longer able to push down her growing anger or her years of frustration. "I am *tired* of keeping my training and abilities hidden. I came here to display them, offer them to the Eternal Queen. If the generals' own pride and ego get in the way, so be it."

She knew her words were dangerous. Knew, as an arbitrator, Auden could hear her words and have reason to slit her throat right where she stood. She also knew that he wouldn't. She did not know who Auden was loyal to, but it was not the generals sleeping outside the walls of the castle. The current argument proved just that.

"Did you? Did you come to offer yourself to the Queen?" He returned the flat emotion she gave him just moments ago.

"Isn't that why we're all here?" she lied in reply.

He stared at her then sighed. He pinched her chin between his fingers and tipped her head up. Leaning down, he whispered a single word into her ear.

"No."

21

Auden walked off, leaving Ellie standing alone amongst the trees.

His "no" lingered in her ear. It was only her first full day in Malavor, and she already knew what had to be done. She would find the book, discover what power hid inside, and she would use it to get the hell out of this place.

She had a warrior, elf, powerful witch, and possibly an arbitrator or two on her side. If Auden was not offering himself to the Queen, why was he here? She still didn't feel she could fully trust him, but she at least knew his loyalty did not belong to the Eternal Queen or her generals.

Ellie slowly made her way back to their tent, stopping to splash her face with cool water from the washing spout. Only Auden sat awake as she made her way to her mat. As soon as she lay down, he did as well.

She lay staring up at the blank canvas ceiling, not fully over her dispute with Auden. If they had gotten caught...She supposed his anger *was* reasonable, and she was thankful for his rescue. As much as she would hate it, she would have to apologize in the morning. She closed her eyes, letting sleep take hold.

"Ellie. Ellie. Come on. It's time to get up." Auden's rich voice spoke as he kicked her bare feet with the tip of his boot.

"Noooo." She groaned. She felt as if she had just barely fallen asleep.

"If you're not out of this tent and in line in five minutes, you'll be joining me in the horse stalls every morning for a week." Auden made his threat as he walked out the front of the tent. She sat up, rubbing the blur from her eyes.

The only ones who were still getting ready were Nate and Kiarhem. The rest of the group must have been in line already.

"Didn't we just go to bed?" Ellie asked, pulling Layla's sack of clothes towards her.

"Yes," Nate grumbled. "It's still mostly dark out. I swear this is his punishment for last night's outing."

"I thought the ear lashing I got last night was punishment enough." Both Nate and Kiarhem gave Ellie a questioning look. "I'll tell you about it later. Kia, could you pick out my outfit while I fix my hair. If I don't wear something from this sack, Layla will give me an actual lashing."

She dumped all the contents on her mat, and a small metal compact dropped free at the end. Inside was a light shade of pink rouge. Kiarhem lit up at the sight of the beautiful pieces of clothing. Leaving her to it, Ellie went out to the back mirror to do both her hair and makeup.

It felt silly, but she trusted Layla and would do it for her continued alliance. Thankfully, she was able to do both rather quickly. Years of helping her sisters with their hair had finally come in handy. She rushed back inside, where Kiarhem held up the outfit she had picked.

"That?" Ellie questioned. It was...not something she would have normally worn, though nothing in the sack was.

"It will look good. Trust me." She handed her the pieces. Nate made his way out of the tent, giving both women the privacy to change.

She had never slid on a pair of leather pants so fast. They fit like a second skin. The cap-sleeved blouse Kia had picked was the deepest shade of blue and also formed perfectly to her body. The new undergarment pushed her breasts just above the blouse's plunging neckline, giving a perfect view of the shiny pendant. She threw on the matching leather corset last, sliding the thin straps over the cap sleeves and placing the bodice underneath her already perky breasts.

Kiarhem helped tie the corset to her body. Despite its tightness, the corset still bent and gave way where it needed. Training and fighting wouldn't be a problem.

"Alright, let's go," Ellie said, picking up her weapon-filled garters and holster. She quickly attached them to her body as she swung open the tent flaps. The slight gasps and explicit murmurs from a silent line were what raised her head from the adjustment of her weapons.

Every male eye was on her. She looked to see Collern quickly move his gaze from the sky to the ground, to basically everywhere but Ellie. Myer's and Kier's gazes were filled with a glee that forced their smiles to reach from ear to ear.

She suddenly became very aware of how tight and exposing the clothes that she wore were. Ellie was not lacking in curves, but they were nothing compared to Layla's. Yes, the two women were around the same height, but that was where the similarity in size stopped. Ellie wondered how the witch's clothes fit as tightly as they did.

She pulled and tugged at the blouse's neckline as her and Kiarhem walked over to a very red Nate. Auden relayed some directions about kitchen duty then herded them off towards the castle. Nate let a little distance fall between them and the group.

"You...uh...You look good. Layla's clothes fit you well." Nate rubbed the back of his neck as he spoke.

"Thank you. My grandfather never had a lesson on using our *assets* as a distraction during a fight, but it might be something to consider. Do you think using my feminine wiles during a fight would work?"

He huffed a laugh and mumbled something under his breath that sounded like, "*It would definitely work on me.*"

They walked the rest of the way in silence. It wasn't until they reached the glass door of the castle that Ellie saw herself in its reflection. Nate was right. She did look good. She looked like a woman. A beautiful, fierce, powerful woman. Ellie was beginning to understand Layla's point of view.

Auden listed the kitchen duties and allowed them to choose between wiping down the Great Hall's tables and chairs, washing dishes, cutting onions, or peeling potatoes. Myer sat peeling potatoes with Kier, Doal, and Kiarhem. Collern and Belig chopped onions with a few other group members, and Nate and her washed dishes.

"So, Ellie," Myer voiced from behind her, "do you mind if I ask you a question that we are all dying to know the answer to?"

"I'm sure I will regret this, but go ahead." Every other man in the room chuckled at her response.

"Are you and Nate here a thing, or do any of the rest of us have a chance to romance you?" Myer's tone was soft, sincere, and seemed full of misguided hope. Nate nearly let a knife slip at the sound of it.

"What makes you think you could have a chance at romancing me either way, *Myer*?" She put unnecessary emphasis on his name. She looked back to see the young, freckled face redden at her friendly jab. He continued with his peeling as the rest of the group carried on with separate conversations.

In the last hour, a few elder witches came to start cooking what would be their first meal of the day. It smelled incredible. The Zye coven might not have been a coven of gifted witches, but they were definitely gifted cooks. Honey rolls, potato hash, and seasoned meats wafted throughout the kitchen as Nate and Ellie washed every dirty dish in sight. Auden entered the kitchen with a dirtied cloth hanging from his left shoulder.

"Alright, ladies." Auden smiled and winked at the witches. A few giggled into their flour-covered aprons. "I think we have done all we can for now. I've got to get these folks going on our run if we're to make it back in time for breakfast."

A run! Ellie's stomach ached and churned for the food that overtook her nose. This was torture. Pure torture. Auden laid his rag on a nearby surface, gave the women one more handsome smile, then waved for designates in the kitchen to follow. The sounds of swooning laughter that filled the kitchen behind her was enough to keep some of her hunger at bay.

"They do realize they're like three times his age, right?" she muttered to Nate.

"That doesn't take away the fact that he's handsome. I'm even willing to admit that he's the best-looking fellow here. Plus, he's..." It seemed to hurt Nate to admit his next words.

"Nice. Most of the other arbitrators treat the witches as servants. Auden treats them as people."

He was right. Auden balanced his authority and kindness well.

They left the Great Hall and immediately began their run. Auden did not force them to stay in line. The group just had to keep up with him.

"Still. He could show kindness without the unnecessary flirting." Ellie's statement sent Nate into a hysteric frenzy. "What?"

"You didn't seem to mind it when *you* were on the receiving end of his flirting." Nate's words stung. Again, he was right. Kiarhem caught up to them as they passed several of their group members and led the pack just behind Auden.

"Fine," she muttered in reply, now feeling utterly ridiculous. She honestly didn't know why she found Auden's coyness with the witches so infuriating. Last night's lashing still left her slightly irritated, though some of the tiff she did need to apologize for.

They ran through the woods towards the back wall of the castle grounds. After some time, the trees broke away to stone. They turned east, running along the immense stone wall.

"For the record, Nate, Auden is not the only handsome man here." Ellie smirked at his growing red cheeks. "Wait back here."

She ran up next to Auden. His steps were quick, quiet, and soft, a run only mastered from years of previous training.

"Yes?" he said with a slight hint of annoyance. Her stubborn pride urged her to fall back.

"I wanted to apologize for last night's adventures."

He continued to look forward, but his expression softened some.

"You were right. My actions put both me and my friends' lives in danger. However, I meant every word I said. I will no longer hide myself or my abilities."

"Clearly," he griped, running a sharp eye over the clothes she adorned. Her face flushed with heat.

"What the hell is your problem!" she growled, releasing the rage that swelled up from that one look. Something about this man made Ellie unable, or unwilling, to control the ever growing anger inside her.

"Do not speak to me in that way, designate!" His face was now equally as flushed.

"Or what?" she sneered, instantly regretting the words that left her mouth. Auden stopped so abruptly, Nate and Kiarhem almost ran into him.

"Everyone keep going!" he yelled. "*Except you.*"

He grabbed her arm and pulled her towards the tree line. Once out of the viewing range of the others, she yanked it free.

He looked down at her with clenched teeth. "I cannot demand respect from the others in our group if I allow you to disrespect me. Do you understand?" he growled.

"Yes. I am sorry," she snapped back and meant it.

Her anger had gotten the best of her, and she was out of line. If another arbitrator or general had heard her speak to him that way, he would be forced to take serious action.

"And I will not apologize for asking you to lie low. I will not apologize for wanting to keep you safe!"

Again, there was worry that laced his words. A wave of confusion washed over her. "Why? It is not your job to keep me safe, Auden. You barely know me."

"It is more my job than you could ever know, Ellienia."

Her name on his lips was like a boulder to the chest. The world around her began to spin. She looked at him with wide, astonished eyes.

"H-how do you know that name?" Fear and anger grew from deep inside her. "*Who are you?*" She spoke with a fierce poison. She was sure no one but her family knew of her true name.

"Your ally. That is all I can say."

"NO! WHO ARE YOU?!" she yelled, pulling her sword free of its sheath.

Auden didn't hesitate. Before she could blink, he had disarmed her with his own sword, his movement faster than her eyes could follow. With her sword on the ground, he grabbed both of her wrists and used his hard body to pin her against a tree.

"I am Auden Reuel, I am your ally, and that is all. I. Can. Say." He spoke with intense power. She looked into the gray eyes before her. They seemed to glow through his rage. His jaw tightened in pain. She sensed his longing, his desire to say more, so she shoved her anger back down. It was not the time or place for this fight.

"Fine," she growled.

He didn't remove himself right away, and she hated how even through her anger and confusion, her body reacted to being pressed up against him. His calloused hands seemed to sear through her leather vambraces. Her heart pounded, and her lower abdomen twisted into a bundle of nerves.

He slowly removed himself from her, his eyes never leaving hers. He picked up her sword and handed it to her. She slid it back into its sheath.

"You will join me for extra stable duty every morning for the remainder of this week."

"What?!" she began to protest.

"There has to be some kind of punishment for your outburst in front of the others. Either you help me in the stables or you can trade Filtmon for bucket duty."

"Fine," she growled again.

"Good. Let's go. We need to catch up with the group." He bolted off with a speed that she would never be able to achieve.

She did catch up to a few designees, but Nate and Kia had returned to the back castle steps way before her.

"What happened? Are you alright?" Kiarhem eagerly asked. It took a lot of restraint not to snap back at her, even though she was not the one Ellie was angry with.

"I'm fine. Just leave it at that, alright," she said softly. Nate gave Kia a warning glance.

Ellie was in a foul mood for the rest of the day. She couldn't even enjoy the delicious breakfast she had looked so forward to or truly acknowledge Layla when she came by their table to commend her outfit. She simply just stewed in her frustration and anger, pushing each wave down deeper and deeper.

The only training they did for the day was some strength building. She was sure Auden chose it as a way to keep her from showing off. She still did more push-ups, more crunches, and more of everything than everyone else in their group just out of straight spite towards their group arbitrator.

Back at the tent, she barely spoke to anyone. She sat with Belig for a little while, learning a few letters and words from his language. After some time, he noticed her tired, frustrated eyes. He waved her off to rest for the last remaining hours of the late afternoon.

She lay on her mat, staring at the portrait they stole from the King's library. *Auden has his own powerful secrets,* Layla had mentioned. Ones that now clearly involved her. Gods, she was so tired of it all. Her whole life seemed to be one big secret, and it seemed the more she uncovered here in Malavor, the more secrets she found.

Why did Auden know her name? A name she had yet to share with Nate, the most important person to her. It was the only reason she hadn't told Layla or Kia yet. Nate deserved to know before the rest of them.

"El." She jumped at Nate's soft-spoken voice. "We're headed to dinner. Did you not hear?"

She hadn't.

The entire tent was empty. She hadn't even noticed the bodies around her leave.

"Sorry." She placed the portrait in her pack and stood for dinner.

Nate gently grabbed her hand, pulling her towards his attention. She looked at him with urging eyes, begging him not to ask if she was alright. She was not, and if anyone else asked her that question, she might break.

He placed a gentle hand on her cheek. "We will figure it all out, El. I promise."

He spoke the words she needed to hear, as if he had read her tortured mind.

"It's Ellienia," she whispered through broken breaths. "My full name is Ellienia Batair. I don't know of its significance, but my grandparents had me hide it. And in the woods today, Auden spoke it as if he has known it his whole life."

Nate said nothing at the reveal of her name. He only wrapped her in a strong embrace. With forced-back sobs, she buried her face in his chest, listening to the comforting beat of his heart.

"To me, you are El. My beautiful, stubborn, strong, witty

best friend. That is who you will always be." He spoke with such soft reassurance. She could not imagine being there without the man that held her. She could not imagine being anywhere without Nate.

She looked up at her handsome dark-haired friend. She pushed herself up onto the balls of her feet, their faces now temptingly close. She could feel the beats of his heart quicken. Feel the warmth of his breath on her lips. She looked into his umber eyes with longing.

"El. We ca—" He was interrupted by the clearing of a throat.

"We are all waiting on you *two*," Auden growled.

She reluctantly removed herself from Nate's comforting arms. "Sorry, *sir,*" she said with equal annoyance, glaring at the officer as she passed through the canvas flaps.

Dinner was uneventful. Auden was in a terrible mood, so what would have usually been filled with his passionate storytelling was now filled with silence. Kiarhem tried to make light conversation, but Ellie too was in no mood to talk, and Nate...Well, Nate sat with a clenched jaw and flushed cheeks completely lost in thought.

The only highlight was seeing the appearance of Officer Shea. Other than some slight bruising around his eye, he seemed to be in perfect health. He sat with their group and ate, giving Ellie reassuring soft smiles. Her reveal of Agilta did not seem to harm anything. Thank the gods.

The next morning, Auden woke her before any sane person should wake.

She threw on a cotton shirt and canvas pants, barely

making any attempt to ready herself completely. It wasn't like anyone else would be up and about at this insane hour.

They walked in silence to the southeast of the castle grounds, where the horse stables were.

"Rakes are over against the far wall. I'll grab the wagon." His tone was still laced with his remaining anger.

Most of the horses barely paid any attention to them. They, too, refused to acknowledge the gods-awful hour. She grabbed a rake and headed to the first stall, which happened to be Tabat's. She slid open the latch.

"Make sure you swing the door inwards, not outwards to avoid—"

"I grew up on a farm, Auden. I think I know how to muck a stall. Plus, I doubt Tabat would go far if she did get out."

"Tabat wouldn't, but some of these other horses would die for some freedom." He looked solemnly around at the other animals.

The rest of the morning was spent mucking and then filling each horse's feeder. Neither one of them wanted to be the first to break their angered silence. Ellie was beginning to wonder if Auden was as stubborn as her or even more so. She didn't even enjoy it when he became so sweaty that he had to remove his shirt. His glistening muscles only made her angrier.

Once back at the tent, she quickly washed fully clothed, as Nate nor Kia were awake yet. She actually enjoyed the extra hour or so of silence before Auden woke the rest of the tent. It gave her time to prepare for the day. She decided to wear an outfit that was a little less revealing, though the pants and blouse still fit like a second skin.

The day went on as the one before: a chore, which was

polishing and sharpening weapons, a run, breakfast, and then training. They once again spent time strength training.

She was still sore from the spite that had pushed her body too far during yesterday's strength building. She ignored the pain and forced herself to endure. After training, they spent the late afternoon in their tent again. Then they headed to another uneventful dinner. The only difference was her need for early sleep, especially since she would again be woken up before all the other living beings.

22

Again, she entered Tabat's stall, pushing the horse back some to give way for the small wood wagon. She nuzzled against Ellie's shoulder as she raked up her droppings.

"She likes you," Auden stated softly, with no hint of any remaining anger. He leaned his arms against the door of Tabat's stall. His white tunic was rolled up, revealing every curve and dip of his strong muscles. Ellie was just glad he was wearing his shirt.

She turned to pat the side of the horse's chestnut face. She ran her fingers down her large muscular neck, stopping below her mane, and gave a good scratch. Tabat whinnied in appreciation.

"I like you too, Tabat. I'm not sure I can say the same for your friend here. It seems he's hiding things, and I'm really tired of things being hidden from me."

Ellie's face looked exactly as she felt: frustrated and despondent.

"I'm sorry, Ellienia. I've already given you the information I'm currently at liberty to give. I should not have even revealed my knowledge of your true name. It was a moment of frustration and weakness. Please. Can we move on and be civil again?"

He revealed more in that statement than he realized.

She didn't answer him; she wasn't sure she was ready to not be angry with him.

"You know, you scrunch your nose when you're frustrated."

She straightened, confused by his statement. "What?"

"That's how I know when you're angry versus frustrated. When you're angry, you have this icy glare that is quite terrifying for such a tiny person. But when you're frustrated, you scrunch your nose as if it's the only way to keep your frustration from turning into that terrifying anger. It's admittedly quite cute. Like a bunny."

Tiny human. Bunny. She was sure that icy glare was now burning in her gaze.

She decided that she was indeed more stubborn than him and wasn't near ready to be "civil" yet. "What's training today? Will I be able to show off my skills? Or will it be something completely useless like yesterday's strength building."

She was skirting a dangerous line. Her lack of sleep made it impossible to control any anger that might rise.

Auden pushed himself off Tabat's wood door. His features remained calm. "If you continue to refuse to proceed with refrain and caution, then yes, I will make sure any training from now until your trials is, as you put it, useless."

"That is cruel. Not just for me, but for the other people who lie sleeping in our tent. They will endure the same trials as me, and they deserve to be trained and prepared properly!" She grasped her rake tightly. The tips of her knuckles turned white.

"None of their lives matter as much as yours, Ellienia."

"WHY?!" she screamed, spooking a few horses. Though, Tabat seemed unphased.

"You will find out soon. Until then, it is your choice whether or not the rest of your group gets proper training. If you promise to at least try to control yourself, then I will promise to prepare them for the upcoming tests." He spoke with a flat expressionless voice.

He knew he had won with his ridiculous ultimatum. She wouldn't risk any number of peoples' lives over her own. They each deserved a fighting chance, even if it meant they would one day fight against her for the wretched Eternal Queen.

"Fine," she growled. "I will hold back. Hide my full potential once more."

"Good."

"You're a proud, infuriating ass, Auden Reuel." His reaction to her words was not one she had expected.

He laughed.

It was the most joyous sound Ellie had ever heard, and his smile...Gods, he was beautiful, but it all quickly ended.

"You are not the first one to call him that," said a smooth voice from farther down the stable stalls. "And I doubt you will be the last."

Ellie wanted to hide behind Tabat at the sound of the oily voice. She knew he was aligned with Auden and Shea, but she did not trust the dark officer who could conceal himself so easily.

"Officer Ames. What is it you need?" Auden's words were filled with annoyance, but there was no hint of fear or tension at the sudden sight of the dark arbitrator.

"I wish to speak to Miss Batair. Alone."

Ellie whipped her head to Auden, eyes begging him not to leave her alone with the threatening, albeit handsome man. He ignored her gaze and merely nodded at the dark officer before leaving them alone.

Ames walked towards her, his gate eerily smooth. Horses shuffled and whinnied in apprehension as he passed by.

"What do you want?" Ellie's tone was harsh. If Auden didn't fear the officer, then neither would she. Additionally, her argument with Auden left her in no mood to deal with his ghastly sneer and disturbing glare. He ignored her tone and leaned against the wood door of Tabat's stall.

"I only wish to see if you are doing well." He curled his lip.

"Why?"

"Why not?" The gaze he wandered over her had Ellie backing into Tabat's warm body.

"Why do you look at me like that?" Ellie bit her lip in surprise to the question she blurted. He raised his brows in interest. "You look at me as if you want to cut me to pieces and feed on my flesh. Or...or roughly take me to your bed."

The sound that came out of the tall, dark man was nothing short of delight. His laugh was surprisingly warm, and Ellie dared to think it was...

Friendly.

Was this the man Auden and Shea saw? Was this hint of humanity the reason they trusted the ghastly officer?

"I admittedly wouldn't mind doing either of those things." His sneer returned, only it seemed less lethal. "Unfortunately, I cannot look at you in the same way Shea or Reuel do. They have always treated designates tough, but kind. The generals and other arbitrators may start to question things if I do the same."

"How is it that Shea and Auden look at me?" Ames's sneer faltered as his brows stitched at the question.

"Shea looks at you like you are his last hope. Like you're the final piece to a long, dangerous game that he has been playing."

"And Auden?"

"With annoyance and frustration mostly." His laugh was once again warm, but it quickly ceased. "Next time you feel his eyes on you, look at him. Really look at him. The poor male deserves some of your attention, especially since you're the only reason he's here."

"What? He—"

"I have things to attend to," Ames interrupted, pushing off the wood gate. "It has been a delight speaking with you in private." He began to turn away, and before Ellie could protest for more information on Auden, Ames said one final thing.

"Miss Batair, I also came to warn you. Be very aware while here. Please listen to Officer Reuel. If you are hurt or, worse killed, by poison, whip, knife, or anything, the generals will only view you as weak and will not pursue or punish the offender. No matter how valuable a few may initially think you are."

"I know."

She did know. They barely batted an eye at Schmilt, and only considered ending him for his inability to be controlled, not for attempting to kill her.

Ames bowed his head and disappeared out the stable doors.

When Auden returned, they spent the rest of the morning saying nothing else to each other. They hardly even looked at one another. Ellie only slightly gazed at Auden when he removed his sweat-soaked shirt, revealing a branded pale scar she hadn't noticed before. It was placed along his right shoulder.

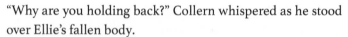

"Why are you holding back?" Collern whispered as he stood over Ellie's fallen body.

Auden had taken the group back to the field in front of their tent. There he paired them up for weaponless sparring. It took more strength than Ellie thought it would to hold back and allow a few of her opponents to beat her. Most of the men didn't even question her sudden inability to fight, especially the extremely young, quiet yet arrogant golden-eyed kid named Kal. Collern was the only one to challenge the change.

"It's complicated," she voiced back, picking herself up from the ground. "I apparently have a large target on my back, and a certain person feels that if I continue showing off, I'll end up dead before the trials even begin."

"Oh." He looked over at Auden, puzzling the pieces of her words together. "You think the generals would really try to kill you? Why?"

"Well, to put it simply...because I plan to kill each and every one of them and get the hell out of here." She smiled viciously through her bold and somewhat sarcastic words. Collern's eyes widened.

"Do you really? How? When?" His eyes filled with hope. Ellie didn't intend for him to take her words seriously, even though they were true.

"Uh...I don't know yet. There are a few things I have to figure out and do before then, and—"

"I'm in," he interrupted. "Whatever it is you're planning, I'm in. I'll follow you in whatever way you lead, and I know

I'm not the only one." He gestured to the other four men in his group.

"Why?" she whispered in astonishment.

"Very few of us actually want to be here and fight for the horrible Queen. You, on the other hand...You would be a queen worth fighting for." He placed a hand on her shoulder. She looked at the innocent eyes of her friend and processed the significance of his words.

"Will you do something for me then?" she asked.

"Of course. Whatever you need."

"Could you and the others find out who here comes from places completely loyal to the Eternal Queen?"

"You mean like Filtmon? He's from Panma. His country views Designation Day as an honor for anyone who gets to sign up. I've heard him say slanderous things about Officer Reuel, stating that he's too soft to be an acceptable arbitrator."

"Yes, exactly like that. Feed me both the people and places you hear of defending these trials and the Queen." Collern nodded with understanding in his eyes.

Auden dismissed the group, allowing them to either continue training with one another in front of the tent or relax inside.

Ellie waved for Belig, who eagerly joined her inside the tent for more lessons on his language.

fter dinner, Ellie walked closely behind Nate.

"Do I scrunch my nose when I'm frustrated?"

Nate turned his head to face her. His brows were raised, and a small smile of amusement graced his lips. "Yes. You're doing it right now. It's adorable."

"Wha—damn it."

She could have sworn she saw Auden's shoulders shake with held-back laughter at the front of the line, but they were much too far away for him to hear.

Back in the tent, Ellie collapsed onto her mat, thankful that the day was finally over. There were only two more days until the second trial, and two more days of wretched stable duty with Auden.

Nate rubbed Agilta's tonic onto her back before falling onto his own mat. The bruising had mostly disappeared, and the black mark in the center had minimized to the size of a coin. Unless she turned a certain way or fell right onto the spot, she forgot the mark was even there.

"Thank you," she whispered to Nate. A soft grunt was

the only reply she got. Ellie lay on her side, slowly falling into a deep restful sleep.

"Are you sure?" the red-haired female questioned. She stood next to King Vedmar in front of a simple, yet beautiful cottage home.

"Yes. It will work. It has to." They both raised their arms to the house and chanted something in the origin tongue: a language hardly heard but that was still used for deep magic. They continued to chant as they circled the entire house. Once through, they released their hands to their sides. "They cannot leave until it is time. Understood?"

"Yes," the Fae known as Millie replied.

"Once they pass through the barrier, it will activate the spell," the King instructed. "Do you still have the book?" Millie nodded in answer. "Good. It will be safe here."

The auburn-haired female stood next to the King, lightly sobbing into a shaking hand.

"I am sorry, Millie. I know this is not the life you planned. It is not the life any of us wanted..." His voice trailed off as Ellie's vision turned black. Then a glowing blue form of a man appeared. His blurred face was urgent as silent words came from his lips.

"WAKE UP!" he finally voiced.

Ellie's eyes shot open. Her hair and neck were wet from either sweat or the moist evening air. She swiftly grabbed the dagger that was still strapped to her thigh and held it at the neck of the man who knelt over her. The dark-eyed man held a liquid just inches from her mouth.

"Do it," he snarled, a gravelly, recognizable sound.

Filtmon.

"If she doesn't, I will." Auden spoke, placing the blade of his sword against the back of the man's neck. "Hand her the vial, Filtmon. Now."

"I doubt either one of you has the gall," he spat back. The vial continued to hang dangerously close to her lips. She didn't dare open her mouth to speak.

Ellie slowly pressed her blade deeper into the man's neck. She could feel the warmth of his blood drip onto her hand.

"*Stop!*" he finally hissed. She held her free hand out to receive the glass bottle. He placed it down harshly.

"Get up," Auden growled. Filtmon stood, finally giving her room to sit up.

She walked over to a stream of moonlight that leaked into the flaps of the back tent. The liquid inside was red and smelled of sweet dirt and raw parsnip. *Shit.*

"It's the sap of a bloodroot and water hemlock." Her breath began to quicken.

Ellie was mere seconds from death. There would be no coming back from even a few drops of the concoction. An all too familiar rage ran up her spine.

"Who gave you this!" Her trembling voice was louder than she intended. A few other tent mates began to stir. Nate woke up completely, shooting to his feet, sword already drawn.

"Ellie, let's take this outside." Auden spoke softly. "Let's go." He jabbed Filtmon with his sword, leading him out the back of the tent. Nate joined, not needing an invitation.

"Answer her question. Where did you get the poison?" Auden asked once clear of the tent.

"Let's just say there's someone who wants you dead before the trials, and I was happy to do their bidding," Filtmon hissed. "And I doubt my failed attempt will keep them from trying again." He smiled with an intense evil glare.

"I doubt that whoever hired you would be pleased with your failed attempt. In fact, I'd be willing to bet they'll be wanting to tie up any loose ends connecting them to this attempted murder." Auden spoke through a calm rage, an anger that mirrored Ellie's own. His tone was dark and terrifying, nothing like Ellie had ever heard from him before. Auden seemed to want Filtmon dead as much as she did. But it was one thing to think of a man's murder, and it was another to actually act on it.

"So, you have two choices, Filtmon. Reveal to us who sent you and we'll end them before they end you or run. Run as far away from this city as you can." He growled the last few words. Filtmon's eyes sparked with terror.

"Either choice makes me a traitor!" he barked.

"You became a traitor the moment you tried to poison one of your fellow designates," Auden voiced back.

"*She* is not a designate loyal to our queen. Her mere presence here is a threat to everything the Eternal Queen has built. They know what you are, Ellie, and they will surely kill you." Filtmon hissed his final words.

"*Run,*" Auden growled, baring his teeth. Ellie resisted the urge to step back at the darkness in his eyes. At the desire to kill that was plastered to his face. He used his blade to push Filtmon towards the tree line. "One...two..."

Filtmon quickly weighed his options and bolted before Auden reached three.

Auden sheathed his sword and removed the flare baton from his belt. Ellie hadn't noticed him wearing it. It was the first time she had seen the weapon hung from his hip. With one swing, it released from its box form.

"Auden, what are you doing?" Ellie's breath caught, her

anger turning into cold dread at the sight of blue sparks. She knew the pain the weapon he held would provide, and she didn't wish it on her worst enemy. Not even one who just tried to take her life.

The center of her spine began to ache at the sound of the weapon's buzzing. Auden's body stood tense and seethed with anger.

"I'm going after an attempted deserter," Auden replied.

Ellie's eyes widened at the sudden realization. "You never planned on letting him live, did you?"

She slowly backed away from where Auden stood.

"No." Auden bolted off after Filtmon, leaving her and Nate standing alone behind the tent.

Ellie's body began to shake as her adrenaline calmed and shock took hold. Nate grabbed her arm and gently led her to the water spout. He disposed of the poison that she still held, helped wash Filtmon's blood from her hand, then walked her back inside to their mats. She lay down, still with uncontrollable shivers. Nate dragged his mat closer to hers, sat on it, and rubbed gentle fingers through her hair.

"You're safe, El," he whispered.

She held back tears, forcing her fear and anger deep within her. She closed her eyes and made herself take deep, cleansing breaths.

"I had another vision. Right before I awoke," she told Nate, relayed the vision, and told of the man cloaked in blue light. The one who saved her life.

"We will discuss the vision more later. For now, you need to rest," he replied.

"I can't just fall back to sleep, not after everything that has just happened. And what about Auden?"

"What about him?" Nate snapped.

"He's out there right now killing a man—"

"That has to die," Nate interrupted. "Ellie, not only did Filtmon try to kill you, but Auden understands the dangers of allowing him to live."

"I know that," she muttered back. "I just...I wasn't prepared to see that side of Auden. It was dark."

"He acted in the same way that I would have in that situation. We will *all* have moments where we will need to act on the darkest parts of ourselves. Even you." Nate grabbed her face between his hands. "But I promise to always be there to pull you out of that darkness, El. To remind you of your kindness and of your love." Nate's hands remained on her face as she sat up.

She had not revealed to Nate the overwhelming anger that she continuously pushed down. She feared that if she were to release the anger, to act on it, she would become something that she would not be able to control or recover from. Ellie also knew she would be forced to release it at some point, but hearing Nate's words made the thought less frightening.

"Thank you," she voiced, barely at a whisper. "I promise to do the same." He wrapped his arms around her.

"Will you lie with me? Until I fall asleep?" she asked, speaking into the warmth of his chest.

"Yes," he answered softly, lying down onto his back. She scooted her mat even closer until they both touched then curled in next to him. He wrapped his arms around her as she rested her head and arm on his chest. They tangled their legs together, and she felt the instant relief of his comfort.

He ran gentle fingers through her hair again, tangling them behind the back of her neck. She could feel the warmth of his breath on the top of her head as he softly kissed her. Her heart swelled. Nate would never know how truly thankful she was for him.

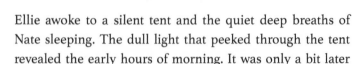

Ellie awoke to a silent tent and the quiet deep breaths of Nate sleeping. The dull light that peeked through the tent revealed the early hours of morning. It was only a bit later than when Auden usually woke her for stable duty.

She removed herself from the arms that were still wrapped protectively around her, sitting up she could see Auden on his mat at the very end of the tent. He was still sound asleep. She dressed and walked over to where he slept. She looked down at the handsome young man. Why did people always look the most innocent and trusting while they were sleeping?

She contemplated not waking him for her own selfish, sleep-deprived reasons. However, after last night's conversation with Nate, she wondered if Auden had anyone to pull him out of the darkness. To remind him of his humanity. Her chest tightened. If he did not have that someone, he would need one, especially today.

"Auden," she whispered while tapping the bottom of his foot with her toe. His only answer was him rolling from his back to his side.

Sitting down between him and the side of the tent, she brought her knees to her chest and wrapped an arm around them. Her other hand combed through his hair with gentle fingers. She did it to softly wake him, but it became more intimate than originally intended. His hair ran through her fingers like rich, dark honey. The ever-present hard lines of his face seemed to soften even more with her touch.

"Auden," she whispered again. He tenderly grabbed the hand that pushed the hair from his face.

"No stable duty today. You can go back to bed." His voice was like sandpaper. Ellie felt the hurt in his tone, felt the tremble in the hand that still held tightly to hers. She knew then, Auden did not enjoy killing. Last night, he did what he had to do to present himself as a faithful arbitrator and to cover up the attempted murder.

"Auden, I'm so sorry." Her whispers became broken as her throat tightened. He opened his eyes, revealing the pain that hid behind his lids. "You were right, and because of my own stubbornness, I have treated you poorly these last few days. I trust you, Auden, even if there is nothing more you can tell me. I trust you."

His eyes filled with both confusion and relief.

"I'm just so tired of the hurt and bitterness that comes with secrets. I want to know something of truth and value about myself."

He slowly sat up, his body tired from the night's events. He placed his other free hand on the one she rested against her knee. "I have only known you for a short while now, though you are incredibly stubborn and infuriating." The corner of his mouth pulled up in a way that made her skin prickle. "You are also a woman of love, mercy, and intense kindness. No matter what else is revealed, that is who you are at your core, Ellienia."

She wanted to throw her arms around his neck, to embrace him for the kind words, but she resisted.

"You saw me at my darkest last night. I saw true fear in your eyes as you looked at me. Yet this morning, you wake me with apologies and reassurance." He moved his hand to her cheek. "Thank you." Tears began to line his gray eyes. "I want you to know everything. You have no idea how much it physically *pains* me not to tell you, but you have to be the one to discover the truth. I made that promise."

Ellie simply just nodded in understanding.

"Can you tell me what happened last night? After Filtmon died." Her question caused Auden to tense.

"I took his body to the generals and presented him as a deserter. Based on both his wounds and a few confirming witches who were hiding in the shadows of the back wall, they didn't question it. I must warn you, though, his body now hangs in the center of the castle courtyard as a warning to the rest of you.

"Just like Remal," Ellie murmured.

"Yes...I'm sorry. Were you close with that man? Remal?"

"When I was much younger, he protected my sisters and me from a man who intended to harm us. Unlike Filtmon, he did not deserve to die."

"I'm sorry." Auden's voice was soft and compassionate.

"Belig says the only one who should apologize for the loss of our loved ones is the Eternal Queen." She smiled. "I'd have to agree with him."

"Yes. It seems you have quite a few men in this tent who have been drawn towards you. I'm pretty sure Myer looks at nothing but you all day long." He looked annoyingly over at a softly-snoring Myer.

"Are you jealous, Officer Reuel?" she teased him. Auden raised a brow, his eyes looking lighter than they had in days.

"Would it delight you if I were?" Ellie didn't know what to say to that. She looked over at Nate, her feelings torn between the two men. Auden lightly shoved her knees. "Come on, my tiny bunny. We have a stable to muck."

24

A uden removed his shirt again as they both mucked out the last and final stall of the morning. Now that she was no longer angry with him, his physique and face were once again very distracting.

She couldn't help but look closer at the faded scar placed on his right, muscular shoulder. It was round, and the center looked as if symbols from the origin tongue were carved inside of it.

"Auden." She laid her rake down and leaned against the tall black silky horse next to her. Darya huffed at the added weight to her side.

Auden wasn't sure who she belonged to, but she had been here alone since he arrived. She always gave Auden a hard time by doing things like nipping at his hair and using her head to shove his shoulder as he raked. Her sass was why Ellie had become slightly attached to the horse in the past few days.

"Should I worry about the person who tried to kill me last night?"

He laughed softly at her question. "What do you think?"

Darya caught his snarky tone and nipped in his direction. Ellie pressed her lips tightly, holding in her laugh

"I think not," Ellie answered. Auden looked at her as if she were crazy. "My grandpa says poison is a coward's kill, and they were the one to choose it as the murder weapon, not Filtmon. Whoever wants me dead, I don't think they will try to kill me themselves. Especially after seeing Filtmon's body hanging in the courtyard."

"Still. I want you to stay by my side for the remainder of your time here. If poison is their weapon of choice, I'll be the one fetching your meals for the next few days," he said, making a good point, which was utterly frustrating. She didn't need to be taken care of and hated that Auden felt he needed to do so.

"Fetching my meals? Interesting. Could I also have you clean my clothes and draw me a bath?" She rolled her eyes, hoping to get a rise out of him. The opposite happened.

That devilish smile appeared, making Ellie's stomach flip. "If there was a bath to draw you, Ellienia, I would gladly do so." He closed the gap between them, ignoring Darya's nipping and nudging. He stood so close to her, Ellie had to crane her head up to look into his gray eyes. "And as for washing your clothes, there are certain garments of yours I definitely wouldn't mind getting my hands on."

Her eyes widened as heat flushed her entire body. She swung out a fist, making contact with his gut. He grunted then filled the stable with his deep, silky laugh.

"You're insufferable." She caught where his eyes had traveled, and she realized what she was doing. She was scrunching her nose.

His laugh was so full, she worried it would wake the rest of the camp. "I think you rather enjoy my teasing, tiny bunny."

She threw the rake at him this time and dearly wished she had her sword. He caught it with such speed and grace, she had to blink to make sure her eyes were working.

He laughed, dropping the tool to the soft ground and leaving her alone in Darya's stall.

Filtmon's body hung from a wooden post at the center of the square. The group walked past the front of the slain man. A sign hung from his pale, decaying neck. It was branded with large letters spelling "DESERTER."

Gasps and whispers broke away throughout the group line, but Ellie didn't notice or even look at the surprised designates. She only looked at the man walking at her side.

Auden's face was flat, emotionless as he led the group to their spot. Ellie held back the urge to reach out and give a reassuring touch. To let him know that he wasn't alone.

"Group twenty-four!" Auden yelled once they had reached the weapons area. "You know the drill! If you don't have a weapon, find one! We will be focusing on blocking and evading techniques, so partner up! Batair, you're with me."

They formed two lines, each of them in the opposite line of their opponent. Auden stood strong with his sword held high. Facing him, Ellie at least didn't have to fake defeat.

"When facing an opponent, your stance and supporting arm are key!" Auden yelled to the line before lunging towards her.

He swung down with his sword. On instinct, she blocked the attack with her blade and used her free arm to shove his parrying arm to the side, simultaneously twisting her body and bringing her sword down onto the back of his neck. A few murmurs and soft exclamations came from the group.

"I'm so sorry. That was a reflex," she whispered, returning to her side of the lines. Her face twisted with regret. She looked around to see if anyone else in the courtyard saw the display. Thankfully, only the eyes of group twenty-four were on her.

From the corner of her eye, Ellie could see Kiarhem elbow Nate as he struggled to hold his glee in.

"Don't be." Auden's eyes were wild with delight. He lunged at her again, with more strength and speed. Their swords met over and over, until she could no longer keep up. He slid his blade down to her hilt then used his free hand to grab her wrist. He spun her around and shoved her back against his chest with his blade now at the base of her neck.

"Don't ever go easy on me, tiny bunny," he breathed into her ear. She bit the inside of her lip, unable to control the sudden desire that ran through her. Her heart raced, and her knees went weak from his words.

Nate was no longer smiling.

Auden released her from his deadly grasp and left her standing alone as he went down the line instructing each person individually.

They finished training and made their ways back to the tent for their usual late-afternoon break. Myer and Kier commended her show of skill against Auden, while Belig itched to teach her more of his language.

She sat with him for a while, learning the necessary words to communicate with him on a basic level. She truly enjoyed his language, somewhat more than her own. There was so much beauty in the movements and the silence. After a bit, she could tell the older gentleman was tired, so she offered to learn more tomorrow. He was thankful for the much-needed rest.

"So," Nate greeted as she sat down on their still conjoined mats. Waking up in his comforting embrace felt like days ago. "That was quite a show. Not as good as ours, but still decent."

She only scoffed in reply. Nate's expression changed from slight amusement to a flat, expressionless face.

"Do you like him?" he whispered.

"Do I like who?" She was truly confused by the question.

"Auden. Do you have romantic feelings for him?"

"Romantic—Nate, I hardly know the man." That was true, though she couldn't ignore the natural desire she felt for him, and the more she got to know of him, the more she admittedly liked. Even his arrogant smiles and the relentless arguing was beginning to grow on her. No one outside of her sister Cammie had ever pushed back or argued with her in the way Auden did. Still, there was so much he was hiding, so much that she still did not know.

"Am I attracted to him? Yes. I mean, look at him. Who's not attracted to that?" Ellie could hear Kiarhem's agreeable giggles behind her. "Why do you care? It's not like you've made your feelings towards me abundantly clear."

"El, we both agreed—"

"No, *you* agreed, Nate." She stood from her mat. A wave of anger hit her chest. She wasn't sure what she felt for Nate, but she was undeniably attracted to him just as much as she was Auden. But Nate's resolve to keep things between them platonic irritated her. He had taken the choice away from her, making the decision of what their relationship was for them both. She agreed with his reasoning for it, but the growing moments of heat between them and last night's comfort only confirmed what she had been feeling for some time now. She cared for Nate, possibly as more than just as a friend, but she would never know if he was never willing to cross the invisible line he had drawn between them.

She kept her voice low, leaning slightly down so only Nate could hear. "You decided to keep whatever the hell you're feeling to yourself to avoid any 'distractions.' Well, guess what? Not knowing the true depths of your feelings for me is incredibly distracting."

She stormed out of the back flaps of the tent. She ignored the naked man bathing in the water spout and headed directly for the tree line.

"El!" Nate yelled from behind her. She ignored him and kept walking. Sticks and leaves crunched beneath her boots.

"Ellie!" He ran up behind her, grabbing her arm and pulling her around to face him.

His eyes met hers, fierce and unrelenting. He looked at her in a way she had never seen before. In a way that had her face instantly heated and her heart pounding.

He spoke through ragged breaths. "There are no words to describe the depths of my feelings for you, El. Love is not a strong enough word for it."

Her eyes widened. *Love.* Her throat started to close. This was the declaration her grandfather had tried to stop. Ellie loved Nate too, but she wondered if it was the same. The fire in his umber eyes said it wasn't.

His nose flared as he slowly stepped closer, sliding his hands to her waist. A small part of Ellie whispered that she should stop this, that a relationship with Nate would only complicate things, but a larger part of her wanted to know how far he would take this. She wanted to know where the fire in his eyes would lead him. "You are all I think about day and night." He gently pulled her closer. The hand on her waist trembled. Their thundering hearts beat as one. "You are the reason I wake up each day. *You* are what I fight for."

He spoke his words onto her lips. A hint of fear began to rise in Ellie's chest. They were about to cross a line in their friendship that would change everything. "Those three days when I thought I had lost you were the worst of my entire life. If you had not woken, I would not have been able to continue." His voice was a broken whisper. "I have loved you deeply for years, El, and I am a coward for not telling you sooner." A strong arm wrapped around her waist, while a gentle hand pulled her face closer, his lips brushing against hers.

Her head spun as the kiss deepened and his lips moved effortlessly with her own. She opened her mouth to him, allowing his tongue to graze hers. A deep groan released from Nate, causing her to dig her fingers deep into his back, wanting him to be closer. Needing more of him.

He slid his lips from her mouth to her jaw and down to her neck. He kissed and licked, and when he ran his teeth along her skin, she couldn't help but say his name through a ragged breath.

It was his undoing. He pushed her against a tree, lifting her so her legs wrapped around him. He claimed her mouth again with even more fervor. With his body pressed tightly to hers, she could feel every inch of his need for her. She ground against him as he ran his hand over every curve and peak of her body. This was a side of Nate she had never seen before. He was powerful, demanding, and confident in how he felt for her.

She could have continued letting him explore her, letting him claim her, if it wasn't for the small clearing of a throat.

Ellie released her lips from Nate's and peered around his

side to see a very amused Kiarhem standing just meters away. "Auden's looking for you two." She smiled with pure delight. Ellie looked up at Nate's eyes that longed for more. Her stomach dipped.

"We'll have to continue this later," she mused, nipping at his lower lip. He made a growling noise that sent her toes curling.

Oh gods.

They arrived back at the tent to Auden, Kier, Myer, and Collern standing outside of the back flaps.

"I informed these men of last night's events. That Filtmon ran after a failed attempt at poisoning you. They have agreed to watch over you during the night. Nate will take first watch, then Kiarhem, Kier, Myer, Collern, and finally me."

"Do you really feel this is necessary, Au—Officer Reuel?" No one seemed to notice the slip in her reference to their group arbitrator.

"Yes. We don't know who it is that wants you dead, Ellie. It's best to be overly precautious at this point." Auden finished the conversation and waved them back into the tent.

She hated the idea of being watched over. She preferred being the one protecting, not protected. Auden grabbed her arm before she could enter the canvas flaps. "You're supposed to stay near me, not run off into the woods." He spoke in a stern but soft tone. "You seemed upset when you left. Are you alright?"

"I'm good. Promise." She tucked in her lips, hoping they weren't noticeably swollen.

He stitched his brows but made no attempt to learn more. He slowly nodded before letting go of her arm.

Ellie sat back on her mat next to Nate and pulled out her sword to polish it. She needed to do something to distract her from the man that currently stared longingly at her.

"So, I guess it's not complicated anymore." Kiarhem chortled. Ellie threw her polishing cloth at her as all three laughed. Though Ellie was certain things between her and Nate were only more complicated now.

25

Nate spent the rest of the evening giving heated glances, hidden soft touches, and quick stolen kisses in the rare moments that he was alone with El. Neither one of them were being very cautious, and they didn't seem to care. He had years of built-up tension and affection to make up for.

So when night came and Nate had to take first watch, they waited for everyone to fall asleep before once again letting out that passion.

Ellie sat in his lap as he placed lazy soft kisses down her neck. Her kiss in the woods had been everything he had dreamed and so much more. It shattered through everything they once were and built something entirely new. It all felt unreal, like he would wake up from this dream and she would just be his friend.

That had always been enough for him: that deep fierce friendship. It still would be, if that was something she one day decided. It would utterly destroy him, but he would never give up his friendship with her.

"I'm sorry," Ellie whispered. He pulled away to look at her. Her eyes gleamed in the soft moonlight.

"For what?"

"For making you feel like you couldn't tell me how you felt." She placed a cool hand on his face. He smiled at her, at the girl he had loved since childhood. He had loved her the moment she laid out a few of his childhood bullies. They had taunted him about his slanted eyes and olive skin. She heard those taunts and swiftly kicked all of their asses. None of the parents found out, as the boys were unwilling to admit they were beat up by a girl half their size.

"I was a coward, El. I should have told you how I felt ages ago. You never made me feel like I couldn't say something, and then your grandpa...Well, I'm not really sure how he knew, but I felt I had to honor his wishes not to say anything. But when I saw you today—" He dared a glance over at Auden. "When I saw your face after he whispered something in your ear, I thought I'd lost my chance."

"We're just friends, Nate." She looked away from him and nibbled on her lower lip—a tell that her words were not wholly true. It stung, but Nate could not control how she felt, and he hoped that he could one day fully win her over.

"I know, but even if you weren't, even if you did have feelings for him..." Which he knew she did. "I just want you to be happy, El. I would still want to murder him, but I wouldn't for your sake." She snorted as she tried to quietly laugh. It was the sweetest sound he had ever heard.

"No more talking," she whispered, barring her neck to him again.

Gods, he wanted all of her, but their first time would never be around so many people, asleep or not, nor would he sneak out the back flaps and take her against a tree. Though he had almost done so earlier. He ran his lips up her soft neck, stopping just under her ear. "You need to get some rest," he whispered, biting the tip of her lobe. She let out a soft moan that had him instantly regretting his words. Through sheer will and care for her, he continued, "You need sleep, and I'll be waking up Kia soon to take my place on watch."

"Ugh. Fine." She placed a gentle kiss on his lips before slowly sliding off his lap and onto her mat. He knew how much she hated this, needing to be watched over, needing to be cared for.

She placed her head on his lap, so he used gentle fingers to play with her nearly white hair, lulling her into a deep sleep.

"Ellie...Ellie..." Auden's deep whispers echoed through her ears.

She was wrapped up in Nate's arms, her back warmly pressed against his chest.

"Come on. Get up. I'll meet you outside."

Ellie slowly opened her eyes, willing herself to wake. When she tried to remove herself from Nate's arms, he pulled her in closer, nuzzling his face into her hair.

"I hate having to share you," he whispered into her ear, his lips caressing the tip. She couldn't control the soft yearning sound that left her body. A deep amusement filled the air behind her.

She rolled over to face Nate's gleaming smile. She ignored the uncomfortable twist in her gut telling her this wasn't right. They had crossed a line in their friendship, and though her body clearly was ready, her heart and mind had yet to realize that Nate was clearly so much more to her now.

This was what she had wanted. Nate's eyes sparked with intense happiness, despite their current circumstances. She couldn't help but return the grin that was plastered onto his face. She playfully nipped at his nose, which resulted in him pulling her chin down for another breathtaking kiss. After a few moments, she forced herself to pull away.

"I hate leaving you, but if I'm not out there in a few minutes, Auden will put most of the mucking on me. Now close your eyes so I can change."

"Fine." He reluctantly let her sit up from the comfort of his arms and turned over to get a few more hours of sleep.

She kissed him on the cheek once more before rushing out the tent.

Auden and she walked silently side by side towards the stables. Her and Nate didn't hide their sudden affection towards one another from the group, so she honestly wondered what Auden's thoughts were. She couldn't get a read off of his angular, expressionless face.

"Auden, is everything okay?" He barely even blinked as he stared at the path before them. After a brief moment, he finally addressed the question.

"Look. I'm happy for you and Nate." His tone sounded the opposite of his statement. "But it's the day before the next trial, and I'm afraid that neither one of you are fully focused now. Pull yourselves together,or you will both end up seriously hurt—or dead."

He was right, but that didn't make her any less angry at the tone in which he spoke towards her.

"Also, it would be wise for you to remember that we weren't all blessed to be here with a loved one. If you continue to flaunt your relationship around, you may lose certain allies that you have worked so hard to gain."

He, again, made a valid point that only led to more anger. He finally looked at her, his rage-filled eyes equal to her own. Nothing about this situation was fair.

He took a shaky breath. "Nate gets to sleep holding *you* —" There was a strange pause before he continued, "He gets to sleep next to the woman he cares about. Not everyone here will get to experience that feeling, Ellienia. I'm not trying to ask you to sacrifice your happiness for the sake of our comfort, but—"

"No." Ellie breathed through her rage. "That is exactly what you are asking of me, and you are right to do so." She clenched her fists but quickly released them. A soft breeze blew past, cooling both of their red, infuriated faces. "If I am to lead these people in whatever way, sacrifices will need to be made."

She swallowed the hurt and fury that came with her realization.

Auden looked shocked at her lack of disagreement. Ellie, too, was shocked, but Auden was right, again, and she was tired of fighting with him.

When Ellie returned back to the tent, she gently woke Nate back up and dragged him out the back. She relayed her and Auden's conversation and voiced her agreement with everything he said. His silence as she talked made her heart sink into her stomach.

"We just have to be more careful. I'm so sorry. I don't ever want to be the one who causes you hurt or disappointment." Her eyes were lined with tears. Nate quickly grabbed her face with his hands.

"El, you are not disappointing me. Is the situation disappointing? Yes, but never you. I'm just happy to know that you may feel for me the way I have felt for you for so long. I can live with just that, at least for now." He took a steady breath. "I do not believe Auden's statements to be fully self-less, but his reasoning is valid. Focusing on the tasks ahead is what is most important right now."

His umber eyes looked down on her with intense compassion. She lifted herself on the balls of her feet to steal one more fervent kiss.

The rest of the day went by as normal. Training was short since Auden didn't want to exhaust them the day before a trial. She made a point to keep some distance from Nate and mingled closer to the men she had allied with. Collern gave her some much-needed information about a few more of Malavor's territories who are in full support of the Queen and her conquests: Panma, Gria, and Forsa. Thankfully, no one in their tent was from those places. At least not anymore now that Filtmon was gone.

She spent some time playfully teasing with Myer and Kier, making sure she also thanked them for watching over her. Lastly, she checked in with Belig and Doal.

After dinner, Auden gathered the group's attention from each of their mats in the tent.

"Tomorrow you will face the second of five trials. Agility was your first, and next you will face a test of strength in both mind and body. Nine of the generals will be present for this trial. I suggest being on your best behavior." He looked directly at Ellie.

"There will be five days between each of your trials here. Tomorrow's trials will test groups one through fifty. The following day will test groups fifty-one to one-hundred, and the third will test one-oh-one through one-fifty. There are over fifteen hundred designates here this year, the largest recruitment since the very first designation, so we cannot test you all at once. Your second trial will begin first thing in the morning. So get some rest. You will need it."

26

The morning came sooner than she wanted. Auden woke each of them up just as the sun broke through the morning dew. He handed them bread and cheese, stating they would not get their normal breakfast on trial days.

Once they were all fed, dressed, and ready, they left the comforts of their tent behind. She led the line next to Auden, as she had done since the attempt on her life.

The morning was dark and filled with a thick layer of mist. The arbitrator beside her looked awful. His eyes were sunken, his normally tan skin had paled, and he slightly hunched over as they walked.

"You look like death," she whispered among the silent line. "Did you sleep at all last night?"

"No," Auden answered softly, then the corner of his mouth rose in a way that always sent both annoyance and desire through her. Even though she couldn't control it, it still seemed like a betrayal to Nate. "But I'm glad to hear you're so concerned for me."

She scoffed and rolled her eyes.

His hand brushed against the back of hers. An unintentional movement, she was sure, but it still sent a shiver up her arm. "I didn't want the others to be tired during today's trial, so I took full watch last night."

"That was stupid." She huffed. "Filtmon's death clearly scared off whoever it was trying to kill me." Ellie looked at the man's long face and considered a more compassionate reply. "But thank you. I appreciate the care and concern."

"It doesn't matter. I would not have been able to sleep either way."

"Why?" Her question caused deep sorrow to fill Auden's tired eyes.

"Today's trial will be barbaric. All of the trials are terrible and inhumane, but today's...Today's is one of the worst." She tried to ignore the dread that his words filled her with, but she began to shake from the rise in adrenaline.

"I can only ask you one thing. Please, do not egg them on. The arbitrators, the generals, none of them. We both know most of them want you dead, so please don't give them a reason to kill you."

She nodded in reply, not trusting her voice to speak clearly. Ellie knew she could handle anything these brutes could throw at her, her grandfather made sure of it, but it didn't make it any less terrifying.

They arrived at the expansive castle courtyard and instantly saw the contraptions built for their trial. Fifty massive wood beams stood horizontally between two supporting posts. Each beam had many small rope loops, and nooses hung directly between each small loop.

There was a large bench placed underneath the beam, and her group took their place behind the row of group twenty-three. They faced the front of the castle, and at the top of the steps sat nine large dark-haired generals—one of those nine being General Dolion. Though they all looked so similar, Ellie only recognized Dolion from the other generals by the dark, hateful gleam in his eyes. Eyes that stared directly at her. An unease stronger than she thought possible ran up her spine.

To Dolion's side stood Officer Ames. His usual sneer was replaced by a face foreign and flat. His sapphire eyes looked dull, lifeless, and unaware of the trial before him.

When all groups had arrived and took their places behind a bench, Dolion rose to address the crowd of designates.

"Good morning, designates! And welcome to your second trial! As you know, the next few weeks you will go through a series of tests that are specifically designed to see how well you will do in our ranks and give us a clear understanding of where to assign you. Today's trial will test your will of strength in both mind and body."

Ellie's stomach sank at the dark delight that pulled at Dolion's ashen lips. "When on the battlefield of war, you will need to find the strength to climb mountains, fight men twice your size, and pull heavy weaponry across miles and miles of land. You will also need to find the strength to fight through pain. Pain that our enemies will surely inflict on you.

"Today's trial will test all of this. You will each step up onto the bench in front of you and place a noose around your head. You will then grab onto the small loops on either side of the noose. Once each of you are hanging with arms at a ninety-degree angle, your arbitrator will kick the bench out from under you. Whoever drops first from each group will hang to their deaths, weeding out any designate too weak to have a chance at being a part of our army." The crowd released a collective gasp. Ellie's heart began to race as she looked wide-eyed at a stone-faced Auden.

Dolion held up a silencing hand before continuing. "Once the first person of your group is removed from the trial, your arbitrator will remove your noose, and you can adjust yourself to hang with straight arms. Your group will also be assigned two more arbitrators to inflict pain when they feel it is needed."

To Ellie's right, two more arbitrators appeared on their line: Schmilt and Ballock. Their presence was not a coincidence. With evil smiles and bright eyes fixed on her, they held their whips and swords at the ready. Neither arbitrator carried a flare baton on his hip. The generals most likely didn't trust the brutes not to use them.

"The longer you last during this trial ignoring your pain and exhaustion, the better. Now, let's begin!" General Dolion held up his arms and grinned with delight.

They stepped up onto the wood bench. It creaked and groaned under the weight of the designates. Standing on the tips of her toes, Ellie reached both the noose and rope handles.

She pulled herself up into the required form with ease. She could thank Cammie for the forced, daily pull-up and hanging challenges along the rafters of their old barn. This part of the test did not scare her, but the two arbitrators' hunger to inflict pain, specifically on her, sent ice through her veins.

The spot in her back had not fully healed. For the most part, it no longer bothered her, but she was sure if a whip landed its mark directly onto the spot, she would be done for.

Auden passed each designate, checking for correct form and placement of each noose. He dragged a gentle hand across her back as he passed. Ellie swore she heard him whisper something, but she could not turn to confirm.

Once he checked each designate, he pulled the bench from under them. To Ellie's surprise, no one in their group fell right away. Unfortunately, that was not the same for most other groups.

She closed her eyes to avoid the scene that took place in front of her. Multiple bodies hung twitching and swinging. Groups twelve and fifteen lost two designates each as their arbitrator could not remove the nooses fast enough.

A man in group twenty-two began to kick and beat the designate beside him, causing him to fall to his death.

"Ellie." A labored voice came from the other side of Kiarhem. Collern hung just two people away from her. "I-I can't," he strained through a tight breath. His face was red, his arms shook, and his eyes were bloodshot.

"Collern. You can do this. Force yourself to do it. It can't be you. It won't be you." She spoke through smooth, confident breaths. Ellie knew the moment she shook Collern's callus-free hand days ago, that these trials would be very difficult for him.

She looked down the line at the other designates of group twenty-four. Most held steady, except Collern and another soft-handed man. He was the only one in the tent to once keep Filtmon company, though she still did not wish for him to die.

"Ballock, who do you wage will fall first?" Schmilt mocked.

"I don't know, but it seems we need to help get this trial moving along." Ballock swung his whip towards the ground, releasing a bone chilling *CRACK*. Both men passed each designate and headed straight towards her.

The mist seemed to thicken around the feet of the two arbitrators. Ballock stood at her front, while Schmilt took his place behind her.

"Hello, Ms. Batair." Ballock smiled with poisonous intent. "It seems you have healed up quite nicely."

"How's the back?" Schmilt sneered.

How brave of him to once again face me from behind, she thought.

She forced herself not to react. Not to release the violent, snarky phrases that ran through her head.

"Not as talkative today, huh?" Ballock smirked. He twirled the large sword in his hand then placed it on Ellie's left thigh. With a quick pull, it effortlessly sliced through leather, skin, and muscle.

She released a forced exhale through a flared nose but refused to show any more of a reaction than that. He placed the sword onto the other thigh and sliced in the same way. Warm blood leaked down her lower legs, dripping onto the stone below. Ballock looked her up and down with a wicked glare.

He placed his weapons down to remove his sweat-soaked white shirt. The morning air was fading, and the humid afternoon heat had begun to move in. Ballock was covered in a variety of small and large scars. Ones he either received during his trial as a designate or from his father who provided the scar on his face and ear. Tying the shirt around his waist and picking up his weapons, he stepped closer to her steady, stone-like body.

"I must admit," he growled softly. "Getting between your legs would allow me to attest to your loyalty. I might consider it if you survive this trial." His eyes gleamed with vile intent. She could feel the anger rising in Nate's body to her right. She, too, could no longer control the rage-filled remarks that crossed through her mind.

She looked down at the man with a vicious smile, one that would make most men flinch in return.

"Have you ever pleased a woman, Ballock? Based on your ugly mug, I would doubt any woman has ever let you try. You wouldn't even know where to put it if I opened my legs to you."

Ellie could see the anger welling up inside the brute. It only worsened when a few of her fellow tent mates snickered. She braced herself for the attack that was now imminent.

"We will break you. Just as I did in Perilin," Ballock growled. He turned to take a few steps back, revealing a dark-black mark on his upper-right shoulder. The same design as Auden's faded scar.

He turned and looked back at Schmilt, signaling to him with a nod. Ellie took a deep breath, forcing all her strength into her arms, willing herself not to fall at the coming pain.

CRACK.

The first blow broke partially through her leather corset and silk blouse. She rested her head on the wood beam that held her up.

CRACK.

The second blow removed the corset completely and slashed deeply into her upper back. She screamed through clenched teeth.

CRACK.

Another lash opened up her lower back. Her vision blurred as her arms now shook and screamed to let go. Ellie desperately wanted to release her arms from their hold. She tried to pull from within but truly felt she had no strength left.

She was about to embrace her death when she felt the pendant that lay between her breasts. Its usual cold touch was replaced by a sensation of burning ice. She felt it sear into her skin, it's cold burn radiating up her chest, shoulders, and arms.

CRACK!

She focused only on the cold and not the pain throbbing and pulsing through her back.

Through a watery haze, Ellie looked to see Nate hanging next to her with horrified tears running down his face. She shook her head slightly, begging him not to protest the torture, or even sacrifice himself to end it as she knew he would.

CRACK!

Another blow came, this time from Ballock, across her now exposed and bleeding torso. The necklace was helping, but the pain was excruciating, and she was growing increasingly weak from the loss of blood.

Ballock gleamed at her with delight. Delight that soon faded at the sound of a rope snapping taught. The young man farther down the line could not last any longer. He now scraped the points of his toes on the dirt below, desperately searching for a hold to help him. Within seconds, he was gone.

"*Damn it,*" Ballock growled under his breath. Auden ran over to remove her noose first. She slowly lowered herself to straight, locked arms, relaxing the muscles in her arms and back and forcing all her strength to her sweat-filled hands.

Ballock's fury proved his ill intent. Some of them wanted her dead and planned for this to be the way she went— hanging in front of everyone. Hoping to prove she wasn't as strong as initially thought. She forced herself to look up. General Dolion glared down at her. She forced a wicked smile and wink towards the fuming general.

Ballock bared his teeth and flared his nostrils as he stormed off to inflict wounds onto the remaining designates of twenty-four. Schmilt stayed.

Ellie contemplated the benefits of staying in the trial, but she had already lost a lot of blood. Her body could not take any more lashes from the man who continued to stand behind her. She dropped, crashing hard into the stone beneath her.

Her useless legs and hands hit the ground first, followed by her head. Ellie's ears rang as the ground beneath her spun. She could feel drops of warm blood rush down her face as she tried to lift herself.

Before she could, another crack rang through her ears.

Ellie dropped back to the ground as pain seared through her shoulders. *CRACK. CRACK. CRACK.* Schmilt released blow after vicious blow. She curled into a ball on her side, protecting her face with her arm. He continued to whip her immobile body. She burned and seethed with pain. A steady flow of tears ran down her face onto the ground beneath her, mixing with the growing puddles of her blood.

"THAT IS ENOUGH, OFFICER! HER TRIAL HAS ENDED!" Auden yelled, running to her aid.

"It is enough when I feel it is enough!" Schmilt sneered, continuing to rain lash after lash down on her.

"STOP!" Auden reached out, grabbing Schmilt by the arm that dealt each lash. "If you continue to disobey the rules of the trial, I will gladly hand you over to a general that will be happy to dole out this same beating on you." Auden gestured to her broken and bleeding body.

"She openly disrespected Officer Ballock. I'm sure the

generals will agree this punishment is reasonable. Now let go of my arm, Officer Reuel," Schmilt snapped.

"*No.*" The growl Auden released didn't sound human. Ellie lifted her face from the blood-soaked ground to see a blurry but terrifying Auden.

He looked at Schmilt with murderous intent. "You have already punished her enough. 'You are proving to be more trouble than you are worth, Schmilt.' Isn't that what General Polage said at your hearing?" Ellie could see Schmilt's growing fear at both Auden's glare and words. "'One more negative report from any other officer and you are finished,' was General Poullig's final statement, wasn't it?"

"How—" Schmilt looked at Auden with wide, enraged eyes.

"You *ever* touch her again, and I'll make sure I am the one performing your execution, Schmilt." Auden growled his name through bared teeth. He released Schmilt's arm and watched as he walked to join Ballock at the other end of the line, doling out one lash to each remaining designate as he walked by. Most of the designates for twenty-four had now fallen. Very few could last after the first or second lashing.

Auden knelt beside her, pushing her blood-soaked hair from her face. He waved over Collern, who had dropped the second his noose was removed. "Go and find a witch named Layla. Have her meet us back at the tent. It is crucial that you get Layla and no other witch. Do you understand?"

"Yes, sir." Collerns words were shaken. "Is she—"

"She'll be fine. Just find Layla." Collern ran off, dodging through injured designates and feral arbitrators. Ellie began to close her eyes as a sudden wave of exhaustion washed over her. "Ellie. Ellie. Hey. Hey. No, stay awake."

"I've lost a lot of blood." Her words were barely audible.

"I know, but you also hit your head pretty hard. I need you to stay awake until Layla examines you. Can you please do that for me, Ellie? Ellienia, please." Panic coated every quiet word that Auden spoke. His voice sounded like an echo in her head. "Nate!" Auden's desperate call for help was the last thing she remembered.

27

"You protected it, didn't you?" Layla's quiet voice rang through her ears. Ellie could feel Layla's hands hovering over the wounds on her back.

"Yes," Auden replied in the same quiet tone.

"That was dangerous. If one of the other arbitrators caught on, you would be dead," Layla remarked.

"And if I hadn't, she would be dead." Auden's voice rose slightly in his anger.

"She deserves to know who you are, Auden. She deserves to know *what* you are," Layla replied with a stern tone.

"She will. When she is the one to figure it out."

"Ugh, stop with that! Stop with all of it! Either you, Shea, or Ames need to tell her or I will!"

"We made a promise, one that cannot be broken. There are things we still do not know. Things that he said only she could figure out. We have to trust him. Even you. You were not meant to find out anything about who she is. You cannot ruin a plan that has been in motion for many years, even before the Eternal Queen took this land. Please, Layla."

"Fine," she growled. "I only concede so you can argue with her about this. She's been awake for the past few minutes."

Ellie could feel Layla's amused grin emanate throughout the empty tent. She, too, couldn't help the smile that grew on her lips.

"I swear, Layla, you are the biggest pain in my ass," Auden growled. Both women laughed at his expense, though it left Ellie in quite a bit of pain. She tried to roll over from her stomach, but agony and the sudden realization that her body was completely bare underneath a lightweight blanket stopped her.

"It's fine, Auden. I already know what you are," Ellie grumbled from her mat.

"You do?"

"Yes. An annoyance," she mused. Layla howled in delight.

"You *both* are a pain in my ass. I'm going to check on the others." Auden began to stand before Ellie groaned for him to stop.

"No. Please stay. I need to talk to both of you while we have a rare moment alone. Layla, could you help me sit up so I can look at you."

"I wouldn't suggest it, Ellie. I've closed most of you up, but the wounds are very fresh. If you move too much, you may start to bleed again. Not to mention the headache that you're probably enduring right now. Too much movement and you may puke up what little you have in your stomach."

She wasn't wrong. Ellie's head felt as if it could explode at any moment. "Fine. Can you at least roll me to the side?"

Layla agreed, rolling her onto the side the whip did not touch. Unfortunately, both of Ellie's thighs had been sliced, and the one she now lay on burned with intense pain. She readjusted as best as possible, eventually finding a position that wasn't so painful.

Auden kicked the mat beside her closer, and he and Layla sat together on it. Both pairs of eyes were focused and watching Ellie's every move.

"First, where are the others?" she asked.

"The Great Hall. The witches have mats set up in there to treat the injured. Once treated, they will be given food to eat. Since we still don't know exactly who is trying to kill you, other than a handful of generals, I thought it was best if Layla treated you here where I could make sure you were safe," Auden replied.

"Shouldn't you be with our group?" she asked, worried his absence may lead to trouble.

"It's fine. Shea and Ames are watching over the group for me."

"Good," Ellie softly muttered. She looked directly in Auden's gray eyes. "Thank you. For stopping Schmilt. For getting me here and—"

"Nate got you here," he interrupted. "I had to stay until the trial was over. He dropped from his ropes at my command, and he carried you the entire way back here. I should have stopped Schmilt faster. I'm so sorry, Ellienia. I should have known the generals would place him and Ballock in our group. I should have prepared you more." Auden's face dropped.

"Auden, there is no way to prepare for a beating like that. None of this is your fault. You risked your life by physically stopping Schmilt. You risked your life by placing some kind of a protection spell on my flare baton mark."

His eyes widened at her last words. Layla smiled with pride.

"How—" he began to ask.

"I'm more intelligent than I may lead on, Auden." She smirked. "I was raised from an early age to solve riddles, puzzles, and mysteries of my grandpa's own invention. I've not just been working on who I am, but I've been piecing you together since we first met. I heard you whisper something as you passed a hand over my back earlier, before the trial began. You are Fae, Auden, and Malavor is your home."

"Wow. She's good." Layla gleamed, elbowing Auden in the ribs.

"Only a Fae with strength and speed could have disarmed me as easily as you did in those woods." Ellie smiled. "And then again during training."

"And you? What have you pieced together about yourself?" he asked with hopeful intent.

"Not enough to form any conclusions I'm willing to say aloud," she said with deep frustration. "All I know for sure is that I'm some form of seer."

"How many have you had now, Ellienia?" Auden asked, completely unsurprised at hearing her mention her power to him for the first time. She saw the way he had looked at her the first night in the Great Hall. He knew what had happened; he knew what she was.

"Six. Four since arriving in Malavor." Ellie told them of her most recent vision of the King and the women, of the spell they cast around the house, and of the book hidden inside. She relayed each and every word exactly. "I think the house in my vision is the cursed house right outside these walls. That's where the book is—"

"Then it is safe," Layla interrupted, her tone filled with solemnity. "The Queen has tried for many years to enter that house. She has risked the lives of many men and witches. If that is where the book is, then it is safe and the Eternal Queen will never get it."

"What book?" Auden spoke slowly and sternly. Ellie had forgotten he did not know of her vision in the library.

"It is a book we believe the Queen has been looking for. One that could lead her to great power," she replied with an urgent tone.

"The one that Mother Talmi searches for? You do not believe it to be in the library, but in this house?" Auden's voice was calm, but she could see his mind working. He somehow already knew about the book. His friendly relationship with Mother Talmi was most likely made to help him find it before she did.

"Yes, and we can't just risk leaving it there. The Queen could have people working on a counter spell. She still could retrieve it one day."

Layla shifted on the mat. "Then we hope we are no longer alive for that day. Ellie, going to that house is literal suicide. I'm sorry to say it, but I think your visions have led you to a dead end. You can still try and find out who that red-haired female is, but we're not going after that book."

Layla grew up on stories of that house. She would know the horrors it provided. Ellie longed to argue with Layla, to convince her otherwise. Ellie instead waited to see what the male beside her would say.

Auden sat clearly processing the new information. "Layla's right. It's not worth the risk."

Ellie nodded, though she was not fully convinced this would be the last time they discussed it.

They sat in silence for a moment. Each processed different things from their conversation. Ellie only had one more thing to ask Auden while Layla was also present.

"Auden." She softly spoke into the silence. "The mark on your right shoulder, it is the same as the one I saw on Ballock today. Yet, yours is now a light scar, and his—"

"You removed your fealty mark?! How?!" Layla exclaimed.

"Shh. Geez, Layla. Yell it for the entire camp to hear," Auden warned.

"Fealty mark? What is that?" Ellie asked.

"It's the final trial. You pledge your fealty, and the witches brand you with the fealty mark. It's a spell that the witches here came up with. It makes it impossible to outright go against the Eternal Queen. If you do—"

"You die an extremely painful, gruesome death," Layla finished for Auden. "How? Who?" Layla tried to collect her scrambling thoughts.

"Agilta," Auden answered with a smile. "Months before Designation Day, Captain Cormel informed Shea that there was a very powerful witch hiding as a healer in the tiny town of Perilin. He befriended her, and after some time, he showed her the mark. When she had successfully removed the curse, he sent word to us. We made sure to be appointed to Perilin for Designation Day. She was able to remove the mark from both me and Ames, but Shea has had his for too long. Agilta claims that the magic is now a part of him. He can skirt the edges of its hold, but never fully go against it."

Captain Cormel was a part of Auden's alliance. Ellie knew this already, but it was the first she had heard it straight from Auden. She wondered if Cormel was the one who kept Auden from revealing things. If he was the one responsible for all the secrets between Auden and her. She shifted her thoughts.

"The healer that I've known for most of my life is...a witch?" Ellie asked in disbelief. Agilta was the kindest soul in all of Perilin. She was incredibly intelligent, witty, and above all caring. Not very different from the witch that she now sat with.

"Yes. An extremely powerful one at that." Auden looked at a wide-eyed Layla.

"So it's true," she whispered. "The other covens have truly separated and hidden themselves. Did she say what coven she belonged to? Is she still in contact with her Mothers and sisters?" Layla edged extremely close to Auden.

"Uh...I didn't ask." Auden leaned back from her.

"YOU DIDN'T ASK!?" Layla jumped from the mat they sat on. "A witch heals you from an incredibly strong curse, and you didn't think to ask those two simple questions."

"Well...No. I did ask where she was from, but she didn't give me a direct answer. She only said—"

"Where the wind blows from the north, and streams flow free in every direction," Ellie finished for Auden. "That is always her answer."

"Ugh. That doesn't help me." Layla stood staring out the crack in the front flaps then down at Ellie's broken and beaten body. "I'm going to get more salve for your cuts. I'll bring back food as well." With that, the young witch was gone.

28

A uden stretched out on the mat beside her. His eyes were still filled with the same exhaustion that plagued him this morning. The top half of his hair was pulled back, revealing every arch and dip of his sculpted face.

Ellie had heard stories of the Fae. Of their strength, speed, and power. She had also heard of their bewitching looks. Auden's good looks only made even more sense to her now, though he seemed to be missing some of the more revealing Fae features.

"You're staring," Auden said through closed eyes.

"Sorry, but there's not much else to look at, and I can't really move."

He laughed, a deep and truly comforting sound. "Excuses, excuses. If you like looking at me, just say so."

Ellie scoffed and rolled her eyes. "If you're done being an arrogant ass, could I ask you some questions? About you and your people?"

"I will never be done annoying you, my tiny bunny. How else could I get those beautiful eyes to roll? Well, I guess there is another, more fun way..." She started to swing at him, but her arm burned as the lacerations stretched at the movement. She winced in pain, drawing her arm back slowly. He moved onto his side, his face lining up to hers. Her heart skipped a beat at how close he now lay next to her. "Sorry. I'll behave so you don't hurt yourself further, and yes. You can ask me anything."

"Why don't you have...you know..." She waved a stiff finger around her ears and bared her teeth.

Auden huffed. "It's a rather simple glamour." His face began to blur and form into something else. Something...more.

His features became more defined, more angled. His ears grew and pointed at the ends, and he slowly ran a tongue along his now sharp canines. But what caught her breath was what stared at her with feral intensity: his gray eyes. They glowed like liquid silver. He was beautiful. He was fully and truly the definition of Fae beauty.

"The Eternal Queen has been looking for Fae for almost two decades now. Hiding my more primitive appearance seemed a wise choice." In a blink, the Fae features were gone and once again replaced by human ones like her own.

"If you're Fae and your hidden colony has yet to be found, why did you join the Queen's Army?" His lips formed a straight line. The painful tightness in his jaw appeared. "You can't tell me."

He shook his head gently.

"Are there a lot of Malavor citizens hidden in Dorumia?"

"Yes, though many died on the day of the attack."

"Are they mostly Fae?"

"Yes. There are some other ancient races, but a few weeks before the siege on Malavor, the King warned the humans and other races of the attack. He advised they go and find refuge in surrounding territories. For the most part, only Fae took refuge in Dorumia."

"How has the Queen not discovered your whereabouts yet?"

He smiled at her question. "Dorumia is very large, with land that easily conceals us."

His answer was not clear, but she decided not to question it more.

"Were you here? The day the Eternal Queen and her men attacked? How old were you? Wait, how old are you now?" Ellie suddenly remembered how long Fae lived and how young they could look despite their age. Fae weren't immortal, but aging was slow and near endless compared to the life of a human.

"I'm only a few years older than you, Ellienia, and have yet to settle."

Settle? She would have to ask more on that later as the look Auden now wore was one of deep sorrow.

"Yes, I was here on the day of the attack. My father was Queen Odina's head general, and my mother..." Auden's lower lip shook. "She was her lady-in-waiting and closest friend. My father had planned to be at the castle when the attack came. He had already sent most of the Royal Army members to Dorumia, as was the King and Queens' order. My father still to this day does not understand why. He believes that if all of his forces had stayed, Malavor would not have been taken. Queen Odina had ordered my mother to escape with my siblings and me. We had packed and were set to leave before the attack, but it came sooner than expected. I was in my home's study with a tutor when I heard the castle's warning bells and the first of many chilling screams."

Ellie's chest began to tighten as visions of burning homes and black-cloaked figures flashed through her head.

"Our tutor ran to find her own family while my brother pulled my sister and me from our house. He dragged us to the woods in the back, and we hid there for what felt like hours. My father arrived just minutes before the Queen's men started burning the town's houses. He pulled us deeper into the woods and farther from our home and deceased mother."

Water escaped the corners of Auden's gray eyes. "We traveled most of the way to Dorumia on foot, staying off crowded and public paths. When we reached a small pasture outside of Panma, we...*borrowed* a few horses that were left out in the hot sun with no food or fresh water."

"Tabat?" Ellie asked. Auden nodded with a slight smile. "I'm sorry for the loss of your mother. I can't fully understand what that must feel like."

He looked at her in confusion. "Did you not lose your mother?"

"I did, but I do not remember her, and I've been told nothing about her or my father. It's hard to mourn the loss of someone you've never been gifted to know."

It was true. Ellie grieved more for what little she knew of her parents than their deaths. Auden looked at her, frustration and grief blanketed his features.

"Do you know where in the castle your mother was killed?"

"Yes. In the Great Hall with the rest of the royals."

Ellie had hoped his answer was different. She had hoped it was in an area she had yet to have a vision. She wanted to see what powers the Eternal Queen had. Ellie wished to see how the Queen could be more powerful than the King and Queens of Malavor. She wondered if there was a way she could summon more of the vision she had already seen in the Great Hall. She wanted to see what exactly happened in that room so many years ago.

"What are your powers, Auden? Do all Fae have magic?" Her questions caught him a bit off guard.

"Umm. Well, yes, all Fae have magic, but at different levels. Most can only perform simple spells like concealing glamours or producing a wisp of light. There are some who can perform more difficult spells, like the protection one I placed around your mark. Then, there are the Benegiménos."

"Be-ne-gim-énos?" Her mouth struggled to form the foreign word.

"It means blessed one. They are the rare few that contain both origin and natural magic. They can perform any number of spells but are also gifted with powers stitched within the nature of their being. It runs through their veins just as naturally as blood."

"So the King and Queens were Benegiménos?"

Auden nodded in response.

"Are there any blessed ones still alive?"

"Yes. A few dozen. One of them being my sister."

That was not the number Ellie had hoped to hear. Auden noticed her sullen expression.

"We are still strong people, Ellienia. We are by far the most skilled warriors among every land, which is why the Eternal Queen still searches for us. We would not be a force the Queen's men could easily defeat."

She knew Auden's words to be true, but Ellie also knew the Queen's men were not what King Vedmar had been worried about. He did not fear her men, but instead, he had feared the Queen herself.

"What are your sister's powers?" Ellie asked, genuinely curious.

His eyes lit up at the thought of his sister, but they soon faded over with a cloud of worry. "She was born with the gift of fire. It is rare among the Benegiménos and one of the most difficult powers to master. In years past, there was always another Fae blessed with fire that could train the younger one. Unfortunately for my sister, the last known fire wielder was killed the day the Queen attacked." He seemed to linger on the thought of the last fire wielder. "I worry that if she is not trained to control her powers soon, they will control her." Auden looked up at the tent ceiling. His eyes filled with hopelessness.

Ellie reached out a shaky, blistered hand towards his. He wrapped his fingers around hers and placed them onto his chest. Her arm ached from the lashes it endured, but she barely noticed over the comforting beat of his steady heart and strong breaths underneath hard, sculpted muscle.

"Could you tell me more about them? Your siblings?" she asked, truly wanting to know.

"Will you tell me about your sisters in return?" She nodded as he began to speak.

"My brother's name is Rovier, and my sister's name is Ianna. We are all very close in age. My mother had a hard time conceiving Rovier. She worried she would have the same difficulty conceiving my sister and me. However, her worries were not needed, as we were both conceived just months after each pregnancy. Her hands were full with us, but my father claims that she loved every minute of the chaos." Auden huffed at the thought.

"Since the day he was born, my father has been training Rovier to follow in his footsteps. He hopes that my brother will one day lead the Malavor Army, but Rovier will do what Rovier wants to do."

Auden laughed to himself. Ellie couldn't help but smile in return. "Ianna, on the other hand, is the leader and fighter my father had hoped Rovier to be. She has a wit and fire in her that goes beyond her natural-born powers." Auden smiled proudly.

Ellie enjoyed seeing his soft expression and small joy in these rare moments alone. After their few mornings in the stables together, she had begun to notice how different Auden was around her. How different he had to be in front of the group and other arbitrators. Auden had to be a firm leader and a fierce fighter, but the man that lay next to her, the one filled with kindness and love for his family, was his true identity.

"Your turn." Auden gently squeezed her blistered hand.

"Cammie..." Her throat instantly tightened at the thought of her sister. At the thought of her screaming out her name just weeks ago. At the thought of her terrified face.

Ellie continued on through burning eyes. "Cammie is my older sister. We're not even a full year apart, and we've been in competition with one another since the day I was born. At least, that is what my grams says. Cam has pushed me to be the person I am today. Her intense desire to fight and protect what is good is everything I strive for. She may go about things with less grace and more grit, but her heart is always in the right place."

Ellie smiled through watering eyes. "Maisie is my younger sister. She is the good that Cammie and I fight for..." Her voice trailed off. She could not control the sorrow that suddenly washed over her. Ellie spoke through sobbing breaths. "I-I could only hope to strive for just an ounce of the gentle kindness that she freely gives. She constantly thinks of others before herself. There would...There would be no war if we were all just a little like her."

Auden placed his free hand on Ellie's soaking wet cheek. He did not say a word. Instead, he allowed her to cry. To release the sorrow and sadness she felt from the isolation from her sisters. To feel the need and desire to be with them again. To truly miss them for the first time since arriving in Malavor. She cried for the two young women that she may never see again.

After a while, her sobbing slowed. Her heart still ached, but Ellie felt a weight slowly lift from her body. Auden rolled closer, placing a gentle kiss onto the top of her head.

"I promise to never let them know how deeply you miss them, if you do the same for me." Auden smiled as Ellie deeply and wholeheartedly laughed.

"Agreed."

They lay there for a moment just staring into each other's sorrow-filled eyes. She was about to ask Auden one more thing when the front flaps swung open and a worried Nate rushed in. Auden quickly untangled his hand from her own and stood from the mat. The sudden motion caused her arms and shoulders to throb.

He awkwardly moved out of the way of Nate's direct path towards her. Ellie hadn't realized how inappropriate they may have looked lying so close to one another, but Nate didn't seem to notice or care. He only looked down at her beaten body, examining every mark carefully.

"I wanted to be here when you awoke. I'm so sorry. Here." He sat in the spot Auden had just vacated and handed her small bites of cheese and bread.

"I saw Layla in the Great Hall grabbing food. I assumed it was for you, so I insisted I be the one to deliver it. It was the only way Shea and Ames would allow me to leave the group." Ellie nibbled on the food in her hands, giving Nate a thankful smile.

"I'll be out back washing up. If you two need anything at all, come get me." Auden ducked out the back flaps, leaving Nate and her alone in the large tent. Nate softly smiled down at her. He ran his fingers through her knotted, bloody hair.

"Should I be worried about you two?" Nate teased with a nod towards the flaps Auden just disappeared through. Real worry and jealousy shined through his eyes. Ellie scoffed before grabbing his collar and pulling him in for a gentle kiss.

"Please. Don't ever do that again," he whispered onto her lips.

"What? Kiss you? Or hang from a wood beam and allow myself to get brutally tortured and beaten?"

He grumbled, clearly annoyed, but leaned in again for one more tender kiss.

"I can't promise that this will be the last time I am hurt like this, Nate." He lay down next to her, resting his forehead on hers. "There are generals, arbitrators, and who knows what else out there trying to kill me." She looked behind Nate to see the tent flaps silently open and close again. Possibly the wind, or a talented and sneaky witch.

"I know," he sullenly whispered. "Let's just hope the next few trials allow for more opportunities to defend ourselves."

"They will," Layla said, popping out of a shadow behind Nate. Layla and Ellie both laughed as Nate's body jumped. He quickly rolled himself away from her face as he voiced a slew of colorful words.

"Wow, Nate, I had no idea you knew such language," Layla said dramatically, placing a free hand woefully over her heart. Nate threw a dagger-like glare her way before slowly sitting up. Layla laid an armful of bandages, tonics, and salves down next to Nate.

"Let me check your wound to make sure you didn't just open it back up," she said to Nate. Ellie had forgotten he was given a lashing by Schmilt.

"I'm fine. The whip barely broke the skin," Nate protested. She ignored him and lifted up his shirt to take a look at the wound.

"That may have been true if you hadn't heroically carried Ellie all the way here, causing the wound to rip and tear open more." She placed small amounts of different salves on his back as she spoke.

"Alright. Your turn." Layla helped Ellie sit up slightly, propping herself onto an elbow. "I brought a strong tonic for both the pain and your head." She placed a small vial filled with a light-purple-hued liquid onto her lips. It didn't taste horrible, which she was extremely thankful for. "It may knock you out for a while, but you should feel at least a little better..."

Her voice trailed off as Ellie's vision turned black.

29

L ayla lifted the blanket that covered Ellie. She rubbed a salve and bandaged the wound across her torso. Once finished, she rolled her over and began working on her badly-wounded back. Deep slashes ran crisscrossed along every inch, except the small black flare mark that was beginning to fade. How this young woman had survived such a weapon and such a beating today was no mystery.

Layla knew the moment she laid eyes on Ellie that she carried power unlike anything she had ever felt or seen before.

"How is she?" Auden asked.

"She'll be fine," Layla said through working hands. She had to apply the salve and quickly cover it with bandage before it dried. "She's healing faster than expected...or rather, to be expected."

"What's that supposed to mean?" Nate stitched his brows at her.

"*Nothing*," Auden growled in warning at her. "I'm sure the protection spell I used on her is helping her heal."

Lie.

"Or maybe it's the power inside her that you felt, Layla," Nate innocently mentioned. "You said you can feel a power within her. Can you also feel how strong it might be? Is it just the power of sight, or something more?" Nate was tiptoeing a dangerous line. Auden glared at her in warning.

Layla ignored his glare and placed a final bandage onto Ellie's back.

"I can feel the power within her, but I cannot see what it will form when fully released."

True.

Layla grabbed a brush from Ellie's pack. She ran it through her tangled hair, making sure to brush out any dried blood and dirt. "Magic moves and flows all around us. I can feel it, hear it, just as easily as the wind, but Ellie's magic is...different. It feels heavy and immovable. Like stone or frozen water waiting to be melted. I can tell, even in its dormant state, the power within her is none like I've ever felt before."

"Maybe that is why she has to be the one to figure out her past. Maybe in doing so, it will free the magic within her," Auden whispered to himself.

"Yes," Layla agreed with him. It was why she had chosen not to reveal what she had learned about the young woman, which was not easy for her.

Layla grew up with gossip and secrets being her only form of entertainment. "I should go. My Mothers and sisters will need more help in the Great Hall."

"Thank you for your help today, Layla. We would not have known what to do without you." Auden held out a hand, helping Layla to her feet. He looked down at Ellie. His eyes were filled with longing and sorrow.

She knew what Auden felt for the young woman. She

knew what both men felt for Ellie. Layla's sleeping friend could never understand the power she held in her beauty both inside and out. Many men and women would love Ellie, but none more than the two men standing in front of her.

30

"Are you sure she's alright?" A familiar tone spoke through the fog in Ellie's head.

"She's fine, Collern. The witch gave her a strong tonic. Sleeping for this long is normal," Nate reassured him.

"Did the witch happen to mention the name of this strong tonic?" Kier asked.

"Yeah. I wouldn't mind a deep sleep. These mats are not easy to get a full night's rest on," Myer added.

"Your snoring says otherwise," Kier jested.

"If you two idiots don't stop talking, I'm going to slice a dagger straight through your tongues," Ellie grumbled through her haze.

"She lives!" Myer exclaimed. Ellie opened her eyes to see a group of faces looking down at her. Nate, Collern, and Kiarhem sat on the mat to her left, while Kier, Myer, Belig, and Doal sat on the mat to her right.

"Myer, make yourself useful and go get Officer Reuel," Nate instructed.

"But—" Nate sent a flat expression towards Myer. "Ugh.

Fine! But don't say anything of interest until I'm back." Myer jumped up from his spot and headed out the front flaps.

"How are you feeling?" Nate asked. Ellie rolled onto the side that was free of lashings. She had forgotten the lack of clothes, but thankfully, the blanket still covered her.

"Stiff, a little sore, and like I have a bunch of deep gashes on my back and thighs. Overall, not too bad. I am starving though. How long was I out?" She could feel her empty stomach churn.

"A little over a day. The witches should be bringing us dinner soon. We're not allowed in the Great Hall since that is where they are treating designates after the trial, so we've been eating all our meals here," Kiarhem answered for Nate. "We're all wondering, Ellie, how did you do it? How did you hold yourself up while they whipped you over and over again?"

Ellie's hand instinctively went to the pendant hanging from her neck.

"Well, most of the lashings happened after I fell." She suddenly became very aware of the number of eyes on her.

"I would rather know why exactly they were targeting you?" Doal asked sternly.

"Well—I—umm." Before she could decide what exactly to say, Auden swung the front flaps open and rushed to where she lay. Myer followed close behind.

"What'd I miss?" he said, taking his place back next to Keir.

"Alright. Everyone up and outside. Collern, go let Layla know she's awake." Auden waved his hands in their direction. They all obeyed, including a reluctant Nate.

"Do you mind if I take a look?" Auden asked, sitting behind her with a hand placed over a bandage.

"Go ahead," she consented. He peeled off the bandages

covering her arm, shoulder and upper back. He took his time looking at each wound, making sure they were all free of possible infection. Once he felt they were good, he removed the bandages on her lower back.

"How's it look?"

"Honestly, really good. Layla was right. You're healing both well and quickly. A few more days, and these wounds will just be another mark in your collection of scars."

"Great," she sighed.

"You should wear them proudly, Ellienia. Scars from battles are highly respected in the Fae culture. It shows your strength, perseverance, and triumph."

"Says the male who's only scar is a mark on his right shoulder."

"Are you checking out my body, Ellienia?" There was deep amusement in Auden's voice. Her face heated as her body betrayed her in hiding the truth. She had in fact been checking out his body every day since arriving in Malavor.

"Fae heal rather quickly, making scars rare unless the wound is severe enough or our magic is impaired in some way." Auden placed the blanket back over her. "Layla can take a look at the lashes and cuts across your torso and legs when she gets here."

"You said you held strong magic. Can you not heal me?"

"No." Auden sighed. "Only some blessed ones wield healing magic, and even if I could, healing too quickly would only put an even bigger target on you. But trust me when I say, I wish I could."

Ellie nodded her understanding as she twirled the cold blue pendant in her fingers.

"It's very beautiful," Auden said, gesturing towards the necklace.

"Thank you. It was a gift from Nate." His eyes drifted

from her to the floor, failing to hide the flash of sadness that crossed his face. "His father told me the liquid inside has healing properties, but after yesterday's trial, I believe it to be more than just that."

His eyes returned to hers. "What do you mean?"

"When I was at my weakest, when I truly felt like falling and accepting my death, the pendant surged its power through me. It restored my strength. I don't know how, but I would have died yesterday without it."

"An Empousîa," Auden whispered in the origin tongue.

"A what?"

"Empousîa. It is beyond rare. It's an item used to enhance one's powers, but..." Auden paused.

"But, what?" she asked, ignoring the calculated thoughts he was clearly having.

The tent flaps burst open as an energetic Layla walked in.

"Hello!" she exclaimed. The smile that was plastered onto her face faded when she took in Auden's serious expression. "Oh, great. What is it now?"

"Nothing that you and I didn't already know," Auden stated to Layla. "Ellie's just figuring out exactly how powerful she might be."

"Oh, okay!" She returned to her chipper self. "Let's take a look, shall we? Auden, the kitchen witches are on their way with food. You may want to get out there and get a few of your men under control. Myer and Kier may have started some kind of wrestling match, and a few other arbitrators have stumbled along to watch. They're now taking bets."

"Of course." With a frustrated growl, Auden left the tent.

Layla re-examined the lash wounds and quickly placed new bandages over them. They both looked at the lash placed across Ellie's torso. It was pink and scabbed over, but mostly healed. Layla left it unbandaged, as it was much further along than the wounds she could not see.

"Layla."

"Mmm," she hummed as she dug through the sack of clothes she had given her.

"Do you know what powers the Eternal Queen possesses or where she came from?"

Layla stopped rummaging, her body becoming like stone at the question.

"No. A few witches have their theories, but no one knows for sure." Her gaze seemed distant as she continued, "Her men are just as much of a mystery. The generals...I can hear their powers, feel it. And it feels—"

"Wrong," Ellie finished. Layla nodded, still staring into the distance. "Malavor is the only place the Queen has ever bothered to show up and fight for. Everywhere else has been taken by her generals only. I need to know what it is she can do, and if she is as powerful as everyone says, why hasn't she gone north. Why does she continue to enslave the South Karmalon people to her army? If she's so powerful, even more powerful than her generals, why does she make us fight her battles? And why hasn't she used her own powers to end this war years ago?"

"How are you going to find all this out?" Layla's attention snapped back to the sack of clothing.

"The Great Hall. That is where the royals of Malavor were murdered, and I assume it was by her hand. I need you to take me there when no one else is around. I need to try and summon a vision from in that room on the day the Queen took this land." Her face lit up at Ellie's request.

"I love it! I'll come and get you tonight." She pulled a beautiful cotton blouse from the bottom of the sack. "Here, put this one on. It's my least favorite of everything in here, so

I don't mind if your wounds get a little blood on it." Ellie slowly sat up, letting the blanket fall from her chest. Layla carefully placed the shirt over her head and arms.

"Come on." She placed a helping arm under Ellie's right shoulder. With great strength, she got her to her feet. "Let's get you some food."

31

Ellie and the rest of her group sat in a circle on the grassy field in front of their tent, shaded by a large tree. Young witchlings laid plates of bread, meats, and cheese in front of the group of designates. Layla sat next to Ellie, inspecting each piece of food for possible poisons. It was all clear, and she quickly devoured each delicious morsel. It was not enough, and thankfully, Nate noticed her eyeing everyone's still-full plates. He slid half of his remaining meal towards her.

"You haven't eaten in a day. You need it more than I," Nate said. She didn't argue with him and took her time eating the extra bit of food given to her.

She looked around at her group. The young chestnut-haired Kal sat silently, staring at his plate of food as he ate. She still had not heard him speak, only ever saw him talk to Auden, and that was only when Auden first spoke to him.

Belig and Doal signed to one another, deep in conversation about something. They signed so quickly, she could only pick out a few useless words. Myer and Keir stuffed their faces and talked to Collern about some girl from back home. Their hair was disheveled, and they were both covered in grass stains.

Auden tried and failed to hold a conversation with Nate about elysium, the metal that Nate's sword was crafted from. Layla and Kiarhem talked quietly about Kia's home and her people. Even Shea and Ames had arrived to check on her and ended up staying to join them for their meal.

Ames merely pushed his food around, as if none of it was to his liking, and talked quietly with Officer Shea. Their presence wasn't odd, as they had now eaten quite a few meals with their group.

Ellie observed each conversation with deep gratitude. She was thankful for the people that surrounded her, but it only made her heart ache more for the sisters she left behind. She wished she could speak with them, tell them all she had endured and learned so far. Ellie was in such deep thought, she barely noticed Belig waving his hands to get her attention. She focused her mind and looked his way.

"How are you?" he signed.

She smiled sweetly at the old man and signed back, "Better."

A young witchling brought a plate of sweet rolls to their group and sat it in the center. Myer didn't hesitate to grab three before he even finished the meal in front of him.

"You smile, yet I see pain in your eyes. Why?" Doal translated as Ellie struggled to fully understand.

"It is the same pain I see in every eye here," she replied. "The longing to be with a loved one." His eyes shone with understanding.

"Who did you leave behind, Ellie?" Doal asked.

"My grandparents and two sisters." She held back tears as a small knot formed in the back of her throat.

"Woah, wait a minute. There's more of you!" Myer

exclaimed from where he sat. She was thankful for his added lightheartedness.

"Yes. Maisie's too young for you, and I don't think you could handle Cammie," she mused.

"That's an understatement," Nate voiced from beside her.

"Really?" Myer's forest-green eyes lit up. "I couldn't imagine her being any more feisty than you, Ellie."

"Ellie's jabs are harmless and playful. When Cammie jabs, it's not subtle, and it is meant to hurt." Nate spoke through a soft smile.

"I'm instantly in love," Myer dramatically voiced through a mouthful of sweet roll. Ellie couldn't help but laugh at the thought of Cammie meeting this kindhearted buffoon. Nate, too, scoffed at the idea.

Both of their smiles faded, though, as Myer's face quickly lost all color. He dropped the half-eaten roll in his hand and began to tremble all over.

"Myer?" Ellie voiced. His eyes widened as he looked directly at her. Then he fell to the ground, convulsing and foaming at the mouth.

"MYER!" Ellie screamed. Auden, Layla, and she rushed to his side.

Shea and Ames bolted into action, herding all other groups back into their tents.

"What's going on?! What's happening?!" Keir panicked as he looked at his poisoned friend.

"Layla, help him!" Ellie cried at the young witch who scanned his body. Layla picked up the roll that fell to the ground and held it to her nose. Her face paled.

"Don't touch the rolls!" Auden commanded the group. Layla looked at the young man. Her eyes filled with panic.

"I-I don't know what was used to poison him." She laid a

shaky hand on his chest. "It smells sickeningly sweet, and his heart is racing faster than it should with any poison I've ever come in contact with. I can't help him if I don't know what poison is inside him." She looked at Ellie in desperation.

Ellie reached through the memories of her training. She knew time was of the essence and desperately thought of every plant that might cause convulsions and a racing heart.

When it hit her.

She crawled towards Myer's face and held it firmly in her hands. She stared fiercely into his dilated eyes.

"Myer, I need you to blink once if the roll tasted slightly bitter and twice if it did not." The young man closed his eyes once. When Ellie did not see a second blink, she turned to the witch. "Foxglove. Is there foxglove in the gardens?"

"Yes!" Layla gasped. She ran into the tent to grab her sack of tonics. She returned with a handful of vials. She first gave Myer one filled with a light-green liquid, then one with a familiar purple hue. He stopped convulsing and closed his eyes, entering a deep sleep.

"Take him inside," Auden told Kier and Collern. Both men did as he commanded, picking Myer up from the ground by his legs and shoulders. "Everyone, back in the tent! Now!" he yelled to the group.

He stopped Layla and Ellie as they began to walk away.

"Will he survive?" he asked the young witch.

"If he makes it through the night, yes. I gave him two different sedatives to slow his heart rate. It will still be fast, but hopefully, it will keep his heart from bursting. He will also run a high fever throughout the night. It will help sweat out the poison, but he will need to be monitored. If his fever gets too high, it will fry his brain."

Shea and Ames returned to Auden's side. Ames failed to

hide the shock in his face, while Shea scanned their surroundings.

"This is my fault," Ellie whispered. "Whoever is trying to kill me doesn't seem to care if someone else gets murdered in the process. Wh-what do I do?"

"This is far from your fault, Ellie." Shea spoke with the softness of a father to a hurting daughter.

"Layla, can you question the young girl who gave us the sweet rolls? Maybe she can give us more information." Layla nodded in reply to Auden's request and headed off to the castle where the young witchling had disappeared.

"I will lurk around and see what I can find out, too." Ames darted his eyes around, as if he could see things they could not. "I am sorry about your friend."

His words were cold, but she knew he truly was sorry. He turned and left, Shea joining close behind.

Ellie stood next to Auden in the now empty field, her body trembling from the events. She looked at him with tears in her eyes. He looked back with equal pain and heartache.

"Ellienia." His voice was barely a whisper. He placed her face gently between the palms of his hands. "You did good. Your knowledge and training most likely saved the young man's life."

"I also am the one that put his life in danger, Auden. The longer I stay here, the longer I go without answers, the more dangerous it will become for them."

"You will have your answers soon, Ellienia." Auden spoke softly. He released her face and looked down at her torso. Small drops of blood leaked through the front of her shirt. She suddenly became aware of the pain in her back, shoulder, and legs. Ellie had forgotten all about her wounds. She almost felt used to the pain that covered her body.

"We should get inside and check on those." He gestured towards her stomach.

The wound on Ellie's stomach was the only one to slightly re-open. The bleeding had stopped minutes after she sat on her mat, so Auden didn't feel the need to call on Layla to return with more salve and bandages. She kept her bloodied blouse on as she sat on her mat watching Keir lay cool damp cloths all over Myer's fevered body. The rest of the tent murmured quietly to one another.

They knew who the poison was intended for. They were aware that some of the generals wanted her dead. That someone had tried to poison her days ago. Again, the murderer failed, but this time they crossed a line that Ellie would be sure to repay.

"It's not your fault," Nate whispered beside her.

"Yes. It is. If anything happens to anyone here, it is on me." Frustration and anger laced the words that Ellie spoke.

"El, that—"

"Don't. I don't want to hear your argument towards this. I don't want you to try and make me feel better. This is my burden. A burden I choose to take." She looked at Nate's wounded umber eyes. "We need to start planning. It's time to figure out how we're going to get out of here, how we are going to get everyone out of here. Alive."

32

"Ellie. Ellie," Layla whispered. Ellie shot up and grimaced in pain. She opened her eyes, but it was hard to see anything in the dull, moonlit tent. She saw Keir silently watching over Myer, and Nate sat to her left, watching over her.

Auden still had a rotation of people watching over her throughout each night. "Scoot back to the edge of the tent so I can shadow cloak you," an invisible Layla instructed.

"Should I even try to stop you?" Nate grumbled.

"I'm just going to the Great Hall. I'll be back in an hour, I promise."

"A little warning would have been nice," Nate growled, his anger beginning to grow. Ellie knew it was pointed at more than just her forgetting to tell him about this venture.

"I'm sorry, Nate. We'll talk about this later. I have to go now before Auden wakes up and stops me." Ellie's choice of words sparked a fire in Nate that she had rarely seen.

"So you'll listen to him and not me? You would stay if he asked you to, but not if I do? Ellie, do realize how that sounds?"

"I wouldn't stay if he asked. I would insist on still going, but he wouldn't trust me to go alone. You, on the other hand, do trust me, as I trust you to not say a word about this."

"Fine. One hour and then I'm waking Auden."

"Deal." Ellie slid towards the edge of the tent walls and disappeared. Layla appeared to her left.

"Trouble in paradise?" she jested.

"Just lead the way, witch," Ellie drawled. "And did you find out anything from the youngling about the sweet rolls?"

Layla walked in front, keeping the two in the safety of the shadows.

"No," she answered quietly. "Sweet rolls were given out to all the groups, but your plate was the only one poisoned. The witchling claims she grabbed it at random from the kitchen and had no idea it was different from the other platefuls of rolls."

Ellie was disappointed with the lack of information Layla had been able to collect. They walked the rest of the way in silence. The moon was not as bright as their first venture to the King's library, so staying concealed was much easier. Shadows along all trees, bushes, and castle walls were darker and longer. The two young women made it to their destination rather quickly.

"All the kitchen witches should be in bed, but I will keep us cloaked just in case. Will you need the room to be lit?"

"No. Just get us as close as possible to where the King and Queens' thrones once sat."

She did as Ellie instructed. They slid through the large glass door and dull moon light that leaked in through the cerulean-blue windows. Layla assured that there was not enough light to reveal them, but they would look more like mist or ghosts passing quickly by until the next full shadow. After walking straight down the center of the Great Hall, the young women now stood on the opposite side of the room under an intricate wooden archway. The floor beyond was slightly lifted, indicating a dais for the missing three thrones.

"This is where the thrones would have sat. This is where the Eternal Queen would have murdered the King and Queens of Malavor. What's your plan?" Layla's whisper seemed to echo through the Great Hall.

"I don't know. I'm just going to focus on that day and hopefully, something will come to me. Can you keep track of time? I only want to try at this for a little while. I'd hate to be back on stall duty with Auden."

"Oh no," Layla droned sarcastically. "How terrible to be alone with a sweaty shirtless Fae."

"How did you know he mucked the stalls shirtless?"

Layla snorted as she held in a laugh. "I didn't, but I'm pretty sure that male would do anything to get your attention, which would include showing off his amazing physique."

"Auden and I are just friends, Layla."

"No. You are just friends with him. He, on the other hand, would burn down the world for you. They both would."

"I hardly know him."

"You hardly know yourself." Layla shrugged. "As for Nate, he loves the girl from your past. The girl who grew up on a farm. I think he's starting to realize that when you leave this place, you will no longer be that girl."

Ellie didn't reply. She needed to focus, and thoughts of Nate or Auden would not allow her to do that. "We can talk about this more later."

Layla stepped back, giving Ellie space. She looked around her. At the beams, the floor, the back wall that was covered with velvet curtains, she desperately searched for something to trigger the vision all while thinking about the King and the Queens.

She thought of Auden's mom standing near Queen Odina and looked in an area where that might have occurred, but nothing. Nothing she thought of or looked at summoned any type of vision. At one point, she closed her eyes and willed within herself for it to occur, but it still didn't work. She could feel the time slipping away from her, and before she was ready, Layla voiced it was time to head back.

Ellie followed with deep frustration. If this was her only power, it was useless. She could not control it. It worked when *it* wanted to, and that drove her insane.

"We can try again tomorrow night if you would like," Layla said once they got back to the tent.

"Yes. At least once more," Ellie agreed. Layla nodded then disappeared as Ellie reappeared in the center of the tent.

"Shi—" Kiarhem threw a hand to her chest. "Ellie, is that you?"

"Yes. Sorry, I didn't mean to scare you." Ellie bent down next to the young elf.

"That took longer than an hour." Nate grumbled from his mat. He was awake even though Kiarhem was on watch. He had worried, but he hadn't sent Auden after her like he said he would.

"You both should get some sleep. I'm going to let Keir get some rest and watch over Myer for a bit."

"Are you sure?" Kia asked. Ellie gave her a reassuring pat on the leg before standing up and heading to where Keir sat, mostly asleep.

She sat next to the young, dark-haired man. Even in the

softly lit tent, she could see the man's puffy eyes and sunken cheeks. She tapped him gently on his slender shoulder. He jumped at her touch.

"Lie down and get some rest, Keir. I can watch him for a bit," she whispered.

"No. I need to change his cloths and force some water into him so he doesn't dehydrate." He reached for the water bucket next to him.

"I've got it, Keir." Ellie placed a hand over his. "Please, you can't care for him properly if you're too tired to do so. I promise, I will wake you if anything changes." He looked between Ellie and Myer before finally agreeing to rest. He lay down on his mat behind her and began to snore just seconds later.

Ellie removed each warm, damp cloth and placed them into the bucket. She brushed Myer's red hair from his forehead, feeling the intense heat from his skin. The cloths were not working. He was still too hot, and Ellie knew that if he continued to run this warm, he would die. She instinctively traced her fingers along the chain of her necklace as she thought. The cool pendant between her breasts called to her. She pulled it from her blouse and placed the liquid pendant in her hand.

If I could get the pendant to work as it did during the trials, it would cool the water down even more.

Ellie focused all her attention, all her desires, frustrations, and sorrows into the pendant. She begged and sent a plea-filled prayer for the pendant to work as she placed the liquid-filled glass into the bucket of water. Moments later, she could feel it's cold burn radiate up the chain. The water in the bucket began to not just cool, but freeze. A slight blue glow emanated from the liquid pendant, causing the water bucket to gleam through the dark tent.

She quickly removed it from the water before it completely froze over.

She held up Myer's sweaty head and pulled out a very cold cloth. Ellie squeezed the liquid carefully onto his chapped lips and into his mouth. A quiet moan released from the back of his throat, showing he was thankful for the freezing-cold liquid. She then placed the cold cloths over his forehead, the back of his neck, arms, chest, and legs.

Ellie spent the rest of the night in a constant rotation of taking off the cloths, giving him water, and putting the cloths back on, only having to cool the water down with the pendant two more times. By the time the sun began to peak, Myer's fever had almost fully reduced to a normal temp.

"We'll never hear the end of it." Auden silently sat next to Ellie. She hadn't noticed he awoke, but based on the soft morning light that now entered the tent, it didn't surprise her.

"Hear the end of what?" she whispered.

"That you were the one to nurse him back to health. He'll be bragging about it to any and all who will hear it for the rest of his life." Auden quietly chuckled. Ellie smirked, knowing it would be true. That is, if the fever hadn't already caused some internal damage. Her smile faded at the thought.

"I can take it from here, if you would like to get some rest," Auden offered.

"No. I'd like to stay until he wakes."

He nodded, not questioning or trying to convince her beyond the first offer. "Aren't you worried Nate might get jealous of the attention you're giving him?"

Ellie knew from the devilish smile Auden gave that the question was not sincere. "I'm pretty sure the only one jealous is you, Auden."

"True. I may inflict stable duty as a punishment again, just to have a bit more of your time." The corner of Auden's mouth went up, his gray eyes gleaming at her.

This was more than flirting, and Ellie knew it. Layla was right; Auden did care for her. She felt it the moment he lay next to her, revealing his true form. She wasn't sure what she felt for him yet, but she still cared for Nate and wouldn't disrespect him by continuing with Auden's bantering.

She turned her head, focusing on the deep breaths of Myer.

Auden seemed to understand, as he changed his tone. "Do you mind if I check a few of your wounds while we wait?"

Auden gestured to her back and shoulder. She turned her back towards him as her reply. With gentle fingers, he lifted her shirt and checked under each bandage to see how all the lashes were healing.

"You're mending well. You should be able to remove all bandages by tomorrow as long as you take time to rest today."

"Will I have time to rest today?" she asked as he ran a soft finger around the center of her back, near the flare baton mark. She tensed as his touch sent a strong ache through every muscle of her back. He jolted his hand away, realizing the pain he had caused her.

"Sorry. I'll grab Agilta's salve." He was silently to her bag and back before she could protest that she was fine. The mark did not hurt as much as it had, and it was bearable even after his touch.

"And, yes. You are healing quickly, but I worry that any hard labor or training would further injure some of the others. We will stick around the tent as we did yesterday."

He handed Ellie her pack. She pulled out the clothes she

brought from home, and no longer wore, and placed them on his lap. Then she pulled out a few daggers, her vambraces, a hairbrush, and the small portrait of the red-haired female and the young male. Finally, she found the small jar of salve Agilta had made.

"Here." Ellie tried to hand Auden the jar, but when he did not take it, she turned to see him holding the small portrait. His face was stone. Unreadable.

"Where did you get this?"

"I found it in the King's desk. In the library. I'm sorry. I shouldn't have taken it, but that female in the portrait is the Fae in my visions, and—" Ellie stopped talking as Auden's eyes shot up from the portrait and stared intensely at her.

"This female is the one from the vision at the house? The one who's home is now cursed and stands alone among the burned ones? This is the Fae that hid the book for the King?" Auden spoke quietly but urgently.

"Yes. Why? Do you know who she is? Who they both are?" Ellie pointed to the young couple in the portrait, but Auden ignored her questions and shoved it back into her sack.

"Listen to me. Your next trial will take place in the city beyond these walls. It will be a test of leadership and skill. While you are out there, you need to map out a way from here to that house. A way that we can all go without being caught. Do you understand?"

"Yes, but Layla said—"

"We need to get you to that house, Ellienia. Despite any curse, that is where you are meant to go. Trust me." She didn't need to trust him. She had felt the desire to go to that house the moment she saw it over a week ago. It was as if it had been calling to her.

"I will ask Nate and Kiarhem to do the same," she said,

knowing multiple eyes mapping out a direction were better than one.

"Good," he agreed, and he finally took the jar of salve that still lay in her open hand.

"When this is all over, Auden, can we agree on no more secrets between us?" Ellie asked as Auden rubbed the soothing tonic onto her back.

"Will you still want me around when all this is over?" Ellie was shocked at his sincere tone. It was not a sarcastic, rhetorical question. He was truly asking for an answer.

"I'm not sure I could get through the rest of this war without you. You're the only one that questions my actions, challenges my thinking, and keeps me out of trouble." They both smirked at her words.

"Then, yes. When we're out of these camps, I promise, no more secrets." He closed the lid to the jar and stuffed it back into her pack. She smiled sweetly at the handsome Fae who looked at her with soft eyes.

"Ellie, there is something you should know. Something that I am not forced to keep from you. I'm not sure if it was simply overlooked or what, but it was not included in the magical vow that I took to keep from revealing certain things to you."

"Magical vow?" Ellie's mind suddenly rushed with a slew of questions.

"It's a spell that keeps me from revealing anything that the counterpart puts down in writing. I swore to—to—" He stopped, struggling to say the words he tried to form. His jaw tightened into a familiar line of pain. "Ugh. There is magic keeping me from saying certain things to you, but for some reason, he didn't include this detail in the vow."

"What is it?" Ellie turned to fully face him. She wondered why he waited until now to reveal whatever it was that needed to be said. Auden fiddled with one of her daggers that still sat in his lap. He bit his inner lip and flared his nostrils. It was a side of him Ellie had never seen before. It was almost as if he were...

Nervous. And not a normal, about to head into battle or address a crowd kind of nervous. This was something else entirely.

"We...Well, we're...umm—" His words were interrupted by the movement of the man who slowly groaned and stirred behind them. Keir was waking, and Auden seemed thankful for the interruption. Whatever it was that Auden knew, he clearly was not ready to share. Though it drove Ellie insane, she would not bring it up or pressure him to tell her until he was ready.

"Hey." Keir spoke through a gravelly voice. "How is he?"

He sat up and placed a hand on his friend's freckled cheek, checking for a fever.

"I got his fever down earlier this morning. He should wake soon." Ellie's words caused Keir's dark eyes to line with silver.

"Thank you," he whispered. "How did you do it? I couldn't keep the water in the bucket cool enough with how hot the cloths were from being on his body." He lifted a cloth from Myer's forehead and placed it in the freezing water. His eyes widened at the touch. "Ellie, this water— how in the world did you get it this cold?"

"Magic," she answered without any hesitation. To her surprise, her answer didn't faze him. He was either too tired to acknowledge the statement or he simply didn't care. He, instead, just nodded with appreciation and continued to remove and replace cloths along Myer's body.

"So..." Nate's familiar voice spoke quietly behind her.

"Are we all going to gather around him until he wakes like we did for you yesterday?"

Ellie smiled and made space for him to sit next to her. He glanced solemnly at Auden before sitting down.

"Yes," she replied. "He'll love the attention."

"So much so he may eat another poison sweet roll." Keir snorted. They all softly laughed and continued to joke as they waited for their friend to wake up.

33

Ellie stood staring at the blue-velvet tapestry that would have once hung behind the King and Queens of Malavor. Myer had awoken in the late morning, and despite his current state of persistent vomiting, Layla had looked him over and voiced he would be fine.

"The vomiting is good," she stated to Myer. "It's your system's way of clearing out any leftover poison, which means your body is doing what it should. As long as you stay hydrated and keep the fever down, you should be better by tomorrow."

Ellie was more than relieved. Myer was going to be fine, and she was determined to keep it that way for all her friends. Which meant another late night helplessly staring into a dark room to hopefully summon up some kind of answer.

She had already been at it for a while now, and she was running out of time again. Ellie impatiently twirled the blue pendant in her fingers. She looked down at it and wondered, *Could I pull enough power from it to summon something?*

She was able to tap into its power the night before, so maybe she could do it again in a different way. Ellie firmly grasped the pendant and closed her eyes.

"King Vedmar, Queen Odina, Queen Akéra, and their death. King Vedmar, Queen Odina, Queen Akéra, and their death," she chanted under her breath over and over again, focusing on the cold glass tucked in her hand. She continued to chant until it became a mindless drone, until her voice began to fade and her vision blurred to somewhere else.

Ellie stood before the three thrones, each filled with its respective royal. King Vedmar was in the middle, and each queen sat to either side. The thrones were simple, but beautiful. The wood was carved with intricate depiction all along the legs, arms, and high backs. They were stories that Ellie assumed pertained to the royal that sat upon it. The golden-haired queen to his left had a bow and arrow carved above her head. Queen Odina the Warrior, Ellie realized. To his right sat Queen Akéra, the Just. A beautiful carving of snow-capped mountains sat above her head, and above the King's was the same carving that was on the door to his library: an owl surrounded by thorns. A young woman with beautiful bronze hair whispered in Queen Odina's ear. When the woman looked up from her queen, Ellie recognized her familiar gray eyes. Auden's mother.

"Most of the citizens in the city have fled, Your Majesty. Just a few more weeks and they will all be safe." A man that stood directly behind Ellie spoke. She turned around to see the Great Hall filled with a few dozen men and women in armor, a few royal children, and their respective parents. They all sat at the large, intricately-carved wooden tables.

"Are you sure this was the best decision, brother? We could still retrieve our forces from Dorumia and fight," Queen Akéra voiced.

"Yes. This is the only way to ensure that this land will one day be free of her evil. I will not have this discussion again." The King spoke with deep authority, not at all in the same way that he spoke to the red-headed female from the portrait, Millie. "Thank you, General Reuel. Continue to evacuate the city at random, with a few families leaving each day." The golden-haired general bowed to the King. His shoulder-length hair was the only similarity to his son. He now stood staring at his wife with amber eyes and a round, clenched jaw.

"When the city is empty, you will also join your families in Dorumia." Queen Odina addressed her forces. The crowd stirred at her words.

"Your Majesty, you are asking us to abandon you, which is against every oath that we have taken," General Reuel voiced for his comrades.

"We are not asking, general. This is an order. Your final order," The King interjected. "You will wait in Dorumia until you are once again called to fight. Until you are once again called upon by a descendant of the Malavor throne. When the Queen of Sondoér comes, the three of us will die, but three more children of the Kiaver line will take our place one day."

This was the first time Ellie had heard the royal family name. She repeated Kiaver, putting the name to memory.

"We will do as you each command. Speselpîda." General Reuel bowed.

"Speselpîda!" the crowd repeated. The three royals each raised a hand in dismissal, when a deep sound rang through the castle. BONG. BONG.

"The warning bell!" Queen Akéra stood.

"She is here." King Vedmar exhaled.

Auden's mother ran off the dais down to his father. She whispered something in his ear, and with tears in her eyes, she yelled, "Go!"

He only hesitated for a moment, his eyes filled with rage. Auden's father ran through the large wooden door that Ellie had entered days ago. She knew what hidden passages and secure exits lay behind that door. Moments later, the large front entry doors swung open to Ellie's left. A young man about her age ran in.

"Your Majesties, she—" He stopped midsentence. His eyes bulged in panic as he clawed at his throat. Queen Akéra raised a hand towards him. She desperately tried to use her powers to fill the man's lungs with air, but failed. His face turned a deep shade of red before his eye rolled into the back of his head.

"No need, darling. I can announce myself." Ellie heard the sweet melodious voice before she saw the Queen that it belonged to. She, along with two of her generals, entered the castle's Great Hall. Moon-white hair that was woven into one large braid dragged behind her deep-violet dress. The pendant that Ellie still held began to burn in her hand. She could feel its power begging her to leave. Ellie backed herself up, taking a place among the armed men and women.

"Hello, my fellow royals. It seems you have been awaiting my arrival." She sent a poisonous smile towards everyone in the room. King Vedmar stood from his throne.

"Allow these men, women, and children to leave here peacefully, and we will freely give Malavor over to you."

"How very gracious of you, but no, I'm afraid that can't happen. And you know exactly why, King Vedmar." She again smiled her evil smile. The King looked down at her with vengeful hate. "Let's not be coy with one another, King. You know what I am, and you know why your people are so important to me."

"*Your Majesty.*" *A familiar foul voice entered the Great Hall. General Dolian rushed to his queen's side. "Most of the city has already been abandoned."*

"*What?!*" *A vile anger filled the room. Its oily touch crawled up Ellie's spine. "Where are they?" she spewed towards the King.*

"*Our people are not yours to claim. Yes, I know what you are, morphling. I also know you will win today's battle, but not this war. Three children of the Kiaver line will rise one day, and they will be your end.*"

"*Burn the city,*" *she barked at Dolion. "Capture all who show any sign of natural power and kill the rest." Dolion ran from the room with a wicked smirk. The Eternal Queen stepped onto the dais and stood inches from the King's face. "Your prophecy means nothing to me. I will win this war, and all of Karmalo and its people will be mine. I will make sure of it." She snapped her fingers. Dozens and dozens of generals entered the room from every direction, outnumbering the Malavor forces two to one. "Kill them all."*

Chaos ensued. The same chaos that Ellie had already envisioned over a week ago, only this time, the details were clearer. Men, women, and the royal children were sliced through one by one. Ellie's heart pounded and breath quickened. She ran towards the dais. Her earlier vision displayed the King and Queens faceless and already slain, but this time she would see everything.

The Eternal Queen thrust her hands towards the royals, blowing each of them back into their throne. With a flick of her wrist, the wood from each throne splintered and stretched to encase their arms and necks. Before the Queen could continue, a blast of blue fire was forced her way. She held up a protective arm that singed at the flames' touch.

"*AUGH!*" *the Queen screamed. Auden's mother stood, ready to send another wave of fire. Before she was able to do so, the Eternal Queen waved her arms, conjuring up every drop of water in the* room. With a forceful push, the water crashed into Auden's mother, throwing her back against the wooden archway. Ellie heard a deep crack come from the mother's body before she crumbled to the ground.

Wind, earth, and water. The Eternal Queen was using the Malavor royals' powers. She held out a hand and began to pull the air from each of the royal's lungs. No, not air. She was drowning them. Using their own saliva and other bodily fluids, the Queen filled each royal lung with water. Odina and Akéra looked past the Queen at their slain children. Tears of agony and great sorrow were silenced as they slowly died. King Vedmar did not look at any children, nor any fallen spouse. He looked directly at Ellie. His eyes stared intently at her until his head fell forward, indicating his death.

The screaming behind Ellie had ceased. She didn't dare turn around to see the fallen men, women, and children. She couldn't bear to view any more bloodshed. She was about to let go of the vision when a general spoke in the direction of Auden's mother.

"This one is still alive, Your Majesty," he said, checking her pulse.

"Good. Put her with the others," the Queen instructed.

General Dolion walked in once more. "There are no other blessed ones, my queen. There was one at a house on the outskirts of the city, but she released a curse that killed herself and five other generals."

"Take me there," she commanded through a fitful rage. The Queen stepped off the dais and walked directly in front of Ellie. She stopped suddenly and slightly turned. Black soulless eyes stared into Ellie's. The Eternal Queen cocked her head and smiled wickedly.

"Hello, there."

.   .   .

With a blinding light, Ellie released the burning cold pendant from her hand and fell to the ground in a panic. She was back in the dark, empty Great Hall, but she could still hear the vile Queen's voice in her head. Her heart pounded as she struggled to breathe through her terror.

"Ellie!" Layla fell to the ground beside her. "What happened?! What did you see?!"

"Sh-She saw me. The Queen...She spoke to me." Ellie's entire body trembled. Layla's eyes widened in fear.

"Come on. We need to get you back to the tent. We need to tell the others." Layla picked Ellie up from the ground and dragged her from the castle. They ran hand in hand back to the tent. Ellie wanted to keep running. She wanted to run straight through the forest, to the back stone wall, and to another land entirely. She wanted to get as far away from this place as possible.

"Stay here. I will go in and wake the others," Layla said as they reached the back side of the tent. Moments later, she emerged through the back flaps with Nate, Kiarhem, and Auden at her heels. They each noticed Ellie's pale face and trembling body at the same time. Nate ran up, wrapping her in his arms. She could not control the fear-induced sobs that overtook her body.

"*What happened*?" Auden commanded. His tone was laced with worry and anger.

"Not here," Layla instructed. "Let's go deeper into the trees."

They each followed her, trusting Layla's ability to sense when others were around.

"Here is good." Auden stopped. "Now, what happened?" he commanded again.

Ellie tried to collect herself, but the Queen's voice continued to echo in her head. "Sh-she saw me."

Layla stepped in to explain how she had taken Ellie to the Great Hall to summon a vision, and how she succeeded in doing so.

"Ellienia." Auden came closer, and Nate reluctantly stepped aside. "I need you to tell us exactly what you saw."

Auden's words sent Ellie into a panic as she realized another crucial terrifying detail from her vision. Auden's mother was still alive. His mother was not killed as his family had thought, but worse. She had been captured over fifteen years ago and most likely was still imprisoned by the Eternal Queen. Ellie did not know how to reveal such knowledge to her friend.

"I-I saw the day the Queen and her men attacked Malavor. I saw her generals slice through men, women, and children of the royal court. And I saw the Eternal Queen single-handedly kill the King and Queens of Malavor using the royals own natural, given magic."

"What? How?" Auden's eyes were wide in disbelief.

"I don't know. The King called her a morphling after stating that she would never claim the Malavor people. She did not only come to take Malavor, but to capture and imprison blessed ones."

A slew of colorful words left Auden's mouth as Ellie spoke.

"When the Queen had finished killing the royals, she stepped off the dais, and that was when she turned. She saw me. I don't know how, but she saw me there and spoke to me."

"She didn't see you," Nate voiced confidently. "Well, she did, but it wasn't you she saw. Hold on." He sprinted to the tent and came back holding a handful of scrolls—the same scrolls he had stuffed into his pocket on the night they went to the King's library. "I've been reading up on seers." He handed a scroll to Ellie.

"But Ellie's not a full seer," Kiarhem voiced. "She only has visions of the past, not the future."

"According to the writings in these scrolls, that doesn't matter. Young seers often start off with only seeing visions of the past. Some seers never even get the ability to look into the future."

"And what about the Queen seeing her?" Auden asked.

"Right. Here." He handed a different scroll to Auden. "Seers have the ability to see and talk to one another through many different ways. If a future seer like El were to summon a vision of the past, any Fae gifted with seeing abilities would be able to sense her presence and possibly see her—"

"As a glowing blue form," Ellie finished for him. "Like the man from my dreams. From the visions in my sleep. The one who woke me up before Filtmon tried to kill me; the same one that called to come find him."

"Yes. Projecting themselves into someone else's vision is another way seers can communicate with one another."

"But that would mean the Eternal Queen was using someone else's gift of sight, and everyone else in the room was dead." Besides Auden's mother, but she would not reveal that yet.

"It could have been leftover power from the last Fae she morphed from," Nate suggested.

She instantly remembered whose power she had possessed last.

"The King. The King was a seer and water wielder." Her voice was barely a whisper. "That's how he knew she was coming. That's how he knew to evacuate the city."

"Yes," Auden confirmed. "Rare, but he was one of a few past Malavor royals to have dual powers. He hid his gift of sight from most everyone but those in his court. Was there anything else from the vision? Anything else we should know, Ellienia?"

Ellie looked around at the others. The information she was about to share was not for their ears. She grabbed Nate's hand.

"Thank you for this." She held up the scroll he had handed her then placed it in her back pocket. She placed a kiss on his cheek and gave him a sweet smile. "I need to speak to Auden alone."

She could see the jealous hurt in Nate's eyes as she spoke, but he didn't question it. He only nodded and walked with Kiarhem and Layla back to the tent.

"Auden. I'm not sure you will want to hear what I have to tell you."

"I'm not sure you could say or do anything else to upset me more, Ellienia." His eyes filled with fear-induced rage. "Why must you continue to act with such reckless behavior? Why must you constantly put yourself at risk? We've already discussed how incredibly dangerous sneaking around the castle is! Why—"

"We are at war, Auden." Ellie spoke with calm confidence. "I will continue to put myself at risk. I will continue to make reckless decisions if they get us even one step closer to getting out of here and fighting against the Eternal Queen. I went to the Great Hall to find answers that we needed, and I got them."

"I was told you would be difficult." Auden ran a frustrated hand over his face. "Ellienia, my one job right now is to keep you alive. Please, make my job easier and at least inform me of the risks you're about to take before taking them."

"Why? So we can fight and you can try to change my mind?" Ellie spoke through her frustration.

"Yes! Exactly! Ellienia, there is a reason kings and queens have advisors, why generals have other generals and captains: to help make the best decisions. Ellienia, I will never keep you from fighting or taking a risk you deem necessary, but at least talk to me about it first." He took a deep breath. "I agree. Your venture tonight was fruitful. I just—I would have felt better if you had let me help. I could have had Shea and Ames make sure the generals were all occupied, or I could have scouted to make sure no other arbitrators could walk in on you. I know Layla can sense when someone is coming, and you are perfectly capable of protecting yourself, I just...I already have to stand aside and watch you risk your life in these trials." Pain contorted the muscles in his face. "Please, Ellienia, let me help you when I can."

Ellie stared at the hurt that radiated from Auden's face. She slowly nodded in agreement and reached for his hand.

"I promise. I will not hide any more plans from you."

Her words allowed his shoulders to relax, until he realized she had still not shared the information from her vision.

"What is it that you saw, Ellienia." He continued to hold her hand with a strong grip.

"I saw your parents." Her words made his muscles tense. "They were both in the Great Hall when the warning bells sounded. Your mom told your dad something before commanding him to leave. I assume he went to find you and your siblings, while she stayed behind to protect the Malavor royals. Your mother was very powerful, but the

Queen was stronger. She threw your mother against a wood beam, knocking her out and potentially breaking her back, but not killing her." Ellie squeezed Auden's hand even tighter. "Your mother's still alive, Auden. She was the one and only blessed one captured that day, and I think it is safe to assume the Eternal Queen still has her."

34

A uden stood in shock at the words Ellienia spoke. He squeezed her hand as a way to keep himself anchored.

"Are you sure?" He spoke after a few moments of contemplative silence.

"Yes. One of the Queen's generals confirmed it." Ellienia shifted uncomfortably in her spot. "I'm sorry," she whispered.

He looked down at her. He wanted to ask more questions, to dwell on the information she gave, but he knew this was not the time or place. "What are your plans once we escape these camps? Will we go north and join their forces, or will we go south to Dorumia where a seer can train you?"

"We?" she questioned.

"I go where you go, Ellienia." Her brows pulled up at his words. She seemed to contemplate them for a moment.

"As a leader to the people in that tent, I feel I should journey with them north, but as someone who has yet to fully tap into her powers, I feel I should learn more from another, stronger seer. Possibly even from the one who calls for me."

"Then we will go south," Auden confirmed. "Nate is your equal and could be an excellent leader to the others. He can be the one to accompany them north."

Ellienia's face contorted and tensed as he spoke. When she stayed silent, he continued to speak.

"If we go south, to Dorumia, I can inform my family of this new information. I can get their counsel on what path we should take in finding and hopefully rescuing my mother, if she truly is still alive." Auden spoke through the knot in his throat. His mother was still alive; she had to be. But after nearly two decades with the Eternal Queen, she would not be the same Mother he once knew. He understood this reasoning for wanting to go south to Dorumia was selfish, but he also truly felt it was the best decision for her as well.

"Then we go south," she agreed.

His eyes filled with tearful relief. He needed to tell his family this news, and the sooner the better.

Ellienia let go of his hand, but instead of turning towards the tent, she surprisingly wrapped her arms around his neck. Her toes barely touched the ground as she held on to him tightly.

He wrapped his arms around her waist, slightly picking her up from the ground. It was an embrace he desperately needed. She provided the comfort of a friend and was someone he was growing to truly admire, no matter how infuriating and stubborn she was, which were both qualities of hers that he reluctantly and secretly liked.

"We should head back and get some rest. Your body still has a bit of healing to do." He spoke into her hair.

She released her arms from his neck, which caused a

slight hint of heartache to hit in the pit of Auden's gut. He hesitated before releasing the hold he had around her waist. Her soft smile up at him sent waves of desire through every inch of his being. He had to remind himself once more, her heart belonged to someone else. Being her friend and ally was enough.

35

Group twenty-four lined up outside of their tent. Ellie stood in front, vambraces and leather garter filled with daggers and her blue-silver sword hung strapped to her back. Weapons were allowed in today's trial and "highly suggested," as Auden put it.

"I will be dividing you up into two groups. These will be your teams for today's trial. Anyone not on your team is considered your enemy. There will be about a hundred teams fighting to retrieve one of only seventy red flags that are hidden throughout the city. This trial is meant to test your ability to lead or be led. Either are fitting qualities for this army. I suggest you pick your leaders now, find a flag quickly, then head back. This sounds simple, but I assure you, a handful of designates may not make it out of this trial alive. If you do complete this trial with no flag found, your team will face punishment," he stated before listing off the teams.

"Team one: Ellie, Kiarhem, Myer, Belig, and Kal."

Ellie controlled her face, not reacting to the blow Auden just gave her. She would be performing this trial *against*

Nate. "Group two: Nate, Collern, Keir, and Doal. You have five minutes to discuss strategy with your group. Go."

Kiarhem, Myer, and Belig all made their way to where Ellie stood. Kal reluctantly followed suit. Ellie hadn't learned much about the quiet young man other than that he looked far too young to be there. His chestnut hair was cut short around the sides and back, but the top was long and tied up in a knot. Shorter strands hung loose against his tan skin.

His upturned golden eyes looked around at the group. He puffed his chest and flared his large nostrils.

"We should search closest to the castle wall. That way we have a shorter and faster route to go to and from the finish line," he claimed with confidence. Ellie's friends all looked at her with raised brows, waiting for her input.

"It's a good idea, Kal. It's most likely the same idea every other team has," she said with kindness laced in authority. "The farther out we go from the castle walls, the less competition we'll have in finding a flag. However, I doubt running out into the city and grabbing a flag is the only thing these generals have planned. I'm sure there will be traps along the way. We will need to be vigilant and watch each other's backs." Ellie began to sign as best she could for Belig to fully understand. "Belig and Myer, I want you flanking my sides, just one step behind. Understood?" Both men nodded. "Kiarhem, I want you directly behind me at all times. Kal, I want you to flank her side in the same way. We need to run close enough together to protect one another, yet far enough apart to fight or dodge flying objects if the situation calls for it. Any questions?"

"Yeah. Why the hell should we listen to you?" Kal voiced. His golden eyes glared down at her. Ellie was about to fire back when all three of her allies lined up next to her.

"Because she is the only one of us that has been training for this every day of her entire life," Kiarhem voiced.

"Because she has shown how skilled she is and strong she can be even through a massive amount of pain. She's also already saved my life once. I know she wouldn't hesitate to do it again." Myer smirked towards her.

"Because she leads for the betterment of all, not just for herself," Ellie translated for Belig. Pride gleamed in his eyes.

"You do not know me, Kal, and I do not expect your trust right away, but I assure you, I am the most equipped to get us all out of this trial unharmed and alive. I will protect you if the situation calls for it, whether or not you plan to do the same for me. You can continue to let your arrogant pride stand in your way and possibly put us all in danger, or you can suck it up and do as I say."

He stared at the four people in front of him, and after a moment of silent contemplation, he finally voiced his agreement.

"Fine."

"LINE UP!" Auden yelled from farther down the field. Each member of Ellie's team followed behind her as they rejoined the rest of group twenty-four. They began their trek to the front entrance of the castle grounds. Ellie led the line as usual, and Auden walked directly beside her, so close his large arm kept brushing against hers.

"What are you aiming at?" Ellie mumbled to him as they walked. "You want me to be safe, yet you place my strongest ally and protector on another team?"

"We both know you do not need Nate to protect you. You are perfectly capable of doing that yourself. Plus, this is the best opportunity for Nate to prove to both you and himself that he can also lead. That he can succeed without you by his side." Ellie knew Auden's decision was admirable, but it didn't make her feel any more comfortable with the situation.

"Fine, but why Kal? His arrogance alone could get us all killed today." Ellie looked back at her teammates.

"He's a good kid, Ellie. He needs you and your alliance more than you need him."

Kid, Ellie thought.

"How old is he?" she whispered.

"Just barely fifteen," Auden solemnly murmured. Ellie loosened a single foul word from her breath. "Get to know him. Having another ally won't hurt."

"Alright." Ellie hated to admit it, but Auden's reasoning was both wise and honorable. The group walked single file through the large courtyard, edging closer to the castle wall exit.

"Don't forget our other plan," Auden whispered, referring to Ellie, Nate, and Kiarhem mapping out a path to the cursed house. "And please be careful out there. I'd hate for you to die on your birthday."

Ellie shot a shocked glance at the young male.

"How—you know what, never mind." She rolled her eyes. "Please don't tell the others. They'll insist on making some kind of fuss. Especially Layla!" Oh gods, Ellie couldn't imagine what Layla would do if she found out it was her birthday.

"I won't say a word." He smirked at her wickedly. They walked the rest of the way in silence. They got close enough to the large stone wall to see all thirty generals standing atop it. Ellie knew the presence of every general stationed at the camp was not a good sign.

They walked through the archway, and witches both young and old stood just out of the shadows. Ellie spotted

Layla standing at the edge of the exit. She glared directly at Ellie, using her eyes to call her attention.

Layla quickly looked up at the trees, then back at her, and up at the trees, and back at her once more. She was warning her of something. Ellie slightly nodded her head in understanding. She now fixed her glance farther down the line. Ellie hoped Layla was giving Nate the same warning.

Arbitrators stood outside the wall, waving their arms in direction. They veered left and took their place with their backs against the stone of the wall. Ellie looked up at the trees. At first, she didn't see anything, until a slight movement from a tree a few yards away caught her eye. Upon closer inspection, she could see multiple trees holding arbitrators with bows and arrows.

"Shit," she voiced under her breath.

"What?" Myer asked.

"Look at the trees." They all did as she commanded, and each breathed their own colorful expressions. "They've most likely been told to injure, not kill, but we're not going to risk it. They will loosen their bows quickly as the trial begins, so we will wait here for three seconds from the starting indicator. Hopefully, we can get through while they're loading their next arrow. Belig and Myer, keep an eye on the trees and tops of buildings." Both men nodded in understanding. "The rest of us will keep our eyes at ground level, watching out for possible traps. We'll head northwest where the city isn't as congested and trees are few and far between."

Everything Ellie said was true, but her reasoning for going that direction was more complicated than most of the others knew. Only Kiarhem was aware of her double strategy.

Once every designate from groups one through fifty

found their spot against the outside of the castle wall, an arbitrator with dark skin and even darker hair spoke.

"Good morning, designates! Your arbitrator should have already given you some instructions for today's trial. It will begin when the castle bells ring."

The warning bells, Ellie thought. She was not ready to hear them so soon after the vision she just experienced.

"Your trial will end when your team either returns a flag to your group arbitrator or the bells ring again, signaling all flags have been found and your team has failed. Flags can be stolen from other teams using whatever force necessary. Just try not to kill each other." The arbitrator walked out of the way.

The whole crowd stood in silence, waiting for the sound of bells. The thundering of Ellie's heart pounded in her head as she grabbed for Kiarhem's hand. She had played a similar game before against her sisters, but it was never this dangerous.

BONG. BONG. BONG. Ellie closed her eyes. Visions of the Great Hall massacre flashed through her head. Cloaked generals slicing through Fae. *One.* The queens silently crying for their slaughtered children. *Two.* Generals dragging Auden's mother away. *Three.*

Ellie shot her eyes open and ran.

Her team followed in their respective positions. Nate's team left the wall only a second later. He had made a similar plan.

Few arrows flew past them as most now lay at the ground or in a designate's arm or leg. Ellie picked up an arrow as she ran. The tip was dull and rounded. If any of them were hit with these arrows, it would hurt, but it would either bounce off or it wouldn't go deep enough to cause any damage. She threw the arrow to the ground and picked up her pace. Teams scurried through the trees and buildings on both sides of the main path into the city. Ellie saw only one team retrieve a flag from the inside of an abandoned store. Unfortunately, another team filled with brute men also saw. They surrounded the flag-holding team and proceeded to beat each individual until the flag was handed over by their leader. The sight of it was disgusting.

They continued running, dodging old buildings and chaotic, gruesome fights. Ellie veered left, leading them down a narrow path. She peered behind her shoulder to check on her teammates. A shuffling of rocks under heavy footsteps shot Ellie's gaze back to the front, but it was too late. She collided into the mass of a large body. They both went down, cursing and sliding against the loose gravel ground. She rolled off, unsheathing her sword, and readied herself in a crouching position.

She was now a wide distance away from her team, who had stopped in time and remained standing. Their weapons were also drawn, and they faced the group filing out of a small two-story townhouse: three other men and a woman twice Ellie's age. The house's windows were filled with broken glass, and its wood was black and charred. Ellie felt if she breathed too hard in its direction, it would crumble to ash. How this team had entered and emerged from it safely was a miracle.

The large man that she collided with struggled to remove himself from the ground, but when he did, Ellie's breath hitched at the sliver of dark-red cloth sticking out of his pants pocket. She shot her eyes to his, but he had seen her glimpse at the flag he carried.

Shit.

"We don't want to fight. You can take your flag and go." Ellie's voice was clear and demanding, but the large man was already rushing her, protecting what he assumed she would take. He was slow and unsteady as he brought the back of his ax down towards her head.

She easily twisted out of the way and behind the man. With a slight jump for reach, she brought the pommel of her sword down onto the back of his head. The ground shook as he fell, but Ellie didn't pause for a single moment. The other opposing teammates had hesitated, watching as she took their leader down with intense speed. They each turned their attention to Ellie's team and away from her. Ellie cut them off before they even began their attack.

Two of the men, both with shaggy dark hair, seemed to be itching for a fight. She knew the look in their eyes, the need they felt to inflict pain. They charged first, the rest of the surrounding designates seeming satisfied to stand back and watch.

"Shouldn't we help her?" Kal's voice was a mixture of awe and a need to act.

"Nah, she's got it handled." Myer was holding back his glee.

"We'd just get in her way." Kiarhem spoke through a satisfied giggle.

Ellie disarmed the two men with ease, using her blade to only cause minor cuts on their arms and legs. They both fell to the ground as she delivered the same knockout blow to their heads as she had done to the first man.

The remaining man and woman stood wide-eyed and unable to move.

"Wh-who are y-you?" The woman spoke through terrified breaths. Ellie turned away from her, knowing neither one would dare to fight her now. She pulled the red flag from the large man's pocket and threw it at their feet.

"I told you I didn't want to fight. You can still take your flag and go."

"What!" Ellie ignored Kal's protest.

"Ellie, we're losing vital time to find our own flag." Myer's voice was low and filled with unusual firmness, but she knew he didn't disagree with the choice she was making.

"I will not win this trial by their barbaric rules. You found this flag, so it's yours."

The woman bent down, picking up the piece of cloth while keeping her eyes on Ellie. "Thank you." She handed the flag to her partner, and both stepped over their fallen teammates and tentatively passed in front of Ellie and her team. Once a safe distance away, the woman turned around. "Watch your step and keep your eyes on the ground."

Her warning was met with a loud *BOOM*. Dust and debris clouded up on the other side of the city. When Ellie returned her gaze to the woman, her and the man were gone.

Ellie knew she had every right to take their flag, but she chose not to. She made the decision to not play by the generals' rules. To win this trial with honor. It may have been a foolish decision, but it was what felt right in the moment.

"Back in formation." Ellie's team did as she instructed.

They continued down the narrow street. She was right. The farther they got away from the wall, the fewer teams they saw. The homes along the road were more destroyed and burnt than the buildings closer to the wall. An arbitrator would have a difficult time finding a stable perch to fire an arrow from here.

"Keep your eyes peeled," she instructed, keeping her own sight on the dirt ground as the woman had warned.

"Do you really think they would hide a flag this far out?" Kal questioned.

Before Ellie could answer, a small gleam from the ground caught her eye. She held out her hand, signaling the group to stop. She cautiously stepped closer. Her eyes followed a thin wire buried slightly under the loose dirt. The end to her left was tied taut around a small metal post that had been nailed deep into the ground. It was hidden underneath decaying porch steps of what would have been a beautiful home. To her right and directly across from the post, the wire led to a small box stuck carefully between two decaying boards of another home. She assumed this box was what caused the boom earlier. The explosion itself would be mostly harmless, but the chain reaction that could occur from its blow would be incredibly dangerous.

"If there weren't flags this far out, there wouldn't be traps like this one," Ellie stated. "Watch your step. Even the slightest bit of extra pressure to this wire could cause the box to blow." Ellie carefully stepped over the wire. Her team followed suit.

"Falling and flying debris from these homes could seriously injure and possibly kill," Belig signed with concern.

"If they're wanting to build up an army, why would they put our lives at risk?" Myer questioned.

"They're trying to win a war. They can't do that with weak, unskilled men," Kal sneered. It took everything in Ellie not to whip around with a snide remark.

"If they wanted to win the war by now, they should have started recruiting women years ago." Kiarhem smirked. "We get shit done."

Myer's deep laugh filled the air. "She's not wrong."

He winked at Kiarhem, who was now the deepest shade of red.

"Shh. Keep your voices down and focus," Ellie instructed. From the corner of her right eye, Ellie saw a figure move swiftly from behind one house to another. "Kiarhem, keep an eye out for any flags," she whispered, keeping her gaze to the right.

They continued on in silence, walking through multiple different streets and stepping over just a few more wires along their way. No one in Ellie's group noticed that they were being followed, but she could feel, hear, and some-times see the man tailing slightly behind them. That was, until they turned down one final city road. The following footsteps ceased, and she could no longer feel his presence.

The road they now walked down opened up to a grass clearing. Ellie knew the small clearing would lay just ahead of an overgrown path. The same path that Ellie saw on her way into the city. The one that would lead to the cursed home. Ellie also remembered the wall of trees that would be waiting just beyond the clearing and path, perfect for any arbitrator to perch from. Perfect for whoever it was that followed them to this side of the city.

They reached the last home at the end of the road, small and held together with blackened wood and crumbling stone. When another loud boom echoed through the air, Ellie turned around to see dust and debris cloud up from the east side of the city. She turned back around just in time to see Myer step on a barely visible wire. She heard the faint click from the hidden box.

"RUN!" she yelled, sprinting and then tackling both Myer and Belig into the tall, dry grass of the clearing. She covered her head as the loud boom led to splintered wood, shards of glass, and crumbled stone falling all around them. None of them dared move until the sounds of the now collapsed home ceased. When Ellie no longer heard movement, she slowly sat up. Dust and debris rolled off her back.

"Is everyone okay?" she called out. Belig and Myer sat up on either side of her. Their hair and faces were covered in dirt and rubble. Ellie was sure she, too, was covered in the same way.

"We're good," Myer voiced for him and Belig. "Sorry." He avoided any eye contact with her.

"I'm fine." Kiarhem popped up just an arm's length below her.

"I'm fine too," Kal called from next to Kia. She brushed off dust from Kal's hair, and Ellie was surprised he allowed the gesture from the young elf. He even sort of smiled at Kia in thanks.

Ellie assessed the damage. The house was thankfully small, and most of the collapse and flying debris went inward instead of out into the street. Ellie whispered a prayer of gratitude to the gods.

"What now?" Kiarhem gestured to the field they now sat in. Ellie looked around. The dry grass was at least knee high —a perfect place to hide both flags and traps. She then looked beyond the clearing. She could see the wall of trees and the overgrown path up ahead. She also knew if they continued northeast, they would hit the road that led out of the city. Escaping now was tempting, but Ellie knew it was not the time, and the road was most likely guarded by officers. She stood, getting a better view of her surroundings. After a bit of scanning, something caught her eye. A dark, rectangular piece of cloth dangled from a low tree branch.

"Hey. What do you see?" Ellie called to her group, pointing towards the tree line.

"A flag!" Myer voiced his excitement.

"Back in formation. This grass is tall and thick, so stay

alert. Belig, Myer, keep your eyes on the trees. There's an arbitrator that has been following us since the city center. If he's going to make a move, this will be the place. Let's go."

She grabbed a handful of rocks and fallen stones and pocketed them. Every few steps, she would throw a few at the path ahead, ensuring that it was safe to step through. There were a couple more combustion boxes hidden in the grass. As her rocks hit one, dirt would fly. The team would duck down each time, but they would stand back up with nary a mark. The closer they got to the tree line, the closer they got to the overgrown path. Ellie's pendant began to freeze beneath her blouse, either warning her or calling her to the home. She was not sure which.

When they stepped out of the grass and onto the path, she didn't dare look down at the abandoned house. She kept her eyes on the trees and the flag that hung just a few feet ahead. She heard the snapping of a bow moments before Belig jumped in front of her. A deep, gargled groan left his throat as an arrow stuck deep within his right shoulder. He tried to point towards where the arrow came from, but pain kept his movement limited.

"GET DOWN!" Ellie yelled, running ahead and away from the group to keep them safe.

She scanned the trees, quickly searching for the arbitrator. She saw slight movement from the corner of her eye. In one smooth movement, she turned and threw a dagger at the same moment the officer loosened an arrow towards her face. She followed through with her throw, twirling and dodging, letting the arrow stick in the dirt behind her. A loud holler and the tumbling of a bow came down from the tree above her. Her dagger had met its mark.

"You bitch!" he yelled from his perch. "I'll have you hanged in the courtyard for this!" he yelled again. Ellie picked up the arrow that sunk deep into the earth. She examined the head. It was not dulled. No, it was sharpened and ready to kill. She placed the arrow in the now empty garter slot.

"I'm pretty sure these arrowheads are supposed to be dulled. Anyways, I'd like my dagger back when you're done with it. I'll be waiting in the courtyard," she spit back.

"Kia! Get the flag!" she sternly yelled back at her group. She saw the blur that was the young elf grab the flag, and then she sprinted back to the group. Ellie stepped forward, grabbing the bow that lay on the ground. With intense force towards her knee, she snapped the weapon in two. She threw the broken bow to the ground, and with that, she turned back towards her team.

Myer stood with Belig's good arm propped around his neck. Kal looked at Belig, his face pale at the sight of the arrow protruding through the elder man's shoulder and back.

Ellie placed a gentle hand near the wound, examining it. It was too deep to try and pull out. "I'm going to need to snap the end and sling your arm. You're going to be fine, Belig, but I need to do this quickly so we're not standing out in the open like this for long."

She stared directly into the man's kind eyes. He nodded his understanding.

"Kal." He whipped his gaze away from Belig. His golden eyes were wide and full of fear. He looked so young, too young to be a part of these horrors. "Keep an eye on that arbitrator. His shoulder is most likely still pinned to the tree, but just in case he makes his way down before we leave, let me know." Kal nodded and took position behind her. He watched her back without hesitation.

"Alright, Belig, on the count of three." Ellie grabbed the

end of the arrow tightly. This was something her grandfather taught her, but she hoped she would never have to do it.

"One. Two." She snapped the wood sticking out of the man's shoulder. He released another deep groan.

"I'm sorry," she whispered with a grimace.

She took a dagger from her vambrace, untucked her blouse, and cut off a large section, revealing her torso and the scar she earned in the last trial. She could feel the stares of Myer and Kia as she wrapped Belig's arm against his chest.

"Can you run?" she asked the elder man. He nodded firmly. "Good. Kiarhem, put the flag underneath your shirt. If at any point we get held up, you run. Don't look back, just run. Understand?"

"But—" Kiarhem began to protest.

"No one in this entire city is as fast as you, so it is your job to hand the flag over to Officer Reuel. It is your job to ensure we finish this trial." Kiarhem hesitantly nodded at Ellie's command. "Let's go. Similar formation, but Myer, help Belig if he needs it." Myer nodded in reply.

They began their run back to the castle courtyard. They went the same way that they came, stepping carefully over blasted dirt mounds, through the wreckage of the small house, and back over each invisible wire. Ellie had made mental notes of where each one was placed for both now and later ventures.

As they once again got closer to the city center, the yelling of designates rang through her ears. They turned the final corner out of the small street and entered what Ellie viewed as a vague warzone. Swords were swinging, punches were thrown, and men were tackling other men. Flags were being ripped from hands and brutally fought over. Ellie stopped her group.

"New plan. We're going to split up," Ellie voiced. "We will look less threatening in lower numbers. Myer, get Belig to the witches. Kal, you and I will flank Kiarhem from either side. We will not take a direct path to the wall or sprint too quickly. Both would indicate what we currently possess, so listen closely for my directions. Kiarhem, if Kal and I get held up in any way, that is your cue to run. Is that clear?"

They're firm understandings echoed around her. She nodded the two men off, and they made their way southeast. Kal took his position on Kiarhem's right. He pulled out the short sword that had hung from his left hip. Ellie did the same with her blue-silver sword, twirling it a few times in her hand.

Kal looked at her with understanding in his eyes. "Sorry. I've been a prick."

"Most men twice your age wouldn't own up to that, Kal." The corner of her mouth rose. "I accept your apology. Let's go."

They ran towards the southwest side of the city, passing scuffling men and the same trees and buildings they ran through at the beginning of the trial. Dull arrows continued to rain down from the tops of the trees. A few hit her leather pants and the straps of her back harness, only leaving what would be some impressive bruising. They finally got within viewing distance of the wall.

"East!" she yelled to her young partners. They glided alongside her as they each turned and now ran east. They're ability to stay together at one speed was quite impressive. Even more impressive was Kal. He used his sword to block and hit any arrow that meant to hit him or Kiarhem. His reflexes were like none Ellie had ever seen before.

They now ran with the wall directly to their right. The entrance road to the castle was filled with brutish teams fighting their way to the arbitrators that stood guard at the castle entrance. Ellie saw a man make his way through the chaos, waving his red flag at the arbitrators. They quickly made an opening for him before closing off the few men that trailed behind, weapons and fists viciously waving in his direction. A couple of his teammates made their way through the entrance a few moments later.

"We're going to have to fight," Ellie voiced through ragged breath. "Kiarhem. We'll get you as close to the entrance as we can. Keep the flag hidden until you reach those arbitrators. Kal, you and I need to make it look like we, too, are fighting for a flag that one of those designates may have. We need to keep all of those men's attention on us."

"How?" Kal asked.

"We have some fun." She smiled at him wickedly. "Continue running east, but let's get closer to the wall with each step." They began running diagonally towards the wall.

Just a few feet from the chaotic gravel road, Ellie yelled, "HE'S GOT A FLAG!"

She looked at Kal and pointed to a random man farther down the road, away from the front entrance. The sounds of *"Go," "Get him,"* and *"Argh"* echoed through the street.

Ellie gave Kiarhem a nod, signaling her to run. She was gone in a flash.

"Let's go." She smiled at Kal, and they ran side by side towards the disarray that she caused.

"THAT FLAG IS OURS!" she yelled, really driving her act home. She sliced through the calves of men, evaded attacks, and crashed the hilt of her sword against the temples of some. She realized that no one really knew what man she pointed at or who she claimed to have a flag. They were all just aimlessly fighting. Ellie almost received an elbow to the face when a blood-curdling scream rang through the air. She dodged the elbow and sent her attacker down with one blow to the nose.

She looked around for Kal. He was successfully fighting a man twice his size, when he too heard the scream.

"GO!" he yelled at her. She didn't hesitate. Ellie knew that scream belonged to Kiarhem. Her heart raced as her entire body filled with fear and anger.

She ran towards the gate, easily evading and taking down any man or woman that approached her. She broke through the tussling crowd to see Kiarhem inches from the wall of arbitrators. She was curled into a ball on the ground. Two men viciously kicked her from behind as one pulled at her arms. Arms that held tightly to their flag.

Something inside Ellie shattered.

A cold, brutal calm took over as her rage washed over her. She sheathed her sword and loosened two daggers from each of her vambraces. She ran towards the heartbreaking scene, releasing the two daggers in her hand. They met their marks in the legs of each man that was kicking Kiarhem. Their screams pulled at a dark delight in Ellie's gut.

The man that pulled on Kia's arms turned. His eyes met her icy stare and his face turned white at the sight of it. He held up his trembling hands in submission.

"It's all yours!" he choked out.

She didn't reply. She held his stare, lips curling into a vicious smile.

"Please, I—"

Her elbow made contact with his cheek, then her fist with his gut. Her leg then swooped his own out from under him. She followed him down with a hand grasped tightly around his neck. He fell, choking and clawing for air. Air that her hand kept him from receiving.

"*Do not ever come near her again,*" she snarled.

The man nodded his head as fear for his life shook through his body. She brought one final blow to his temple, knocking him out. Ellie stood to see the wide eyes of every arbitrator that stood blocking the castle entrance. She revelled in their terror. Ignoring their stares, she bent down and picked up the young elf, cradling her in her arms. Kiarhem's tear-stained face looked up at her.

"You're safe," Ellie whispered.

The young elf closed her eyes, letting her body go limp. The tether that was holding on to Ellie's anger was fraying. Once snapped, she knew she would kill. She walked over to the two whimpering men. They scrambled back, avoiding her deathly glare.

"If she does not make a full recovery, I will take those daggers and slowly gut you from end to end." It wasn't a threat. It was a promise.

"Ellie." Kal softly spoke from behind her. "Let's go."

His tone was gentle, yet urgent. She had not noticed his presence and wondered how much he had seen. Ellie slowly turned away from the terrified men and headed for the wall of officers. The arbitrators did not hesitate to let the three of them in. They had their flag, and her trial was over.

36

A uden intently watched the castle entrance. Myer had dragged a wounded Belig through the shadowed archway just moments ago. An arbitrator had made another attempt on Ellienia's life, most likely following the orders of General Dolion.

Nate and his team had emerged from the shadowed archway sometime ago, but she still had yet to return. Team after team ran their flags in, leaving very few left in the city beyond the wall. A scream of excruciating pain sent Auden's mind into a panic. He hoped and prayed to the gods that it was not Ellienia.

"She'll be fine," Nate voiced to his left. Auden knew the statement was not meant just for him. He could see the worry on Nate's face. The tension in his arms and shoulders. It took everything in Auden to not display the same feelings. Something too deep in the shadows of the archway caused commotion among the witches. They emerged from their shadows yelling urgent demands.

"Where's Layla!"

"She will only let Layla near her!"

"Find her now!" multiple witches commanded. Auden released a breath of relief as he saw the young woman emerge from the scrambling of witches. His relief was short-lived as he noticed the limp elf she held in her arms. Both he and Nate ran towards them. As they got closer, he noticed the hard, icy expression on Ellienia's face. The rage in her eyes alone would send any sane person running. It was no wonder the witches listened to her demands for Layla.

"Here's your flag," she snarled at him. He clenched his jaw, keeping his hurt and worry for her at bay. He carefully grabbed the flag that Kiarhem still barely clung to. Kal stood behind Ellienia. His face was filled with awe, respect, and a bit of fear for his group leader.

"Where is she?" Layla's voice shouted from behind him. Auden turned to see Layla and five other young witches headed their way. Ellienia passed between him and Nate, handing the young elf off to the capable hands of their witch friend.

"I only saw her back being kicked and beaten. I do not know if she endured any other wounds before I arrived." Ellienia spoke quickly. Her words were short and filled with irate worry. The witch simply nodded and headed towards the Great Hall.

"What happened? Why were you not with her?" Nate asked.

Auden was unaware if Nate knew how condemning his tone was. He braced himself for the rage that Ellienia was sure to throw his way.

She whipped around. Her icy glare sent shivers down Auden's spine. He was impressed that Nate was able to stand his ground and not flinch at the fury in her eyes.

"I made a choice that I felt was the best one at the time.

Clearly, I was wrong. I do not need you to point it out to me," she spit back. Her hands clenched at her side.

"El, I didn't—" Nate's words were interrupted by a deep and poisonous tone.

"Miss Batair."

Auden turned to see the dark towering figure to his left. General Dolion sneered down at Ellienia. "We have a bit of an issue. It seems you attacked and injured an officer during your trial, which is means for immediate disqualification and severe punishment." He purred out the last few words of his sentence. "I'll need you to come with me."

"She only did so in defense, general." Auden stepped between Ellienia and the large beast.

"She will have her opportunity to state her case in front of the other generals," Dolion remarked. The generals had the taste and desire for cruel punishment. If they already deemed Ellienia guilty, there would be no changing their minds. At least not without hard evidence.

"Then I will accompany her. As my designate, I am responsible for her actions." Auden spoke with confidence. He would not let these brutes harm her, even if it meant taking on the punishment himself.

"You will do no such thing. The trial has yet to end, and—"

The castle bells rang. One final group ran through the shadowed archway, their flag waving in the air. The trial was over.

"I can watch over group twenty-four." Shea appeared from nowhere. The redheaded man had a way of making his presence known whenever Auden needed him. General Dolion looked furiously at the two arbitrators.

"Fine," he growled. "You may accompany Miss Batair, but she will be the one to answer for her crimes. And as her appointed officer, you will watch silently as she receives her just punishment."

Auden's heart sank into his stomach. He turned to see Ellienia's icy glare replaced by a flat, unreadable expression. General Dolion walked off, not waiting to see if the two of them followed.

"El...I'm sorry. I—"

"Go watch after Kiarhem. I'll be there soon," Ellienia flatly instructed Nate before they both quickly caught up to the general.

He led them through the crowd of bloody and bruised designates. Auden couldn't help but notice the eyes that followed as he and Ellienia walked by. Their stares were usually filled with awe and infatuation towards the young, gifted female, but Auden could see they were now filled with confusion and worry. Being escorted by a general was never a good thing.

Auden looked over at Ellienia. She walked straight, with confidence and strength. Not an inkling of fear showed on her beautiful face. He noticed her right arm stayed directly next to her right thigh, over her garter of daggers. He prayed she would not attempt an attack, but Auden never knew what to expect from Ellienia.

They walked up towards a small wooden door at the far east side of the castle wall. General Dolion pushed the door open, leaving it ajar for both to enter behind him. They climbed up stone steps that twisted and turned in the way Auden knew could make one dizzy. He went to grab for her arm in the dimly-lit stairwell, but she discreetly dodged his touch. She then walked ahead, keeping herself at least two steps above him. Once they reached the top of the stairs, Dolion pushed open another wooden door. One that opened to the top of the castle wall that was lined with the remaining twenty-nine generals that were stationed in Malavor under the Eternal Queen's orders.

They all turned to face the three figures that emerged from the dark stairwell. Auden's heart began to race. In all his time in Malavor and among the Queen's ranks, he had never been in front of so many generals at once. A strange, cold dread crawled up his spine.

Each general towered over him by at least two feet. All of their eyes were filled with the same evil darkness, and their faces were a mix of scars and black facial hair. They gathered around them, each getting a good look at Ellienia. From the middle of the crowd came a pale, blonde-haired arbitrator. Auden knew the young, irritating man to be Officer Trudge. He held his limp arm, as Ellienia's silver dagger still protruded from his left shoulder.

"Is this the designate who attacked you, Officer Trudge?" He nodded in reply to Dolion's question.

"I was hidden in a tree and shot arrows down at her team as instructed, sir." He stared viciously at Ellienia, who returned his glare with a vengeful smile. "Look! Even now she smirks at her work."

"I smile because you know of the proof I have against your accusations." She spoke back coolly.

In one quick smooth motion, Ellienia removed the item she kept hidden in her right garter. Without hesitation or warning, she threw it at Trudge.

It all happened so quickly, the generals barely had time to react. They each drew their large swords but resheathed them at the sight of one glistening sharp arrow that planted itself in the stone at Trudge's feet.

"I assume all arbitrators were ordered to use dull, mostly harmless arrows. However, the head of this arrow, the arrow you shot and missed with, is quite sharp."

Auden could see the anger rising in General Dolion's face as his fellow men discussed the new evidence in hushed, deep whispers.

"Why should we believe this designate over one of our own officers? She could have easily picked up one of these arrows from the armory," Dolion interjected.

"That could be true." She kept her venomous stare on the officer. "Except one of my teammates took on the first arrow shot by Officer Trudge. He is now in the Great Hall waiting to have the arrow removed from his upper chest. I assure you, the arrow stuck in him is a match to the one that lays at Officer Trudge's feet. My actions were made in defense of my and my team's lives. Nothing more."

Ellienia spoke with authority and power. Auden thought she was done, but she opened her mouth to speak once more.

"I understand that more than a few of you view me as a threat. I also understand the rest of you view me as a weapon. At this point, I have proven my skill, strength, and leadership. I am here to serve in the Eternal Queen's Army and nothing more. If I wanted you dead, your bodies would already be hanging from the crenels of this wall." She sneered at each of the generals, her eyes filled with a cruel darkness that terrified Auden.

The air went silent at Ellienia's threat. Every muscle in Auden's body tensed. He didn't move or dare to react at all to her words. The sound of his thundering heartbeat was interrupted by the deep rumble of...*laughter*.

General Polage stepped forward from his spot across from Ellienia. "This is why I like her!" His deep voice boomed. "She threatens us as effortlessly as we threaten each other! And that display you made against those three men at the castle entrance! Beautiful! You will fit in well among our ranks, girl." He gave Ellienia an evil, green-toothed smile. "Who is the man that took on an arrow?"

"Belig Smeh, sir," Auden answered for her.

General Polage snapped his fingers. Officer Ames appeared from directly behind his shadow, hidden effortlessly behind the mass of the dark general. He looked at Ellienia with a playful sneer—one that Auden wished his ally would stop doing.

"Go and confirm Miss Batair's story," Polage commanded. Ames ran off without hesitation. "Officer Trudge, your orders today were to injure and allow the designates to tear each other apart. If it is revealed that you used unauthorized arrows in today's trial, you will endure a traitor's punishment. Either way, we get to kill someone today."

Polage smirked down at a wide-eyed Trudge. He frantically looked to General Dolion and a few other generals, who all looked back with clenched, murder-filled gazes.

"But, I—" His face begged for a rescue that would never come. "General Dolion—he—"

"Gave you the same orders, *officer*," Dolion growled out. "Any actions you made to harm Miss Batair were of your own doing. It makes sense, really. You've had it out for Miss Batair since she showed off her swordsmanship in the courtyard. You constantly mock and confuse her skill and comprehension for arrogance. Such a shame, Officer Trudge. I had viewed you as one of the good ones."

"But...No! I was doing what I was told!" Tears escaped Trudge's panic-ridden eyes.

"You will have to deal with these lies in front of your gods." Dolion whipped out his flare baton. Two other generals swooped in to hold Trudge in place. He kicked and screamed for help. Auden could see Ellienia look at the terrified man with no emotion on her own face.

"PLEASE! I DID WHAT I WAS TOLD! I DID WHAT I WAS—" Trudge's silent scream filled the air. Dolion had placed the baton directly on the man's heart. The mark would instantly kill him.

"It would seem we don't need to confirm your story, Miss Batair. You are free to go." Polage grinned in delight at Trudge's motionless body. Ellienia stepped forward, towards the deceased man. Her path was blocked by Dolion. She mockingly smiled up at the general.

"I told the man I wanted my dagger back when he was done with it. I think it's safe to say he's done." Her face filled with a wicked amusement Auden had never seen before. She stepped around and pulled her dagger from the man's stiff shoulder.

Polage's deep laugh filled the air once more. She held her bloody knife and winked at the general, really convincing him of her act. Her cruel careless sneer nearly had Auden believing as well. She wouldn't make eye contact with him as she led their way back through the wooden doorway, wiping her dagger on her already ripped and ruined shirt.

"re you alright?" Auden timidly whispered as they made their way down the winding steps to the courtyard.

Ellie didn't answer. She wasn't sure how.

In rescuing Kiarhem, she let a lot of her anger free in a way she had never done before. It was blind rage that fully consumed her.

It terrified her. More than the sudden appearance of General Dolion.

The moment the general arrived, Ellie remembered her grandfather's lessons on masking.

"At some point, you may have to become someone else. You may have to emanate a completely different person than who you truly are. You must put on a metaphorical mask and become that person."

It was one of her favorite lessons. She excelled at it when put to practice against her sisters. She even, reluctantly, had made Maisie cry once.

Today, she had gambled on the generals reacting better

to a cruel, powerful demeanor than the pleading, gentle approach she wanted to take. Ellie felt as if she'd lost herself on the battlefield, and again on the top of the wall. She now struggled to remove the mask she had placed. She struggled to find a piece of herself as she walked down the winding steps.

She had dug deep into the darkest parts of herself, and the act she portrayed was almost too easy for her. She enjoyed seeing the arbitrator that hurt her friend be killed, and she hated herself for feeling that way.

She clenched her fist tightly around her dagger, not feeling safe enough to sheath it yet. Her speed quickened down the stone steps. Auden followed close behind. She appreciated his presence, but she wished he had never seen that side of her.

A wave of overwhelming guilt washed over her: for Belig, for Kiarhem, and for the darkness she had to call upon. Everything bad that had happened the last few weeks had been her fault. Her grandfather sent her here because he felt she was the most equipped.

He was wrong, she thought. *All I've done is hurt the friends and allies I have obtained. If I can't protect them, I am a failure to this mission.*

Her thoughts had her head spinning. She wanted to crash into the stone beneath her feet. She wanted to scream and cry out in her emotional torment. She almost did until a gentle, firm hand wrapped around her wrist, stopping her downward descent both physically and emotionally.

"Ellienia," Auden whispered, turning her around to face him. Her eyes blurred from the growing tears.

He placed his free hand on her wet cheek. "You are not alone, and you are not at fault for today's events. Belig jumped in front of what should have been a dulled arrow.

You sent the fastest member of your team ahead, the same strategic decision I would have made. And you just became someone you had to for your own safety. If you remember, I, too, had to become someone...darker to do something dark."

Auden referred to his dealings with Filtmon. His words were like a soothing salve to her wounded heart. She ran a dry sleeve over her damp face.

"Even though I know the pain of those flare batons and wouldn't wish that onto my worst enemy, I still...I felt satisfaction seeing Trudge killed for what he did to Belig and for trying to kill me." She didn't know why she admitted this to Auden, but to her surprise, he nodded in agreement.

"I felt the same satisfaction in Filtmon's death. I took no pleasure in ending a man's life, and for days I felt guilt from it. When I realized my satisfaction came from the fact that he could no longer hurt you and you were safer with him gone, I felt less guilty about the actions I had to take." Ellie nodded, thankful for Auden's understanding. She began to voice her appreciation when the sound of voices and footsteps descended from above them. "We should head to the Great Hall."

She turned in agreement, and they continued their quick pace down the winding steps.

Kiarhem lay motionless on a cot near the back door of the Great Hall. Ellie and Auden stood watching as Layla worked diligently with herbs, tonics, and salves. Upon their arrival to the Great Hall, Auden had ordered Nate and a few of the others to join the rest of their friends at Belig's cot. Belig was in high spirits and enjoyed the unnecessary company.

"She has two broken ribs and some internal bleeding.

She will be fine, but she will need constant monitoring for the next week." Layla placed a final salve onto Kiarhem's chest before looking up at Ellie with tired eyes. "I know you may not like this, but I highly suggest she comes to stay in my quarters for that time. I share a room with five other witches that are completely trustworthy. They can help me watch over and heal her."

Ellie contemplated Layla's request. She knew Layla was right. Kiarhem needed the best care possible, and that would not happen in the tent. However, Ellie still didn't know who was trying to poison her, and after what happened to Myer, she wasn't keen on letting another one of her friends near the possible killer.

"I trust *you*, Layla, but I do not know if I can trust the other witches you speak of. Not when someone is out there trying to harm me or anyone else I may be in alliance with. I will agree to letting Kiarhem stay in your care if you allow two of my allies to come and watch over her as well. They will rotate their watch, so none grow too weary."

"Convincing any of the Mothers to allow a man into our quarters may prove to be difficult, especially allowing them to come at night."

"I'll take care of it." Auden spoke from his place behind Ellie. "The Mothers have to listen to an officer's order, and I hold quite a bit of persuasion among these women." He sent a wink towards Layla.

"Fine. Who will you send tonight?" she asked Ellie.

"Collern and Keir." Ellie lowered her voice and leaned over closer to Layla. "Once they are in place, you will need to meet us at the tent. We need you to shadow cloak us out into the city."

"Why?" she questioned with a furrowed brow. Ellie bit

the inside of her lip. She knew Layla wasn't going to like the next thing to come from her mouth.

"We're going to the cursed house."

"Like hell you are!" Layla's voice carried in the large room. A few eyes nearby glanced their way. Nate's gaze was the only one to remain fixed on the two women's conversation.

"Shh!" Ellie shot a vile glare at her friend. "Look. We're going to that house with or without you. You can either join us and give us the added protection of your cloaking, or you can stay behind and we have a higher chance of getting caught."

"Guilting me? Really?" The two women glared at one another. They stood there for a moment, neither one daring to break eye contact. Until Layla flared her nostrils and finally blinked away her stubbornness.

"Fine," she growled. "I'll take you, but I will not go near that house. If you want to get yourselves killed, that's your choice." She snapped her fingers and two witches appeared —a familiar one with strawberry-red hair, and one with raven-black. A twin to Layla's. "Take the young elf to our quarters. She will be in our care for the next week."

They nodded, but before they lifted the young elf, the familiar witch held something before Ellie. "I pulled these from two rather fragile men."

The gleam to the witch's smile was almost as bright as the silver daggers she held. Ellie's daggers.

She took the blades, remembering the witch's name and her love of late-night sweet rolls. "Thank you, Hannabella."

Her eyes lit up at Ellie's knowledge of her name. Ellie turned her attention to Kia, and she leaned down and placed a kiss upon the young elf's brow.

"I'm sorry," she whispered before Kiarhem was whisked away.

"You better have a solid plan for tonight," Layla warned.

"Don't worry. We will."

38

Nate sat on his mat resisting the urge to grovel at El's feet.

Their group spent the rest of the late afternoon and early evening in the quiet tent. Auden, El, and Nate were divulging and working out a plan.

Nate had found no way to the house from the far west side of the city. Traps and other teams had made it impossible for him to skirt the west side and head north to the house. Going through the center of the city, as El had done earlier that day, would be the safest path.

She mapped out their direction on a spare piece of parchment. There were a total of eight explosive boxes that they would have to pass among the old abandoned houses, and they would just have to hope no more were placed for the trials that would happen the following day.

"Arbitrators should be done placing flags for tomorrow's trial before midnight. I will inform Layla of our intent to go after that," Auden stated.

"And if we make it through the city unseen, what then?" Nate asked, his voice stern and filled with cynicism. "If the stories are to be trusted, we won't get two feet near that house without wanting to off ourselves."

"Don't worry about the curse. I know how to take care of it. I'll just need each of you to trust me. Can you do that?" Auden looked directly at him when asking his question. He didn't want to hate the guy, but he clearly had strong feelings for El, and Nate was beginning to think...

No.

He *knew* she had feelings for him too. She may not even realize it yet, but she looks at Auden in the way Nate always wanted her to look at him. Nate at least knew Auden would never harm El, which made his agreement to trust him easy. He nodded his head once.

With their plan made, Auden returned to his mat at the front of the tent to get some much-needed rest. El and Nate lay down to do the same.

"I am sorry for my reaction earlier today. You are not to blame for what happened to Kia," Nate whispered towards El. Her back faced him. "Please, El. Talk to me."

She didn't move. Auden had pulled him aside earlier in the Great Hall. He had told him what happened in the city, and then on the top of the wall. El's trial was much harder than his, and he knew he would not have survived it or the meeting among the generals.

"I'm proud of you," she whispered, her words hitting him like a strong wave. It both shocked and confused him.

"What?" was the only word he could think of in reply.

"I'm proud of you." She finally turned around to face him. The crystal-blue eyes that stared back at him were filled with exhaustion. "You led well today. You were one of the only teams to return with little to no bruising."

"My teammates' lack of injuries does not make me a good leader." Nate's guilt grew in the pit of his stomach. He had questioned her ability to lead, and now, here she was, complimenting him.

"No, but their willingness to trust and listen to you shows that you are a leader, Nate. They stayed at the wall after the starting bells, which I assume was your order." He nodded. "Then I assume they continued to listen to your guidance through the rest of today's trial."

She was correct. Everyone in his group had freely appointed him as their leader, even Doal, to his surprise. They all listened to him without hesitation or question through the entire trial. He had never been put in that type of position, but he more than thrived under the pressure of it all. However, when faced with a difficult decision, he asked himself what El would have done.

"I would not have known how to lead them if it had not been for your guidance and training over all these years. Thank you."

She smiled in return and placed a heavy hand on his. "Let's get some rest. I'm sure we will need it."

She went to close her eyes, but Nate grabbed her attention once more. "I haven't had the opportunity to tell you yet today, but happy birthday. I'm really glad the fates allowed you to be born, El."

She scoffed but held his hand even tighter. "I'm not sure I feel the same, but thank you. What do I get for this gratitude towards my life?"

She looked at him with eyes that sent his stomach straight to his throat.

"Hopefully, tonight, you get answers." Nate reluctantly let go of her hand to dig in his pocket. "And this." He held out intricately woven white flowers, formed into a bracelet. "Layla picked them for me. I know it won't last long, but you deserve at least one gift for your birthday." He slid the bracelet onto her wrist. "I love you, El"

She brushed tears from her cheeks. "Thank you, Nate."

Ellie woke up to the light sound of raindrops hitting the roof of their tent. Her hand was still lightly intertwined with a sleeping Nate, and the flowers that had encased her wrist had already wilted and broken away. She slowly sat up and waited for her eyes to adjust to the darkness around her. A small lantern had been lit and hung from the center post of the tent. Once adjusted, Ellie's eyes could see all of group twenty-four asleep on their mats. All except Collern and Keir.

"It's almost time," Auden whispered as he sat at the end of her mat. "Is there a cloak in the sack of clothes Layla gave you?" Ellie nodded. "Good. The rain will most likely get worse while we're out there. We're going to get wet and cold, but it will add an extra bit of coverage from our own sound."

Ellie never minded rain. Actually, she loved it. Its cooling touch, fresh smell, and calming sound soothed her more than anything else in the world. This was the first rainfall since being in Malavor, and she couldn't wait to be out in it.

"Should you wake him, or should I?" Auden pointed at a lightly-snoring Nate.

"I got it. Is Layla here?" Ellie asked as she gently shook Nate's shoulders.

"Unfortunately, yes," Layla grumbled quietly from the shadows behind her. "I still strongly advise against this."

"We know." Nate sat up. His hair was knotted and sticking up in all different directions. Layla reached a hand out of the shadows and attempted to brush it through Nate's mangled locks. "Stop!" he whispered, batting her hand away.

Ellie couldn't help but laugh at the exchange. She was thankful for the current friends that surrounded her, but her heart twisted for the friend that was missing.

She grabbed the cloak from the sack and swung it around herself. She placed daggers and her sword in their rightful holsters then grabbed her emptied bag for the book she planned to bring back.

"Let's go."

39

The fresh rain that dripped onto Ellie's face was like water for her soul. It soaked through her cloak and into the mostly-healed wounds on her back. The feel of its cool touch was life-giving. The others didn't seem to feel the same way. Layla huffed and grumbled as she led their way on the west side of the castle. They could barely see the massive castle to their right and kept their hands on its smooth stone to help guide their way. The rain clouds gave them full coverage, blanketing the night air in complete darkness. Hiding in the shadows was the easiest it had ever been. Behind Ellie, she could hear the chattering teeth of a freezing Nate. She could feel both his and Auden's misery. They reached the end of the castle and stopped at Layla's command.

"There is little to no coverage through the courtyard. We will be out in the open from here to the entrance of the city. I can still shadow cloak us with how dark it is, but there are about twenty witches hiding and waiting at the entrance. So, what's your plan?" Layla's words were laced with annoyance and anger.

"Just wait," Auden commanded. A moment later, a man holding a small, lit lantern descended the front steps of the castle. "Officer Shea will lead our way. Stay out of the light of his lantern and we'll be good." Layla growled but did as Auden instructed. They walked in a straight line behind the redheaded officer.

"Are you all back there?" Shea mumbled behind them.

"Yes," Auden answered in return.

"I'm surprised, Officer Shea. I thought you would be against us going to the cursed house," Ellie voiced, remembering the warning he gave her weeks ago.

"I am." His voice was deep and easy to hear over the large drops of rain. "But if what Officer Reuel has told me is true, then his plan to break the curse will work. It has to."

What plan? What did Auden tell him? Ellie desperately wished she knew what Auden was hiding, especially since she had just recently agreed to include Auden in any of her plans going forward. She understood there were still things he could not tell her, that this plan involved those things. She wanted to know all the information he was being forced to keep from her. She even more wanted to know who made Auden take the magical vow.

They made their way down the center of the large courtyard. Ellie thanked the gods that there was no lightning to accompany the rain. One strike and they would be revealed.

When close to the entrance, Shea stopped and waved a discrete hand behind him. They followed his signal and made their way towards the cold stone wall. They placed their backs against it and waited to see how Shea lured out the witches that hid beyond the dark archway.

"Hello? Is there a witch that could possibly help me?" Shea called out towards the archway. Seconds later, an elder witch emerged from the darkness.

"What is it you need, Officer Shea?" The elder witch's voice was rough, but not unkind.

"Mother Paya." Shea bowed his head in respect. The woman smiled in appreciation. "I wasn't sure who to get since the kitchen witches are in their quarters, and I felt it inappropriate to disturb them there. But this onset of rain has caused a leak or a pipe to burst, and the kitchen is now quite flooded."

"What?!" Mother Paya urgently waved her hands behind her. A flood of witches ran with her towards the castle steps. Shea, too, joined the clambering of women towards the castle kitchen.

"How many witches are left in there?" Auden asked Layla.

"Five."

"Good." Ellie could see Auden's gentle smirk through the dark night air. "Go ahead."

"What? We'll get caught by the five still in there," Layla protested.

"Layla, where are your five most trusted friends and roommates? Are they in your room, inappropriately spending the night with two designates, Kier and Collern. Or did the Mothers decide it best to put the five on night watch until Kiarhem is healed and the presence of men are no longer needed?"

Ellie could feel the arrogant pride oozing off Auden. He had planned all of this, and so far, it was working. However, Layla was not pleased with his actions.

"You made a plan involving my friends...my sisters. They will now be put into danger with the lies they will each have to tell! Not only that! Kiarhem is now left in a room without a proper healer watching over her! How dare you do this without telling me first!" Her voice was becoming dangerously loud.

"Layla, you have told me that there are other witchlings that believe as you do. They believe in the power given by the goddess of magic, not the god of death. If they truly want to fight, their fight starts now. As for Kia..." Ellie's heart twisted again as Auden spoke. "Collern and Kier have been instructed on what to do if she needs immediate attention. She will be fine for the next few hours while you are away."

Ellie grabbed her friend's hand. "Please, we cannot get through this step without their willingness to help, or yours for that matter."

Layla slowly nodded and led the group into the dark archway. Five silver-lined figures stood against the left side of the entrance walls. One graceful figure stepped forward, and Ellie recognized her from her twin raven hair. They were all shadow cloaked, making every one visible to one another through their magic.

"Layla. Officer Reuel has informed us of your plan. Is it true? Are you taking them to that house?" The young witch gestured towards them.

"Yes. I don't have time to explain. I just need you to let us through and to please trust me as you have always done." Layla's voice was shaky. Ellie realized what Layla was asking of her sisters. If their plan failed and the five were caught letting them through, their punishment would be death.

Ellie would not have forced Layla into this position, and she resented Auden for doing so. To Ellie's surprise, though, the young witch didn't hesitate as she nodded and waved them through.

"For the Mother." She placed four fingers to her brow then lifted them to the sky. Layla repeated her, performing the same motion.

"Thank you," Ellie whispered to the young witch. She

stared at her for a moment, then politely nodded in reply. They made their way through the archway, which Ellie thought would be the hardest part. She was wrong. What she saw when she emerged from the dark entrance to the city crushed her.

Lights from arbitrators' and generals' tents shined just enough brightness to view the horrors in front of them. Each team that had failed the trials earlier that day stood around the trunks of the city trees. Their hands and ankles were bound to one another, their arms and legs stretched to reach the teammate next to them, and many softly groaned in pain. Ellie began to step towards the group closest to her, but Nate caught her arm, reminding her to stay in the safety of Layla's shadow cloak. Her eyes stung from the water that filled her eyes.

"*This.* This is their punishment?" she quietly growled.

"Yes," Auden softly replied.

"They could get sick in this weather. And what of their wounds? Were any of them treated before being tied up and bound like animals?"

"No," Layla voiced. "If they survive the night, we are allowed to treat them in the morning."

"This is vile." Nate stated the words they were all thinking. They began to walk down the pathway towards the city center. Ellie desperately wanted to do something to help, but there were people and trees for as far as her eyes could see in the darkness. Small balls of light floated through the crowd.

"There are arbitrators on watch, to make sure no one out here escapes. We will need to keep our distance from them," Auden instructed. It, thankfully, wasn't a problem. They made it to the center of the city with ease. Layla released them from her cloaked protection.

"There aren't any arbitrators this far out, so there's no need to be cloaked. However, there's also no light out here, making it impossible to see our path," Layla grumbled.

"And if we make too strong of a light, someone atop of the wall may see us." Auden pointed up. Sure enough, a few more lanterns floated back and forth atop the large stone wall. Ellie felt the cold pendant beneath her shirt. She remembered her night looking over Myer. She pulled it out and surged a little magic towards the pendant. It began to softly glow. She led the way without a word or question from her friends.

She took the exact path she had taken earlier that day. The lines of the combustion boxes were impossible to see, but she remembered the houses they each sat between and was able to recognize their dark forms. They walked quickly through the streets of the city, carefully stepping over eight invisible lines. They finally reached the last street that led to the open field.

"There are combustion boxes hidden among the tall grass, so step exactly where I step," she instructed the others. They did as she said and were able to easily make it through the field. They now gathered onto the overgrown path that led to the cursed house. They slowly walked towards it. Ellie could feel her pendant grow even colder. Its magic surged in response to the growing magic around them.

The small house came into view, but its details were clouded by the dark and rain. All she could see were the lines and shadows of small citrus trees encircling the sides of the building.

"Stop." Layla held out her arms in command. "Any closer and we'll all go mad."

"Are you sure?" Ellie questioned. "When the King and

the woman placed their spell, it was much closer to the house," she said, referring to the vision she had many nights ago. They were still a few yards from the house, and it was hard to view in the growing darkness.

"I'm sure. I can feel it. Feel how it was formed. This curse was made with a broken heart and deep, deep sorrow." Layla took a few steps back. Fear laced her green eyes. "Magic formed from strong emotion is the darkest and most powerful known. It is rarely taught among witches, as it can be temperamental and dangerous."

"So what now?" Nate asked, pointing his question at Auden. With a deep breath, Auden turned towards Ellie.

"When we met weeks ago, we talked about the curse around this house. Do you remember what I said about it?" Auden looked at her with kind eyes. Ellie searched her memory.

"You said the Queen had tried and failed to break the curse, because only the blood of the Fae who cast it can break it."

"Exactly." Auden softly smiled.

"So...what are you wanting me to do? Use my powers to somehow summon the past red-haired female here? Can my powers even do that?"

"No—well I don't know, but no. That's not what I'm trying to tell you. Ellienia, close your eyes." She followed his instructions. "Picture the portrait. Picture the red-haired Fae and all of her features. Do the same for the male."

She saw the beautiful couple vividly—Millie's red hair and delicate features. She saw the male's golden-blonde hair and strong jaw.

"Now replace the female with a vision of Maisie and replace the male with Cammie. What do you see?"

Ellie shot a confused glare at Auden.

"Yes, I know what your sisters look like. I saw them when I was in Perilin. Three equally stunning women are hard to miss in such a small town."

Ellie shut her lids, picturing her sisters and the couple in the portrait as Auden instructed. Ellie's heart began to race as she realized what Auden was implying. Sure enough, Ellie pictured Maisie with the same auburn hair and delicate features of Millie. Cammie had the identical hair and broad features of the male, but the eyes were switched. Cammie had the same electric green eyes as the female Fae, while Maisie's deep-blue ones were a match to the male's.

Ellie shot her watery eyes open. "They're my parents."

She spoke through broken sobs. Auden only nodded in reply. How had he known?

"Millie...my mother...she was Fae?"

"Yes."

"And my father?"

"Everything you need to know is in that house, Ellienia. Break the spell and all your questions will be answered."

"And you knew? When you saw the portrait, you knew who they were?" He nodded again. "And you know their relation to the King?"

He didn't nod this time. He, instead, just stared at her with the same look he had whenever he urgently desired to speak something he was not allowed to say.

Anger and hurt began to rise in Ellie. She hated whoever placed the horrible vow on Auden. She hated that he couldn't just speak freely with her. And most of all, she hated that it had taken her this long to realize who the two people in the portrait were.

"You've known this whole time. Known who I am...what I am." Her mother was Fae. She was Fae.

"I've known you since the day you were born." His words

were a shock to her ears. "Please, Ellienia. When we get into the house, I can tell you more."

"The blood of the Fae that cast the curse runs through my veins, so you think I can break it. That's your plan?" Ellie's voice trembled.

"Yes."

"I don't know how to cast a curse, let alone break one!" she yelled in her frustration.

"Breaking a curse that belongs to you is relatively easy compared to forming one," Layla interjected. "I hate to admit it, but it's actually a solid plan."

Ellie looked at her friend, the witch that knew too much. She had known what she was, had somehow figured it out, and also hid it from her, but without some spell keeping her from revealing the truth.

"I had my reasons, Ellie," Layla claimed as if reading her mind.

Ellie looked at a silent Nate. His expression was flat, revealing none of his possible thoughts.

She then moved towards the shadow of the house. Her house. She looked down at the path before her. The same path that she envisioned her grams and grandpa running away down. She realized the last time she saw this road, she was stuffed into the back of a carriage with her sisters. The Queen had taken so much from her, and she intended to take it back.

"Tell me what to do."

40

Auden had Ellie hold out her hands, with palms facing upwards.

"Your mom was what we call an empath Fae," Auden voiced, pulling a small dagger out of one of Ellie's vambraces.

"A what?" Ellie questioned.

"An empath. She could feel what others felt, and even change their emotions to anything she wished." Auden cut small slits into the palm of Ellie's hand. She clenched her teeth at the slight pain.

"How do you know this?" Auden didn't answer. He continued to carve a few more slits in each palm. "Right. Another thing you can't tell me. So this spell and its ability to force someone to...end things, was it part of her powers?"

"In a way, yes. She released the curse under great duress. Like Layla said, magic formed from raw emotion can be temperamental and dangerous. It takes most empaths a lifetime to master their powers. She most likely didn't mean to release a spell so...brutal." He finished his work with a small circle carved into the center of each palm. The markings looked like small suns.

Ellie breathed deeply, looking down at the blood as it slowly seeped out of her hands.

"I do not blame her if she did mean to release a curse this cruel. It has kept the Eternal Queen and her generals away for this long. It has kept the book safe for all these years."

Auden nodded his agreement. "You'll need to get as close to the house as possible, which means you'll need to remove any weapons that could be used to harm yourself."

Ellie nodded, removing all holsters and vambraces. She handed them to Nate, who looked at her with true fear in his eyes.

"I'll be fine," she assured him. "What do I do once I'm close to the house?"

"That's the difficult part." Layla stepped in. "Because the curse was formed with emotional magic, it will need to be broken in the same way. How did you summon the vision in the Great Hall and the soft light of your pendant?"

"I don't know. I just...did it."

Layla looked at her with furrowed brows. "Well, this time you'll need to force your magic out with rage, sadness, or despair. Whatever you feel is the strongest at the time, focus it on overpowering the curse. With it being your mother's creation, it should be rather easy to overcome."

"Got it," Ellie said, though she wasn't sure she actually did. She stepped towards the invisible wall of despair but was stopped by a strong hand.

"If at any moment it becomes too much, *run* back. Understand?" Auden, too, couldn't hide his fear. "I have no doubts you can do this Ellienia, but you need to be the one who believes it can be done."

She looked down, and small drops of rain splashed in the blood that pooled in her hands. This was her mother's blood. This was her home, and this curse was intended to be broken by her.

She stepped forward. A wave of sadness crept into her soul. A darkness like none she'd ever felt settled deep in her bones. A rush of whispers swirled around her, each word becoming clearer with every step she took. Her own thoughts took form into chants of her deepest worries.

Your grandpa should have chosen Cammie. All you have done is get people hurt. You can't help these people. You're worthless, scared, and your powers are useless. You can't control them. They will always control you. You will never be strong enough to do what needs to be done.

Ellie focused on getting one foot in front of the other, but she couldn't block out the despair that was beginning to take over her entire body. She allowed her ever-present anger to rise, but the emotion seemed to feed the curse. It made it stronger as disappointed faces of her family and friends flashed across her eyes.

You failed us, Camie and Maisie voiced.

I should have never chosen you. Her grandfather spoke.

You could never be as good as your sisters, Grams snarled.

We should have never trusted you. Layla and Kiarhem spoke as one.

You are unlovable. Nate and Auden's faces were the last to flash across her mind.

She fell to the ground as the weight of the curse grew heavier. A silent scream tore through her at the despair that wracked her body and soul. She clawed at the mud as every harsh statement was repeated over and over again. She felt the truth in their words.

ELLIE!

A distant voice tried to break through her anguish and torment. With an iron will, she turned her head, meeting the umber eyes she'd known for years. Nate mouthed her name again, but the sound was lost to the whispers swirling in her head.

"ELLIE!" She snapped her gaze to the voice that made it through the chaos. Auden's own body knelt in the mud. His hands were clenched at his sides, but his eyes were clear. There was a strength in his gaze. A certainty that was directed towards her. At that moment, she found the feeling she would force out with her magic. The light to drive out the darkness.

Ellie was not unlovable. The words the curse spoke were all lies, and though her emotions didn't match the logic in her head, she forced herself to focus on one thing.

Hope.

Hope for a future with no tyrant queen. Hope to be with her sisters once more. Hope for her people, and all people of Karmalo.

She closed her tear-soaked eyes and raised her bloodied hands.

She pictured Cammie's wild green eyes as they sparred, Maisie's gentle, kind smile, and the two sisters meeting her new friends. Her new family.

She pictured Nate laughing as they sparred late into the night. She pictured Auden's half smile that she both loved and hated, and his incredible Fae features. She pictured Layla and Kai and their fierce, unrelenting spirits. And she pictured Shea's familiar, kind eyes.

She could feel the curse fighting her. It questioned her right to overpower it. It burnt and ached in the fresh wounds of her palms. She forced her emotions to push back at it, willing it to bend. Forcing it to break.

Ellie continued to kneel in the mud as the voices in her head were replaced by her uneven breaths and the soft pitter-patter of the rain. The sound of splashing footsteps came just moments before three pairs of arms wrapped around her.

"You did it," Layla whispered in disbelief. "What emotion did you force back at it?" They released her from their embrace. She looked at each of them and smiled.

"Hope."

They let out a soft laugh in relief. Ellie looked down at her hands. The marks were gone and covered only by a bit of dried blood.

"The spell recognized your mother's blood, so it healed you," Auden answered her question before hearing it.

"Come on." Nate held out his hand. "Let's get you home."

41

Ellie stood, ready to face anything else this place had to throw at her. She went to take a few more steps when Layla grabbed her arm to stop her.

"I feel another spell placed around the house." She spoke quietly, as if not to spook it.

"Is it dangerous?" Auden asked.

"No. It feels like...But that wouldn't make sense..." Layla spoke quietly to herself. She turned and ran an eye over Ellie. "You need to go first."

Ellie didn't question her. With careful steps, she inched closer and closer to the house. Just a few steps from the wraparound porch, the faded blue light of the teardrop pendant glowed brighter. It revealed the beautiful eggshell home with paint chipped blue shutters and a small, splintered oak door.

Ellie stepped onto the old wood deck, and that was when she felt it. Something deep within her shattered. Her breath was stolen as the world spun around her. She fell to her knees at a weight that seemed to be lifted from her body. A pressure within her that she was so unaware of was now overwhelmingly set free.

Then the pain came. Every inch of her burned as if her skin melted and reformed over and over again. The spot in her back ached as it had when the flare baton wound was fresh. She held in every urge to scream out.

The pain ceased as quickly as it came.

"El! Ellie!" Nate placed Ellie's face between his hands. His eyes were wide and filled with panic.

"It's been freed." Layla gasped. Her eyes were not on the panting girl on the deck before her, but on the sky.

"Ellienia." Auden softly spoke from behind her. "Look around you."

She forced herself to focus not on the change within her, but on the world around her.

The rain that had been falling freely was now frozen. Drops hung in the air completely motionless.

"What the—" Nate helped Ellie to her feet.

She held out a curious hand. Multiple suspended drops soaked into her skin.

"Ellienia." Auden spoke softly again. "Look at me."

She did as he asked. Auden stood strong, water dripping from his soaked hair. She gazed into his gray eyes as she had done many times in the last weeks. Looking into them now felt different. *He* felt different.

She could feel his tension, sense his worry and awe in the power that now surrounded them. Worse, she could hear the thunder of his heart. The thunder of all of their hearts.

"Breathe, Ellienia. Breathe with me."

She had not noticed the air still struggling to reach her lungs.

"Focus on the sounds of the rain outside your magic," Auden instructed.

Her magic. This was her doing. The rain did continue to fall mere feet away, but around them it stood still. She had done this. The world began to spin again.

"Close your eyes and listen."

She shut her eyes. Pushed through the sounds of their hearts, focusing only on the soft pats of the falling drops.

"Now breathe." Auden rushed air through his lungs. She struggled to do the same. "Again."

They stood there breathing until it was no longer an effort for her. Until she opened her eyes and the rain once more fell at her feet.

"I-I don't understand..." Ellie stood, allowing the cold water to soak every inch of her. She still felt lighter. Stronger.

"It was a power-dampening spell meant specifically for you," Layla voiced. "And I assume your sisters as well. A dampening spell of this magnitude would have to have been placed by two very powerful Fae."

"Like the King and my mother. But why?"

"To keep you hidden." Auden stepped closer. She could feel his growing tension.

"How does it work?" Nate asked. His eyes seemed to look at everything but her.

"It seems this specific spell was formed as a gateway spell. Meaning you pass through it once to activate it and back through it to break it. As you just did, Ellie."

"And my sisters?" Ellie tried not to panic as she thought of her sisters facing this with no information.

"You broke the spell. We can assume any powers they may hold have also been released."

Ellie now only heard her own thundering heartbeat. She

stepped back onto the deck. A sense of urgency ran through her veins.

She reached a shaky hand towards the small oak door. It slowly creaked open. The light of her pendant gave way to a dusty, open foyer. In the center were steps that Ellie assumed led to bedrooms. To her left was a large open doorway. Through it sat a large dining table, identical to the intricately-carved tables in the Great Hall. Farther down her left was another door that led to the kitchen.

Their footsteps were near silent on the thick dusty floors. Auden whispered a spell into his cupped hands, forming several wisps that lit up the interior. The surrounding trees and distance from the castle wall would make seeing them from this far out impossible, and the added light allowed Ellie to take in the quaint beauty of her childhood home.

A wall to her right displayed a collection of small portraits. She gently wiped away the dust to reveal the faces of her sisters, herself, and her parents. Cammie and Maisie's young eyes stared back at her. She allowed the tears to flow at the sight. It was unfair for her to be in their home without them. To see pictures of their parents before them.

She walked a few steps more stopping at an oval mirror. The glass was oxidized and clouded at the bottom, but she could still clearly see the female it reflected. The Fae it reflected.

"This is your true form," Auden said from behind her.

She ran slender fingers over her pointed ears. They were much longer than the small delicate ones of her elf friend. Her tongue ran along her slightly longer canines, and her eyes... Her crystal-blue eyes glowed in the darkness. She was the beautiful Fae that she always admired.

"The King must have entwined a glamour within the

dampening spell. To keep your and your sisters' features human until it was broken."

Ellie nodded in agreement. "When the spell broke, the spot on my back burned. It burned as it did the day I was struck."

Auden ran a gentle hand down the side of her cloak. He pulled it up and draped it over her shoulder. "May I?"

Her nod of approval was met with a warm hand gliding down the center of her back. He stopped where pain should have radiated, but it didn't. Ellie only felt the idle circles Auden ran across her back and the warming of her core at his touch.

He lifted her shirt, now placing those idle circles directly onto her skin. Her breath got caught in her tightening chest. His touch...Gods. Why was his touch affecting her so much?

"It's scarred, but no black remains." His fingers slid lower to her left hip. Her gut formed into a bundle of nerves. "The slashes are also fully healed. Their scars aren't as visible."

She turned around to face him, his hand remaining on her bare back.

When had he released the glamour on his features?

Those molten silver eyes of his burned into hers. His hard chest rose and fell in uneven breaths as he flattened the hand on her back, pulling her closer to him.

"El," Nate called from an open doorway at the back of the house.

She froze. Any warmth she felt from Auden was washed away at the sound of Nate's voice. She removed herself from his hold. "Thank you." She straightened her cloak. "For checking."

They all gathered at the entrance to a small library. The walls were lined with broken and decaying shelves. The pages of books barely held on to their bindings. Rolls of parchment lay scattered across the entire room.

To Ellie's left was a leather chair covered in dust and cobwebs. It, along with a small wooden table, were nestled underneath a wide-open window.

This was where her father sat.

She walked over to the chair and ran a finger through the thick layer of dust. On the side table lay her father's pipe. The smell of tobacco still lingered in the air. Parchment, tobacco, all that was missing was...

A light evening breeze blew through the window. It carried the sweet smell of citrus blossoms.

She was now standing in a warm line of daylight that stretched through the windows of the small library. Her very first vision flashed in front of her, only this time it was crystal clear.

The handsome man read in a large leather chair. His short golden hair shifted slightly as a soft breeze from the open window blew in.

Her father.

His deep-blue eyes looked up at the two young girls playing on the wood floor before him.

"I am Ewienia! Sthord master! On guarwd!" Her three-year-old self held a delicate wooden sword towards a small, enraged Cammie. Young Ellie's icy-blonde hair was pulled back into one long braid, but thick strands stuck out and hung loose, as if she had tried to pull it free.

"Dad! She won't stop poking me with that stupid thing! Stop! Ellie! Stop! ARGH!" Young Cammie started to throw the charcoals she had been using to draw. Young Ellie used her sword to hit

away the flying objects. It became a game that left both the girls and their father laughing.

"Girls." The soft voice echoed through the library door. Her mother stood at the threshold, the infant Maisie asleep in her arms.

Ellie's father stood and gracefully made his way towards her mother. Ellie couldn't help but blush at the love in his eyes and the gentle kiss he placed on her mother's lips.

"Has he called for you today?" Her father's gaze turned to worry.

"No. His calling on me is over. Now we wait."

"We should leave with the other families and not wait here to be slaughtered like cattle."

"He is our king, Mika. We will do as he has commanded. It is the only way to ensure their safety. To ensure that they will have a future." She looked down at the young girls, both drawing now, ignorant of their parents' conversation.

"It is a future and a life we chose to separate them from many years ago, Millie. We wanted them to have a life full of freedom and choices. Not the life our king is forcing upon them."

"He is at least providing them with a life, Mika. He has seen their future. It will not be one of ease, but it will at least be one."

"You know I would die a thousand deaths for these girls, but the King's visions have been wrong before." They both walked towards the desk in the center of the room. Ellie watched as the two Fae moved as one.

"He is not wrong, Mika. He has spent the last year envisioning possible future after possible future. This is the only way." She pulled out the green and gold embossed book from the drawer of the desk. "And this book will be her guide." Her mother gestured down to the young Ellie. "This book will reveal the truth. She will discover who she is, who the three of them are meant to be. And it

will remain here until she is ready, until all three are ready for the truth it holds."

"And what about the Reuel's? What about Auden?"

Her mother stiffened at her father's question. "Ellie—"

The castle bells began to ring throughout the small cottage.

"She's here." A young, beautiful Grams ran into the room, panic covering her face. Her mother slammed the book back into the drawer.

"It's time," her mother said, handing Maisie over. "You must go now. Go!" her mother yelled. Ellie's young self stood, tears of fear running down her face. Her father knelt before her and her older sister. He held their faces in his hands.

"You are loved beyond measure, and you will remember us when the time is right." He whispered a spell onto their brows. When he removed his face from theirs, the girls looked at him with vacant, unknowing eyes. He had spelled them to forget.

They each ran after their grams, willingly leaving their parents behind.

Ellie stood in the library, watching as her parents mourned their children. The daughters they would never get to raise. Ellie stood there and cried with them until a dark figure appeared at the threshold.

Her father attacked the general. A sword seemingly appeared in his hand from nowhere. Another general rushed into the room. Ellie's mother held out a hand, and the general crashed down to his knees, weeping.

Ellie's father moved and parried in the same way she had been taught, though he was quicker, stronger, and years of training made him a fierce opponent. A third general entered the room, and her mother brought him down in the same way as the second.

"Mika," she whispered through a ragged breath. "It's time." Her father's tense muscles seem to sag at her words. He slowed his

pace, pulled his swings, and failed to block an upward attack into his gut.

Ellie's own sobs were silenced by the screams of her mother. She could feel her mother's agony. It was unbearable. She couldn't think. She couldn't breathe. A blinding light flared from her mother's chest, and she knew the vision was ending.

She was on her knees, sobbing into her hands. They were all on their knees sobbing.

"El," Nate whispered. "H-how did you do that?"

She shot her head up, brow stitched at the sight of them.

"We saw," Layla voiced breathlessly. "We saw it all."

"I'm so sorry, Ellienia." Auden's voice broke. She had somehow shared the vision with them. They saw what she saw, and now felt what she felt.

"We need to hurry." She wiped the tears from her face. They all three looked at her with concern, but she needed to find the book. She needed to know why her parents sacrificed themselves.

She found it exactly where her mother had left it: hidden in the drawer of the library room's desk. Ellie pulled out the green and gold bound book. Its weight and size were much more than she expected. She traced a slender finger over the golden tree filled with animals, which she now realized were house sigils.

She opened it up. Each page was titled with a family crest and name, and below them were the faces and names of the Fae that belonged to that family.

"It's a genealogy book," Auden stated from over her shoulder. "It's of any and every Fae family with a blessed one in their lineage." Nate and Layla joined them.

"I thought this book was a way for the Eternal Queen to gain more power," Nate voiced.

"It is," Auden answered. "If the Queen had this, she would have the names and faces of all blessed ones. The names of every Fae she desires to imprison and steal power from. If she knew their names, she could do a simple locator spell and...If she ever gained this information, this book, those Fae, she would be unstoppable."

"That's not the only reason your mother agreed to hide it, though. Is it, Ellie?" Layla already knew the answer to that question.

Ellie quickly flipped through the pages. The Batair name, the family stag, was nowhere to be found, but she knew where to look. She now knew why King Vedmar trusted her mother so much. Why hiding her true name was so important. It was clear what Ellie was from her stunning features and her dual powers of water and sight.

She was a Kiaver. She was a Queen of Malavor.

42

S he stared down at the page before her. Her gentle fingers ran over the royal crest. A phoenix of ruby and gold was pictured with its wings spread wide, as three silver linked rings hung from its talons.

The pictures, names, odd symbols, and connecting lines only confirmed what she knew to be true. Under the portrait and name of Queen Clara Kiaver was a line that led to the portraits and names of Queen Odina Kiaver, King Vedmar Kiaver, and her mother, Amilliety Kiaver. The younger sister of the King and Queen.

Ellie stared for a moment at the portrait of her uncle. Her gentle features, mousy nose, and round lips came from her mother, but her crystal eyes and icy hair, they came from him. She didn't notice it before, that night in the King's library, but she was undoubtedly his niece.

Below her mother's portrait were her and her sisters' names. Cammiellé Batair Kiaver. Ellienia Batair Kiaver. Maisiel Batair Kiaver. Blank spaces were left for their portraits.

"You and your sisters, you're the heirs to the Malavor throne." Nate breathed his disbelief.

"What do these symbols mean?" Ellie ignored Nate's gaping stare.

Different simple symbols were placed at the end of each name. Some looked like a wave, some rocks, some swirls, and a few others.

"They're symbols signifying the power you hold." Auden pointed a finger to her mother's name. "This symbol signifies the empath power. Your sister Maisiel has the same symbol." An "X" with three dots in the top and side corners was placed next to her younger sister's name.

Ellie almost asked how their powers were already known at such young ages, but she remembered her uncle. The powerful seer. The King.

Three stones were drawn next to Cammie's name. Earth powers like their cousin, Queen Akéra.

"Why does El's name have so many symbols?" Nate's finger hovered over her name. Three different markings were placed after it: a wave, an eye, and a circle with an "A" in the center.

"She is a Kiaver seer. Meaning she has also been blessed with the ability to control water."

"And the last one?" Ellie could feel Auden tense and heard his heart rate spike.

"It's...complicated."

Ellie began to flip the pages of the book once more. Her father had asked specifically about Auden. His family, her family, they had known each other.

She found the Reuel line and the familiar blue eagle holding a dagger in its talons. It was the same crest she had seen on a scroll atop her grandfather's desk not so long ago.

A fire symbol lay next to both Auden's mother's and

sister's name. Next to Auden's was the same "A" in a circle.

"It's a symbol unique and rare to our race. It's a gift only given to two Fae every few hundred years. It stands for Anychî."

A soft gasp released from Layla's throat at the sound of the ancient word. He flashed her a flat warning.

"We can discuss it more in private, but any other questions I can now answer for you. My oath only had to be kept until you found out your royal namesake."

"Who made you take the magical vow?"

"Your grandfather."

Ellie's chest tightened.

"I guess he's not your grandpa...He was your mother and father's guard." Ellie instantly remembered the words King Vedmar had said in her vision in the library. *A plan has been made by your guard. When the time comes, do everything that he has instructed.* Bile began to burn in Ellie's throat.

"Before he was your parents' guard, he was a general in Queen Odina's ranks. He would work closely with my father, who claimed Ackerley to be the most skilled tactician he had ever known."

Ellie tried not to let the hurt show through her face. She knew this to be true. Ackerley's favorite lessons included the strategies of war, both on and off the battlefield.

"Your grams was your mother's lady-in-waiting."

Grams. Not her grams, but Tulli Pyer. She always assumed Pyer was her mother's maiden name, but no. It was Kiaver.

"*Why?*" was all she could choke out through the lump in her throat and the icy rage building in her gut. In an instant, she remembered another lesson. One she never thought would include her grandparents.

Anyone and everyone has the potential to betray you, Ellie.

You have to be smart enough to decide what their betrayal might be. You have to be strong enough to handle that betrayal.

His lessons. Their life on the farm. Her grandparents. It was all a deception. It was all a means to an end.

"Him, your parents, the King. It was a plan made almost two decades ago to hide you and your sisters from everyone, even yourselves.

"The King had many visions of the future, but only one where Malavor and all of Karmalo were free of this terrible queen: a vision of you and your sisters sitting on the thrones. I was told this when I came to Perilin before your Designation Day. Ames, Shea, Cormel, and I met with your grand umm...with Ackerley."

She swallowed hard at the name. *Ackerley Pyer.* The man who raised her, the man that claimed to raise her mother. It was all a lie. She and her sisters were just pawns in one of his many strategic schemes.

Auden continued. His voice sounded distant over the growing ringing in her head. "We met with him, and he revealed to us who you were right before he had us take an oath not to reveal any of it to you.

"I've known your name and title since the day you were born, but most of our people thought the daughters of Amilliety to be dead along with the rest of the royal heirs. That was until a few years ago. Ackerley reached out to my father, revealing that the three daughters of Amilliety were in fact alive and you were almost ready to take back Malavor. I volunteered as a designate the following year. I rose in ranks fast enough to be here when you came."

Ellie shook her head, trying to understand everything Ackerley had done. "When I came? The Queen's ruling to allow women as designates was decreed this year. How would Ackerley know she would make such a decree?"

"It was his idea. Ackerley and Officer Shea have been working with one another since the day Shea enlisted. Shea never moved up in ranks so he could stay close to the generals here in Malavor. He whispered among the generals what a good idea it would be to let women join. That having men enlist wasn't enough. The generals seemed to agree and easily convinced the Queen to decree it.

"Ackerley never revealed to us why you had to come back to Malavor. I didn't understand it at first, until I saw the portrait of your parents and realized it was your own house you had envisioned. That the powerful Fae that had placed the terrible curse on this house was your mother.

"You needed to come back. You had to be the one to break your mother's curse and the dampening spell placed on you and your sisters. Enrolling in the Queen's Army was the only way."

"He planned this..." Her words were barely audible.

Her grandfather's...No. Ackerley's voice rang in her ears again.

"You three will be the end to this war," she whispered.

But not as warriors. As queens.

She had known for some time that he could have been involved, but she never thought it would be to this extent. The walls began to close in around her. She needed air. Room to breathe and think. She ran from the library, book in hand.

Ellie sat on the steps of the front porch. The rain had stopped, and she desperately wished for its cooling touch.

She heard him coming from far down the hall. Her Fae hearing and his heart and steps gave him away.

"How can I lead—no, rule a people group I know nearly nothing about." Nate sat next to her, still avoiding her gaze. "I have no knowledge of their culture, *my* own culture. I have not been taught our ways. They are only my people by blood, but nothing more! I'm just a girl who grew up on a farm. I can't do this. I can't lead a kingdom." Nate reached over to grab her slender hand.

"El, you have never been just a girl from a farm." He loosened a soft breath. "From the moment I met you, I knew you and your sisters were destined for greatness. All of Perilin knew it. You are a fighter, not just for yourself, but for all people. You are a leader for every person in our tent, and you gained that leadership without your title. They follow you because of your kindness, strength, and knowledge. You gained their respect. You gained their trust. You gained their alliance. Only you could have done that, El. This is who you are meant to be. Not a young girl from a farm, but a powerful queen."

Decide what role you want to play in this war. Ackerley's words rang in her head. Icy rage twisted her gut again as she thought of the man who raised her, trained her. He had cried the night before she left, looked at her with both love and fear in his eyes. She had never doubted the man cared for her, even now. It still did not change the anger she felt for being used and lied to, for having her entire life planned and mapped out for her. Not just by him, but by the King and her parents.

Though, she remembered her visions. Her mother had begged King Vedmar to find another way. She had begged for her daughter's freedom, and it was ultimately Ackerley that had planned and schemed for all these years.

Ellie knew she could hide her title, ignore her destiny. Choose to only be the warrior she had been trained to be.

Or she could use that title. Use it to gain alliances, to instill hope for a better future with better leaders, to change the tide of the war. Use it how her uncle and adopted grandfather wanted her to.

It wasn't a choice.

She knew who she was and what role she now had to play.

"A Queen of Malavor," She whispered, allowing the title to sink in. "Cammie's going to hate this." Nate's deep laugh filled her broken heart, but he still would not look at her.

"Is this form not to your liking?" she ground out.

His brows raised, and he finally turned his face towards her. His expression was soft, but she could see pain in his umber eyes.

"You are more beautiful, more appealing than you have ever been, El. Which makes what I have to say even harder." He pulled at a strand of her near-white hair, twirling it gently around his finger. "El, I love you."

Love. Why did that word make her so uncomfortable?

"Do you realize you have never said it back?"

Ellie's heart sunk into her stomach. She knew she hadn't said it back but didn't know why.

"I know you care for me, El, but do you merely care for me because of convenience, dependence, and circumstance? Or am I the only one in this entire world that you deeply and desperately want?" His questions lingered in the air for a moment before he continued. "You deserve—we both deserve to figure that out."

Ellie knew it then. Nate was comfortable, familiar, and though she was attracted to him, she admittedly didn't love him. At least not in the way he loved her.

"What are you saying?" Ellie choked on the question.

"I'm saying that I love you. As a friend and so much

more. I will love you for the rest of my life no matter what... even if we choose to be with other people."

Her eyes blurred at the silver in his. She wanted to tell him to stop talking. She wanted to plead with him to stop as he was ending things between them. Her heart could take no more sadness. No more change. No more surprises. Even if she knew now, he was not meant to be more than what he always was.

"You and Auden have been drawn to one another since the day he took your arm on that path into the city. I see how he looks at you. I see how many of the men here look at you. You are a queen whose entire life has been planned out for her. You deserve to at least choose who you love."

Choose. She could no longer hold back as she sobbed into her hands. She sobbed for her parents, for her sisters, for the life she would no longer get to choose. And she sobbed at the gift Nate now gave her.

"Thank you," she whispered. He wrapped his arms around her, placing a kiss into her hair.

"Plus, when I'm old and gray, you're still going to look like *this*." He waved a hand over her body. "My pride couldn't handle that."

She elbowed him in the waist as they both huffed out a laugh.

"How touching." A vile, oily voice rose from behind a hedge.

Nate and Ellie jumped to their feet. She rose with such speed, she nearly lost her balance. Her body was not used to the freed magic and all that being a Fae entailed.

She stuffed the book into the bag hung against her hip. Auden and Layla quickly ran out of the house.

Gray hair, violet eyes, and a crooked smile emerged from the shadows. Mother Ubel now stood before them. Her skin looked near translucent from the small lantern of light she held in her hand.

"What are you doing here, Mother Ubel?" Layla sneered.

"I wanted to ask you the same thing, child. How dare you choose these traitors over your coven!"

"How dare you put your trust in the Father over the Mother," Layla bit back. "There is a reason I'm more powerful than you. More powerful than all the Mothers before me." Layla held out her hands with a rhythmic spell on her lips. They began to glow. Not with the soft light Ubel held, but with a fierce roaring fire.

"Stop!" Auden demanded. Layla extinguished the light from her hands. "Your light will signal the generals. It will call them here."

"You always were a smart male, Auden. Though, I never found you attractive like my idiot sisters."

"How did you know we were here?" Ellie growled, shifting the Mother's eyes onto hers.

"I felt you would be a threat the moment you arrived, child. I never imagined you would be a Fae, a royal Fae at that. Nonetheless, I still felt your power," she answered, ignoring the question. "I tried to warn the generals, urged them to take immediate action, but they wanted a more public slaughter." Auden took a step closer to the witch, only to be hissed at. "One step closer and I raise this light into the air."

She inched closer to Ellie. "I knew you would not be so easy to kill in their trials and games, and so did General Dolion. He was the only one interested in what I might do to end you before you could raise an army against them."

"How did you know we were here?" Ellie repeated.

"*Who sent you?*" Auden's question was a near growl.

"I did."

43

G eneral Dolion stepped out of the tree-lined shadows to their left. His familiar sneer gleamed in the soft light that Mother Ubel held.

"I followed them, sir. Like you said. I stayed far enough behind that Layla would not detect my presence." Ubel bowed to the brute.

His face was cruel, his large body pulsed with strength and power, but all Ellie could stare at was the sneer on his face. Her heart did not race as the others did. She could hear them and smell their terror.

"You've done well, witch," he praised.

"*Coward,*" Auden barked. "You would poison her as she slept, as she ate, instead of giving her a chance to fight! You are a weak, spineless coward," he spit.

"Should I call for the others?" Ubel raised her glowing hand in the air, keeping her eyes on them.

"No," he said simply.

She whipped her gaze towards him. "She has her powers now, sir. They could defeat you without help from the others." She scanned the general, assessing what Ellie already noticed.

"Here's the thing." He silently and smoothly walked towards the witch. "I never intended to kill Ellie."

He grabbed the witch's wrist and twisted it around, forcing her to release the magic in her hand. With one smooth move, the witch now lay on the ground with his sword hovering inches from the back of her neck.

"Stop!" Layla yelled through her shock. "We feel when one of our own is slain. If you kill her, they will come to avenge her death."

The general's face twisted, blurred, and reduced to a slender beautiful face. The recognizable sneer of Officer Ames remained.

Both Auden and Nate let out a slew of colorful words. Ellie just stood there smiling at the officer, his sneer a mirror of her own.

"We can't let her live now that she knows one of the Queens of Malavor walks these camps," he said, but he made no attempts to move his weapon closer to the Mother's neck.

"We can tie her up. Hide her." Layla's voice was thick with panic. "We're literally standing in a house that no one would go looking in."

"*Traitors!*" Mother Ubel hissed.

"Take her inside," Ellie ordered flatly. "I have an idea."

They took her while Ellie picked small purple wildflowers that grew around the front porch. The same purple wildflowers that grew on her farm.

She found the group in the dining room. Auden had found old sheets and ripped them apart. He now worked on tying the Mother witch up to one of the decaying wood chairs, while Layla and Nate kept a watchful eye on Ames.

Ellie dug through the kitchen cabinets before joining the group, teacup in hand filled with water she had to summon with great effort. Her multiple attempts to pull water from a puddle just outside the kitchen window would have shown if it wasn't for her already rain-soaked cloak.

The magic inside her seemed to fight her control, unwilling to give up its newfound freedom. A ringing in her ears had started the moment she broke the dampening spell, and it only worsened the longer they stayed in the house.

She shook her head as she entered the dining room. She picked the petals off the small flowers and threw them in the water.

"Can you heat this with your magic?" she asked Layla, handing the delicate cup to her.

"What is it?"

"Purple poppies. Stewing the petals in hot water will create a strong sleep tonic. She will be in a comatose state until she receives an antidote or withers away from hunger and dehydration." Both witches' eyes widened at her statement. "Come get me when it's done. You." She pointed at Ames. "Come with me."

"Ellienia—"

"You can come too, Auden. Or stay, I really do not care." Her words were sharp. It was late, she was tired, and her head...Gods above. It wouldn't stop pounding.

Ellienia led them back into the library.

Auden watched her walk effortlessly down the hall, her Fae form silent as she moved. He couldn't get a read from her flat expression, though he knew she had to be tired emotionally, physically, and mentally.

She made her way to the desk and planted herself into the wood chair behind it. She pulled a dagger from her vambrace and twirled it between her fingers.

"Why? And how?" she questioned. Her face was blank and unyielding.

"Dolion and a few other generals wanted to get rid of you the moment they realized you were impervious to their new flare batons. I convinced them to wait. I even convinced them not to listen to Ubels claims on you, but keeping them convinced became impossible. As you know, most of them wanted you to fail in your trials. They wanted your death to be public.

"Ubel was determined to be rid of you as quickly as possible, so I posed as General Dolion. I pressed her for information on her plans, but all she did was assure me that you would be taken care of, and soon.

"I found out she was going to poison you. I was hidden in the shadows when I overheard that idiot Filtmon bragging about it to a few of the men from his home. I stayed close by, then snuck into your dreams that night to wake you. I hadn't used that power in a very long time, and it wasn't easy."

"Snuck into her dreams? What the hell are you?" Auden questioned.

He had met Ames the day he had arrived in Malavor. The apparent young man had already earned Shea's loyalty, so Auden didn't question him further despite his cruel demeanor, odd comings and goings, and willingness to share a bed with the generals to gain freedom and information.

"He's a Nokken," Ellienia answered with slight amusement in her eyes. Ames's returning smile was the only confirmation Auden needed.

A Nokken. The creatures that could use light and water to change their forms and mist to sneak into another's mind. They had disappeared centuries ago. Auden couldn't help but wonder why one now stood next to him.

"Was it you in my first vision as well? The man that called me to come find him?" Ellienia asked.

"No. That was the only time I misted into your dreams, and I hope it will be the last." Ames's face was apologetic. "I don't enjoy invading one's mind. It's too...personal.

"Anyways, I knew you were a seer at that point, similar to the one that sent me here years ago, so I knew if I presented myself in that glowing blue form, you would listen and wake. Unfortunately, I did not know about the poison in the sweet rolls. I was just as shocked as you.

"But tonight, I found Ubel standing in the courtyard. I approached her as General Dolion. I threatened her and asked why her attempts at killing you were failures. She said you had already gained allies. That Auden killed Filtmon for you, and the sweet rolls were the only way she could get poison close enough to you again. She even gave one of her own witchlings a potion to forget that she handed them to her so your allies couldn't trace the poison back to her.

"She realized how trained you were that day. She underestimated your knowledge of poisons and expected you or at least one of your allies to die. She then claimed that she had figured out another way to kill you. That poisoning wouldn't work, but the Father had her look out her window this evening and saw the glimmer of a person pass through the stone archway, conveniently after Shea called upon a handful of witches.

"I thought she was insane, but I told her to go out into the city to see what she could find. And if she found you out here, it would be enough for the generals to all agree on killing you for attempted desertion. I only followed her out of pure curiosity. I in no way expected to find you in your true form." He bowed from the waist up. "The Queens of Malavor have returned."

"Not yet." Ellienia spoke flatly. "And what about the generals? You claim you knew of their plans to slaughter me in the trials. Did you not think to warn me of those added ploys."

"I did warn you of the archer in your leadership trial. I was the one tracking you. I made my presence known so you would think the archer had been following you, but the officer had been placed in that tree for hours before the trial even started. He wasn't the only one. Dolion had placed a handful of arbitrators around the city and instructed them to fire upon you the moment they saw you. Following you and making you aware of my presence was the only warning I could give you at the time.

"As for the strength trial...I took matters into my own hands."

"The mist," Auden whispered from beside the Nokken. He was in awe of the power Ames could produce. The morning of that trial, the entire camp had been filled with mist, *his* mist.

"I had heard Ballock and Schmilt would be placed at your station. There wasn't a way for me to change that, not without calling attention to myself. With my mist at the ready, I waited until the moment was right and snuck into the mind of one of the other young designates." Ames's eyes flashed with regret. "All eyes were so focused on you and your torture that no one even noticed when my mist slightly rose above the young man. He fought back. He didn't want to die, but you held on. Through every brutal slash, you stayed put. Seeing you endure that was the strength I needed to fight him. A sacrifice needed to bring my queens home."

"*Your* queens?" Auden questioned, keenly aware of the guilt in Ellienia's eyes.

"We want our land back, territory once ruled by the Kings and Queens of Malavor. We want to help you win this war so you may grant us this request."

"And what land would that be?" Auden asked for the silent Ellienia. Her eyes had gone dark at the mention of Ames's sacrifice.

"Panma."

The Malavor territory ruled by selfish brutes and cruel men would never willingly hand their land over to the Nokken.

"Where is it that you and your people have been hiding all these centuries?" Ellienia asked, her blade dancing effortlessly between her fingers.

"On an island between this continent and *hers.*"

Her blade stopped moving. "The Eternal Queen? You know where she came from?"

Ames nodded as his reply. Auden's mouth hung open, as he was unable to hide his shock. No one had known where the mysterious Queen came from. No one.

"It is yours." Ellienia stood, placing her dagger back in her vambrace.

"Ellienia—"

"Despite the fact that Ames carries incredibly valuable information, the land belongs to the Nokken, Auden. It was never for the humans to claim. Giving it back is the right thing to do."

He knew she was right but, "You are making a promise you may not be able to uphold. The citizens of Panma will fight against this, fight against your reign because of it. You cannot end one war by promising something that could start another one."

"The land is theirs. My decision is final. If your people help us win this war, Ames, then you can come home."

Ames smiled with silver lining his eyes, a glimmer of humanity shining through the dark mask he wore.

45

Nokken.

Nate stood staring at Ames in the dark study. The Nokken had posed as General Dolion to protect El, had played a huge role in protecting her during the last two trials. He was who they saw on their way to the King's library many nights ago.

Nate had never heard of the ancient race before, and he was glad. Knowing that creatures like this existed would have given his younger self nightmares.

The Mother witch was now fast asleep, and the five of them stood silently working through their next move.

"Well, at the very least, Auden needs to teach you how to glamour your features. You can't walk back into camp looking like that." Layla waved a hand over El's newly-formed body.

She truly was a sight to behold. Beauty like none Nate had ever seen before. Her hair was brighter, her curves and muscles more defined, and those crystal eyes literally glowed in the dull nighttime. It took everything in Nate not to glare at Auden and Ames as they, too, admired every inch of her.

"It might be easier if I glamour for you," Auden suggested. "At least until your magic settles in a bit more. It has been dormant for so many years, And I'm not exactly sure how it will *react*."

Without even a wave of his hand, El's features blurred and melted back to the human form Nate had known for years. Layla's mouth gaped slightly at the ease in which Auden wielded his power.

"How are we going to walk back into camp? I doubt Officer Shea has been able to occupy the witches for this long." Nate was certain Auden would not be careless enough to not have a plan back in, but they had surely taken longer than the male Fae had planned.

"Do we need to go back?" Ames's innocent question was met with an icy glare by El. One that would have sent any sane man stepping back a few, but Ames was no sane man.

"*Yes.* We need to go back. Kiarhem, Shea, Myer, Kier, Belig, Doal, Collern, Kal...They're all in there, and *if* we are planning to escape, we are not leaving without them."

"*If?*" Auden looked at El with lowered brows. "What do you mean by *if*?"

El stayed silent. The air in the small library grew more tense with each passing second.

"How many people, arbitrators and designates alike, are truly loyal to the Eternal Queen? How many from Malavor territories and beyond desire to leave this army?" El's voice was strong. She spoke in a way that Nate had never heard her speak before. She spoke like a true queen. "If we leave now, how many more people will continue to enter these camps? Continue to fight against the north as if it is their only option."

"What are you saying, El?" It was a question Nate didn't need to ask. He knew this was her plan from the very beginning.

"I'm saying destroy it all. Make it impossible to be rebuilt. Impossible for the Queen to continue to use my home as a training facility to grow her forces. Make an undeniable statement to all of Karmalo that there is another choice for them. I'm saying we take those who want to fight against the Eternal Queen north."

"And we kill the rest?" Ames's question caused El to flinch. Only slightly, but enough that Nate noticed. She was raised to fight, to kill, but Nate knew the latter would change her, destroy her. She would not leave this place the same in more ways than any of them could know.

"Yes," she softly replied. "If they fight us, fight for the generals and the Queen, we will have to take action against them."

"We will need to be cautious. I've spent years getting close to the generals to see what they are and what they're capable of." Nate cringed at the thought of how *close* Ames was willing to get to the generals. "They are not human, and they're not like any race from our land. I never learned what hides beneath their dark, large exteriors, but I fear it's far worse than any of us could imagine. Why else would the Queen only assign thirty of her generals and a few hundred arbitrators to a camp of over fifteen hundred designates."

"Not all designates are against the Eternal Queen's reign," Nate pointed out.

"No, but enough are that they could easily overtake the generals and arbitrators under normal circumstances." Auden adjusted his stance, shifting him closer to El. Nate's gut twisted at the movement. "Ames is right. We saw how fast they could move in Ellienia's vision. Just because they don't use any other power, doesn't mean they can't. We'll need to keep that in mind while we sort out the plan."

"What is the plan?" Nate leaned against the shelves of destroyed books and scrolls.

El's eyes danced at his question. The slight pull at the corner of her mouth told Nate that she knew *exactly* what to do.

46

A fter minutes of debating and honing in on their plan, Ames assured Ellie that he could get them back through the wall unseen. She allowed him to lead the way through the grassy field and over any potential traps. With his thick mist and Layla's shadow cloaking, their path through the tied-up designates and on watch arbitrators was effortless.

When they reached the large archway, Ames asked Layla to continue shadow cloaking them while he used his powers to reach into each of the witches' minds. He hid them from their view. He explained that the witches would look at them but see nothing.

Layla had cringed at the obvious violation towards her Mothers and sisters, but she didn't say a word to argue it.

They made it back to their tent where Shea stood half asleep, leaning heavily against one of the wood beams. Layla released her magic only meters away from him. He startled, straightening as he reached for a weapon.

"It's just us, Shea." Auden held out his hands in submission. There was no sigh of relief, or even a relax in Shea's shoulders as his stare met Ellie's.

"My queen." He bowed. When he rose, his eyes were lined with tears, his smile filled with unrelenting hope. Ellie couldn't ignore the weight in that one look.

She wasn't upset with Shea. He was just another pawn in Ackerley's plan, one that had sacrificed so much. He had spent most of his life in these camps, waiting for when Ackerley decided it was time for her to break her mother's curse. Knowing that Ackerley would use him in such a way made her both angry and sad.

"Thank you," she whispered, her words catching on the lump forming in her throat. She walked forward and placed the man's face in her hands. His red beard scratched against her newly-sensitive skin. Though she still looked human, her magic now ran freely, and she was fully Fae. Everything was heightened, even touch. "I want to hear your story. I want to hear of your sacrifices. I want to hear every detail that led to me standing before you now."

"I will tell you everything, Queen Ellienia, but after you have rested." She saw the teal eyes that scanned her and knew what he saw. She was exhausted, more so than she had ever been. "Come. Inside, all of you. It's not wise for us to be standing in the open like this, even at night." She released his face and happily followed his waving hands towards the tent flaps.

She couldn't get to her mat fast enough. She didn't even remove her muddied boots and sodden cloak before crashing down to the floor.

The remaining designates of tent twenty-four stayed asleep even as Layla and Ames said their hushed goodnights and Auden gave multiple thank yous to Shea for distracting the witches and watching over the tent while he was gone.

Nate had whispered something to her, but his words were muddled as sleep took its hold.

Ellie awoke to gentle hands brushing through her hair. Her head was still pounding, and the ringing had yet to subside. She rubbed at her temples before sitting up to stretch.

Her boots had been removed, she wore fresh, dry clothes, and the tent was empty aside from her and the young witch that sat beside her.

Ellie sat up, fingering the soft cotton of her shirt.

"Auden didn't want the others to know you had been out all night, so he had me change you early this morning," Layla answered her silent question. The witch's emerald eyes were sunken in, showing her lack of sleep.

"Where is everyone?" Ellie blinked away the sleep that remained in her own eyes.

"The Great Hall. Auden volunteered the group to help the witches mend the designates who failed yesterday's trial." A shadow of grief passed over Layla's features.

"How many?"

"So far...a few dozen."

A few dozen.

More than thirty designees had not made it through the night.

"Why did he let me sleep? I should be with them. I should be helping." Ellie grabbed her sack of clothes, swiftly pulling out garments to wear. Layla placed a gentle hand, halting Ellie's panic.

"You went through a lot last night, Ellie. The amount of magic you had to wield to break your mothers curse—" Layla pursed her lips. "Ellie, you did that before your magic was even fully released. I've felt your power for some time now. I've seen it drip out slowly since arriving here, but now...Ellie, you have no idea how powerful you are. With no training, it makes you—"

"Dangerous," Ellie answered for her friend.

"Yes. Any deep emotion—fear, anger, sorrow—could set you off. I'm here to teach you what I can. To try and help you control it. I will come every morning and evening to work with you, but first..." Layla grabbed her hands and held them tight. "How are you? Honest and true, what are you feeling?"

Ellie hadn't had much time to really reflect on all of last night's events. She hadn't allowed herself to react to it, but now—

Layla's question sent a wave crashing over her. The air became colder, the morning dew gathered around her legs, and her body shook with overwhelm.

In one night, she had become something new and foreign: a Fae and a queen. She had wielded magic like never before. She had watched her parents be murdered and sacrificed for a plan made decades ago. And she had found herself surrounded by people, by allies and friends, willing to fight alongside her. She was sad, angry, but most surprising of all, grateful.

"Honest and true," she said roughly through a knot in her throat. "Despite a splitting headache, I'm surprisingly okay. I want to mourn my parents more, and even the life I had before coming here, but now is not the time. I have a purpose now, one that goes beyond the warrior I was trained to be. I'm ready to fight for my people and for all of Karmalo. So honest and true, Layla, I'm okay." The sound of her own words washed over her like soothing waters.

Layla looked at her with gleaming eyes. The smile on her lips was pure pride, and Ellie accepted it fully.

"Good, and I think I can help with the headache." Layla dropped her hands and grabbed the sack of clothes. "Get dressed. We have work to do, starting with speaking to the man that waits just outside, then seeing our dear friend Kia."

47

The outfit Layla had picked for Ellie was both elegant, and terrifying. The tight brown leather trousers had delicate silver buttons that ran up the outside of each leg. The crystal-blue blouse fit tight around her chest and torso, and around her upper arms, but the lace sleeves flowed and lightly billowed out at the ends. The matching brown leather corset had the same silver buttons running up the front, stopping just at the center of her breasts. It was tighter than any of the other corsets Layla gave her, and the low-collared blouse hid none of the full chest that overflowed over the leather.

Layla had weaved her hair in a single loose braid that lay flat over her shoulder. Soft natural waves framed her freshly-painted face. After getting all her vambraces and weapons in place, Layla had looked at her in complete awe.

Ellie walked out of the tent to see Shea leaning on the same wooden post he had leaned on the night before. "Good morning, ladies. Shall I escort you to the castle?"

Ellie wasn't quite sure why, but Shea looked younger. His

teal eyes looked as if years of stress had finally been released. "You look quite well this morning, Officer Shea."

His smile was broad behind the curtain of orange-red hair. "Though it was short, I slept more soundly than I have in many years."

Ellie's chest tightened at knowing she was the cause of his relief. They began to walk across the large field to the witches' garden.

"Why?" she softly asked.

He looked down at her with a gentle smile. He took a steady breath, the warmth of it reaching her right shoulder. "As you know, Perilin was one of the few territories to not be outright attacked by the Eternal Queen's men. We willingly gave our land over to the Queen to avoid the bloodshed and destruction that so many of our neighboring lands dealt with. It's why it prospered for so many years after, and why the Queen often overlooked it.

"I met your grandfather—sorry, Ackerley. I only just recently learned he wasn't really your grandpa. Anyways, I met Ackerley a few weeks after you had moved to the town. He was looking for someone to help develop the farm he had bought and was willing to pay handsomely for the work. As a young man with a new bride, I jumped at the opportunity."

A new bride. Ellie's heart sank.

"A couple years later, a few generals came to town. They revealed the Queen's decree." The first Designation Day. "Men would be called to enlist, and some of them did not take the news well. They voiced their outrage, and a few days later, the generals burned their homes down." Shea swallowed hard. "One of the homes was next to mine. It was early morning, and I was away working on the farm with

Ackerley. My wife and newborn baby boy peacefully slept when the flames from the neighboring house caught ours."

Ellie's breath caught in her throat. Her eyes misted with the man's she now held hands with. "I'm so sorry."

He squeezed her hand gently. "I lost everything that day, including myself. I wanted to murder every one of those generals and still do." He rubbed the fealty mark on his shoulder. "It was Ackerley that found me kneeling in the ashes of my home. He took me back to the farm and talked me through my rage and despair. He revealed to me that he still served the Malavor royals, that they were not dead as the world now believed. He told me if I was willing, I could help bring back peace and destroy the Eternal Queen and her men. Ackerley gave me a purpose to live again.

"I enlisted a few days later, on the first Designation Day. The first few years after I received my fealty mark, I cut ties with Ackerley. Once I learned how to skirt the lines of the curse, I started informing him and building alliances. Ames was the first one, then Captain Cormel, and finally Reuel. We arrived early for your Designation Day. Ames, Cormel, and Reuel had their fealty marks removed by Agilta, then we met with Ackerley. He revealed the truth. That the tiny girls, the little warriors that I once watched run recklessly around the farm, were the rightful Queens of Malavor."

Little warriors. Ellie began to sob. She knew now why Shea seemed so familiar. He was the man from her vision, the one she had on the afternoon of her Designation Day.

"I...I remember you. You didn't have a beard back then, and your nose...well, it was quite a bit straighter." Shea laughed, shaking the hand he held. "My gods. You have sacrificed so much, Shea. I could never repay you."

"The only repayment I need is seeing you and your

sisters seated in that Great Hall." He pointed towards the castle. "You do want to be queen, don't you?"

Ellie stopped walking, her sobs halted. No one had yet to ask her if she *wanted* to be queen. "I never wanted my life planned out for me. My parents never wanted this life, this role placed upon me and my sisters." Her heart sank at the thought of the life she would never get to choose. "But I know what my sisters and I are capable of. I know the peace and goodness we can bring back to these lands. So yes, I want to be queen."

Her shoulders relaxed. She may not have chosen this path, but at least it was something she wanted. "I may not agree with how Ackerley went about all of this, with all of the lies, secrets, and oaths, but I appreciate everything you have done for him, Shea. All the work you have done for your queens."

His smile was a warmth that seeped into her bones. He would have made an amazing father. The smile faltered as he saw the glint of anger in Ellie's eyes. Anger she couldn't help but feel towards her adopted grandfather.

"You're angry with him?" There was a hint of shock laced with his question, as if she had no right to be.

"I feel—I feel as if he used my sisters and me. That we were just pawns in a long game of strategy. A game I know he enjoyed playing. I feel there were lies and secrets that weren't needed, so yes, I am angry with him. I am angry with my uncle as well, but I have to trust in the decision he made."

To Ellie's surprise, Shea didn't argue against her claims. There was only understanding in his eyes. They were still standing at the edge of the witches' garden. The tall hedges provided them some shade. She kept his strong hand in hers, and when she looked down at those hands, she realized how comforting the touch was. Shea was a father without a child, and she was a daughter without a father.

"You would have made an amazing dad." She choked on her words and the truth they spoke. She could hear Shea's breath catch in his throat, but she didn't dare look at his teal eyes. Ones she knew would be filled with sadness.

"When this war is all over, there will be many children without a father. Maybe...that can be my next calling. My next purpose."

She didn't know when it had happened, but the strong arms that wrapped around her kept her shoulders steady as she sobbed. She could do it. She could be the end of this war, the end of the mindless slaughter of mothers and fathers. The ringing in her head deepened, causing the front of her brow to pinch.

"It may not matter," Shea continued, "but I am very proud of you and all that you have done here."

"It matters," Ellie breathed. "It matters more than you could know."

He released their embrace and stepped back from her. After a moment of silence, he sighed, running a hand through his beard. "I, unfortunately, need to find Ames and ready myself for groups fifty-one through one hundred's leadership trial. Will you ladies be alright from here?"

"We will be fine, Officer Shea. Thank you." Ellie was slightly alarmed at Layla's voice, as she had not spoken since leaving the tent.

Shea bowed his head before leaving them standing in the shadows of the hedges.

Layla and Ellie walked in silence for a while after Shea left. The moment with him and the words they spoke, it was a conversation Ellie didn't know she needed.

"So, do you want to talk about you and Nate?" Layla's abrupt question followed after she had picked a pink rose petal from a nearby bush.

"There's nothing to talk about," Ellie flatly answered. Though she agreed with Nate's choice and was truly thankful for it, it still hurt, and she wasn't in the mood to talk about it.

"Mmm. Okay, then should we talk about you and Auden?" Ellie shot her an annoyed glare. Layla was fingering the soft rose petal in the same way she had done some weeks back. Their first conversation in this garden seemed like years ago.

"Again, there's nothing to talk about."

"You're Anychî. That's definitely something worth talking about."

Admittedly, Ellie had forgotten about the symbol by their names. The book was now hidden somewhere only Ames knew. He seemed like the best choice to keep it hidden as that was what he was most skilled at. The others thought her crazy to trust him with it, but Ellie knew something about the Nokken that the others didn't. She wasn't worried about the dark male in the least.

"I don't know what being an Anychî means, or why Auden and I were gifted with...whatever it is. More power maybe?"

"It's not what you are individually, Ellie. Anychî is what you and Auden are together. It's what you are for one another."

"You're speaking in riddles, Layla." Ellie let out a soft

exhale. "Auden said it was something we needed to discuss in private. Until then, I think it's best if you and I table this discussion."

Layla nodded, though her eyes begged to say more.

"You know what it is and it's killing you not to say anything, isn't it?" Ellie prodded at her friend.

"You. Have. No. Idea."

Their laughs filled the air. Layla hooked her arm under Ellie's, and they walked through the garden with more peace than Ellie had felt in a very long time. When they reached the stone steps of the castle, Layla whispered a prayer onto the rose petal and placed it in her mouth, just as she had done before.

"May I ask...Why do you do that?" Ellie's question was asked with less tact than she wanted, but Layla lit up at her curiosity.

"It's a way for me to feel closer to the Mother. I eat plants known for good and healing, plants that the other covens were possibly made from. I whisper a prayer for blessings and guidance before consuming the flowers. I feel that is why I am more powerful than the others. It is why...," Layla trailed off, biting her lip in contemplation.

"Why what?"

"It's why I can hear the Mother speak. She whispers to me. I know it sounds ridiculous—"

"No. It doesn't," Ellie interrupted. She had never been truly religious. She sometimes prayed to any god that might hear her, but there were so many gods from every different race. She lacked the faith and understanding in knowing which gods were real. For the first time, she thought maybe they all were. "You acknowledge a goddess who acknowledges you in return. It's the least ridiculous thing I've heard in a long time."

Layla gave a thankful smile before walking up the steps and through the large glass door. Ellie was not prepared for what lay behind it.

The stench hit her before she could focus on the chaos that was the Great Hall. Blood, rot, bile—it took everything in her not to bring up the small piece of bread she had eaten for breakfast. She softly cursed her new Fae sense of smell.

Hundreds of men and women lined the floor of the Great Hall. Most lay unconscious; others groaned at their infected wounds. Weaving in and out of the maze of people were witches and members of group twenty-four. At the far end of the room, by the abandoned dais, knelt Auden. His hands were stained red, his brow drenched with sweat, but his vacant eyes met hers. The ringing in her head increased, and the pull in that stare begged her towards him, pleading for her to help.

Layla's voice in her ear reminded Ellie to breathe. She forced herself to look away from Auden, though she could feel his gaze linger. "They only have a few hours to treat the wounded before the next set of designees from today's trial flood in."

Groups fifty-one to one hundred would perform their leadership trial today, and Ellie cringed at the memory of hers just the day before.

Layla led her through the web of bodies. She met the stares of many and tried to give a reassuring smile. Nate passed her by without even a glance as he carried bottles of tonic and armfuls of gauze and cloth. Her entire tent worked tirelessly, and Ellie couldn't hide the guilt she felt in not joining them.

"Why aren't any other groups helping?" Ellie carefully stepped over a man's gnarled, bleeding arm.

"Why would they? The generals and most arbitrators see

these designates as weaklings. If they survive this trial, their rank will be the lowest in the army. Either they die here in this room or in a few months on the battlefield."

Ellie swallowed the bile that lingered in her throat. These people, mothers, daughters, fathers, and sons, the generals saw them as cattle. The first to be shipped out for slaughter.

Layla quickened their pace, pulling Ellie through the large oak door and the glass-lined hallway. She wanted to turn around, wanted to go back and help, and she would after first seeing Kiarhem.

Layla's room was only a few doors down from what was Mother Ubel's room. It was small but fit six beds, three of which lay on tall wooden planks above the other three mattresses. Deep-green ivy grew up the beams of the beds, as well as around the seal of the one bedroom window. Bottles and jars of tonics and salves were spread across a small desk in the middle of the room.

Kal and Myer sat on the floor below the bed Kia lay on. They both jumped to their feet at the sight of Ellie and Layla, while a young witch stayed reclined and relaxed on her lofted bed.

"Ellie!" Myer's eyes scanned her from head to toe, a hint of heat brushing across his cheeks.

"Myer, Kal." Ellie softly smiled in greeting. "How long have you been here?"

"We traded with Collern and Kier a few hours before the sun rose," Kal answered, as Myer still stood wide-eyed and gaping at Ellie. It had only been a little over a day, and the once young ,arrogant boy who now stood before her seemed willing to do anything she or her allies asked. She had seen the look on Kal's face after the last trial: respect, appreciation, and fear. Fear of her and the *thing* she became at seeing Kia's broken and beaten body.

"How is she?" Ellie crossed between them and sat on the edge of Kia's bed.

"Nothing has changed since Layla left this morning."

"And nothing will," the young witch murmured.

48

S ilver braided hair cascaded over the edge of the lofted bed. The young witch sat propped up on a pillow, picking at her black nails with a stick.

"Hush, Polli," Layla spit.

The young witch jumped down from her bed in a smooth, quick motion. She landed silently on the stone floor. Ellie struggled to hide her shock as familiar violet eyes met hers. She was tanner than Ubel, but her angled face, slender nose, round lips, and petite figure was identical to the elder Mother.

"You're Mother Ubel's daughter." Not a question, but a statement filled with panic as Ellie darted her eyes between the two witches.

"Don't worry," Polli sneered. "I hated the old bat more than you. In fact, I owe you for not yet killing the beast. I still hope to be the one to claim her last breath."

She knew.

Layla had told her where her mother now sat unconscious and tied up.

"Polli, go make yourself useful in the Great Hall," Layla firmly directed with no hint of kindness.

"Thank the Mother. These two are a true bore." She waved a slender hand at Kal and Myer. She walked towards the door but stopped just before opening it. "It was nice meeting you, Your Majesty." She flared her wrist and dramatically curtsied before swiftly escaping Layla's cursing and cruel gestures. All color was gone from Layla's face as she apologetically met Ellie's wide eyes.

"I'm sorry. I cannot lie to the five sisters who live in this room. They know everything."

"Know what, exactly?" Kal looked at the two women with lowered brows, and Myer's face was a mirror of Kal's confusion.

"It's fine. If you trust them and they're on our side in this, then they will find out soon enough anyway. But why did she comment that nothing will change with Kia? Is there something wrong?"

Layla bit the inside of her cheek, and her face paled even further. "I wasn't honest with Kiarhem's initial exam. She had more internal bleeding than I led on, and I've had to put her in a very deep sleep that keeps her heart rate and blood flow down. Unfortunately, none of my magic or tonics are helping, and there's only one more thing I can think of to try."

"Sh—she's dying?" Ellie's beating heart was drowned out by the sorrow and anger that rushed to her pounding head.

The temperature of the small room dropped significantly, plumes of mist seeped in through the window seal and encircled Ellie's legs. Pipes groaned and creaked in the walls around her. Vials filled with every shade of liquid exploded from the desk in the center of the room. Ellie could barely hear Kal's and Myers's colorful words as they dropped to the floor, avoiding the shards of glass.

"Ellienia! Breathe!" Layla yelled. "She's not dying! Not yet! You can save her!"

She shot her head towards Layla, her powers calming slightly. "What do you mean I can save her?"

Ellie's voice was foreign. It was laced with her anger and power and filled every corner of the room. She tried and failed to calm her magic even more as she saw the fear in Layla's eyes.

"Your pendant." She pointed a trembling finger at Ellie's chest. "It's an Empousîa. Empousîas are rare objects filled with their own untapped magic. They've only ever been wielded by extremely powerful Fae whose powers are similar to the magic found in the Empousîa. The pendant holds healing water, right? I think there is a way for you to feel the healing magic in the water and duplicate it."

"How?"

"Every bit of magic is unique. If you focus hard enough, you can feel the difference, hear it, then in theory, you could manipulate, form, and duplicate it." Layla disappeared into the adjoining washroom and returned with a small glass of water. Kal and Myer still sat on the floor in shocked silence. "Focus on the magic in your pendant."

Ellie now held the glass in one hand and her pendant in the other, the ringing in her head growing at the contact. Her vision began to blur from the pain. She was sure her magic was trying to kill her.

"I don't even know how my own magic feels, let alone control or manipulate it," she said through clenched teeth.

"Just focus, Ellienia. Everything is new to you right now. Your senses are so heightened that it's muddling everything in you together. Your magic is overwhelming you, begging you to use it." The ringing in her ears changed its tone, as if confirming what Layla said. "Close your eyes. Think of a place familiar and comforting. Relax your mind and focus."

Ellie looked down at Kiarhem. Her dark, coiled hair had been tied up in a bun above her head. She looked so young, so fragile. Her breaths were shallow, infrequent on her small chest. Ellie took a shaky breath and closed her eyes.

She transported herself to the brook on the outskirts of her family's farm. Atop Henry, the moss-covered bolder, she sat, hanging her legs over the streaming water. The creek had always brought her comfort. Its sound, movement, and cool touch were life-giving.

But here, in the vision she forced in her head, its constant flowing sounded distant, its quick movement a blur before her eyes, and she knew if she reached down, she would feel nothing on her fingertips.

The ringing in her ears grew stronger, deafening. She pushed against her magic, willing it to calm. It pushed back, putting more and more pressure in her head. She felt as if it would explode at any moment.

"Manipulate it. Mold and form it to your will, Ellienia," a male voice whispered in her head. *"Don't fight it. Accept it. Let it wash over you."*

Tears flowed from Ellie's eyes. She knew the voice. It had become so familiar to her—the male from her visions, her uncle, the King.

"How?" The single word was more than an effort to get out.

"The seer in Dorumia will explain, my darling niece." His voice began to fade. *"I'm so sorry, Ellienia. I wish I had more time."*

And he was gone. Only the overwhelming ringing remained. It grew stronger, but she didn't push back this time. She allowed it to rise. She let its reverberation take over her head, then her neck and shoulders, eventually finding its place along every inch of her, down into her very bones.

She focused her eyes on the stream before her. Its sound grew nearer, its flow clearer. The ringing in her head, her body, became a soft hum before she willed it into a constant ripple: the sound of water bubbling over rocks both large and small.

Instantly, the brook was as it had always been. She reached down from Henry and placed her fingers into the water. Its cool touch caressed her skin as it flowed by. She watched it for a moment. Watched as the water effortlessly changed its course and flowed around each of her fingertips.

Its movement, its sound, this was her magic.

She sat up, pulled the pendant from her chest, stared at the crystal-blue water, and listened. It grew colder in her hand, reacting to the attention and recognition she gave.

The soft sound of lapping water on a frozen shore, that was the magic inside the pendant. That was what the power inside hummed.

Ellie knew what to do as she blurred the vision from her head and returned to the witches' room.

49

Layla audibly gasped at the blue light streaming from both liquids in Ellienia's hands. Her eyes were still closed, focused, but Layla knew she had done it. She could feel the power shift in Ellienia. See her friend accept it into her bones. Now she truly was a queen to be feared.

The young men remained on the floor, looking in awe at the beauty before them. They had no clue what lay underneath the glamour placed on her. They could never fathom the true beauty that she possessed. In her Fae form, Layla knew both men and women would gladly bow down to that beauty.

The glowing faded. Ellienia shot her eyes open, and a light gasp escaped her throat. She turned and placed the now crystal-blue liquid onto Kiarhem's lips.

Moments passed. Either seconds, minutes, or hours, Layla didn't know.

"It's working." Ellienia relaxed her shoulders. A small tear escaped the corner of her eye. "I can hear her heart. It's beating much stronger now."

Layla placed a gentle hand on Kiarhem's chest. Both the beat of her heart and the rise and fall of her chest were much more powerful. Ellienia stood from the young elf's bed and sat in front of the two young men. She placed a hand on each of their faces.

"My name is Ellienia Batair Kiaver. I am the niece of Queen Odina and King Vedmar. My sisters and I are the last remaining heirs to the Malavor throne."

"Holy shi—"

"You're Fae," Kal interrupted Myer's slew of curses.

"Yes. Officer Reuel is also Fae and has placed a glamour over our features."

"Wh-why are you here?"

Layla could see the look in Kal's eyes. The horror in knowing the danger Ellienia was in for being there, and the danger he was in for knowing her truth.

"I'm here to take back my home. To take back Malavor, its surrounding territories, and all of South Karmalo. And I would like your help in doing so."

"HELL YEAH!" Myer's voice rang through the small room. Kia stirred slightly at the noise.

Ellienia stood, pulling both men up with her. "Do either of you have a wineskin or flask? I need it to discreetly give the healing water to the injured out in the Great Hall."

Myer was already untying a skin from his belt before Ellienia finished her sentence.

"Thank you." Ellienia placed a kiss on the poor gent's cheek. His face went as red as his hair. She turned to face Layla, her crystal eyes more clear than Layla had ever seen. "Myer and I will head to the Great Hall, while you and Kal stay here with Kia."

Ellienia also saw Kal's fear. Exposing him to the horrors of the Great Hall would only worsen it. "When she is ready, meet us in the woods behind our tent. It's time the rest of our alliance knows who I am."

Ellie and Myer walked shoulder to shoulder in silence. Witches that passed by them didn't question their presence. They knew of the deal Layla made with her, and they didn't dare argue against it. Not with Auden, their favorite arbitrator, enforcing it.

They reached the large oak door to the Great Hall. Ellie stopped just a few steps before it.

"Myer." She reached out to squeeze his rough hand. "You cannot speak freely about what you just learned, not yet. Understand?"

"I would never do anything to endanger you."

My queen, his eyes seem to say.

She gave him a nervous, grateful smile. He grabbed the oak handle and held the door open for her. She took a steady breath before stepping through.

"My gods," Myer gasped from behind her. Without a second thought, he ran past her, grabbing gauze and tonics from a nearby table and hurrying them to the nearest working witch.

Ellie began her work, scanning for the more seriously injured, the ones she knew would not make it much longer. She would sit, stroke their brow as if checking for a fever, then place the wineskin of water to their mouths. A woman simply hydrating the sick. That was what it would look like.

Each person only needed a single drop, but the water was limited, and she wouldn't risk making more. Not here. She had healed a few dozen designates when she felt the water run low. She stood in the middle of the Great Hall, scanning the many hurt and dying faces. Staring at the sheer amount of people she knew she could not save.

She heard his approach and the familiar stride of his steps. Felt his stare and smelled his woodsy scent as he walked up behind her. What surprised her was the sound of his magic. Now that she was clearheaded, she could hear the faint sound of a soft breeze through trees and the rustling of leaves. The same sound she heard when she first touched him weeks ago. It reminded her of the trees that banked the stream in which her own magic emanated. She didn't dare turn to look at Auden. Seeing those vacant gray eyes again, it would break the current hold she had on her powers.

"That is no ordinary water, is it?" His words were barely a whisper, but her Fae ears heard him perfectly.

"No, it is not."

"How much is left?"

"Only enough for one."

They stood there silently for a moment. Ellie knew he was seeing the same lost, dying faces.

"Come with me." Auden's voice was rough and filled with exhaustion. She went to grab for his hand but stopped herself. This was not the place to comfort him. He was still her arbitrator, and every witch in the room kept a watchful, longing eye on him.

She followed him through the maze of people. A few of the men and women she had given the water to began to stir. A young witch knelt down to check on a man, and her face filled with confusion and shock. She lifted his shirt and arms, checking for wounds that were no longer there. She looked around wildly but didn't bring the miracle to any other witch's attention.

"You're playing a dangerous game with that water,

Ellienia." Again, his words were only loud enough for her Fae hearing to register.

"I can't just stand aside and let these people die. If I have the power to save them, even if it's not all of them, I will."

He didn't reply. He only stopped before a young girl. Her hair was a dusty brown and drenched in her own blood. A deep cut ran from the crown of her head to the tip of her brow. The rest of her body was covered in cuts and bruises, and Ellie truly wondered how this young woman had made it through the night.

It took a moment, but Ellie recognized the pale, lifeless face. She was from Perilin, the fierce girl that had been so brutally beaten by Schmilt on their first trial.

Beside the young woman sat a familiar silver-haired witch. She looked up from the bandages she wrapped around a too-skinny arm. She glanced at the wineskin in Ellie's hand before looking at her face. Delight danced in those violet eyes.

"You saved your little elf."

"I did."

The smile that reached Polli's eyes was not filled with joy, but wicked surprise.

"Polli. There are a large handful of designates who seem to be doing much, *much,* better. See to it that you and your sisters tend to them before the others have to." Auden's words were careful, direct, and Polli understood without question.

She was gone in a flash, whispering to a few young witches before tending to the miraculously-healed designates.

Ellie didn't care if they took credit for the healing. She didn't care what the young witches made up to convince the other witches that it was their work. Their knowledge of herbs and potions that saved the lives of those she gifted with healing water. All Ellie cared about were the lives that didn't yet deserve to die.

"She has your fire." Auden gestured to the girl. "Who you give the last drop to is your choice, but she is a fighter. One that could be an asset in this war."

"She may have the heart of a warrior, Auden, but I've seen her fight. It would take years to hone that fire into something useful." Ellie felt the guilt of her words as she said them. This young woman's life could have a greater purpose, but so could the life of anyone in the Great Hall.

"Like I said, it's your choice." Auden's head dropped. Ellie had been avoiding his gaze, avoiding his vacant eyes, but now...now she wished he would look up at her.

She knelt to the ground and pushed the blood-soaked hair away from the young woman's skin. Drops of that blood covered Ellie's fingers. A knot formed in her throat.

She should be dead, Ellie thought. With the amount of blood loss and the undeniable trauma to her head, at this point, she truly should have been dead.

At that moment, Ellie understood. This girl had already fought for this long to stay alive, arguably harder than anyone else in the room, and therefore deserved the last drop of healing water.

She placed the wineskin to the girl's chapped lips and emptied the skin into her mouth. With how far gone she was, the magic would take a while to heal her broken body.

Auden had lifted his head, but his gaze did not meet Ellie's. He looked past her at the line of arbitrators and their designates filing into the crowded room. They were there to take the injured back to their tents. Any recovery or lack of would be finished in their respective group tent.

Arbitrators began pointing and directing designates

towards broken bodies, and Ellie wondered if the other groups would continue to tend for their wounded.

"We should go." Auden stood, waving a hand at the rest of group twenty-four. "There is nothing else we can do for them."

"What will happen to those who have passed?" She scanned the broken bodies again. She knew quite a few would be gone in the next couple hours.

"Their bodies will be placed in the field before our tents, and the witches will burn them."

"And her?" She gestured a hand to the bloodied young woman. The cuts and bruises on her body were near gone, but the deep gash to her head remained.

"I will have Ames discreetly check on her at dinner, but I have no doubts she will be fine." Ellie nodded her agreement as they weaved their way to the back door of the Great Hall. She lowered her voice, so only he could hear.

"It's time our allies knew our plan. It's time they knew everything."

He nodded. "Where?"

50

_____

She had done it.

How, Auden didn't know. He was in awe of the female, the queen that sat watching him place wards around their planned meeting place. Creating healing water, manipulating and duplicating an Empousîa's magic, he was sure it had never been done before. When Ellienia had told him of all that happened in Layla's room, he couldn't hide his shock.

"You're incredible," he had breathed, causing her face to turn the slightest shade of pink.

She proceeded to say that Layla, Kal, and Kia would join them, most likely before Nate finished gathering up the rest of their allies, the entirety of group twenty-four, having them join only two or three at a time. The entire group gathering in the woods at once would surely cause suspicions.

"So how does this work?" She sat, leaning her back against a large tree trunk, analyzing his every move. She nibbled at a piece of bread, forcing herself to eat despite the earlier sights and smell that he was sure stole away her hunger.

"When everyone is present, I will activate the wards. A shield will go up, and no one outside this ring of trees will be able to see or hear us." He dragged his hands in the air, connecting the final two trees to one another with an invisible wall.

"Can I perform this same magic?"

He stopped and turned, giving her a knowing smile. "After today, I'm pretty sure you could produce any kind of magic you set your mind to."

She didn't return the smile. Her crystal eyes pierced into his as if contemplating her next words. She gestured for him to sit with her.

"What does it mean?"

He paused his movement. Auden knew what she was asking. Knew he had to tell her. He sat, leaves and sticks rustling beneath him as he shifted to get comfortable. She tore off a piece of her bread and handed it to him. His fingers brushed against hers, sending a rush of desire to his core.

"Being Anychî, what does that mean?"

He bit into the bread, allowing the full mouth to give him time to think on his answer.

"I am your Anychî and you are mine," he finally said. He wasn't sure how detailed he should be, and he knew there wasn't the time for it. "If you accept me as your Anychî, Ellienia, and I accept you, then there will be a bond of magic between the two of us. One very few possess. It will be like a tunnel where our magic flows back and forth between each other, allowing either of us to use your magic or mine."

Her brows raised. "It seems like you would be getting the better end of that deal, seeing as I am a bit more powerful." She went to poke his chest, but he grabbed the slender finger.

"You have no idea how powerful I am, Ellienia." He released her finger with a wink and grin that had her eyes rolling. "The Anychî bond can also enhance both Fae's original magic. We won't know exactly how until we accept it."

"Was the bond the thing my grandfather failed to include in his oath?"

"In part. Yes." He had thought of a way to tell her about some of the bond without revealing who or what she was. However, it would have revealed more than Auden was willing to admit. Even now, he hesitated to reveal the full truth of the bond.

"Why is it so hard for you to talk about?"

"I...I felt you a few months ago."

Her eyes widened, the crystal-blue irises gleaming in the soft sunlight. "You *felt* me?"

"I didn't necessarily feel you, but my magic felt your magic. It pushed and pulled against my skin, as if trying to guide me to you." Auden's heart raced as he saw Ellie's breathing become uneven. "I think you and your sisters' magic was beginning to grow beyond what the dampening spell could contain. It's why Ackerley reached out to my father when he did. In one of the letters Ackerley wrote, he spoke of your sister Maisiel stating she had the same powers as your mother.

"Anyways, the Anychî bond can be very...personal. We'll be able to send more than just magic down the bond: words, emotions, thoughts. There's no hiding things from your Anychî."

She placed the last bit of bread in her mouth. Auden watched her silently contemplate the information. Finally, she spoke.

"My visions started a few months ago," she stated as if confirming what he said about her magic and the dampening spell. "So our magic, it wants to be connected. It wants us to accept the bond?"

"Yes. There are stories of the gods and their designing of the Anychî bond. They help explain why our magic wants to be connected, but we don't have time to go over them."

She nodded, and a few strands of her hair fell in front of her face as she did. "You did promise no more lies between us."

She held out her palm. He grabbed it, fully encasing the petite hand. He resisted the urge to bring it up and caress his lips along her delicate skin.

"I did." And he meant it. As his queen and friend, he would not betray her trust.

"How do you accept the bond?"

His eyes widened at her question. "You're actually considering it?"

She shrugged her shoulders. "Any extra bit of magic to use against the Eternal Queen seems a wise thing to consider."

He agreed, even if the Queen could possibly morph it and use it against them. He wanted to say more, reveal more, but the sound of multiple footsteps approaching stopped him. They both stood in tandem, readying themselves.

Layla entered the ring of trees first. Her glance went straight to their still-entwined hands. To Auden's pleasant surprise, Ellienia didn't release her grip at the teasing smile Layla gave. It wasn't until the small elf and young man walking arm in arm entered the ring of trees. Then she let go and ran to her friend. Ellienia wrapped Kiarhem up in her arms, kissing her dark brow.

"Are you alright? Are you still in any pain?" There was a slight tremble in Ellienia's voice that had Auden's own heart sinking.

"I'm fine, I promise. Just a bit sore." Kiarhem pushed Ellienia off slightly, not to leave her embrace, but so she could look into Ellienia's eyes. "Thank you." Her hazel eyes lined with tears.

"You missed out on quite a bit while you were out." Ellienia released her.

"So I've heard." Kiarhem gestured her head towards Layla. "She didn't tell me everything. I think she left most of the good stuff for you."

"She knows your magic healed her, and that's about it," Layla informed.

"Yes, but don't be surprised when I don't react to your true form." Kia waved a finger over Ellienia's face. Ellienia stitched her brows. Auden, too, was surprised by the claim. "Glamour doesn't work on all elves. I've known what you are from day one, and you too." She turned to Auden and winked.

"You've known we were Fae and never said anything? Why?" She shrugged her shoulders at Auden's question.

"It didn't seem like my place to say anything."

More footsteps shuffled towards them. Ellienia pulled Kia and Kal further into the ring before returning to her place next to Auden. He hadn't planned on standing by her side during whatever speech she had planned, but she had asked him to. Moments after sending Nate off to gather the group, she had asked him to stand with her.

You were sent here to be my guard, but you have been so much more. You question my actions, argue my choices, and I need that. I need you to keep questioning me, keep being brave enough to counsel your queen. And as the only other Fae here, having you on my right side seems the logical choice.

He knew even if he wasn't the only Fae there, she would have still asked him. And it was the look she gave him after he promised to stand with her that had him questioning everything.

Her heart belonged to Nate, despite their current decision to part. But that look...

He wouldn't allow it to give him false hope.

The bond between them pulled, begging to be connected. His need to touch her and be near her had heightened. The bond amplified what he already felt for her, and he now wondered what the need for their magic to be connected felt like for her.

Auden had been taught that the bond would feel different for each person. That what he felt would be different then what she felt. He wondered if she even felt the bond's need to connect over her overwhelming rush of power.

The last of their allies filed into the ring of trees: Layla, Kiarhem, Kal, Myer, Kier, Belig, Doal, Collern, Nate, and even Shea, who leaned against a tree in the back of the group. His weary eyes remained solely on Ellienia.

"Are you ready?" Auden tilted down, whispering into her ear.

"Not yet." She smiled up at him with a gleam in her eyes. "We're still missing one, who seems satisfied with remaining behind this tree for the entirety of this gathering."

From the shadows behind them, Ames appeared. No. Materialized before them. Like mist forming into a solid dark cloud.

The shocked gasps and slur of colorful words had both Ames and Ellienia beaming.

"You could sense me?" Ames peered at her with a raised brow.

"Yes. Unfortunately for you, my magic now *reacts* when you're around." Her playful sneer was a mirror to Ames's.

"How...*delightful.*" He grabbed for her hand, placing a kiss atop it. When he pulled away, Auden's stomach curled at the look he gave Ellienia. He tensed at the desire to growl at him.

"Now we're ready." She gave him a nod. With a wave of his hand, the shield was up, and they were invisible to the outside world.

51

E llie hadn't much time to think on what she would say to her friends and allies. She only wished to tell them the truth, and so she did. She started with her name, title, and the entirety of her adopted grandfather's plan. She told them of his alliance with Officer Shea, and the part they played in getting women enlisted. She spoke of everything from the royal library to her cursed house; there was no detail she left out. When she was done, she looked towards the male standing to her right.

"Remove our glamours, Auden."

"Did she just call him Auden?" Myer whispered to Keir. "Are we allowed to call him that?"

The glamour was removed in tandem to Auden growling and baring his Fae teeth at Myer. He smirked at the multiple steps back both Myer and Keir took.

A few extra exhales echoed throughout the circle of trees. She could feel their eyes scanning her every inch.

"We have a plan. I will not lie to you. It could free you from the Eternal Queen's ranks or get you killed trying."

"Our town was told your people had all been killed." Doal spoke through a shallow exhale.

"We've done a good job at making it seem that way." Auden gave a reassuring smile. "King Vedmar sent our people into hiding to save us from being used and slaughtered by the Queen."

"King Vedmar wasn't just the King of Fae. The Malavor royals ruled over all of Malavor and its surrounding territories. Territories that called upon their king and queens for help in this war. Help that never came. They let hundreds of others die at the hands of the Eternal Queen's men. This entire land knew how strong your armies were. We all knew you would be our only hope in surviving any attack made by the Queen. But instead of fighting or aiding any allies, *your* royals chose to have their armies run and hide like cowards. Why should we fight with two young Fae of Malavor in their time of need when you would not do the same for us?" Doal's dark eyes glowed with anger. Belig's eyes did not mirror his friend's, but he did nod with agreement.

The initial battles of this war were less than two decades ago. Doal and Belig were present for the attacks on their home. She knew the resentment they held on their faces was not towards her, but the avoidable slaughter they endured. Auden began to protest, but Ellie waved a silencing hand.

"Because—" She shifted at the weight their gaze held. "—fighting with us now means getting yourselves out of this hell. It will get you out of fighting for the Eternal Queen and instead lead you to fighting against her. I understand your anger, Doal. I do not agree with every decision the Malavor King and Queens made, but I can't go back and change those decisions. None of us can. We can only move forward, hopefully as continued allies through whatever future paths we face." She stared at the two men from Turgo.

Collern stepped forward, shoulders back and green eyes focused. "You are not defined by your ancestors." He wisely spoke. Ellie couldn't believe this was the same man she punched weeks ago. "The kindness and strength you've displayed these past weeks proves you are a queen worth serving. I will serve you, Queen Ellienia." He bowed gracefully.

Ellie breathed through the tightness in her chest. "I am not asking you to serve me as a Queen of Malavor. I am asking for your alliance as my equals. I am asking for your help as my friends."

"Then as your friends, you don't even have to ask." Myer beamed as he swung an arm around Kier's shoulders.

"We'll help with whatever you need, Ellie," Kier added.

Belig and Doal looked at one another, and an unspoken agreement laced their eyes.

"We will fight for you, Ellienia, but only you," Belig signed. It felt like a promise and a warning. She could not let them down in the same way the previous royals had.

"Thank you." She bowed her head to the two men.

All eyes were now on Kal, the newest and youngest alliance.

"If you succeed in whatever plan you have, what then? Where will you go? Where do you expect us to go?"

It was a valid question. One she had thought through thoroughly.

"It will be your choice," she said simply. "Nate and Layla will lead any who wish to go north and fight. If you want to go home to your loved ones, you can." Ellie wasn't sure what actions the Eternal Queen would take once her training camp was *inoperative*, but she knew each and every one of their family members were at risk. "Fighting and risking your lives, and the lives of those you love, will always be your choice."

"And you? Where will you go?" Kal asked again.

"Ames, Kiarhem, Auden, and I will go south. To the elf colonies and to where the Malavor Fae have been hiding."

She glanced at Nate. He lowered his head to look at the ground, shifting his weight at her words. They argued about this part of the plan for what felt like ages last night. He had pleaded with her, begged her to take him south with the others, with her. She couldn't though. Not when she needed someone she trusted to lead her allies north. To ready the northern armies for the Malavor Fae and hopefully a few other forces.

She swallowed a knot that formed in her throat at the thought of his pleading umber eyes. "There is work to be done there before we also join the northern armies."

Vague, but she didn't have time to go through everything they had planned to do in Delmi.

Kiarhem squeezed Kal's arm. She looked at him with a soft, reassuring smile. She saw something in him the rest did not. Ellie took a closer look at the young man, hoping to see what Kia saw.

"I would like to go south with you," he finally voiced.

Auden stepped forward, to either accept or deny his request, Ellie didn't know, but she once again stopped him with a gentle gesture of her hand.

She slowly walked towards Kal, inspecting every inch of him. He had been fast, so fast in the last trial. She hadn't questioned his inhuman reflexes until now. Her scanning snagged at his eyes. Golden eyes like she had never seen before. So bright that they seemed to...*glow*.

She whipped her head towards Auden. He smiled and nodded once.

"You're Fae." Ellie took another step towards the young male, a gentle smile gracing her lips.

"Half." He shifted on his feet at the growing attention from all who were gathered. "My mother was human."

Was. Ellie saw the silver lining his eyes. She reached for his hand. She would not question him or force him to tell more. Not now, as so many eyes peered at him.

"Yes. You will join us south." Her words caused his shoulders to relax.

"So, then what's the plan, my queen." Myer gave a mocking bow. Kier elbowed him in the ribs for the gesture, but Ellie replied with a wicked smile.

"It's time for the generals to participate in their own trial."

52

F our days.

      After talking to the entire alliance, they had only four days to perfect their plan. It was now the night before their attack and the fourth trial.

The apathy trial. Ellie didn't want to think about what that meant.

Every night, Auden would take their group to pay respects to the fallen. They were the only group to do so. The smell of charred hair and skin still burned her throat, and her eyes had remained swollen and red from her constant shed of tears. She couldn't help but look at the fallen, see their blank stares, and think of their loved ones.

It had kept her up despite the fact that Layla and Auden had her training late at night and early in the mornings.

Her first lesson had been learning her limit. Like a muscle, her magic had to be built up or it would tire her easily. The more she used it, the longer she could go without feeling the effects of it draining her. Auden constantly reminded Ellie of the consequences of her using too much of her powers and draining herself mid battle. She would be too tired to physically defend herself, so knowing her limit and not reaching it was the first and most important lesson.

Then came the easy part: wielding her magic that so desperately wanted to be used. Now that she had fully accepted her power, parts of controlling it were easy. She could form water from the humid air and direct it effortlessly. All she had to do was think about what she wanted the water to do and it would do it.

What became difficult were the moments where her Empousîa would react to the power she used. One moment she would be jetting a powerful stream of water towards a tree, and the next that jet of water would be turned into a deadly shard of gleaming, hard ice, shattering and splintering large chunks of bark from the tree.

Ellie hadn't seen it as a problem. She admittedly wouldn't mind seeing a general impaled with her ice. Until she held two large bubbles of water, readying to release them, when the water turned to ice and completely encased her hands. It took Auden ages to carefully chisel and melt all of it off. It was a miracle her fingers weren't frostbit by the time he finished.

"Unfortunately, I don't know much about Empousîas. And I've never heard of a water Fae being able to wield both water and ice," Auden had admitted. He and Layla both sat next to her on the forest ground. They stared at her chest, trying to figure out how to stop the pendant from acting out.

"It seems to have a mind of its own," Ellie stated.

"Most magic does." Layla reached forward and grabbed the pendant in her hand, inspecting its invisible power. "At least in its own way. It's most likely tied to emotion, as more unruly magic usually is. You need to feel absolutely nothing when you wield your powers."

"That's like asking me not to breathe, Layla."

She bit the inside of her cheek. "I know. I just don't know what else to do."

She dropped the pendant. Its cold touch slammed into Ellie's chest.

"We're out of time." Ellie stood from the hard ground, dusting dirt and leaves from her backside. "We just have to hope it *behaves* tomorrow."

"And if it doesn't?" Auden stood, offering his hand to Layla. She batted it away, standing without his help.

Ellie couldn't hide her smirk. "I'll only use my left arm to wield my powers if the pendant acts up." *And her hand becomes encased in freezing ice.* "I'll still have my right hand free to wield my sword. Problem solved."

"My definition of *solved* is different from yours," Auden scoffed. "I need to relieve Shea. He'll need to help Ames set up for tomorrow's trial. Shall we?" He held out a bent arm.

Shea had watched over group twenty-four anytime Auden was away.

Ellie wasn't sure why, but Auden had seemed more at ease since their talk a few days ago. The pain that once lined his jaw had disappeared. He had joked more with Myer and Kier. Openly laughed when Kiarhem surprisingly took Kal down during a heated sparring match. He then spent some one-on-one time training him. Even now, hours before their possible demise, he smiled at her with gleaming eyes.

She hooked her arm with his.

"I'd actually like a moment alone with Ellie. Could I escort her to the tent?" Layla crossed in front of them, linking Ellie's free arm with hers.

"Of course, but don't be long. We all need our rest before tomorrow." Auden unhooked his arm, squeezing her hand gently and giving her a playful wink as he did.

She snorted and rolled her eyes.

Both women watched him, Ellie eyes shamefully spent too long looking at his backside as he walked away.

"So." Layla's voice broke her gaze. "You talked to Auden about being Anychî?"

"I did."

"And?"

"And what?" Ellie wasn't sure what Layla needed to know. Yes, being bonded to Auden would be extremely intimate, but she was comfortable with it. She couldn't explain why, but having that bond with him didn't scare her. And knowing the bond would result in more power to be used against the Queen was an added bonus.

"Wow, I'm shocked at how well you're handling it."

"It's not a big deal, Layla."

"Being told you're mated seems like a rather big deal, Ellienia."

Ellie's gut twisted. "What?"

"Anychî. As in a magical bond of both love and power created by the gods. A soulmate. It's why you're both so drawn to one another. You don't really have a choice. It's the gods' design and destiny for you two to be together. Didn't he tell you all this?"

She saw red. "No. He did not."

Layla stepped to the side fully, viewing Ellie's building rage. "I'm so sorry," she whispered. "I thought he told you. Please, Ellienia, forget what I just said. Focus on tomorrow."

Focus on tomorrow. Her entire body was trembling. Her fingertips covered with frost. How could she focus on anything when another choice, her last remaining choice, had just been ripped away from her. She never had a chance to choose her future, and now she'd never get to choose who she loved. The fucking gods chose for her.

"Ellienia, he's a good male who does care for you—"

"Shut it, Layla. You've said enough." Her growl was feral. She didn't care if it hurt her friend.

Layla had been right. She had to focus, which meant no more talking about a future she may not even have after tomorrow's fight.

53

"Are you ready?" Nate placed his onyx sword through the sheath on his hip.

Ellie looked at what should have been her father's weapon. Today, Nate would use it for the purpose it had initially been forged for. Today, it would kill. Today, Nate would kill.

Her chest tightened.

The tent was eerily quiet as each person readied themselves for the trial. The members of her alliance didn't hide their apprehension. Their eyes were more focused, muscles more tense, and faces more somber than in days past.

"Do you remember when your father compared me to a rose?"

Nate stitched his brows. "What?"

"The day we left." She pulled her beautiful leather harness and sheath from the end of her mat and ran a finger along the engraved rose. "He spoke of the rose being a symbol of love and hope, but also a protector of itself and others. At the time, I don't think he realized how accurate his comparison was. I don't think he knew I was a Queen of Malavor...or maybe he did."

She placed the harness on her back and buckled it to her front. "He also told me about its thorns, how they could over grow and kill what it was meant to protect. That its need to fight and overtake would take control. It would become unbalanced without the beauty of the rose.

A metaphor for what I could become with this constant anger within me. What I could become without love and hope and friendship."

"El..."

"As a queen at war, *I* won't just be killing. Others will be killing and sacrificing for me. And as Queen, every one of those deaths will be on my hands." Her eyes burned at the emotion she held in. "Please, Nate. Don't let me lose sight of who I am. Don't let me become like the cruel Queen we currently fight."

Nate was on her instantly. His long arms wrapped around her in a powerful embrace. "You will never be her. The fact that you hold life in such high regard proves that."

He held her for not long enough, but Ellie could feel their gazes. When he released her, every eye of her alliance was on her.

She straightened her shoulders, hardened her face, became the fierce Queen, the powerful symbol they needed to fight for.

"Everyone out. It's time to leave," Auden announced from the front tent flaps.

Beyond the flaps lay a thin layer of mist, familiar and comforting. They lined up as they always did, following behind other groups of designates. Auden walked beside her, his shoulder brushing against hers with each step.

She hadn't had time to process what Layla had revealed.

She knew she was angry—at the gods and at Auden. He purposely did not tell her that accepting the bond of power would also mean accepting him as a mate.

Beyond her anger was confusion. She admittedly did have a growing affection for Auden. However, she now questioned whether or not those feelings were sincere. Was it the bond between them making her feel such things?

"Are you alright?" he whispered as they walked.

She shook her head to refocus. "I'm fine."

"He's right. You will never become *her*."

Ellie clenched her teeth. "You shouldn't listen to conversations that do not involve you."

Beyond her apprehension and anger for the battle ahead, she was annoyed. She wondered how many earlier conversations Auden's Fae ears picked up.

"Anything that involves you questioning yourself in any way also involves me." He brushed a hand against hers, causing her gut to twist and her skin to prickle.

His touch. It had always caused her body to react in ways it had never done before. She now understood why, and the realization only angered her more.

"*Don't.* Don't touch me." Her tone was vicious, and if she wasn't so angry with him, she might have regretted it.

His eyes widened in surprise. He moved farther from her shoulder, allowing distance between them as they walked. "Whatever's going on, Ellienia, you need to forget it and focus on the task ahead."

He was right. Gods. Why was he always right?

She focused on her steps, replaying the plan in her head. This would work. It had to. Too many lives were depending on this plan to succeed, but she couldn't focus on that. It only caused the aching in her stomach to grow. Nerves ran through her body as each step brought her closer to the courtyard. To where the fourth trial was set to take place.

Rows of short leather whips lay in lines across the stone ground. She found herself standing a few feet behind one of the short whips. Collern stood across from her, another few feet away from the whip placed eerily between them. This was the apathy trial. Ellie didn't need much more information to conclude what the generals expected the designates to do with the whips.

She looked up at the front castle steps to see all thirty generals seated. Beside the green-toothed General Polage stood Ames. The mist around her legs tickled at her ankles as she made eye contact with the Nokken.

Dolion stood at the center of them, ready to make his speech. His final speech, Ellie hoped. Auden claimed that this trial was the general's favorite and no one would miss it. Thankfully, he was correct.

"Good morning, designates." Dolion's sneer was brighter, filled with more wicked delight than usual. "Today is your apathy trial. You should each be facing a fellow designate, and between you should lay a leather whip. There will be five rounds to today's trial. At the beginning of each round, you will hear a whistle. When you hear that whistle, you will race to the whip. Whoever gets to the whip first will administer five lashes to the opposing designate. Fighting and using weapons are allowed to gain access to the whip. However, once the whip is fully in the hands of either you or your opponent, the fighting must end." Collern held his sword at the ready, though Ellie knew it was not for her. All eight of her allies held their weapons, their eyes focused and ready for battle. She could not fail them. She prayed for their protection to any god that would hear her.

No designate in the entire courtyard dared to voice a

disgust or concern. Barely a breath was heard, but Ellie scanned the surrounding faces. More than a few wore sneers of delight and excitement, the citizens from territories loyal to the Eternal Queen, but most looked up at the generals with expressions of anger and horror.

"If you do not stand still while lashes are being distributed, or you refuse to inflict the five lashes, your group arbitrator will be forced to take action."

The sounds of short clicks and dull buzzing radiated throughout the courtyard. Ellie looked around to see every group arbitrator encircle the designates with their flare batons at the ready. She swallowed down the bile that rose in her throat.

She had warned her allies, basically begging them to stay as far away from the batons as possible. Unfortunately, she knew these were the weapons they would face. Them and the generals.

"We will not have soldiers of weak heart or mind in this army. You are expected to hurt, inflict, and kill in this army, and that is what you will do today."

Ellie tried not to cringe at how truthful Dolion's last words were.

Dolion took his seat and pursed his lips, but the whistle never came.

54

A sound deeper and more terrifying shook the ground beneath them. Stones from the surrounding wall burst outwards, pieces of it crumbling to the ground. An explosion, one after another, took more and more stones from the wall.

Ellie knew the combustion boxes that Shea and Ames placed all along the stone wall would not be strong enough to tear it down completely, or even really cause too much damage, but it was enough to cause just the right amount of panic and diversion.

Designates from all other groups ran screaming from their tents, gathering to the center of the courtyard, away from the falling debris. Just as she had planned, every single designee, arbitrator, and witch pushed and squeezed their way into the courtyard.

The generals stood, faces enraged at the scene before them.

"Go!" Nate yelled into Ellie's ear.

She ran for the center of the courtyard, weaving through the mass of people. She headed straight for the wood post, the beam that last held Filtmon's limp body up as a deserter. She jumped onto its circular solid base and scaled the post. It was large enough in circumference to easily crouch down on top of or stand, as she planned to do. She would be an easy target, one she hoped someone would be foolish enough to engage.

The explosions ended, and only the sounds of crumbling rocks and worried voices remained. Ellie stood on the beam, releasing the whistle Dolion never got to carry out. It was their trial now, not hers. She unsheathed her blue-silver sword, holding upright at her side. The generals' eyes were all on her, as was the quieting crowd. She felt the slight warmth in her face and body as Auden released his glamour.

She had picked a terrifyingly beautiful outfit for today's battle, but it was not the outfit the generals gaped at. It was the small circlet of braided silver that was in Ellie's hair. The gleaming cerulean fluorite gem in the shape of a teardrop lay just between her brows. The piece was one of the royal jewels found and restored by Layla and presented to Ellie just days ago.

Many of the generals stood, the shock clear on all of their faces. She held their stares, a wicked smile gracing her lips.

"I am Ellienia Batair Kiaver. One of three living Queens of Malavor." She let the statement sink into the crowd. "I've come to destroy these camps, to free the Karmalo people of these abhorrent trials, and to take back my home!"

She raised her sword. Shouts of her allies and many more came from the crowd below.

"For years you have been forced to watch loved one after loved one die for a cruel, wicked queen. Die for a faceless and nameless leader! I will fight against her reign, and I vow to end it!"

More shouts of approval rang, so loud she barely heard the snap of a string and the whistle of an arrow. Someone took the bait. She whipped her head around, and her Fae speed dodged the arrow slightly before pulling it out of the air. She held it in her hand, twirling it once before snapping it in two.

The crowd murmured at the display. Ellie scanned the area from where the arrow came, and she saw the small, round arbitrator just as he took another shot. This time, she used her sword to knock it from her path. His eyes were wide with panic as he scrambled to nock another arrow.

She hoped someone would attack first, making her display of power justified.

"Officer Schmilt, again you try to kill me from behind." She clicked her tongue in disapproval. "I tire of your attempts."

She held out a hand, feeling the thrum of her magic. She pictured what she wanted her powers to do, and Schmilt's sudden inability to breathe told her it was working. He fell to his knees, grabbing at his chest as water dripped from his mouth. She was drowning him, and not just him. Many arbitrators fell to their knees, any and all that Ellie saw being cruel at one point, including Officer Ballock. He fell towards her right. His eyes glared at her with so much hate, Ellie nearly looked away.

She didn't. She gazed at him with equal hate and rage. She held his stare as her pendant began to run cold. She didn't know what it would do, and she didn't care as she looked at Ballock's enraged face. Icicles began to form from his nostrils and mouth. His eyes bulged then shattered as ice exploded out of him. His large body fell to the ground, his horrible flare baton dropping with him. Ellie dropped her arm. A bit of fatigue ran through her muscles at the substantial display of her power.

Gasps of shock and horror rang near the now-lifeless arbitrators. Ellie turned back to face the generals.

"A Benegiménos," General Dolion mouthed.

Before any of them could take action, she gave Ames her signal. Every bit of mist was pulled from the ground and now formed a wall around the generals. Their hollers of outrage turned to screams of horror. Ellie didn't know what the Nokken made them see, but she was thankful for it.

She jumped from the beam and ran towards the steps as chaos ensued. Fighting broke out all around her: designate against crueler designate or designate against arbitrator. A few arbitrators tried to stop her as she ran for the castle steps, but she easily evaded and brought them down.

The witches ran for the castle walls, wanting to hide in their shadows. They soon realized five young, beautiful witches made it impossible. Layla stood arms raised with her sisters chanting towards their Mother witches.

From another direction a high-pitched bird call rose over the clash of weapons and screams of pain. A blur of dark bodies ran past Ellie towards the call, towards Kiarhem. The elves cut through man after man as if they were stalks of wheat. They encircled Kia like lions protecting their cub and readied themselves for an attack coming from a larger, more feral-looking group of elves. Those aligned with the Eternal Queen.

Ellie stopped a few feet from the front steps. The mist was fading; Ames's power was weakening. He emerged from the haze holding two curved blades in each of his hands as he ran down the steps to join her. Two other bodies flanked her from either side before Ames took his place behind her.

"That was incredible." Nate smiled proudly to her left.

Ames breathlessly laughed behind her. "Incredible! No, that was perfection! I will have daydreams of Ballock's face exploding."

She could feel Ames's sincere sneer from behind her, but she tried not to cringe at his words.

"You did good, Ellienia."

She didn't dare look at Auden. She couldn't risk losing her focus, especially now that the mist had disappeared.

55

Ten dark figures lay at the feet of the remaining twenty generals.

Ames had killed *ten* generals by himself. Ellie wasn't sure if she was terrified or impressed. She admittedly felt both.

The remaining generals rubbed the mist from their eyes, shaking their heads to clear them. Ellie readied herself, flipping her sword in her hand to feel its weight. Dolion's eyes were the first to clear.

"I figured you'd want to be the one to end him," Ames growled. Ellie was sure Ames had just as much right to end Dolion as she had, possibly more.

"I don't care who kills him. As long as he dies."

"Good."

They darted up the steps, each aiming for their own general.

Delight danced on Dolion's lips as he glared at her with rage. She thrust a wave of water towards the dark figure. One moment she looked at those dark eyes, and the next she saw it blur and disappear into a cloud of black smoke. Her water blasted through it, splashing against the stone ground.

She didn't have time to react as the black smoke curled behind her and a strong hand reached through it and grabbed her hair, throwing her backwards. Her body screamed as she slammed down multiple steps. She stopped herself from rolling but took too long to regain her bearings. Dolion was already on her. He slammed his knee up into her chin. She flew back, falling down the remainder of the stone steps.

A metallic taste coated her tongue, and warmth ran down the side of her face. She forced herself to stand, to focus on her surroundings.

Screams of terror erupted through the crowd as plumes of black smoke, then generals appeared randomly throughout the battle ground. With swords and flare batons, they slaughtered anyone and everyone, too enthralled with their rage and bloodlust to care who was fighting on their side.

Auden, Ames, and Nate made it to the top of the steps. Ames took on two generals next to Nate who stood his ground against General Polage.

Auden took on two more generals, moving through the air with inhuman speed and grace. But the generals were just as fast. One sliced through his lower back, causing a deep howl to echo in the air. The sound of his screams shifted something inside Ellie. A feral rage-filled focus took over her body. Her need to fight for him and all her friends took hold. Her magic pushed against her skin, feeding off her anger and begging to be used.

"I can't decide if I should kill you or take you to my queen." Dolion took his time walking down the stairs, unsheathing his sword with one hand and releasing his flare baton with the other. The sight of the blue sparks coming at her had Ellie swallowing bile that formed in her throat.

"She has been waiting many years for another blessed one and will have much *fun* with you." Ellie cringed, ignoring the growing ringing in her head. "But you're a Kiaver. A royal line we thought had been eradicated."

"Looks like you were wrong." Her growl was unrecognizable.

"Clearly. So who is it that birthed you, little princess? Queen Odina? Queen Akéra?"

"Neither." The corners of her mouth grew upward, despite the pounding in her head. "King Vedmar and Queen Odina had a younger sister. A powerful Fae who killed many of your men even after her death."

There was no smile that remained on the general's cruel face. He glanced beyond the castle towards her childhood home. "The empath."

When his eyes returned to hers, they were filled with terror and rage. They had feared her mother. They would fear her, too.

"I am much more powerful than the King and Queens you slaughtered. I am the second daughter of Amilliety Batair Kiaver, and you will die for what you did to my parents, my family, and my people. You all will."

She rushed him, and when she swung her sword towards his face, he didn't turn to smoke. No, he met her sword with his, easily pushing her back. General Dolion was incredibly strong, and his ability to quickly disappear and reappear at any moment made tracking his movement near impossible. Ellie had no advantage against the beast she battled. The only thing that was stronger than his was her rage and desire to kill him.

They slammed their weapons together, attacking and

blocking over and over again. She used every bit of her training against him, but she knew it would not be enough. She reached her magic out multiple times, pushing him back with intense bursts of water.

"You can kill me, little princess, but she will raise me again. Form me as she once did. She will continue to do so until every last blessed one is hers and all of Karmalo is enslaved."

Little princess. She threw her magic at him again. This time the water turned to ice as it had done many times before. She was enraged, and the pendant seemed equal to her anger as it burned against her chest. Dolion sidestepped the dagger of ice, and it crashed against the stone steps.

His eyes were wild. "Such unique magic you wield, blessed one."

She growled at the general, ready for another attack. From the corner of her eye, the mass of a body came tumbling down the castle steps. His head knocked against the hard stone of each stair. His arms and legs thrashed with no control. His lifeless, mutilated body rolled and stopped mere inches from where she stood.

Nate.

Layla stood hand in hand with her sisters, arms raised and chanting in the origin tongue.

An invisible wall stretched from her to the surrounding castle walls. She would force her Mothers and sisters to endure this battle. Watch as the monsters they aligned themselves with brutally murder hundreds.

"This! This is what you chose! You turned your backs on

the Mother, and she will never forgive you for it," Layla yelled as her sisters continued to chant.

"Let us pass or you are the one who is doomed," an elder witch sneered. She grabbed the hands of the witches next to her. "The Father will grant us power to put you in your place."

A chorus of voices chanted as one, louder than Layla and her sisters ever could. Layla was indeed stronger than any other witch in her coven, but with their voices united, she was uncertain her magic would hold.

Layla raised her voice over the chanting of witches and screaming of designates. "All the Father has granted our coven is death. My sisters, the Mothers are blind to the misfortunes we have endured since aligning with the Queen. They have set us on a path of failure, they have forgotten the goddess of magic, our Mother, and she has forgotten them. If you remember every stillborn, every daughter lost since living in these castle walls, I beg you to join us. Support Queen Ellienia in taking back her throne. Earn the Mother's love once again."

"Zye witches do not beg, Layla," the mother witch growled.

"But she is right." A young witch to the Mother's right released her hand. The Mother witch snarled in outrage as the young one joined the line of Layla's sisters. A few more followed, ones Layla knew would, and others she was surprised to see join her, but it was not enough. It was only a matter of time before the Mothers' chants overpowered theirs. It was only a matter of time until whatever death spell they sang took hold.

Kiarhem swung two short blades, slicing through man after man. She had little training before arriving at the Malavor camps, so she left any elves to the Arimos and fellow Dorumia warriors that surrounded her. She'd known the Dorumia elves would hear her call for help.

Unfortunately, she did not expect every other elf in Malavor to hear and understand her call. Esvanora, Thanoré, Lalenor, Arimos, and Dorumia elves gathered, ready to fight for their colony and against any that stood in opposition of the Queen they aligned with. The discord of Delmi and its colonies battling on Malavor soil.

Though the warriors from Arimos and Dorumia were fierce forces, so were the others, and there were more of them. They were encircled and herded into an immovable space, too close to one another to get a good hit or jab in.

"Your parents would be very proud of you, little one." A familiar Dorumia voice spoke. Kia's vision blurred with tears, knowing her end was coming.

Auden's magic felt Ellienia's anguish before hearing her earth-shattering cry. It stirred him into action like never before. His speed and efficiency increased, allowing him to slice through one of the two generals he fought. His black blood coated Auden's golden sword and sprayed in his face.

He whispered in the origin tongue, releasing a spell that stilled the second general. Auden whirled around to slice the general in two but stopped as he viewed the curved blade that protruded from the general's neck.

"Seriously, Ames. That was my kill."

The Nokken stepped out from behind the slain general. "No. It wasn't."

The look in Ames's eyes told Auden enough. This was one of the many generals that had used him, so it was indeed his life to claim. They both stood at the top of the castle stairs, looking over the chaos and slaughter.

"She's going to lose control, isn't she?"

Auden didn't answer him. He rushed down the steps towards a still Nate and a struggling Ellienia.

The sound that came from Ellie was inhuman. She shook as her power begged to be released, begged to react to the rage and despair that she felt. Her growing anger held on by a single thread. She went to kneel towards Nate's body, but a sword against her left leg stopped her. It sliced deep and long. Her leg burned as she forced herself to stay standing. She lost control of some of her power, and it released in shards of ice straight towards the general. He cursed as a few icicles met their mark.

She turned towards Dolion, viewing the damage her ice caused. Dozens of small shards of glistening ice stuck from every inch of the general, like pieces of broken glass. Black oily blood dripped out of each wound. He rushed towards her but was stopped by the gathering of black smoke.

A scream caught in Ellie's throat as a sword came through the smoke, headed straight for her neck. It never made its mark as it clanged against metal.

Ellie twisted to see the orange-red hair of Officer Shea as he pushed back against General Polage.

She refocused and rushed General Dolion as he gazed at Shea and Polage. She released another wave of magic, the icy daggers making their mark in Dolion's gut. He roared in outrage.

Their swords met again. The clanging of metal was near deafening. He swung towards her with the flare baton, but she dodged with ease.

Ellie watched Shea from the corner of her eye. He parried and attacked better than any man she had ever seen —a warrior with decades of training, and it showed. However, it was not his skillful fighting that caught Ellie's attention. It was boils and red blisters that formed across the man's arms, neck, and face.

He knocked Polage to the ground as smoke began to appear. Not black and consuming like the smoke of the generals, but gray, and it seeped from every inch of Officer Shea.

It was killing him: fighting against the generals, against his fealty mark. If he continued to do so, he would die.

"Shea! Stop! STOP!" She pushed back against Dolion, guiding him closer to Polage and to Shea.

Polage's black smoke began to appear, his only way out of Shea's killing blow, but he wasn't fast enough. Shea turned his head towards Ellie and smiled. Tears gleamed in his eyes. "You were worth the wait, my queen."

"NO!"

Her screams echoed as he swung his sword down at Polage's face and instantly went up in flames. Shea let out a battle cry as he dove from the slain Polage to the shocked General Dolion. He caught the general's cloak before he could move through his smoke. They both burned together. Their cries of agony filled Ellie's head.

She fell to her knees and screamed. Agony ripped through her for the man that gave so much, gave too much of himself.

She crawled across the ground as her screaming continued. Ellie grabbed at Nate's broken body. Her Fae hearing picked up his barely-beating heart.

"*Please,*" she cried. "*Please, don't die.*"

She placed her brow onto his as she continued to plead for his life. Ellie didn't know when she had grabbed her pendant, but the throbbing cold liquid burned her hand.

She ignored the two male bodies that knelt beside her and focused on the magic within her pendant. She tried to hear its power, the familiar lapping of water on an icy shore, but she couldn't hear anything over her horrified screaming and the battle that surrounded her. She couldn't focus past the smell of blood and slain bodies.

Shea was dead. Against the back wall, Layla and her sisters were being overpowered. Most of the elves fighting with Kia had fallen, and she couldn't place Kal, Myer, Keir, Belig, or Doal. Nate was going to die; they were all going to die. Her plan had failed.

The thread holding back her anger finally snapped.

Her screams of agony and rage again filled the air. She let go of the control she had on her magic. She let it rush out of her with every broken heartbeat. Her vision blurred, and her mind came undone. The power inside her completely took over.

She heard Auden and Ames curse as they dove to the ground.

She stood on shaky, tired legs, her veins coursing with the burning cold of the liquid in her pendant. She met the wide eyes of many generals and screamed again. Blades of ice flew through the air, decapitating a large handful. Black, oily blood sprayed from their necks. Heads and bodies fell to the ground. Plumes of black smoke appeared, but never reappeared.

She turned towards the castle. Its walls were tainted and destroyed by decades of trials, by innocent blood. She wanted to tear it down brick by brick. She wanted to erase what had been done to her home, what had been done to her and the people she cared for. Visions of the Great Hall and generals slaughtering the royals flashed through her head. They weren't just royals that were killed that day. They were her family.

A final scream of rage filled the air as she let the remaining bit of her power free. She didn't know what she was doing, and she didn't care. She let the magic guide her, she let it do as it wished, and when the final dregs of power were spent, she crashed to her knees.

A pair of strong arms caught her quick descent before her head slammed to the ground. The faint sounds of chaos rang through her ears before she allowed darkness to take hold.

56

Auden stood clenching and unclenching his fists. The heavy use of his magic left him more fatigued than the use of his sword and fighting skill.

"What she did was extremely dangerous, Auden." Layla stood to Auden's right, viewing the incredible display of power Ellienia created—the object and statement she unintentionally made.

"I know."

The generals that disappeared never came back, fearful that their heads would also roll. Layla claimed that most of the witches also ran as soon as they saw the power Ellienia wielded. Where they went, she didn't know. Once all the generals were gone and Ellienia had finished her work, any designate and arbitrator that remained loyal to the Eternal Queen laid down their weapons.

"She can't wield that kind of power with that much emotion again."

"I know."

"It will destroy her. It could destroy us all."

"I know, Layla. I know." Everything Layla said were words Auden had already spoken to himself.

Layla, her sisters, and a few other young witches that stayed worked endlessly on the hurt and wounded. Their resources were limited now that they couldn't get in the castle doors. They had no access to their workspace or the many premade tonics and salves. Even if they did, their tonics would be useless to the many designates struck with flare batons.

Ellienia had not been of sound mind when she did what she did. She had lost control, and Auden didn't blame her for it. Even in her manic state, she still created something incredible—a symbol the Eternal Queen would not mistake.

Ellienia currently lay resting next to Nate in a tent nearby. Her strong alliance rotated their watch over them. How they had survived the battle, only the gods knew.

"When she wakes, she can't know what she did. She can't know how many innocents she killed. It will only worsen her state of mind."

"She will need to know, Layla. It will be a mark on her soul for as long as she may live, but she needs to know so it may never happen again."

57

"Did you see when Kal came from out of nowhere and stabbed a general from behind? It was amazing." Myer's voice was rough in Ellie's throbbing head.

"Not nearly as amazing as Kia taking on two men by herself. You're a badass, little elf."

Ellie didn't need to open her eyes to see Kiarhem's smile at Kier's words.

"I would not have aligned myself with any of you if I didn't think you were amazing." Ellie opened her eyes and tried to sit up, but the weight of multiple bodies crashed into hers. She fell back, knocking her head against the mat beneath her. "Ow."

"She wakes! Finally!" Myer's voice and the joyous laughs of many rang through her ears. The sound of small steps and tent flaps opening and closing came from her right. She waited a moment, enjoying their hold, before pushing them off.

"You all smell like you've been drinking." Sure enough, each of them held a glass filled with a dark-amber liquid. All except Kia and Kal, who sat rather close to one another. Doal and Belig raised their glass to her, and Collern, Kier, and Myer did the same.

"We found it in one of the general's tents." Kier smiled.

Myer drank the amber liquid from his glass in one swallow. "They may have been brutes, but they were brutes with good taste."

"They're all gone?" she whispered in disbelief. They all nodded at her question. Their clothes were still ripped and stained with a mixture of red and black blood. Most of them had bandages covering larger wounds and glistening salves over smaller ones.

How long had she been out?

"It's evening. You've been out for about nine hours," Kiarhem answered as if reading her mind. "You gave them quite a scare," she said, referring to the generals. "You gave all of us quite a scare."

Each man shifted their weight uncomfortably.

"Wh-what did I do?"

"There are more pressing things to worry about, Ellie," Belig signed and gestured to the mat next to her. To the unconscious, barely-breathing Nate.

She crawled over to him, a light sob escaping her lips. She ran her fingers through his black wavy hair, but they got caught by chunks of dried blood and dirt. His face was swollen, near unrecognizable, and his shoulder and exposed torso were wrapped in thick layers of gauze.

"He was beaten, stabbed in the gut, and has head trauma from falling down the castle steps, but what keeps him unconscious is the mark on his left shoulder." Kia crawled closer to her side, pulling down the gauze to reveal the black cluster of bolts on Nate's shoulder. "No normal healer can help him, Ellie."

Before Ellie could respond, the tent flaps flew open and tiny footsteps belonging to a familiar freckled face walked towards her. The young brunette woman from Perilin held a glass of water in her hands. No scars and bruises remained from the wounds Ellie had healed a week ago. She smiled at her hesitantly as she knelt down beside Nate, opposite of Ellie.

"Here." She held out the glass of water. "Officer Reuel told me you are the one who healed me. I–I would be dead if it wasn't for you, so thank you."

Ellie took the glass of water from the woman's trembling hands. Her soft smile did not reach her leather-brown eyes. Eyes that were filled with fear. She was scared of Ellie, despite the fact that she had once healed her.

Ellie could not blame the young woman. From what she could remember...from what she did on that battlefield, Ellie was also terrified of herself.

"Thank you." Ellie forced a gentle smile to grace her lips. She placed a hand on her pendant and closed her eyes. The sound of lapping water on an icy shore instantly came to her, as if the pendant's power recognized her own and was excited to be used. After only seconds, Ellie had once again succeeded in duplicating the liquid's healing power. However, this time she felt her fatigue immediately. Despite her rest, her magic had yet to fully recoup.

She opened her eyes, ignoring the shocked gazes on her. She wondered if they would ever not be shocked by her powers. She placed the water onto Nate's lips, allowing more than just a drop to pass through his mouth. She sat back, watching as bruises slowly disappeared from Nate's face.

"Here." She handed the glass of water back to the young woman. "There are more injured. Ones without a flare baton mark only need a drop. Give those with a mark more, just in case. Look for the injured with marks closest to their hearts first. They will have less time than the others, and when you run out, come find me. I will make as much healing water as is needed."

"D-do you not need any?" Her questioning gaze traveled over Ellie's body.

Ellie's face and left leg were still covered in blood. Other than a slight pounding in her head, Ellie's Fae magic had healed her rather quickly. She shook her head at the young, round face.

"I'm fine."

"You don't want to distribute the water?"

"No. I see your fear, even as you try to hide it. I am sure many share that fear. I doubt they will let me near them to help."

The young woman nodded, not denying her terror. "I used to hate you, without even knowing you," she whispered. "I was jealous of your beauty. Jealous of how he and many of the men in Perilin looked at you and your sisters. But I understand now that there is much more to you than that."

Ellie was shocked at her admittance. The young woman was far from unattractive.

"I don't know why I'm telling you this. I guess—I just now understand why he loves you, why he has always loved you."

She looked down at Nate as she stood, the glass of water tucked safely in both hands. "My name is Catel, but please call me Cate." She curtsied down at Ellie. "I will find you when this runs dry, Your Majesty."

She left the tent before Ellie could say more, before she could request she didn't call her *Your Majesty*.

"Come, Ellie." Kiarhem pulled her up from the ground.

"The boys will watch over Nate. There is something you need to see."

Kia held tightly to her hand as they walked out of the tent flaps. Ellie released a sharp breath at what she saw before her. At what her magic...At what *she* had done.

58

A n enormous dome of clear, thick ice encased the Malavor castle. It glistened brightly against the setting sun. No one could enter; no one could escape.

"Is there anyone in there?"

"No. Any witch that had remained in the castle during the battle escaped before the dome was complete." Kia squeezed Ellie's hand. They walked closer to the dome's edge. "You're amazing, Ellie. You did exactly what you set out to do. You made Malavor unusable for any further trials. If the Queen wants to continue enlisting Karmalo citizens, she will have to build her training camps elsewhere. Not only that, you've made one hell of a statement with this display of magic."

"What do you mean?"

"In the elfin culture, and even from what I know of the Fae, symbols are extremely important. When I look at this dome, I see your immense power. I see your claim on Malavor. I see your declaration of war. If the Eternal Queen visits here, she will see the same. Everyone will."

They reached its edge. Ellie placed a hand on the cold ice. It did not feel wet or slick as normal ice would. Normal ice would melt, but this ice, her ice, would not. Not until she wanted it to. "I feel like this is a speech Layla or Auden should be giving me."

Ellie looked down at the small elf as she laughed. It was a beautiful sound that reminded Ellie of how her and her sisters would laugh as young girls. Kia was no longer a young elf, though. These camps, this battle, had changed her as it had changed them all.

"Those two do like to hear themselves talk, don't they."

It was Ellie's turn to laugh. Her body ached at the jolting movement, but she felt freer, lighter than she had in over a month.

"I would be offended, elf, if it wasn't so true." The deep voice that came from behind Ellie caused her heart to skip. She whipped around to Auden, seeing his clothes were cut and ripped in places where wounds already healed. His shirt and hair were stained with the vile, oily, black blood of the generals he killed. The smile that graced his lips was strained, full of uncertainty as he met Ellie's gaze.

She had been so enraged with him before the battle, but now...she wanted to look at him and feel anger. She wanted to feel upset for what he failed to mention to her. But that pit of rage that normally welled inside her was empty. She had used it all to form the dome behind her, and she admittedly only felt relief when she met his silver eyes.

Before she realized what she was doing, she was running towards him, crashing into his hard body and wrapping her arms around his neck. He didn't hesitate as he folded his large arms around her waist, lifting her slightly as he did.

She felt him nod to Kia and heard her steps as she walked away, leaving them alone in their embrace.

For just a moment, she would pretend that what she felt for Auden was real. She would pretend that there was no bond forcing her to feel the way she did for him. She would allow herself to enjoy the embrace, to appreciate the comfort it gave.

"This wasn't my original plan." She pulled slightly away from him, their faces incredibly close.

"No, but it is arguably way better." His breath was hot against her face. She hadn't realized until his warmth surrounded her, that her body was still quite cold from the power the pendant coursed through her veins.

"Shea...he—"

"I know. I saw." He rested his brow onto hers. "Shea knew the risks. He knew what it would mean to fight for you, and I'm sure it was a choice he gladly made."

A knot formed in her throat at the thought of Shea—a man that deserved so much more from life. A man who truly would have been an incredible father. "I'm going to tear down that stupid deserter beam and replace it with a statue in his honor."

The corner of Auden's mouth pulled up in a way she both hated and loved. "I like that idea, but seeing as it's your only current platform to stand on and address your new army, it'll have to wait, *little princess*."

His reference to what Dolion had called her formed an entirely new pit of rage within her. She pushed him off, punching him in the gut as she did. "Don't call me that."

Her threat was silenced by Auden's deep joyous laugh. "The man was a horrible beast and terrible at pet names. You are clearly no princess, Ellienia. You are a queen." Ellie sucked in a breath. *A queen.* It still all felt surreal. "Though, I'd have to agree with the little part." He smirked at the daggered glare she gave him.

He once again closed the gap between them, placing both of his palms on either side of her face and tipping her head up. "As much as I would like to stand here and continue teasing you, you really do have an army to address."

"Then let go of my face and lead the way."

He smiled. A real, and true smile that reached his silver eyes. He was truly breathtaking in his Fae form. It was impossible for Ellie to look away. Leaning closer to her face, the tips of his lips brushed against her brow. He waited for a moment, as if seeing if she would push him away. She should have, but her body and heart rejected anything her mind screamed at her to do.

Her lower abdomen warmed as he finally placed his full lips on her temple. She hated how her heart sank when he pulled away from her.

"What was that for?"

"For staying alive."

59

Ellie had once hidden with two chickens for multiple hours in the rafters of their farm's old barn. The chickens had soiled her clothes, pecked until her arms bled, and made the wait near unbearable. It was all worth it when she dropped those birds onto the unexpected heads of her sisters. A lesson in being more aware of their surroundings, Ackerley claimed when he thought of the idea. And a lesson in patience for Ellie.

She had never once thought that her years of sparring, pretend war games, riddle and puzzle solving, and other odd lessons would lead to where she currently stood: a Malavor queen addressing the people she just liberated. The thought sent a cold wave down her spine.

Over a thousand lives were lost during the trials and in the courtyard earlier that day. Most were killed in the generals' lust for blood. Just under six hundred remained. A small percentage of that were arbitrators and designates still loyal to the Eternal Queen and her cruel generals.

Hundreds of tired eyes looked up at her, patiently waiting for her to speak. Cate had worked quickly, and most of the previously wounded were now standing alert and present. All except those who were marked with the flare baton. The healing magic was taking longer for those to heal. Ellie honestly wondered if they would. If Nate would.

She shook her head to focus, not allowing herself to worry or think of Nate. She looked back up at the hundreds of waiting faces.

Ackerley had failed to give any lessons on public speaking, and Ellie cursed him for it. Of course she had done it just yesterday, but that was different. That was in the heat of battle. That was a promise of war and death.

"I know—" She paused, not exactly sure of what to say. These people, in an instant they had fought for her, fought to free themselves from the Eternal Queen's enslavement. That was what the army was—a well disguised form of slavery. The Queen had *forced* men to enlist for years. *Forced* them to die in her grasp for power.

They feared the Eternal Queen and her unimaginable powers. Feared the queen that once destroyed the strongest kingdom in all Karmalo. Now Ellie stood before them, and she easily saw the same terror in each of their eyes: fear of a new, unknown powerful queen. A Fae queen so strong that she had intentionally slaughtered thirteen generals and unintentionally killed dozens of innocents.

She had lost control of herself and her magic. She had murdered fathers, sons, mothers, and daughters.

The shredded, cut areas on Auden's clothes weren't from the sword of a general, but from her initial burst of uncontrolled power. Shards of her ice sprayed out of her, hitting and slicing through anyone more than ten feet away. When Auden had told her, she felt no different than the terrible queen she planned to overthrow.

A heavy weight sat on her chest and refused to lift.

I am not her, Ellie reminded herself. She swallowed down the knot forming in her throat.

"I know most of you stand before me and fear what you see. I do not blame you for it." She adjusted her weight, hitting her back on the wood beam behind her. The silver circlet she adorned felt heavier than it had earlier that day. "I am not here to force any of you into joining my fight against the Queen. Nor will I ask you to support my or my sisters' claim to the Malavor throne. We have not earned that right. Not yet. So what happens next is your choice." There were whispers of confusion and concern.

"The Queen will not be happy with what happened here. She will plan an attack, a retribution, on every one of your towns, so here are your choices. You can leave here today and go home. Warn your town and prepare your loved ones for the coming attacks. You can cross the Boroug border, where rumors of refugee camps have been built. Or head north with my allies to the Kotesque Mountains, where the northern armies currently gather and fight against the Queen's Army. Again, the decision is yours, but every person that heads north to fight will be greatly appreciated and considerably rewarded when the war is over. You will have until first light tomorrow morning to decide."

She stepped down from the platform, allowing the voices and conversations of many to ring in her ears.

"Very well done, my little queen."

Ellie was too tired to react to Auden's quip. Tired and saddened by the deaths she had caused.

"You are not her," Auden repeated her earlier thought. "Ellienia, look at me."

She didn't lift her head. She couldn't bear to look into his silver eyes. Eyes that made her feel way too many conflicting emotions. He grabbed her chin, pulling it up. She shut her lids, avoiding his gaze.

"Ellienia, young blessed ones always struggle with controlling their powers, and they are nothing compared to yours. We will find a Fae who can help you. You will receive the training you need to control it. I swear, what happened yesterday will not happen again."

She shot her eyes open, thankful for the tears that blurred his face from her vision. "You cannot promise that, Auden. You didn't feel what I felt. I was so enraged, felt so much agony, that I wanted my powers to be free. I wanted my magic to kill and destroy everyone and everything."

"You thought Nate was lost, and Shea sacrificed himself in front of your eyes. You are valid in those feelings, Ellienia. But knowing what you know now, knowing you could kill innocent men and women, would you try harder to control it?"

Yes. No matter how angry or emotional she got, she would at least try to prevent her magic from taking over as it had. She would try to save others, even from herself.

"Come on." Auden dropped her chin. "We have one other thing to deal with before we head out."

60

S tanding in the grassy field between the gardens and tents one through fifty were Layla, Kia, and Ames and six taller, darker, unfamiliar figures. They encircled a large group of men and some women, each seated and contained, tied and bound to one another. Arbitrators and designates still loyal to the Queen and her generals.

As Auden and her got closer, she realized who the six dark figures were: the elves that protected Kiarhem, at least the ones that remained alive.

"Holy gods, they're beautiful."

Auden softly laughed as she took in the tall, dark-skinned elves. They were different shades of beautiful brown. Two, whose complexions were similar to Kia's and shared her hazel eyes, were adorned with what seemed like hundreds of golden hoops. They wore gold bangles on their wrists, gold cuffs on their upper arms, their pointed ears were lined with tiny gold hooped earrings, and there were even gold loops braided into their dark hair.

The other four elves had even darker skin tones, with pale silver tattoos of intricate designs and foreign symbols that lined their arms and necks. Ellie was sure that beneath their fighting leathers, she would find more of the same tattoos.

They each stood at the same height or taller than Auden. Ellie felt incredibly tiny as they gathered around her.

Tiny bunny. Little queen. She knew these were the names Auden was thinking when she quickly glanced at his silver eyes.

"Your Majesty." One of the golden-adorned elves bowed. The other five followed suit.

"Please, there is no need to bow, and my name is Ellie or Ellienia. You can call me whichever you please."

The other of the two elves with golden accents stepped forward. Her full lips pulled into a gentle smile. "We owe you a great thanks for protecting and healing one of our own."

A small arm linked with Ellie's. She looked down to see Kiarhem smiling up at her. Would this tiny elf grow to match the height of the fierce ones she now faced?

"This is Luixa and Ondrej. They are also from Dorumia."

Ellie inclined her head. "It is an honor to meet you. All of you. What colony in Delmi do you derive from?"

One of the four tattooed elves stepped forward. His features remained flat, unreadable. "We are from the Arimos Colony, north of Dorumia."

He stepped back in line with the other Arimos elves. He gave no other information, and Ellie had a strong feeling that if she asked their names, they would not give them.

Instead, Ellie turned to look at the faces of her enemies. Auden and the six elves stayed to her right, while Ames and Layla joined Kiarhem on the left.

Ellie noticed the lack of a few dozen opposers. "Where are the elves who attacked you?"

"They've been taken care of." One of the Arimos elves spoke. There was no emotion on the beautiful female's face. "We don't take prisoners. Neither do the Fae."

There was a cold insinuation in her words. Ellie turned to see Auden slightly nod in confirmation.

"What do you plan to do with them, Ellienia?" Luixa asked, her tone kind and gentle. Nothing like the Arimos elves.

"Ames, what are your thoughts?" Ellie turned to the Nokken. His dark brows rising was the only shock he showed in being included in the decision she faced.

"As much as we all admire your compassion and regard for life, my queen, most of these men have the fealty mark. They will have no choice but to serve the Eternal Queen. Either end them now or we end them later on another battlefield."

A few arbitrators had blisters and burns on their faces and arms, as if at some point they had tried to fight against their mark, whether for their own protection from the generals' bloodlust or for more admirable reasons.

"And the designates who do not wear the mark?"

"They saw the generals slaughtering men and women on both sides. They ignored that cruelty. They do not have the fealty mark yet continue to support, continue to be loyal to the cruel Queen and her generals, making their actions far more serious."

Ellie agreed with Ames. The faces of the men and few women that looked up at her were wicked, holding no guilt for the choices they made. But they had at least been able to make that choice, as horrible and terrible as it was.

The arbitrators, on the other hand, did not.

"I was once reminded that each arbitrator in the Queen's Army was once a designate like us." A knot formed in Ellie's throat at the thought of Shea and their first conversation. "Without that reminder, I may have never trusted you." Ellie elbowed Auden, who released one deep laugh. "And I definitely would have never trusted you, Ames."

"That's fair." The sneer on Ames's face was one Ellie would never get used to, but truly grew to like.

"Layla, how quickly can you and your sisters make that disgusting truth serum you gave us when entering the camp?"

"If we had a usable workspace, a few hours."

"Good. There are plenty of desks and tables in the generals' tents. Find one that suits you and get to work." Layla went to leave, but Ellie held up a hand. "Take Ames with you." They both gave her questioning stares. "Ames, do you remember much of how Agilta removed your fealty mark?"

"I remember every detail of it."

"Thank the Mother. At least one of you has a brain." Layla stuck a tongue out at Auden.

"You asked if I knew what coven Agilta was from. Not if I remembered how she removed the mark." Ellie's lips tightened at Auden's protest.

"She's from the Érra coven."

Ames so nonchalantly answered Layla's question, it took a second for any of them to register what he said.

Layla's mouth gaped so wide, Ellie thought her jaw would fall off.

"What?" Ames looked at Layla's wide eyes. "She was an extremely gifted witch. Asking what coven she was from seemed like an obvious question."

"*See*! Thank you!" Layla grabbed Ames's face and kissed him on the cheek. "A male with a brain!"

Ellie could no longer hide her laugh as Auden waved his arms in submission. When he lowered them again, he placed a hand on the curve of her lower back, reminding her of the elves that watched. She stiffened, not at his touch, though it was both welcomed and unwelcomed, but at the examining eyes that watched her.

She composed herself. "Take Ames with you and see if removing the fealty mark is something you might be able to do."

"Woah. I'm not an Érra witch, Ellienia."

"No, but you are a Zye witch chosen and blessed by the Mother. I have no doubts you are powerful enough to remove the mark."

Shock and appreciation covered Layla's face. "Thank you."

Ellie nodded, ignoring the knot that formed in her throat at the sight of Layla's appreciative tears. "Go."

Layla and Ames bowed their heads slightly before turning to leave.

"So you plan on removing all of their fealty marks and freeing them?" one of the Arimos elves questioned, not hiding the displeasure in his voice.

"No. There are a few arbitrators here that have blisters and burns showing that they at least tried to fight against the mark and the generals. Auden and I will question those arbitrators and see how admirable their reasons were for their actions. If they prove to be honorable and pledge their loyalty to me, then they will go north as prisoners until their marks can be removed by Layla."

"And the rest?"

Ellie wasn't sure who asked that final question. It sounded a bit like Kia, but it echoed in her head as she viewed the group of people before her. Ackerley had taught her that in times of war, lives would be lost, either in battle or by the command of the royal they fought against. She never once thought it would be her. She would be the royal to order the execution of these people, and even if they were cruel and far from innocent, it was still a life that she would be responsible for ending.

She swallowed and drew in a breath. With her exhale, she allowed a bit of anger and darkness to rise. She changed her face to the mask she wore a week ago. To the dark, cruel woman who stood before the generals atop of the wall.

"The rest. The rest will die for the Queen they chose to follow."

61

Kiarhem held Ellie's arm as they walked to the tent their alliance occupied on the western side of the castle grounds. Luixa and Ondrej walked a few steps behind them. The elves from Arimos volunteered their "services," and Auden stayed to pick out the arbitrators inflicted with burns and blisters and to watch over said services.

"You made the right choice," Kia whispered.

Ellie's face was a mask of darkness and pain. Her eyes were filled with a cruel shadow Kia had never viewed before. She had seen Ellie's icy glare, but this...this was something different.

"The warriors from Arimos will be forever grateful to you." That seemed to catch Ellie's attention as she finally met Kia's eyes. "Not all Arimos elves are like the four you met, but the warriors...they enjoy killing. Using them to end the lives of your enemies is a great honor. One they will not forget."

Ellie nodded, but that dark mask remained. Kia knew the conflict happening inside her friend was not one she could counter with logic or encouragement. There were no words she could give that would erase the burden Ellie carried for the lives, both innocent and full of blame, that she had taken.

"Luixa and Ondrej plan to return to Dorumia. I was wondering if they could travel with us? They could be useful in knowing the land we're to travel through, and—"

Ellie squeezed her arm, a slight smile breaking through the dark mask. "Anyone who protects and fights for you, Kia, is welcome with us." She turned to give that same slight smile to the elves behind her. "It would be an honor to have you join us. I'm sure you are eager to return home."

"The honor is ours, and I'm sure you are just as eager to see your people, Ellienia." Luixa's voice was filled with kindness, and Kia could see Ellie struggle to not frown at her words.

"I grew up among humans, only hearing stories of the Fae, and now I am supposed to be their queen. Eager would not be the word I would use to describe how I feel about going to Dorumia."

Kia nearly jumped as a silent Ondrej appeared beside her. He was so fast, faster than Kia could ever imagine becoming.

"You may not have been raised among your people, Queen Ellienia, but you have the fierce, unrelenting heart of a Fae. Anyone who has seen you fight would agree." There was so much strength in the soft way Ondrej spoke. His slight Delmi accent was stronger than Kia's, and it reminded her of her father.

Kia's throat tightened at the thought. She knew deep in her bones that her parents were still alive somewhere. She knew that a few arbitrators would have an impossible time taking down two fierce elves.

"Thank you." Ellie's mask had fully disappeared, and her shoulders relaxed as she smiled at the male elf. "What groups were you placed in? It's hard to believe I've spent over a month here and Kia is the only elf I've seen."

Luixa walked to the other side of Ellie and smiled over at Ondrej. "We were one of the last groups to arrive. Every elf was placed on the eastern grounds in groups one hundred to one-fifty. You may not have seen us, but we had definitely heard about you. The beautiful young woman that could easily kick some ass." Luixa's smile was one of admiration. "We were placed in group one-oh-two. That raven-haired witch Layla made it possible for us to be in the same group."

"But she did say we owed her for it," Ondrej added.

Ellie laughed, a full and melodic sound. Kia had never heard her laugh so freely. It was beautiful. *She* was beautiful. "Layla gave me my number too. I wonder why and how she knew to put me in group twenty-four?"

Ellie draped an arm over Kia's shoulders, pulling her in close. "The goddess of magic whispers in Layla's ears. I guess she knew I would need a fierce elf at my side to protect and fight with, but to also gawk at Nate and Auden with."

Ellie's wink had Kia snorting as they both laughed.

Luixa smiled at them as they giggled. "I don't know who Nate is, but that male Fae *is* incredibly handsome."

"Agreed." Ondrej's wide eyes and sincere smile had all of them howling.

Kia curled her arms around Ellie's waste. Between her friend and the two familiar elves, it felt a little like home.

62

Ellie sat atop Darya, who shifted beneath her, eager to begin their journey.

"Easy, girl." She leaned down, patting the black mare's neck.

"Are you ready, Ellienia?" Auden rode up next to her, and Tabat nuzzled her head against Darya, who nipped at her in return.

The sun had barely begun to rise, and it was time for them to leave.

Auden and Ellie spent hours questioning arbitrators. With the help of the witch's truth tonic, they discovered only three men had honorable intentions for their burns and blisters. The Arimos elves dealt with the rest.

Ellie returned to her mat next to Nate late into the night.

He had still not awoken. Many of the people who were struck with the batons remained unconscious. Her magic was working, as some with marks farther from their hearts woke early that morning, but she knew the ones with marks closer, the ones closer to death, would take more time to heal.

"We'll watch over him," Collern had said as she gave her goodbyes to each of them.

They had already stayed in Malavor for too long. The general's may have disappeared, but they could reappear just as quickly. Ellie didn't know if the Queen would send them back to deal with any that remained, but she wasn't willing to risk the lives of her allies. They needed to leave as soon as possible, despite her desire to stay until Nate awoke.

She placed a kiss on Nate's brow and hugged each and every one of her allies, her friends.

She held Belig's and Doal's faces in each of her palms. "You two are in charge until he wakes. I've already discussed it with Layla and her sisters. They're gathering what food they can from the gardens, but I'm afraid you will have to hunt and gather as you travel."

"You don't have to worry, Ellie. We will arrive in Kotesque with all four hundred and six persons who have vowed to fight for you." Doal smiled as he translated for Belig.

Four hundred and six. Ellie thought Ames had lied when he gave her the final number. It was way more people than she thought would go north, and though she was incredibly grateful, she was also incredibly worried. She knew that traveling with such a large group would be near impossible to hide from the Eternal Queen's men. The travels would also be slow with that many people, and food was already limited.

"I am extremely grateful for each and every one of you." She allowed her tears to fall freely. Showing her care for each of them was not a weakness. "I will see each of you soon. I promise."

She looked down at Nate again.

He is healing. The magic is working, she told herself as she studied his face. It was no longer swollen, and no bruises remained. He just looked like he was sleeping.

"Go get stronger and become even more of a badass, Ellienia." Myer's bright smile was the last thing Ellie saw before she stepped out of the tent flaps.

Layla had been waiting for them at the stables when they came to ready the horses. She held a large leather saddlebag in her hands.

"I brought this here a few days ago, in case things went badly and you had to make a quick getaway." She handed Ellie the leather bags. "There's food, emergency tonics, some books, and clothes that will be more suitable for the warmer climate." Ellie grew concerned by Layla's devilish smirk. She wouldn't dare open the bags in front of the others. "I had Hannabella make a few new things for you. She's an excellent seamstress."

Ellie threw her arms around the young witch. "Thank you, Layla. For everything."

Ellie felt Layla's tears fall onto her shoulder. "No. Thank you, Ellienia. You freed me. You freed us all."

When Ellie pulled away, she saw her friend smile in a way she never had before. "I will see you in Kotesque."

"Yes, you will, my queen." She curtsied and ran to say her goodbyes to the others.

Ellie now sat on her horse viewing the dome she created. The symbol she would leave. Ames and Auden sat beside her, while Kia, Kal, and the Arimos elves waited patiently behind her.

"The book?" She looked over at Ames, his dark hair blowing in the early-morning breeze.

"It's somewhere safe."

"It's in the King's library, isn't it?"

"No. It's in *your* library."

Ellie laughed. "Then it is definitely safe."

She turned to look at Auden, and his silver eyes glowed in the dull morning light.

"Ready?" he repeated his earlier question.

There were things concerning Auden she was definitely not ready for, the bond being the main concern, but there were things Ellie was sure of. She was ready to see her people, to prepare the Fae armies, and bring Karmalo hope in a better world. She was ready to be a Queen of Malavor.

"Let's go."

CONTINUE READING FOR A SNEAK PEEK OF THE FORSAKEN KINGDOM SERIES BOOK 2

I mages of her sister's silent scream, bloodied face, and broken body crumbling to the ground replayed over and over in Cammie's head as her own desperate cry of warning rang in her ears.

ELLIE!

Cammie screamed the moment she saw the small brute release his horrifying weapon. She jumped to her feet, ready to rush towards her sister, despite the fact that it would not change Ellie's fate. Cammie was too far away to stop the arbitrator from completing the dishonorable blow and marking Ellie with whatever terrible wound that weapon created.

She could, however, still take down each and every arbitrator that participated in that appalling trial. Given the chance, she would have killed the small one that struck her sister from behind, while she was weak and wounded. Cammie would have enjoyed the feeling of retribution that came from watching him beg her for mercy, knowing he had absolutely no chance against her. If Ellie had been allowed to fight back, she too could have destroyed any man on that mockery of a stage.

None of those thoughts mattered though. A firm hand grabbed Cammie's wrist the moment she stood. The iron grip kept her from moving even an inch at that time. Now, that same hold dragged her from their carriage and into the safety of their small farm home.

The old man released her the moment they walked over the threshold. "Go to your room and wait."

Cammie could only look at her grandfather in stunned silence. There was no kindness in his demand, no hint of worry or anger either. The man had just watched his grand-daughter be publicly and brutally beaten, and there was hardly any emotion in his face.

She wanted to scream at him, and punch him for choosing Ellie to enlist in the Queen's brutal army. She wanted him to feel her rage.

Cammie swung out her arm, her fist aiming for the old man's slender nose. It never met its mark as he caught her hand, grabbed her opposite shoulder, and twisted her around. He clipped her ankles, and pushed her towards the wood floor. It all happened so quickly, Cammie only had time to register what happened after her face hit the ground.

"Ackerley!" Grams rushed into the house, Maisie, the youngest sister followed close behind. "That is enough! Girls go to your room while I speak with your Grandfather. Then we will *all* have a long overdue talk."

"It's not time." Her grandpa's voice was low, and unaffected by Cammie's attack.

She sat up, her cheek throbbing and already swelling, but the look grams shot towards her grandpa had Cammie wanting to sink back to the floor.

"It is time. They need to be prepared, Ackerley."

"Tulli..."

"This is not up for discussion. I am telling them, with or without you."

Cammie and Maisie sat on their separate beds in silence, both admiring the new gifts that had been carefully laid out on each of their mattresses. Gifts similar to those Ellie received that same morning. New fighting leathers, a single sheath garter, a dagger, and their favorite weapon.

Ellie had received an assortment of throwing knives, daggers, and, to Cammie's dismay, their mother's sword. Blades had always been Ellie's thing. Cammie preferred her own two hands if possible, but her grandpa had drilled into her at a very young age that every warrior needed to be proficient in all weapons. They also needed a favorite weapon, one they could put the time into learning until they truly excelled in wielding it. For Cammie, that weapon was a bow.

She ran fingers over the leather quiver filled with arrows of golden shafts and deep burgundy fletchlings. There was a rose branded into the front of the quiver, identical to that stamped into Ellie's sheath. Clearly the work of Mr. Gadeu.

"Do you have a rose branded on anything?" Cammie asked Maisie, breaking the eerie silence. Without lifting her gaze, Maisie threw a small black cylinder towards Cammie. It landed in her open hand with impressive precision. The leather pouch was only slightly longer than her hand, it was narrow, and a small flap of leather snapped open and closed at the top. It too had a rose branded along the length.

"What's it for?" Cammie rotated the strange leather case, inspecting every inch.

"This." Maisie held up a dark green cylinder. The strange metal gleamed in the evening sunlight pouring in through their bedroom window.

"What is it?"

"Something I asked Grandpa for a long time ago." The look in Maisie's eyes was cold and flat, as it often was, but a hint of a smile pulled at the corner of her mouth. Cammie threw the leather case back to her peculiar sister. "Do you think..." Maisie breathed, sheathing her strange weapon with immense care. "Will Ellie be alright?"

"They would have taken her to Agilta's. I'm sure she will be fine." The lie tasted bitter on Cammie's tongue. She'd heard whispers during the trial that a few men and women who had been struck with that horrible buzzing weapon had already died, and Mr. Remal...Cammie would never forget that terrible sight.

"I wish we could see her, and talk to her. Just one more time." Masie said softly.

Me too. Cammie thought, though she wished for more than just one more talk with Ellie. She wished to take her place, or better yet that neither one of them had to go and they could all three still be together.

The air in the room felt strange, as if it too felt the missing presence of the middle Batair sister and didn't approve. Cammie studied the empty bed between Maisie's and hers. It had been nicely made with the top of the light blue sheets folded neatly over the cream quilt. At the foot of the bed Cammie noticed the many holes and grooves splintering from the wood, damage from repetitive knife throwing as Ellie relaxed on her mattress. Cammie could hear the repetitive thudding. Over and over again.

"Let's go see her." Cammie hopped off her bed.

"What?" said Maisie, looking up at her sister.

"New designates always eat and sleep in The Ring, then they head out at first light. Family members always line up along the road towards Malavor and wave their good-byes. If Ellie is at Agilta's, then we have an opportunity to give her more than a pathetic wave farewell. We can talk to her one last time," and more importantly, Cammie had a chance to apologize to Ellie.

Cammie had treated her sister horribly that morning. Jealous that she was going to leave the farm and see some action, and too prideful to admit Ellie *was* the better choice to go.

"We can't just go see her. Families aren't allowed to see designates after the first trial. There will be arbitrators standing guard outside Agilta's home." Maisie's cold navy eyes began to fill with panic. She knew Cammie would go, no matter what argument she gave.

"Ellie was going to break that rule for Nate. They had plans to see each other after his trial. If she was willing to do that for him, shouldn't we be willing to do it for her?"

A hard line formed in Maisie's jaw at the mention of Ellie's best friend Nate. He was more than just Ellie's friend, and he had become like a brother to both Cammie and Maisie.

"What about Grandpa and Grams? They seem to have something important to talk to us about."

"They can tell us when we get back. They've waited this long, I'm sure it can wait just a little bit longer. Are you coming or not?" Cammie threw on her new leathers and weapons, unlatched their bedroom window and swung it open.

"Fine, but you're saddling the horses."

ACKNOWLEDGMENTS

First, and most importantly, I want to thank my husband. Sean, this book would not exist without your constant support and encouragement. Thank you for being my sounding board, for reading my terrible first draft, and for your constructive criticism that I said was mean, but was actually really helpful.

Second, Norma Gambini, thank you for perfecting this story and adding more comma's than I could count. You were the first person outside of my husband to read this story, and your kind words and encouragement meant more than you could ever know!

I also want to thank my sweet kiddos. You've had to listen to mommy talk about this book for over two years, and though you know you're not old enough to read it yet, you both were still so excited for its release. I love you both, forever and always.

Last, but certainly not least, I want to thank the readers. You are making my dreams come true. I hope you love this book as much as I loved writing it.

Ingram Content Group UK Ltd.
Milton Keynes UK
UKHW010849100323
418370UK00004B/490